More Praise for
Katie MacAlister

"Ms. MacAlister entertains readers with a captivating romance, supernatural politics, and her always present touch of humor."
— Darque Reviews

"MacAlister delivers the fun, even in the drama. The characters are engaging, quick, and inhabit a universe that only a genius can imagine."
— Romance Reader at Heart

"Fantastic . . . not a book to be missed by lovers of paranormal romance."
— Enchanting Reviews

"Action-packed . . . zany."
— *Midwest Book Review*

"Pure escapist pleasure!"
— *Romantic Times*

"Laugh-out-loud funny . . . a whimsical, upbeat humor-filled paranormal romance . . . delightful."
— Romance Junkies

"A nonstop thrill ride full of sarcastic wit, verve, and action right to the end."
— A Romance Review

Also by Katie MacAlister*

*May not be appropriate for readers of all ages.

CONFESSIONS
OF A
VAMPIRE'S
GIRLFRIEND

Got Fangs?

and

Circus of the Darned

KATIE MacALISTER
WRITING AS KATIE MAXWELL

 NEW AMERICAN LIBRARY

NEW AMERICAN LIBRARY
Published by New American Library, a division of
Penguin Group (USA) Inc., 375 Hudson Street,
New York, New York 10014, USA
Penguin Group (Canada), 90 Eglinton Avenue East, Suite 700, Toronto,
Ontario M4P 2Y3, Canada (a division of Pearson Penguin Canada Inc.)
Penguin Books Ltd., 80 Strand, London WC2R 0RL, England
Penguin Ireland, 25 St. Stephen's Green, Dublin 2,
Ireland (a division of Penguin Books Ltd.)
Penguin Group (Australia), 250 Camberwell Road, Camberwell, Victoria 3124,
Australia (a division of Pearson Australia Group Pty. Ltd.)
Penguin Books India Pvt. Ltd., 11 Community Centre, Panchsheel Park,
New Delhi - 110 017, India
Penguin Group (NZ), 67 Apollo Drive, Rosedale, North Shore 0632,
New Zealand (a division of Pearson New Zealand Ltd.)
Penguin Books (South Africa) (Pty.) Ltd., 24 Sturdee Avenue,
Rosebank, Johannesburg 2196, South Africa

Penguin Books Ltd., Registered Offices:
80 Strand, London WC2R 0RL, England

Published by New American Library, a division of Penguin Group (USA) Inc. *Got Fangs?* and
Circus of the Darned were previously published in separate Smooch editions by Dorchester Publishing
Co., Inc.

First New American Library Printing, November 2010
10 9 8 7 6 5 4 3 2 1

Got Fangs? copyright © Marthe Arends, 2005
Circus of the Darned copyright © Marthe Arends, 2006
All rights reserved

NAL
REGISTERED TRADEMARK—MARCA REGISTRADA

Set in Cochin
Designed by Ginger Legato

Printed in the United States of America

*To all of the Ben and Fran fans
who wrote to me saying they couldn't find one or the other
of these books — I hope you enjoy this new edition!*

AUTHOR'S NOTE

Greetings, readers!

I'm sure there are at least a couple of you squinting at the cover of this book and saying to yourself, "Something about this looks familiar. . . ." There *is* something familiar about this book—well, familiar if you happened to read the previous incarnation of it: two slim volumes going by the titles *Got Fangs?* and *Circus of the Darned*, originally published in 2005 and 2006, respectively.

Those two books were intended to be the start of a young-adult paranormal series based on the world created in my adult Dark Ones books, but unfortunately, the fates were against the series going any farther than two books; the young-adult line that was publishing them closed up, and Ben and Fran, the hero and heroine, were left hanging around, waiting for the time to be right for them to make a reappearance.

In November 2010, Benedikt Czerny and Francesca Ghetti will transition into adult fiction with the publication of *In the Company of Vampires*, but since their roots are firmly dug into the young-adult world, I'm pleased that the folks at New American Library will be releasing the two young-adult books in this one handy volume, newly retitled, but containing all the original text from both *Got Fangs?* and *Circus of the Darned*. In addition, I've written a glossary to ensure everyone will be up to speed with all the odd people and ideas contained in the books.

For those of you new to the world of the Goth-Faire and Dark Ones, welcome! I hope you enjoy acquainting yourselves with the denizens of my Otherworld.

Katie MacAlister/Maxwell

Got Fangs?

CHAPTER ONE

"What do you want to do first—have your aura photographed, or see the witch and have her cast a spell?" a girl asked.

You know that creepy kid who saw dead people in *Sixth Sense?* He's Norman P. Normal compared to me.

A guy wearing a backpack answered the girl's question. "I want to see the demonologist. I've had a bad run of luck lately; it could be due to demons. He can tell me if I've been demonized."

Okay, so the kid could see ghosts—I'll give him that—but was his mom a bona fide witch?

"I don't know that demons would give you bad luck, John," the girl said, frowning. "That sounds more like a curse. Maybe we should see the witch first and have her check you over for curses."

Did he spend his days traveling around Europe with a group of people who knew more about ghosts, demons, and various assorted weird things than stuff like ATM machines and cell phones and the latest hottie on *American Idol?*

The girl's voice cut through my mental rant. "I heard they have a vampire who drinks the blood of a volunteer each night! I'd love to see that!"

Oh, yeah, I forgot the vampires. Not that GothFaire had any, but still, what was I thinking?

"Hey, Lynsay, take a look at that girl. She looks odd. You think she's part of the show?"

I bet the *Sixth Sense* kid got to live in a normal home with a normal mom, and go to a normal school with other normal kids. Shoot, I'd be willing to put up with a little "I see dead people"-ing in order to have all that normal around me.

"Shhh, she might hear you."

The two people stopped in front of me, a girl and a guy probably a few years older than me using the opportunity to give me the once-over. I tried to look like there wasn't anything unusual at all about standing in front of a tent with a big red hand painted on the side, shoving my own hands in my pockets just to make sure I didn't touch anything. Don't touch, don't tell; that's my policy.

"It's okay; she probably doesn't even speak English. She sure doesn't look normal, not with all that white skin and black hair. Maybe she's one of the Goths?"

Or maybe I just happen to have an Italian father and a fair-skinned Scandinavian mother? Ya think?

The girl giggled. I sent up a little prayer to the Goddess that Imogen would get her butt in gear and come back to her booth so I didn't have to stand here and let the rubes gawk at me.

Rube—that's one of those words you pick up when you travel with a freak show. It means the uncool, people not hip to the way of the Faire.

"Maybe she's one of the vampires! She looks like one, don't you think? I can see her drinking your blood."

I turned my back so they wouldn't see me roll my eyes. It might be rare to find Americans this far into Hungary, but I wasn't so desperate to see my countrymen that I wanted to drink their blood. Besides, everyone knew only guys were vamps.

"Francesca, I'm so sorry!" Imogen hurried past the couple, her long blond hair streaming behind her as she dodged behind the table and grabbed the sign and easel that announced she was available to read palms and rune stones. She ignored the couple watching as she set the easel at the edge of the tent, popping the sign onto it as she chattered in her trademark Imogen style—breathy, soft accent that was part British, part something I couldn't put my finger on, not that I'd been in Europe long enough to learn how to say anything, more than: *hello, good-bye, thank you, how much is that,* and *I wouldn't let my dog use that toilet; where is a clean one?* in three different languages (German, French, and Hungarian, for those of you who are aching to know).

"Thank you so much for watching my things. Absinthe insisted on seeing me—evidently there's been another robbery. Oh, bless you, you didn't touch anything. You know I don't like anyone to touch the stones, and Elvis was after me again to help set up, which is ridiculous, because you know he has an orange aura, and orange auraed people are absolutely death to me before I'm supposed to read. But I have something exciting to tell you! My brother is coming to see me!"

I straightened up out of my perpetual slouch and gave the couple a big, toothy grin to show them I didn't have fangs. I was as tall as the guy (six feet), and as big as or bigger than him. He looked a little worried about that fact. The girl blushed a little and grabbed her boyfriend's arm, dragging him off toward the large tent, the one where the band plays after the magic shows.

The irony of me trying to prove I was normal didn't escape me. I'm like that. I see irony a lot. You know what? It's a pain in the butt. "They thought I was a vamp," I told Imogen as she shook out her blue casting cloth.

She cocked one golden eyebrow. "You? You're a female."

I resumed the slouch that made me look less like a burly football player, and tugged at my T-shirt in an attempt to make myself look smaller, prettier, thinner . . . you know, like a girl. "Yeah. Guess they don't know the rules."

She muttered something that sounded like *peons*, and arranged three ceramic bowls of rune stones along one side of the casting cloth. "Absinthe says the band ran off in the night with the last week's take, but Peter said they didn't, that only he and Absinthe know the combination to the safe, and that it wasn't forced. She's gone to Germany to find a new band."

I chewed on the chapped skin on my lower lip. This was the third theft in the last ten days. Although I hated to agree with Absinthe, if the band skipped out during the night, it did sound like they were guilty. "What are they going to do about tonight?"

"Peter is hiring a local band. I hope they're good; the last few bands he's hired have been abysmal beyond belief."

I tipped my head to the side, tucking my hair behind my ear, wishing for the one thousandth time that it was anything but straight, straight, straight. Other people have curly hair—even my own mother has curly hair. Why can't I? "You're the only person I know who's heard Mozart play in person, and still thinks Goth bands are the best."

Imogen gave me one of her sly smiles. "Mozart was a brat. Gifted, but still a brat. But the Cure—now *that's* music!"

See what I'm talking about? Is it normal for your best girl-friend to be a four-hundred-year-old immortal?

"What's wrong, Fran? You look upset about something all of a sudden. Has Elvis been bothering you again? Would you like me to—"

I shook my head. "You know he doesn't see anyone but you. And besides, I'm bigger than him. I think he's afraid I'll beat him up if he tries to get busy with me."

Imogen stepped back from lighting scented candles, tipping her head as she looked me over. Her head tip was much nicer than mine, since she had long, curly hair, whereas I had a short, jaw-length pageboy full of straight black hair that refused either hot rollers or a perm's chemical wooing to give it body. "I see. You're feeling inadequate again."

I couldn't help but laugh at that. Nicely, because I like Imogen, but still, I had to laugh. "Again. Yeah, like when am I ever *not* inadequate?"

"I think the question is, rather, why do you feel you are?"

I glanced around to make sure no one was near to overhear us—not that some of the people connected with the GothFaire had to be near you to listen in (I'll bet you my whole summer's allowance that the *Sixth Sense* kid didn't have mind readers eavesdropping on *his* thoughts). "You want the list? You got it! First, I'm approximately the size and shape of your average high school linebacker."

"Don't be silly; you are not. You're a lovely girl, tall and statuesque. Men are going to be falling at your feet in a few years."

"Yeah, falling over in fright," I said, then quickly moved on before she was forced to say other nice things about me. You only have to look at me to see I am a big, hulking monstrosity. I didn't need tiny little petite pity from tiny little petite Imogen. "Second, my dad remarried a girl only a couple of years older than me and told me he needed six months alone with her to get settled, which meant that when my mom took a job with a European traveling fair, I had to go with her."

"I'm sorry about your father," she said, her forehead all frowny, like it really mattered to her. That's one of the things I like so much about Imogen — she's honest. If she likes you, she *really* likes you, all of you, and stands up for you against who- or whatever is making your life a living nightmare. "That is wrong of him to banish you from his life. He should know better."

I made a face that my mother called a moue. "Mom says he's having a midlife crisis, and that's why he bought a sports car and got himself a trophy wife. It's okay. I didn't really like staying with him very much." *Bzzzt!* Big fat lie. I hoped Imogen's lie detector wouldn't catch me on that one. I hurried into the next complaint in case it did. "Third, the fair isn't a normal fair, the kind with popcorn and cotton candy and hokey country singers. Oh, no, this fair is filled with people who can talk to the dead, do real magic, read minds, and other weirdo stuff like that. One minute I had a relatively normal life with normal friends and a normal school, living with an almost normal mom in Oregon, and the next I'm Fran the Freak Queen, spending the summer hanging out with people who would give most people a case of the willies that would last them a lifetime. If *that* isn't something to look upset about, I don't know what is."

"The people here aren't freaks, Fran. You've been with us long enough to see that. They're gifted with rare talents, just as you are."

I stuffed my hands deeper into my pockets, the soft silk of the latex gloves brushing against my fingertips. My "talent" was something I didn't like talking about. To anyone, not that anyone but Imogen and my mom knew about it. I think Absinthe suspected, but she couldn't do anything about it. She was afraid of what Mom might do to her if she tried to mess with me.

Okay, sometimes it was handy having a witch for a mom. Most of the time it just sucked, though. What I wouldn't give for a mom who was a secretary and knew how to bake cookies. . . .

"You don't think *I'm* a freak, do you?" Imogen's blue eyes went black. That was one of the things her kind could do, she told me. Their eyes changed colors with strong emotions.

"No, not you—you can't help it if your dad was a vampire."

"Dark One," she corrected, fussing with the candles. They were special ones Mom made, invocation candles, bound with spells and herbs to enhance clarity of mind and communication with the Goddess.

I nodded. One of the first things Imogen had told me about the vamps was that they like to be referred to by their proper name: Moravian Dark Ones. Only the guys were Dark Ones, though; the women were just called Moravians. "You're not a freak just because your dad was damned by some demon lord. It's not like you drink blood or anything."

Imogen shrugged. "I have. It's not very good. I prefer Frankovka." That was Imogen's favorite wine, the only thing she drank. She had cases of the stuff she hauled around with her from town to town. She said it reminded her of her home in the Czech Republic. "I think, dear Francesca, that what you need most is a friend."

I kicked at a lump in the grass, and watched out of the corner of my eye as she made a few symbols in the air. Wards, she called them, protective devices like a spell that you had to draw in the air. All vamps—excuse me, *Moravians*—could draw wards. Mom had been nagging Imogen to teach her how to do it, but for some reason she had refused. "I've got friends, lots of friends."

That was another lie. I had no real friends back home, but I figured I didn't need to make myself sound any more pathetic than I already did.

"Not in Oregon—here. You need friends here." She didn't look up as she traced another symbol into the casting cloth.

"I have friends here, too. There's you."

She smiled and beckoned me toward her. I leaned forward, the back of my neck tingling as her fingers danced in the air a few molecules away from my forehead. She'd drawn a protection ward for me once before, when I first arrived and Elvis— the resident flirtmeister—tried to hit on me. Having a ward protect you was a strange feeling, as if the air surrounding you were thick and heavy, like a cocoon. I'd never seen a ward actually work (Mom had a few words with Elvis, words like "manhood shriveling up and dropping off if you ever lay a finger on her"), but still, it was a nice gesture for Imogen to use up a little of her power on me. "I am flattered, Fran. You are, indeed, one of my best buds."

I tried not to smile. Imogen spoke like something out of an old English movie—very rich vowels, all proper and perfect grammar, with a lot of big words like a professor who dated Mom used, but mixed into that was a handful of hip slang that sounded odd in comparison. She didn't know that, though, and I didn't want to hurt her feelings. "And I like Peter, too. He's nice, when he's not groveling around Absinthe."

"Yes, he is. They are the strangest pair. . . ." She set the little box where she kept her reading money beneath the table, and dusted off the chair. "Did you know that they are twins?"

I shook my head. They didn't look like twins. Absinthe had pink hair, pencil-thin eyebrows, and a brittle smile, while Peter was short, balding, and had nice, gentle eyes. I had heard they had bought the Faire off of the group of people who used to work here, a group that scattered when it turned out the previous owners were psycho killers, who had murdered a bunch of women all over Europe.

Do you wonder that I want to go home?

"They are, despite not looking like each other. It's almost as if one has all the good traits, and the other the regrettable ones."

I grinned after a quick check to make sure no one was nearby (you can't be too careful where Absinthe is concerned). "And then there's Soren. He's a friend, too."

"Yes, there is Soren," she said as she sat down, straightening her Stevie Nicks retro-seventies frilly lace shirt. I could tell she was trying not to look all-knowing, the way adults do whenever you talk about a guy your own age. The thing is, Imogen looks like she is just a few years older than me, about twenty, so sometimes I forgot that she'd lived as long as she has, making her more adult than any adult I knew. "He is a very sweet boy."

"He's okay," I said, really nonchalant. I didn't need Imogen telling everyone I had a crush on Soren. I didn't, in case you were wondering. Soren was fifteen (a year younger than me), had sandy hair and a face full of freckles, and was three inches shorter and probably fifty pounds lighter. He was, however, the only other person in the Faire who was close to my age, so we hung together.

"I think perhaps . . ." Imogen looked up and smiled brightly at three young women who approached her table. They asked her something in Hungarian, and after giving me an apologetic glance, she answered and waved them into the chairs on the opposite side of the table. Customers. I was a bit lonely and would have liked to stay and chat with Imogen, but one of the first things I'd learned when Mom dragged me here a month ago was that paying customers came first. I gave Imogen a little wave and went off to see what Soren was up to.

The GothFaire is usually set up in a basic U shape, with the big tent at the bottom of the U, and two long wings containing the individual tents, with all the "talent" along one side, and vendor tents along the other. The tents weren't camping tents; they were made of heavy canvas, painted in wild colors with even wilder designs, all of them open-fronted, some also having wooden panels for strength. Most could be quickly set up or torn down, and packed into long canvas bags. Soren mostly helped with the setting-up and tearing-down part, but he also did odd jobs, stuff his dad (Peter) was supposed to do, but never had time to get done.

I wandered down the line of tents, weaving in and out of the early Fairegoers, listening to, but not understanding, the different languages around me. The big lights lining the aisles had been turned on, since the sun had just gone down, casting eerie shadows in the little dips and hollows of the grassy field that held the Faire. Enticing, spicy scents came from the food-vendor tents, blending with the faint lingering smell of the sun-warmed earth beneath my sandals. I waved at Mom as she counseled someone with a spell. Davide, her cat, sat looking like a black meat loaf on her table, his front paws tucked under his chest, his white whiskers twitching as he watched me walk by. Davide doesn't really like me, but I put up with him mostly because I like cats, but also because Mom said he was very wise.

A cat. Wise. What*ever*.

I found Soren down with a bunch of guys in matching denim jackets unloading amps and sound equipment from a battered old truck. The replacement band had arrived.

"Hey," I said.

"Hey," Soren said back. We're cool that way.

"What's the band called?" I asked as he struggled with an amp that was almost as tall as he was. I hefted one side of it onto my shoulder and helped him ease it off the truck and onto a dolly.

"Crying Orcs. They look great, don't they?"

We both looked at the guys clustered around a soundboard. I shrugged. "They look like all the other bands." I'd die before I admitted it, but Goth wasn't really my style. I was a ballad girl. I liked Loreena McKennitt and Sarah McLachlan, women like them. Guys singing about wanting to slash someone's wrists and watch their blood drip away forever just left me kind of cold.

"I heard them last night. They're good. You'll like them." I shrugged again. "Take this in for me, please. Give it to Stefan; he's the man with one ear."

Soren dumped a heavy coil of cable in my arms. I grunted a little when he did. Darned thing weighed a ton. I carefully edged around the amps, stacks of sound equipment, and assorted crates, and stepped out into the alley between the truck and the tent.

Right into the path of a motorcycle.

CHAPTER TWO

"Narng."

Darkness swirled through my head, but it wasn't the familiar darkness of the inside of my eyelids, or even the twice-experienced darkness of anesthesia, but a really black darkness that was filled with sorrow . . . and concern.

Are you injured? Does anything hurt?

"Gark," I said. At least I think it was me. I felt my lips move and all, but I don't think I've ever said the word "gark" before in my life, so really, why would I be saying it now, to this sad blackness that talked directly into my head?

Gark. I'm not familiar with that word. Is it something new?

"Mmrfm." Yep, that was me speaking, I recognized the "mmrfm." I said that every morning when the clock radio went off. I'm a heavy sleeper. I hate being woken up.

You don't look injured. Did you strike your head?

The motorcycle! I had been run over. I was probably dead. Or dying. Or delirious.

You stepped directly in front of me. I had no time to avoid you. You really should learn to look before you walk out from behind trucks.

You shouldn't have been driving so freakin' fast, I thought back to the voice that rubbed like the softest velvet against my brain, not in the least bit surprised or shocked or even weirded out that someone could talk to me without using words. I'd been with the GothFaire for a whole month. I've seen stranger things.

The voice smiled. I know that sounds stupid, because how can a voice smile, but it did. I felt the smile in my head just as clearly as I felt the hands running down my arms, obviously checking me over for injury.

Eeek! Someone was touching me! The second my hands were touched . . .

My brain was flooded with images, like a slide show of strange, unconnected moments in time. There was a man in one of those long, ornately embroidered coats like Revolutionary guys wore. This guy was waving his arms around and looking really smug about something, but just as soon as I got a good look at him, he dissolved into mud and rain, and blood dripping from a dead guy in World War I clothes. He was sprawled backward in a ditch, his eyes open, unseeing as the rain ran down from his cheeks into his hair. It was night, and the air was full of the smell of sulfur and urine and other stuff that I didn't want to identify. That dissolved, too (thank goodness), this time into a lady with a huge, and I mean *huge*, like a yard-high, powdered white wig and a giganto-hipped dress with her boobs almost popping out of it. She was lifting up the bottom of her skirt, peeling it back slowly, exposing her leg as if it were something special (it wasn't), saying something in French about pleasure.

I jerked my hand back from the man touching it at the same time I opened my eyes. Vampire. Moravian. Nosferatu. Dark One. Call him what you want; this man was a bloodsucker.

His eyes met mine and I sucked in my breath.

He was also the cutest guy I had ever seen in my whole entire life. We're talking open-your-mouth-and-let-the-drool-flow-out cute. We're talking hottie. Major hottie. The hottest of all hotties. He wasn't just good-looking; he was fall-to-the-ground-dead gorgeous. He had brown-black hair pulled back into a ponytail, black eyes with lashes so long it made him look like he was wearing mascara, a fashionable amount of manly stubble, and he was young, or at least he looked young, maybe nineteen. Twenty at the most. Earrings in both ears. Black leather jacket. Black tee. Silver chain with an ornate Celtic cross hanging on his chest. Oh, yes, this was one drool-worthy guy bending over me, and just my luck, he was one of the undead.

"Some days I just can't win," I said, pushing myself into a sitting position.

"Some days I don't even try," he answered, his voice the same as the one that had brushed my mind. It was faintly foreign, not German, like Soren's and Peter's, but something else, maybe Slavic? I haven't been in Eastern Europe long enough to be able to tell accents very well, and since everyone in the Faire speaks English, I haven't really had to learn much. "You are unhurt."

"Was that a question or a comment?" I asked, ignoring his hand as I got to my feet, brushing off my jeans and testing my legs for any possible compound fractures or dismemberment or anything like that.

"Both." He stood up and flicked the dirt and grass off my back.

"Oh, lucky me, I got to be run over by a comedian," I growled. "Hey! Hands to yourself, buster!"

His hand, in the act of brushing grass off my legs, paused. Both of his eyebrows went up. "My apology."

I tugged down my T-shirt and gave him a look to let him know that he might be a vamp, but I was on to him. That was when it struck me that I had to look up to glare at him. Up. As in . . . up. "You're taller than me."

"I'm glad to see that you aren't suffering any brain damage. What is your name?"

"Fran. Uh . . . Francesca. My dad's parents are Italian. I was named for my grandma. She's in Italy." God, could I sound any more stupid? Babbling. I was positively babbling like an idiot, to a man who at some point in his life had a big-haired French Revolution babe baring her legs at him. *Oh, brilliant, Fran. Make him think you're a raving lunatic.*

"That's a very pretty name. I like it." He smiled when he said that last bit, showing very white teeth. Nonpointy teeth. As in no fangs. I wanted to ask him what happened to his fangs, but Soren and some of the band guys had just noticed us standing with the cable spilled all over, and the motorcycle lying on its side.

"Fran, are you all right?" Soren asked, jumping off the truck and limping toward me. One leg is shorter than the other, but he's really touchy about his limp, so we don't say anything about it.

The vamp glanced at Soren, then back at me. "Boyfriend?"

I snorted, then wished I hadn't. I mean, how uncool is snorting in front of a vamp? "Not! He's younger than me."

"Is something wrong, Fran?" Soren said, limping up really quickly, giving the dark-haired guy a look like he was trying to take a favorite toy away. To tell you the truth, I was kind of touched by the squinty-eyed, suspicious look Soren was giving the guy.

"It's okay. I was just run over. The cable isn't hurt, though."

"Run over?" Two of the band guys hurried around Soren and grabbed the cable, examining the ends of it.

"Joke, Soren. I'm not hurt. This is Imogen's brother."

The dark-haired vamp gave me a curious look before holding out his hand to Soren. He didn't deny it, so I gathered my guess was right. It was no surprise, though. I mean, how many authentic Dark Ones were going to be hanging around the Faire on the very same evening Imogen was expecting her brother? "Benedikt Czerny."

"Chairnee?" I asked.

"It's spelled C-Z-E-R-N-Y. It's Czech."

"Oh. That's right. Imogen said she's from the CR. How come her last name is Sorik?"

"Females in my family take their mother's surname," Benedikt said smoothly, then pulled his bike upright. He was talking about Moravians. I wondered if anyone else knew what he really was. Imogen said only Absinthe knew about her—I had discovered it by accident one night when we both reached for the same piece of berry cobbler and my hand brushed hers.

"I'm Soren Sauber. My father and aunt own the GothFaire."

Soren had puffed himself up, his normally nice blue eyes all hard as he glared at Benedikt. I'd never seen him like that; usually he was all smiley and friendly, kind of like a giant blond puppy who wants to tag along.

"It is a pleasure to meet you," Benedikt said politely. He turned to me and offered his hand.

I stuck mine behind my back. "Sorry. I have this thing

about touching people. It's . . . uh . . . a skin problem." A skin problem. *A skin problem!* Great, now he'd think I had leprosy or something.

His left eyebrow bobbled for a moment before it settled down. He looked back at Soren. "Is there somewhere I can park . . . ? Yes, I see. Thank you." His black eyes flickered over to me. I sucked in my cheeks and tried to look like I wasn't the sort of leprosy-riddled babbling idiot who walks out in front of motorcycles. "I look forward to seeing you both again."

"Wow," I said as he walked his bike over to where a horse trailer was parked next to Peter and Soren's bus. "Is he, like, major cool, or what?"

"Major cool?" Soren looked after Benedikt. The guy had a really nice walk. I mean, *niiiiiiice*. Course, his skintight black jeans didn't hurt any. "I suppose so."

I hugged my arms around my ribs, vaguely surprised that they didn't hurt despite my being slammed to the ground. Nothing on me hurt. To tell the truth, I felt kind of . . . tingly.

"You should stay away from him," Soren said. I dug the latex gloves out of my pocket and put them on, then pulled the black lace gloves from my back pockets. I had bought them from one of the vendors because they looked suitably Goth. No one would look twice at someone wearing black lace gloves, but experience taught me that if you go around wearing latex doctor's gloves, people start to give you strange looks. Soren watched me put on the gloves without saying anything. I told him I had hypersensitive skin (not terribly far from the truth) the first day we met, and he's never said anything about my gloves since. I guess what with his limp, he figured it wasn't kosher to comment on my gloves.

"Why? He seemed okay to me."

"I don't like him. You should stay away from him. He could be . . . dangerous."

I grinned and socked him on the shoulder in a friendly buddy sort of way. "Yeah, right, I know the truth; you're jealous."

His eyes got all startled-looking. "What?"

"His bike. You're jealous 'cause he came roaring up on a big Harley or whatever it is, and your dad won't let you get a Vespa until you're sixteen."

He just stared at me for a second, then turned back to the truck. "Are you going to help unload or not?"

"Sure." I smiled to myself. Guys hate it when you get them pegged so quickly. I spent the next hour helping the band set up behind the big black curtain that hid the back of the stage from the front, where the magic acts were held. GothFaire got two basic kinds of customers—average people who were excited to see a traveling fair come to town (and we went to some really small towns)—people who wanted to have their palms read and fortunes told, and buy some crystals and aura pictures and all that cheesy stuff—and the rockers who traveled from around whatever country we were in to hear the bands. The last band we had was from Holland and they were really popular, bringing in lots of people for the shows, but as the Crying Orcs were local boys, I figured the crowd wouldn't be as big for them.

I wandered around for a bit, watching the visitors (they were much more interesting than the people they came to see), more than a little bored. I thought about going to see if Tallulah had manifested any interesting ectoplasm (lately it's all been coming out in the shape of Matt Damon—she's got a bit of a crush), when I realized that it was a quarter to eleven. I hung around the outside of my mother's tent until her customer went off clutching a bottle of happiness. (Mom's most popular potion—it really works, too. I drank a big jug of it when I just learned how to crawl. She said I laughed for a week straight.)

"Franny, could you watch things for a couple of minutes? I have a few premade vials of happiness and luck, but ran out of blessings. I'll just run to the bathroom and be back in two shakes of a cat's tail."

I swear Davide rolled his eyes. "Sure, no problem. Hey, Mom, do you know anything about Imogen's brother?"

"Imogen's brother? I didn't know she had a brother. Now, where did I put those keys . . . ?" She bent over, searching through the huge mom-bag she carries, looking for the keys to our trailer. The first week we were here, when I was going through the horrible shock of having to move from our nice house outside of Portland to a small trailer in the middle of Germany, she told me I could pick out what to paint on the trailer. Everyone in the Faire had their trailer painted with their own emblems on it. Imogen's was gold and white, with scarlet hands and runes. Absinthe's was pink and green (a horrible combination), while Soren and Peter's bus-turned-into-home-on-wheels was a soft sky blue with a castle and knights on horseback stretching down the length. Soren told me the town in Germany where he was born had a big ruined castle that he used to love playing in.

Mom wanted a representation of the Goddess on ours. I decided on a midnight-blue background with gold stars and crescent moons on it. She put all sorts of metaphysical meaning into it, saying I had chosen to portray the mystery of the unknown, yadda yadda yadda.

I just thought it was pretty.

"Drat it all, I know I had my keys when I left the trailer; I remember locking up after you left. Honey?"

"I gave you my keys two days ago, Mom. Don't tell me you've lost those, too?"

"Bullfrogs!" Mom takes this witch stuff seriously. She doesn't swear, because most swear words have their origins in curses, and she won't dabble in anything dark like a curse. She practices only good magic. It gets a bit tedious sometimes. I mean, I could have really used a couple of quality curses during my sophomore year.

She held out her hand. "Would you?"

"Mom!"

"Please."

"I am not the Clapper! You'll have to find your own keys."

"I know, baby, but I have to use the bathroom, and I want to change into my invocation gown. Just this once, please?"

I turned my back to the opening of the tent so no one would see me as I peeled off the lace glove, then the latex one beneath it. "You know I hate doing this. It makes me feel like a big fat freak."

"You're not big or fat or a freak; you've been blessed by the Goddess."

I took a deep breath and tried to clear my mind, like she said I was supposed to do in order to open myself up to all the possibilities. "Is anyone looking?"

"Not a soul."

I took her hand in mine, and tried to ignore the rush of thoughts that filled my mind. Mom arguing with Absinthe about the band stealing the Faire money. Her worries about me not being happy here battling with her desire to be with the Faire, all mixed up with the fear that the Faire would close if the thefts didn't stop. Her pain over Dad remarrying so quickly after the divorce. The sudden thought that she hadn't changed Davide's litter box, a growl of hunger, a sense of loneliness that so closely resembled my own that I almost dropped her hand . . . I gritted my teeth and tried to focus my mind to pick through hers until I found what I wanted to know.

"You dropped them just outside of the trailer. They're in a tall clump of grass beneath a candy wrapper," I said, letting go of her hand with a sigh of relief. Mom was the only person I could touch who didn't leave me feeling all creepy . . . until Benedikt. I blinked at that thought, and realized it was true. Touching him didn't freak me out like it did when I touched anyone else—he was warm and soft, inviting, a bit mysterious, but oddly comfortable, considering I'd only just met him.

And, of course, there was the fact that he was a vampire.

"You're such an angel," Mom said, kissing my forehead and rushing off to the trailer, pausing to tell the group of people approaching the tent that she'd be back in ten minutes.

"If I'm an angel, where are my wings?" I whispered. It was what I always said whenever she called me an angel, starting from the time when I was little and she would swing me around and around, and tell me I was an angel sent to bring heaven to earth.

I looked down at my hand. It wasn't small and slender like hers, or long and graceful like Imogen's. It was big, and my fingers had blunt tips. A musician's hand, someone had once told me, but I had to stop piano lessons when I was twelve because I couldn't stand touching Mrs. Stone's piano. Too many kids used it for their weekly lessons—I'd go home afterward shaking and near tears. That was when Mom finally figured out what had happened to me.

"How long have you been a psychometrist?"

I turned around slowly, wondering if Benedikt had read my mind .

"Since I was twelve."

He stood on the other side of the table, a large black shape blocking my view of the sky turned indigo and black. "Puberty?"

I nodded and tried to look away, but couldn't. It was something about his eyes, glowing with an inner light as they watched me fiddle with my gloves. I didn't want to talk to him about the weird things I could do. I didn't want him to think I belonged in the freak show.

You're not a freak.

"Stop that," I said, taking a couple of steps backward, as if distance would keep him out of my mind.

Are you afraid of me?

His eyes were the color of dark oak, little golden flecks against the warm honey brown, flecks I could see even though his face was thrown into shadow. "Why should I be afraid of you? If anyone should be afraid, it's you. I know your secret."

And I know yours, he said into my head as he started coming toward me.

I backed up a couple more steps, straightening my shoulders, trying to look big and tough and mean. "Yours is worse than mine, so if you don't want to end up on the business end of a sharp stake, you'd just better back off and leave me alone."

I don't want to leave you alone.

"You don't know who you're messing with—" I started to say, then shrieked when he lunged toward me, grabbing my arms and pulling me toward him. We stood together like that for a second, me braced and ready for him to bite me, him looking down on me with eyes that were changing into glittering ebony.

"I don't want to mess with you at all, Fran." Slowly, very slowly, his hand slid down my arm. I watched it as it headed for my naked hand, my bare hand, my hand that kept me from being happy like any other kid.

"Don't," I said, ashamed it came out a whimper.

"Trust me," he said softly. His fingers trailed along the back of my bare hand, then curved under, pushing my arm up so that our palms rested together. I gasped and held my breath, waiting for the rush of images, waiting for the *everything* that would pour from his mind into mine.

There was nothing. I was touching him, hand to hand, and I felt nothing, saw nothing.

I looked from our hands to his face. "How do you do that? How do you turn yourself off like that?"

His fingers twined through mine, and all of a sudden I was aware that he was a guy and I was a girl, and we were standing together holding hands.

"You know who I am."

"I know what you are, if that's what you mean."

He nodded. "What do you know about us?"

"I know that you're a vampire . . ." His fingers tightened on mine. *Poop. Used the V-word.* ". . . but that you prefer to be called Dark Ones. I know that you drink people's blood to survive, and you're probably a couple of hundred years old—is Imogen your older sister, or younger?"

"Older."

I don't know why that made me feel better, considering he was probably at least three hundred years old, but it did. "And I know that you are really sad most of the time, but somehow, you can block the images in your mind from me at the same time you can talk into my head."

"Do you know anything about how a Dark One is created? How he can be redeemed?"

"Um . . . you're created . . . something about a demon lord cursing you?"

I thought his eyes were black before, but they went absolutely obsidian. "My father was cursed by a demon lord."

"Oh, that's right. Imogen said something about the sins of the father being passed on to the sons, but not the daughters. I don't know anything about redemption."

He looked at our hands, still locked together. It was strange touching him, feeling his warm fingers twined through mine, and not having my head filled with his thoughts and memories and everything else I felt when I touched people. "For every Dark One there is one woman, called a Beloved, who can redeem his soul, a woman who can balance his darkness with her light, and make him whole again."

"Oh," I said. So it wasn't the smartest thing I could say. The guy was holding my hand—it was hard to think about anything but how warm his hand was.

"You are my Beloved."

I snatched my hand out of his, jumping backward straight into the metal rods that held the tent up. The pointy bit of bone on my wrist whacked into it, making me yelp in pain. "You're crazy!" I said as I rubbed my sore wrist. "You're psycho! You're a total nutball! You're some sort of stalker!"

He stepped forward. "I don't have a choice in the matter. Dark Ones have only one Beloved—many never find them. I had almost given up hope that I would ever find mine. Let me see your wrist."

"Why, so you can bite it? No! I don't want you touching me. You're some sort of weirdo vamp perv. Leave me alone."

"I swear to you I will not hurt you, and that I am not a weirdo vamp perv. Let me see your wrist."

He stood in front of me, close enough to grab my wrist but not touching me, just waiting for me to offer up my wrist like a good little sheep.

I am *so* not a sheep.

I made a fist with my right hand at the same time I stomped on his foot as hard as I could, kneed him in the happy sacs, and as he doubled over to clutch his crotch, punched him in the Adam's apple like Mom showed me in case some guy ever got nasty with me.

I just don't think she anticipated that guy being a vamp.

CHAPTER THREE

I know what you're thinking. You're thinking, *Hey, I didn't know you could bring a vampire to his knees by kicking him in the noogies.*

Well, you can. I mean, they might be the walking undead and all that, but they are just guys, you know? They have the same outdoor plumbing as nonvamp guys, and I gathered from the way Benedikt writhed around on the ground that getting whomped there hurt him just as much as it would a normal guy.

Which is probably why I hesitated for a few seconds rather than running off, watching him roll on the ground clutching his groin, clearly in pain but not saying a single, solitary word. He was absolutely silent. The only other guy I've ever kneed (my first and only date) was screaming obscenities at me after I kicked him, but not Benedikt. Guilt washed over me as I watched him, guilt and a horrible urge to laugh. Not at Benedikt, but at me, at my life. All I've ever wanted is to fit in, to be like everyone else, to not be the odd one, the one who is different from all the other kids, and what happens? I meet a vamp who tells me I'm the only one who can redeem his soul. Oh, yeah, like I bet *that* happens to every other girl who goes to Europe.

"I just want a normal life," I yelled at Benedikt. "Is that so wrong? I am *not* Buffy the Vampire Slayer!"

A little grunt escaped him as he got to his knees. "Good. I'm not up to playing Angel if you're going to be attacking me very often."

I stood at the front of the tent, part of me twitching to get away from him, the other part wanting to apologize. All he had done was be nice to me, and I repaid that kindness by kicking him where it counts. *Oh, good one, Fran.*

"You watch *Buffy*?" my stupid mouth asked. It was like I was possessed or something. I should have been running or apologizing, not standing there talking TV with an honest-to-Goddess Moravian Dark One. "Which season was your fave?"

"Third." He got to his feet, breathing heavily as he stood doubled over, his hands on his knees.

"Oh. I like the fourth. Spike rocks." He didn't say anything, just slowly straightened up until he was standing more or less normally. "Um. Are you okay?"

He nodded, his hand twitching like he wanted to rub himself but couldn't because I was there. I felt guiltier than ever.

"I'm sorry."

I stared at him, blinking like an idiot. "What?"

"I said I'm sorry."

I blinked even more until I realized what I was doing. "You're apologizing to me? For what?"

"Frightening you. I shouldn't have dumped it all on you so soon."

"Oh." My inner Fran, the annoying one who always tries to make me do the right thing, nudged me hard. "Um. I'm sorry, too. I didn't mean to hurt you. Well, I did because you were getting bossy with me, but now I'm sorry you did. I mean, I'm sorry I did. We both did." Great, now I sounded like a lunatic. If he was in any doubt that I was the queen freak of all freaks before, he wouldn't be now. A lunatic freak.

"You're not a freak," he said tiredly, like it was something he said a lot.

"Will you stop that! No one gets into my mind unless I invite them."

"I'm sorry," he said again, and rubbed his neck.

Before I knew what I was doing, I stepped forward and touched the red mark on his neck where I had hit him. He stood still, his hands at his sides as I gently felt around his Adam's apple. His skin was warm. "I thought vamps were supposed to be dead. How come you're warm?"

He placed my hand on his chest, over his heart. I could feel it thumping away in there just like anyone else's heart. "Do I feel dead?"

"No." I let my fingers wander over to the silver Celtic cross that hung from his neck. "You can wear a cross."

"I can."

"You're not dead and you can wear a cross." I gave him my best squinty eyes. "Are you sure you're a Dark One?"

Quite sure. He laughed into my mind.

"Hey!"

He held up a hand and grinned. "Sorry. Won't happen again. Not unless you invite me first."

"It'd better not." I took a step back and nibbled my lip as I looked at him. "How come you're not mad at me for hitting you?"

"I frightened you. I don't blame you for what you did."

"Why not?"

His eyes had lightened while we were talking, but they suddenly went black again. He didn't say anything.

"Anyone else would have been pissed at me, but you're not. Why? Because you think I'm you're salvation?"

He just stood there, one hand in his jeans pocket, the other hanging open and relaxed, his eyes glittering like those shiny black stones Mom sometimes uses—hematite, they're called.

"I'm sixteen, Ben."

His eyebrows raised. "Ben?"

"Benedikt is kind of a mouthful."

He smiled. "I know how old you are."

"I don't even want a boyfriend, let alone to get married to you or whatever it is you Moravians do to get your soul back. I just want to be left alone. I just want to get through this summer so I can go live with my dad in the fall and go to school and not have to travel all over Europe with Mom tutoring me, like she's threatening to do. Besides, you're . . . you're . . ." I stopped. I'd rather die than tell him that he was so gorgeous he probably had to pry the girls off him with a two-by-four, whereas I was . . . me. Okay, people didn't actually barf when they saw me, but I was *not* gorgeous.

"I'm what?"

I shrugged. "A vamp."

He tucked one side of my hair behind my ear. It was an oddly intimate gesture, and left me feeling hot, then cold, then hot again. "I don't want anything from you, Fran. The only reason I told you that you were my Beloved is so you understand that you can trust me. A Dark One can never harm his Beloved."

"Oh, really? So if I had a stake and started pounding it on your chest, what would you do?"

He pursed his lips as he thought it over. He looked so funny, I couldn't keep from smiling. "Depends. Where would you be pounding?"

"Right over your heart."

"Then I'd die."

My smile faded. "Really? The stake thing works?"

"Yes, it works. So does beheading."

"And you'd let me kill you? You'd just stand there and let me kill you?"

He nodded. "If it was in your heart to see me dead, yes, I'd stand there and let you kill me."

Wow. Talk about a head trip. I decided I wasn't ready to think about that and pushed it aside. "How about sunlight?"

He made a face. "It wouldn't kill me, not unless I was out in it for several hours, but I do my best to avoid it. Gives me a hell of a sunburn."

"Huh." I looked him over. He'd taken his leather jacket off earlier and was now wearing a sleeveless black tee. His arms were tan. So was his face. He had a tattoo of words in a fancy script twined around in a circle on his shoulder. "So, what, they have Moravian sunlamps to keep you from looking fish-belly white?"

He laughed. I liked it; it was a nice laugh. It made me want to laugh, too.

"Something like that." He looked over my shoulder, then bent down to pick up the gloves I had dropped, handing them to me as he added, "Maybe we can talk about this another time."

"Sure. I promise I won't hit you again." I meant it, too. It might be stupid to believe what he said about not stopping me if I wanted to kill him (as if!), but I did believe him when he said he wouldn't hurt me.

He started toward me, toward the exit behind me. I chewed on my lip for a few seconds before I blurted out, "Would you take me for a ride on your bike?"

He was right next to me when he paused. His eyes were back to their normal dark oak color, the gold flecks clearly visible as he stared down at me; then they lifted to look beyond me. "If your mother says it's all right, yes."

I turned to see what he was looking at. Mom stood in the entrance to the tent, dressed in her white-and-silver invocation gown, the layers of light gauze fluttering around behind her in the breeze. She had a crown of white flowers in her hair, ribbons trailing down her back. In one hand, on a piece of scarlet velvet, she held her silver scrying bowl; in the other was a handful of invocation candles. Davide sat next to her, his mouth open in a silent hiss at Ben.

I sighed and plopped myself down in the nearest chair. Why did I even try to act normal when everyone around me was so weird?

Mom grilled me about Ben for the rest of the night and most of the next morning. Who was he, what did he want, why had I mentioned hitting him, yadda yadda yadda. I answered her questions because it was the first normal mom-type thing she'd done since I was in the sixth grade, and reassured her that she didn't need to cast a spell on Ben (not that I was sure it would work—maybe Dark Ones are spell-resistant? I'd have to ask Imogen).

Then she started in on stuff that really made me uncomfortable.

It was around eleven in the morning. We had just gotten up (the GothFaire closes at two in the morning during the summer), and Mom was standing at the tiny little stove that she sometimes cooked on. When she absolutely had to. She may be a great witch, but she's a pretty bad cook. Usually I do it, but this morning I had been too busy being grilled about Ben.

"I don't like the thought of you seeing a boy that much older than you," she said once she started to wind down.

"I'm not seeing him; we were just talking." Yeah, okay, so he expected me to salvage his soul at some point, but hey, that didn't mean we were dating or anything, right? "Is there any more hot water?"

Mom shook the electric teakettle and handed it over to me. I made another cup of tea (Earl Grey — I may be a freak, but I'm a civilized freak) and squeezed a quarter of a lemon into it.

"How old is he?"

I looked at her over the top of my mug. She was standing in front of the stove alcove, poking at some fruit hanging from a wire basket. The trailer we shared had one bedroom (hers) and a second bed (where I slept) that was converted from the tiny table and couch I was sitting at now. Mom has a very good lie radar. I figured she was suspicious enough without my saying something that would get her undies in a bunch. "Um . . . he's younger than Imogen."

"Is he? Then he must be about eighteen or nineteen." *Give or take a couple of hundred years, yeah.* "That's still too old for you. I'll have a little chat with him. What would you say to French toast this morning?"

Now *my* radar went off. She was offering to make me break-fast? "Sounds good. You don't have to talk to Ben, Mom. I'm not dating him or anything."

"Mmm. Do we have any eggs?"

"In the fridge." I watched her for a few minutes as she hummed a little song to herself while she whipped up a couple of eggs, sniffed a small carton of milk and decided it wasn't too old, added a sprinkle of cinnamon, then started slicing thick slabs of bread from the loaf she'd picked up a half hour earlier. "Okay. What are you up to?"

She turned around to look at me, her eyebrows doing a pretty good job of looking surprised. "What do you mean?"

"You're cooking breakfast. You never cook breakfast for me."

"I most certainly do! I cooked breakfast for you just last . . . last . . ."

"Uh-huh. You can't remember, can you? It's been that long."

She waved an eggy spatula at me. "I remember like it was yesterday. It was when you broke your arm riding your bike to school. I made you eggs Benedict. You loved it."

I smiled into my tea. "Mom, I was in the fifth grade then."

She turned back to the stove with a self-righteous sniff. "I merely pointed out that I have, upon occasion, made you breakfast."

"Usually only when you want something from me, so dish. What do you want me to do? If it involves dressing up as a naiad and frolicking around a stream like you made me do last summer, the answer is no. One round of poison ivy is enough to last me a lifetime."

She flipped the French toast in the skillet, not saying any-thing until she put it on a plate and handed it to me. To my surprise, she sat down across the table rather than making a plate for herself. "Franny, I'm worried about the Faire. It's these thefts—if they continue, the Faire will go bankrupt, and we'll have to go home."

Home! Oh, man, how I wanted to go home! Home to our little house with the tiny little flower garden, home to my room with the two leaks when it rained hard, home to everything familiar and normal, where I had my place and no one bothered me in it. Home sounded just fine to me.

Unfortunately, Mom didn't feel the same way. She'd signed a year's contract to tour with the Faire, dispensing her potions and spells while she got in touch with the European Wiccan community. She had looked forward to this year with an excitement I'd never seen in her. For three long months she yammered about how thrilling it was to be able to see Europe, and what an education I'd have going with her. She even had the school district convinced that her Ph.D. in education was good enough to tutor me for the school year while I was dragged all over Eastern and Western Europe.

Don't get me wrong; it's not like I love school or anything, but at least there I fit in. Relatively. As long as I didn't touch anyone. Most of the kids thought I was just shy, which was fine with me. At least no one thought I was a weirdo.

"I thought Absinthe said the last band ran off with the money. If they're gone, how can they steal more money?"

She fretted with her teacup, her spoon clinking against the side as she stirred it a gazillion more times. The sound of it set my teeth on edge. I buttered my French toast and spread raspberry jam on it. "Peter said this morning—this is in the strictest confidence, Fran; you can't breathe a word of this to anyone, not even Imogen—that the safe was rifled again sometime after

Absinthe had put the evening's take in it. He said he was going to have to call in the police, but I don't see how that's going to do any good. Whoever is stealing the money is very clever. He or she wouldn't be so stupid as to leave their fingerprints on the safe. Especially not if—"

She stopped and looked down at her tea as she shook the spoon and set it on the table.

"If what?" I asked around a mouthful of French toast.

Her light gray eyes lifted to meet mine. "If someone is using their special powers to steal the money."

I swallowed. "Like who?"

"I don't know. Absinthe doesn't know. Peter doesn't know. No one knows."

I made a half shrug, unwilling to admit that I would be perfectly happy if the Faire went under and we had to go home. "The police will probably find whoever it is."

"This is beyond the police, Fran. There's only one person who can possibly determine who the thief is."

I didn't see it coming. I didn't see it at all, which should prove once and for all that I don't have a single, solitary psychic cell in my body. At least not of the precognitive kind. I stuffed another chunk of French toast into my mouth. "Who's that?"

"You."

I choked, tears streaming from my eyes as I wheezed, trying to get air into my lungs around the big lump of French toast that was stuck in my throat.

"You're the only one who can find the thief, Fran."

"I'm not going to be able to do anything if I choke to death," I gasped.

She frowned. "I'm serious."

"So'm I!"

She handed me my mug of tea. "Franny, you have to do this. I know you don't like touching anyone—"

I wiped my streaming eyes with the back of my hand. "No."

"—but this is an emergency."

I shook my head, coughed, took a sip of tea, coughed again, and snarfed back the runny nose that always came with a near choking. "No!"

"I wouldn't ask you if it wasn't very important."

"It's not our problem! Absinthe and Peter can figure it out for themselves, or the police can."

"They can't, baby. If they could, they already would have. You have to help them."

"I don't have to do anything," I muttered to my half-eaten French toast.

"Please, Franny. Our whole future is at stake—"

"This isn't our future!" I shouted, slamming my hand down on the table so the mugs rattled. I was suddenly so mad I couldn't see straight. "Home is our future, not this freak show! I won't let you turn me into a monster like them! I just want to be normal like everyone else. You do understand normal, don't you? It's what you're not!"

Her eyes widened and I realized she was about to go into the "you're not a freak; you've been blessed, gifted with a skill that others would cherish" lecture. I knew it well; I heard it on the average of once a month, and at least once every couple of days after we arrived at the Faire, but I couldn't take it again. Not now. Not when I was so confused about Ben and everything.

"Where are you going?" she yelled as I jumped up from the table and grabbed my bag.

"Out."

"Francesca Marie—"

I slammed the door to the trailer on her words, jumping off the metal steps, holding my bag tight across my chest as I ran through the maze of trailers situated at the far end of the big meadow that held the Faire. Several of the Faire people said good morning to me, but I ignored all of them and settled down into a steady lope that I knew could last me a couple of miles. I ran through the trees ringing the meadow, down a small grassy slope, then onto the road that led to the town of Kapuvár.

Cars passed by on their way in and out of town, kicking up dust that swept over me, leaving my mouth and hair gritty. I slowed my lope to a trot, then a walk, trudging past field after field of cows, horses, goats, and some sheep. I rehashed the argument with my mother, changing it so I had all the good lines, my arguments so convincing she had to bow before my superior reasoning and admit that we belonged back home, not in the middle of Hungary. I muttered to myself as I passed a big white truck with wooden slatted sides, the kind they use to haul livestock. An old man who held a lead on a dirty gray horse was arguing with a tall, thin guy in expensive shoes. The tall guy kept looking around him as if he smelled something bad. A girl a few years younger than me was standing next to the fence, obviously trying not to cry.

I stopped because I like horses, and the old gray horse had lovely lines, a thickly curved neck, rounded haunch, deep chest, and big, big, soulful brown eyes.

"What's going on?" I asked the girl, forgetting for a moment that I wasn't back home where everyone spoke English. She turned and sniffed.

"It's Tesla, my *ópapi's*—grandfather's—horse. Milos is taking him away. You are American?"

"Yeah. Who's Milos?"

She pointed to the old man, who was now holding out his hand. The tall, thin guy was arguing with him as he doled out Hungarian forints (their dollars). "I study English in school. We are very good, yes? Milos, he is a . . ." She said something in Hungarian then.

"A what?" I asked.

She sniffled again. "He takes old horses, you know? And they make them into dog meat."

I stared in horror at the old man. "My God, that's horrible. Isn't that illegal or something? Why is that other guy letting him do it?"

"He is my uncle Tarvic. He says he can't afford to feed Tesla anymore, now that *ópapi* is dead, but it makes me so sad. Tesla is old, but he is special. My *ópapi* loved him more than all the other horses."

"Hey!" I yelled, scrabbling through my bag with one hand as I hurried through the gate toward the two men and the horse. The old horse nickered at me, nodding his head up and down as if he understood what I was going to do. I hoped he did, 'cause I sure didn't. "Hey, mister, I'll give you . . . uh . . . I have two hundred and forty dollars. U.S. cash. I'll give it to you for the horse."

The girl stood behind me, jabbering in Hungarian. I assumed she was translating for me, because the tall man turned and scowled at me. I dug out my wallet and waved the year's allowance that Dad had given me as a going-away present (or bribe, however you wanted to look at it). I held out the money.

"Tell your uncle that I'll give him the money if he sells the horse to me, instead. That way he won't have to pay the knacker."

"Knacker?"

"Milos."

She turned and said something to her uncle. He eyed my cash with an avid gleam in his eye, but the old man started yelling at me, shoving me backward. I held the money out to Uncle Tarvic by the very tips of the ends. "Tell your uncle that I'm with the Faire just down the road, and that the horse will be fine; he'll be treated really well."

The girl hesitated. "He won't care; he doesn't like horses."

I made an exasperated noise. "Look, you can tell him whatever you want; just get him to take my money and give me the horse."

Milos the knacker was back to trying to shove me from the field, waving his hands around wildly. Tesla laid his ears back and snorted a warning at the gestures.

"You will treat him well? You will care for him?"

"Would I be willing to give up my whole year's allowance if I was going to be mean to him?" I asked. "Yes, I'll treat him really well. I've always wanted a horse, and since Peter has a horse trailer for the horse he uses in his magic act, hauling Tesla around won't be a problem. Please."

The girl nodded and turned back to her uncle, pleading with him. Evidently the sight of my money was too much, because Uncle Tarvic snatched his money back from Milos, and handed me the lead to the horse at the same time he grabbed the money from my hand. One finger of his brushed mine, but I jerked my hand back before I could pick up anything about him.

"*Köszönöm,*" I said (Hungarian for "thank you"). "*Köszönöm.*"

I gave the lead a slight tug and the old horse started forward. I tried to remember on which side Soren walked when he led his dad's horse, Bruno, but Tesla evidently knew the ropes. He marched by my right side, heading for the road like he knew where he was going. Milos yelled and screamed a lot, but I only smiled as I led Tesla to the road, turning toward the way I had just come.

"What is your name?" the girl asked. Tesla stopped and looked back at her.

"Fran. What's yours?"

"Panna." She stepped up to Tesla, cupping her hands around his whiskery nose. He snorted on her hands. Her eyes were all weepy again, like she was going to cry. "He will be a very good horse, yes?"

"Yes, he will be a very good horse. If you like, you can come visit him while we're in town. We're going to be here three more days; then we go to Budapest."

She gave me a watery smile. "I will like that. Thank you, Fran. You are my friend."

"Sure thing. Well, come on, Tesla; we'd better get you back so I can start working on Mom."

"Working on Mom?" Panna asked.

"Nothing. I'll see you later?"

"As soon as I am able."

"'Kay. See you."

I tugged on the lead and Tesla started walking amiably enough. I looked back once. Panna was getting in the car with her uncle. Milos was grinding the gears on his truck, driving in the opposite direction. I looked at Tesla. His long white eyelashes hid his eyes as he walked along next to me, periodically stopping to graze a particularly succulent-looking patch of grass.

I had a horse. An old horse. In the middle of Europe, where I had no home but a trailer, I bought a horse. I tried to think of a reason Mom shouldn't throw the hissy fit to end all hissy fits when she saw Tesla, but knew it was a lost cause. I had only one thing I could use as bargaining power. I sighed. Tesla, drowsing as we strolled along in the morning heat, bobbed his head and rolled an eye over to look at me. "You're going to cost me a whole lot more than money, horse. A whole lot more."

We walked the rest of the way to the Faire in silence, Tesla thinking horsey-type thoughts and paying no attention to the cars as they zoomed by us, me dreading the deal I was going to have to cut. I'd have to do what Mom wanted me to do.

I'd have to find out who the thief was.

CHAPTER FOUR

"Hey," Soren said, and set a bucket of water down beside me before plopping to the ground.

"Hey," I said back. "Thanks for the water. I'm sure Tesla will appreciate it when he's done stuffing his face."

We were sitting on a bank at the far edge of the meadow, beyond the area the cars used to park. Tesla was grazing happily away in the long shadows cast by the sun as it started to dip below the trees. I had spent most of the day just sitting there, watching him. He moved stiffly and slowly, but I didn't see any signs that he was deathly ill or ready to keel over any second, both of which Mom had suggested once she got over the shock of my arriving back at the trailer with a horse in tow.

"How did your mother take it?'

I shrugged and plucked a piece of rail grass from the bank. "She threw a hissy."

Soren's freckled nose scrunched up. "A hissy?"

"A hissy fit. She had kittens. A cow. You know—she ranted."

"Oh, ranted, yes, I'm familiar with ranted. My father rants always."

"Yeah, well, when your father rants, I bet flowers don't wilt and milk doesn't turn sour." That wasn't the worst of it. Once, when she got really mad at me because I went out to a club after she said I couldn't, every mirror in the house shattered. I was grounded for a month after that. Talk about your seven years' bad luck.

"No," Soren said thoughtfully. "Although once the doves all died."

Peter was one of the three magicians who practiced magic. He was the only one of the three who could do real magic, the kind you almost never see. His grand finale was turning a box of doves into Bruno, their horse, only that was an illusion, not real magic. The real magic . . . well, it gave you goose bumps to watch it.

"I suppose sour milk is better than dead birds."

Soren selected a big piece of grass, splitting it down the middle to make a reed out of it. He blew. It sounded wet and slobbery. I folded my blade of grass carefully, put it to my lips, and sent a stream of air through the narrow gap. A high, sharp squeal silenced the nearby bird chatter for a moment. Tesla lifted his head and looked at me. I tapped the water bucket with my toes. He wandered over and plunged his gray-black muzzle into it, drinking and snorting to himself.

"Miranda said you could keep him?"

I thought back to the hour-long argument we'd had once I returned. "Well . . . she said I'd have to get a job in the Faire to pay for his food and vet bills. And she said your dad had to okay him traveling with Bruno when we're on the road, and that a vet would have to look at him to make sure he didn't have a horrible horse disease. And I have to find him a home when it's time for us to go back to Oregon. But yes, she said I could keep him."

There was, of course, one other condition, the most important condition, the one that clinched the deal for me. I agreed to become Miss Touchy-Feely in an effort to figure out which one of the Faire employees (if any) was robbing Absinthe and Peter.

I frowned at Tesla, trying to decide if he was worth all the agony he was going to cost me. He pulled his nose out of the bucket, snuffled my feet, then lifted his head and blew horse snot and water all over my legs.

"You would have been a dog's dinner without me, Tesla. You just remember that little fact!" I grabbed a handful of long grass and wiped the snot and water off my right leg.

Soren sat resting his arms on his knees. "I saw Imogen this morning."

I threw away my handful of grass and got another one, glaring at Tesla as I wiped my other leg. "Yeah? So did I. She was getting a tan."

Soren tried to make a whistle out of another piece of grass, but it fell apart. He threw it at Tesla, who promptly ate it. "She said her brother is staying with her for a few days."

I knew that. Imogen had mentioned it to me the night before. It seemed they hadn't seen each other in a long time. I wondered how many hundreds of years "a long time" was to a vamp. I threw away my grass and stood up, walking over to pat Tesla's neck. "Yeah, I know."

Soren slid a sidelong glace at me. "I don't like him. He's too . . ." He said something in German.

"What?"

He waved his hands around. "Slippery. Slick. Fast. I don't think he is nice."

"Really?" I held on to Tesla's halter and stroked my hand down his lovely curved chest. It was thick with muscles, even at his age. He turned his head and nuzzled my hand. I scratched his ears for a minute, then slid my hand under his mane and ran it down his neck, enjoying the feeling of warm horse beneath my fingertips. "I like him. He's—What the heck?"

I pushed aside a dirty length of mane and looked at the spot where Tesla's shoulder met his neck. Nothing looked different— it was all dirty gray horse hair—but running my fingers lightly along his upper left shoulder, I felt something, a thickening, like a big scar. "He must have hurt himself a long time ago," I said to myself.

"Who, Benedikt?"

"No, Tesla. Touch him here. What do you feel?"

Soren limped over and ran his hand over the horse's shoulder. "Horse."

"Try again."

Soren did, made a face, and wiped his hand on his shorts. "Sweaty horse. About Benedikt—"

I tipped the water over with my foot. Soren jumped back out of the way of the creeping puddle. I scooped the bucket up and handed it to him, clipping the lead onto Tesla's halter. "Come on, I want to give him a bath. You can help before the evening rush starts. The vet is going to see him tomorrow, so he has to look healthy."

Soren frowned, but followed me as I led Tesla across the grassy parking area. "You're avoiding the subject."

"Yeah, I know. I'm doing pretty good at it, too, huh?"

He sighed one of those dramatic sighs that guys who are fifteen sigh. "I warned you. When you come crying to me that he did something terrible to you, don't tell me I didn't warn you."

I smiled and nudged him with my elbow. "Deal."

I'll say this for Soren—he might be jealous of Ben's very cool motorcycle (and working on Mom to let me go for a ride on it was next on my list), but he was willing to let it go in order to show me how to take care of a horse. Bruno, Peter's flashy Andalusian, looked positively sparkly white compared to Tesla's dingy gray, but an hour later, after having soaped him up and rinsed him off (much to Tesla's delight—I swear that horse positively moaned with happiness when Soren produced a curry comb), he looked less gray and more like a true white. I spent another half hour combing out his mane and tail, so he was looking pretty spiffy by the time Peter stopped to check Tesla's feet and mouth.

"He's old," Peter said as he peered into Tesla's open mouth. "Probably twenty, twenty-five years. But he looks in fairly good shape." He let go of the horse's lips and patted him on the neck. Tesla arched it and did a stiff little prance-in-place move. Peter laughed. "Nice old boy. He should cause us no trouble. Your mother says you will work to pay for his feed, true?"

"True." I nodded, feeling all warm and fuzzy because Tesla was showing off. The big galoot. "I can do concessions, or tickets, or move stuff, or—"

Peter shook his head. "You will learn the palm reading from Imogen. Your mother tells me you will be good at it, and Imogen wishes to read the runes only. You will learn from her. I will pay you in feed for Tesla while you learn; then you will get real wages, yes?"

My stomach wadded up into a little ball at the thought of reading people's palms. That would mean I'd have to touch them! Sneaky, sneaky Mom. She had been trying for the last couple of years to get me to do readings for people. Now she had me right where she wanted me.

Man, you buy one horse and all of a sudden your life goes all complicated! I patted Tesla, thinking that before that morning, everything was crystal-clear to me—more than anything, I wanted to go back home. Of course, there was Ben . . . but there was nothing to stop him from going to Oregon, was there?

Tesla, however, was another subject. I was pretty sure I couldn't take him home with me; that would be way too expensive. So that meant either I had to stay and give in to my mother's evil plan to make me one of Them, or I could stay and just refuse to do anything, and mope and pout until everyone got sick of me and sent me back to live with my dad (which, to be honest, wasn't looking that good, what with the new trophy wife in the picture), or I could give up Tesla and make the best of things.

I looked at Tesla. He looked back at me with his big, liquid brown eyes. There was nothing wrong with him; he was just old. Did he deserve to be chopped up into dog food just because I didn't want to do a little investigating and some stupid palm reading? I sighed again (I really have to stop; it's getting to be a bad habit), and nodded at Peter. "All right. I'll let Imogen teach me to read palms." On my own terms— I'd wear my gloves.

"Good, good. Soren, come with me; I have much work for you. . . ."

They hurried off to the little trailer that served as an office. The generator behind the main tent hummed, then snapped into life, the big lights running down either side of the fairway buzzing on one after the other. Shadows sprang up, their edges crisp and clear in the bright blue-white light that flooded the ground, turning the green grass silvery black. Tesla whinnied, pawing the ground with one hoof as I ran the brush over him one last time.

"Found a new friend, have you?"

Ben's voice curled alongside me, almost as if it were actually touching my skin. I looked over Tesla's back. "Yep. I bought him earlier today. He's mine."

"You bought him?" Ben's black eyebrows rose as he approached us. Tesla snorted and tossed his head up and down, trying to pull away from where I had tied him to the bumper of Peter's bus. "You bought a horse. A little souvenir of Hungary?"

"Something like that." Ben put a hand out and caught Tesla's halter, murmuring soothing things as he stroked the horse's head, calming him down.

"Don't tell me: Dark Ones have a special ability to calm horses?"

He grinned that infectious grin that made me want to smile back. "Nothing so exciting. I just happen to like horses. What's his name?"

"Tesla."

"Hmm." Ben stroked Tesla's neck just as I had done. I bent over to brush his legs, and when I stood up, Ben was frowning at the horse's shoulder.

"There's a scar there," I pointed out to him.

"Yes, I noticed," Ben said. His fingers traced out the letter P, two Xs, and beneath it, a wavy line.

"What's that?" I asked. Ben looked up at me. "The symbols you were drawing. Were you warding him?"

A slow smile spread across his face. "What do you know about wards?"

I put the brush back into the bucket and stepped back from Tesla. He looked pretty good, if I did say so myself. "Not a lot. Imogen said she'd show me how to draw them sometime, but she's always so busy. Did you ward Tesla?"

"No," Ben said. "Where did you get him?"

I explained my morning's adventure, leaving out all the stuff about Mom and my promise to help find the thief. He wasn't going to be around long enough for that to matter to him.

"You know nothing about where the girl's grandfather got him?"

"Nope."

"Not even his name?"

"Tesla's?"

"The grandfather's."

I shook my head. "Nope. Is it important? Should I have gotten a receipt? My mother says I should have, that someone could claim I stole him, but I have Panna as a witness."

"I don't think a receipt would tell you anything," Ben said slowly, still stroking Tesla. He traced something on the horse's cheek. "If you like, I can look into finding out where he originated."

Tesla turned and bumped me with his head. I peeled off my gloves and scratched behind his ears. "Why?"

Ben raised an eyebrow. He was looking just as nummy as he had the night before, although this time he had on black pants and a bloodred shirt that looked soft and shimmery, like it was silk. He had two little black stone earrings in his left ear, and a diamond in his right. We are talking *major* cool, here. "Do you always ask *why* when someone offers to do you a favor?"

"Sometimes. If I think the favor is going to cost me something."

He smiled again. "This will cost you."

I walked around behind Tesla, being sure to stay clear of his back legs just in case he was a kicker. "How much? I spent all my money on him."

"Think you can convince your mother to give you permission to come on a ride with me?"

I sucked in my breath. "On your bike?" He nodded, his fingers still gently stroking Tesla's neck. "That's an awfully strange payment. How about we just go on the ride and not worry about the okay?"

"No." He shook his head and held out his hand for me. "You must get permission or there will be no ride."

I hesitated, chewing my lip as I looked at it. It was just a hand, just five fingers and a palm. I had touched him before, and I had been okay. There was no reason not to trust him now. I took a step closer to him, stretching out my arm, my hand poised over his.

I swear the air between our hands got hot.

"Are you turned off?" I asked.

He didn't say anything, just looked at me with pitch-black eyes. I let two of my fingers droop down to touch him.

It was just a hand.

"You never have anything to fear from me," he said softly, his thumb rubbing the back of my hand. "If you ever find yourself in trouble, I will help you. Without any questions."

"And all I have to do is save your soul in return?" I asked, pulling my hand out of his.

He shook his head. "I ask nothing of you. I never will, Fran."

I pretended my arm itched, and scratched at it just to break the moment. His unblinking gaze made me uncomfortable, leaving me very aware that he was a gorgeous guy in a red silk shirt and I was a big lump of a girl in a dirty pair of jeans and a sweaty T-shirt.

I picked up the bucket of grooming tools and turned toward the horse trailer, saying over my shoulder, "I'll ask my mom about the ride in the morning. She's not too happy with me tonight. At least she won't be until I start—" I stopped. It was just so easy to talk to Ben, I forgot that I didn't need to blab every thought I had to him.

"Until you start what?"

He followed me around to the front of the horse trailer, where Soren told me they kept Bruno's grain. I measured out the amount he'd mentioned, dumping it into a bucket. "Here, you carry this."

Ben took the bucket, watching as I frowned at a bale of hay. "How much is a flake? Soren just said a flake. Half, do you think?"

"No, look, you can see the natural divisions in the bale. That's a flake."

"How do you know so much about horses?"

He did a half smile. "I told you—you're not the only one who likes them."

"Oh. Have you had one? I mean, like, long ago? You know, when everyone had horses?" He looked so normal (an understatement if there ever was one) that it was hard to remember that he was walking around a couple of centuries ago, before they had cars, before they had electricity, before stuff like penicillin and anesthetic. I wanted to ask him about a gazillion questions, but figured that would have to wait.

"Yeah, I've had horses."

"I guess you would have to, huh? Did you take care of them yourself?"

His half smile got a bit quirkier. "No. I had grooms."

"Grooms? Like servants?"

He nodded.

I just stood there with my mouth hanging open like a big dumb girl. "Are you royalty or something?"

He laughed and chucked me under the chin, just like you do to a little kid. "No, I'm not royalty, Fran. You don't have to look so appalled."

I turned away, yelling at myself for being such a boob as I pulled loose a chunk about six inches wide and carried it over to the opposite side of the trailer, where Bruno was munching down on his dinner. Ben set the bucket down, then went and fetched a second with water for the horses while I brought Tesla over and tied him on a long lead to the trailer. "Din-dins! Bon appetit."

"Fran? What is it you have to start?"

I turned and faced Ben. Just what I needed in my life, a vamp with a one-track mind. "It's nothing, okay? Just a little project I have to do for my mother. Something I had to agree to in order to keep Tesla. So you can stop prying and leave me alone."

Sometimes I'd like to kick myself. Other times I just want to step out of my skin, point to my body, and say, "I'm not with her." This was one of the times when I wanted to do both.

"Sorry," Ben said, and without giving me anything more than a quick glance, he turned around and walked off.

Crap, crap, and double crap! Could I be any more stupid? The cutest guy in the whole universe—okay, he's a bloodsucker, but no one's perfect—and I have to snap at him until he goes off to talk to smaller, shorter, prettier girls, girls he doesn't have to pretend to like just because they can save his soul.

"My life totally sucks," I told Tesla. He twitched his tail aside and pooped. "Thank you. I so needed that."

I scooped the horse poop out of the way, made sure Tesla was okay for a while, then figured, as long as I was miserable and unhappy and depressed, I might as well be *really* miserable and unhappy and depressed.

Fran Ghetti, the Nancy Drew of the twenty-first century. *Not!*

CHAPTER FIVE

"Miranda says you have agreed to find the thief who steals our money. She vill not tell me how it is you are to do this. I am naturally curious. You vill tell me now." Absinthe set her overnight bag down next to her trailer, and turned to bark something in German to Karl, who had picked her up from the train station. Imogen says that Karl is Absinthe's boy toy, but I have a hard time believing that. It isn't that Absinthe is ugly, but her spiky pink hair doesn't quite go with the hard jaw and mean little eyes.

Her German accent was a lot heavier than Peter's and Soren's, but even so, when she turned her washed-out pale-blue eyes on you, you got her meaning. She was also a mind reader, a fact that made me really nervous around her. Much as I disliked Ben marching in and rifling through my mind, at least I trusted him. To a certain extent. Absinthe I didn't trust farther than I could spit. "Um . . . actually, I don't think I will tell you. Mom didn't say that was part of the bargain."

"Bargain?" Absinthe spun around and narrowed her eyes at me. It was late morning, and she'd just returned from her trip to Germany to find a replacement band. Most of the Faire people were just waking up, but I figured I'd get a start on my new role as detective, and fire up the investigation . . . such as it was. "Vat bargain is this?"

"The bargain that says I get to keep my horse if I help you. I figured the first thing I need to do is talk to you about the thefts, and maybe see the safe and stuff like that."

She gave me another narrow-eyed look, then turned and entered the trailer. I assumed I was supposed to follow, and climbed up after her. I figured the inside of the trailer would look like the outside (pink and green, remember?) —in other words, garish— but it was surprisingly uncluttered. There was an awful lot of that shade of tan called taupe, but the little couch, two chairs, and tiny table that made up the main part of the trailer were actually pretty tasteful. Absinthe set her overnight bag down on the table and waved at the curved bank of the couch.

"This is the safe. As you can see, it is a good safe, very reliable, *ja*? In the morning ven I come awake, I open the safe to take out the money for food, but there was no money, only newspaper. It was that Josef, in the band, you know? *Verdammter Schweinehund!* He is trying to ruin us!"

I squatted down in front of the safe. It was big, about two feet high, made of white-painted metal, with the usual spin dial thingy on the front, a metal handle to open it, and not a lot else. I prodded it with my toe. It probably weighed a couple of hundred pounds.

"Who has the combination to the safe?"

"Peter and I do." She shook out her linen jacket and hung it up in a tiny closet.

"No one else?"

"Of course not; do you take us for the fools?"

I tried to think of what I would do if I wanted to break into the safe. "Um . . . when do you normally open it?"

She grabbed her bag and brushed past me, opening the door behind me to her bedroom. "In the morning, to pay out such money as ve need to Elvis and Kurt for purchasing food and anything ve need for the shows."

Kurt was Karl's brother. Another boy toy, or so Imogen said.

"And you put money into it at night?"

"I do it, *ja*. I put it in a bag like this, you see?" She held up an empty black money bag, the kind with a zipper and a lock on the end. "The money goes in once ven I count up the ticket sales, and also after the fair closes, ven all the money comes from the employees."

The Faire contract called for all the performers to split their takes with Peter and Absinthe. In return they had their travel expenses paid, and were guaranteed a minimum amount each month.

"Ven I look in the morning, fffft! The money is gone, and the bag is filled vith newspaper."

I chewed on my lip as I watched Absinthe unzip her travel bag. I didn't want her to see me touching the safe—if she knew about my little curse, she'd demand I be put to work as the resident Teen Freak. With my back to her, I peeled off the gloves from my right hand and reached for the safe handle. With Absinthe liable to finish putting away her stuff any second, I didn't have time to brace myself for the onslaught of images. I just grabbed the handle and hoped for the best.

It was awful. Worse than I thought. At least seven different people had touched the safe in the last few weeks: Absinthe and Peter were the strongest, but I could also feel Karl, Elvis,

Soren, even Imogen and my mom had touched the safe at some time or another. Inanimate objects can't hold on to memories the way people do, but if someone was feeling a very strong emotion when he or she touched it, sometimes that was imprinted onto the object.

Indecision and frustration were there on the safe handle, but the overwhelming feeling, the emotion that swamped my mind was a cold, quiet desperation, the kind of desperation that makes your palms prick with sweat. One of the people who'd touched the safe was emotionally in a state so bad that touching the memory of it now left me slightly sick to my stomach.

I pulled my hand away, but didn't have time to get the glove back on before Absinthe popped into the room. "I am not seeing how you can help us if you vill not tell me how you work. Do you read the minds, eh? Can you see someone's guilt in their aura? Are you a human . . . what do you call it . . . lie detector?"

I gave her a feeble smile and shoved my bare hand behind my back, slowly backing down the narrow aisle of the trailer so she wouldn't see it. "None of that, sorry. Mom just thinks I can help. I read a lot of Agatha Christies."

Absinthe crossed her arms and glared at me. "I don't think that is at all the amusing. How vill you help us now?"

I reached for the door with my gloved hand, still keeping my back away from her. "I'll probably talk to everyone and see if anyone has noticed anything."

"Bah!" She threw her hands in the air in a gesture of annoyance. "Useless, that is useless. I have questioned everyone and no one sees anything—no one notices anything wrong. This is a vaste of my time."

I let one shoulder twitch in a half a shrug. "Yeah, well, I

made a bargain with my mother, and I'll stick to it." *No matter how much it destroys me*, I added silently. "I'll let you know if I find out anything."

Absinthe thinned her lips at me, her eyes glittering brightly. I stood with one foot on the step, one in the trailer, suddenly unable to move, locked into place by that look. My scalp tingled as I realized what she was doing. I could feel her nudging against my consciousness, trying to find a way into my mind. I wanted to yell at her to stay out of my head, but I felt as if I were caught in a big vat of molasses, as if everything going on around me had been switched into slow motion. Panic, dark and cold, gripped me as I could feel her sliding around me, surrounding me, suffocating me. She was going to get in, and then she'd know everything about me! I couldn't breathe; my lungs couldn't get any air in them. I felt squashed flat by her power, by her ability to just push aside my feeble resistance and march into my head. Everything started to go gray as I was swept up in wave of dizziness.

No! my brain shrieked.

Fran?

Warmth filled me, eased the stranglehold Absinthe held on me, allowed my lungs to expand and suck in much-needed air. I clutched at the warmth. *Ben?*

Is something wrong? He sounded sleepy, a warm, comfortable sleepy, as if he were snuggled down in a warm bed on a cold winter morning. The touch of his mind on mine was reassuring, pushing away the gray dizziness, blanketing me in security.

Absinthe is trying to get into my mind. She'll find out about me — about you, too.

She already knows about me. Don't worry; she won't get in. Imagine yourself in a sealed chamber, with no way in and no way out. Just you. Imagine yourself in that, and she won't be able to get into your mind.

I took a deep breath, my eyes still on Absinthe's as she made a big push at my mind. My knees almost buckled under the attack. *Ben!*

Think of the sealed room, Fran. His voice was so soothing, so filled with confidence, it helped push some of the black panic away. I pictured a room made of stainless steel, all rounded corners, the seams of which were welded together. There wasn't a crack, wasn't a space anywhere that anything could get in or out. It was absolutely airtight, sealed, and I stood in the middle of it.

Absinthe's hold on me snapped just as if I severed a taut rope. She snarled in German, but I didn't wait around to see what else she had to say. I babbled something about seeing her later, and ran for my life.

Ben?

He didn't answer. I couldn't feel him, either. I couldn't feel anything, not one single thing. There was just me in my brain. *Ben, are you angry because I woke you up? I'm sorry if you are, but I wanted to let you know that your idea worked. Absinthe didn't get into my head. Everything's okay now. Um. Unless you're mad at me, and then I guess everything is not okay.*

Nothing. *Nada.* Not one blessed thing. He didn't even think angry at me, the way he could think a smile.

I sighed and looked around. There're not a lot of places to hide when you're living in a big, open, grassy meadow with a bunch of tents and a cluster of trailers. I had no idea where I was going, but weaved through the trailers until I arrived at one with Norse symbols painted in gold and black. I knocked on the door as I turned the handle and slid through the door, glancing over my shoulder to make sure that no one saw me going into Imogen's trailer. "Imogen? You up? I really need to talk to you."

The shades were up, sunlight slanting into the trailer, highlighting the remains of a bagel on the tiny little table, so I gathered Imogen was up and about.

"You getting dressed?" I headed for the closed door to her bedroom. "Listen, I have a question for you— Ohmigosh!"

It wasn't Imogen in the bedroom; it was Ben. With a bare chest. Sitting up in Imogen's bed with a sleepy, surprised look on his face. Until I moved and a tendril of sunlight snaked past me into the room, falling on his bare arm. He yelped and jerked the blanket up, squinting at me.

"I'm so sorry!" I tried to move to block the sunlight, but more came in around the other side of me. "Geez, I'm sorry. I can't . . . stupid sun . . ."

"Get in and close the door," he snapped. I jumped into the room and slammed the door shut behind me.

That was when I realized that I was standing in a tiny little dimly lit bedroom with a naked vampire who looked really, really mad.

He clicked the bedside light on, pushing the blanket down to look at his arm. At the sight of the blisters that streaked up his arm I forgot all about being embarrassed that he was naked. "Did I do that? Oh, Ben, I'm so sorry. What should I . . . Ice, that's what you put on a burn."

"Don't open that door again!" he yelled just as I was about to go hunt for ice. "I don't need anything; it will be all right."

"Don't be stupid; those are like third . . . degree . . . wow." Ben stroked his burned arm. With each pass of his hand, the blisters lessened until all that remained were faintly red angry marks on his nummy tan skin. "That's amazing! You're a healer!"

"Not really." He slumped back against the wall. "I have limited regenerative powers. The weaker I am, the less I am able to heal."

"Weak?" I reached out to touch his arm, realized I had my gloves on, and yanked them off. The second my fingers touched his skin I was filled with hunger, gnawing at me, biting me with sharp, painful stabs, a need building within me to take what I needed, to subdue that animal that growled within. I jerked my fingers back and stared at Ben. "You're hungry. Is that what you meant by weak?"

He ran his hand through his hair and looked peeved. "Yes. Is there a reason you're here?"

I stared at him, unable to look away. Okay, so I was looking a lot at his bare chest, but still, even with drooling over that, I couldn't help but wonder how he could have so much pain locked inside him, yet seem so normal on the outside. "I was looking for Imogen."

"She's not here."

"Yeah, I figured that out. How come you're hungry? I mean, why aren't you . . . *you know* . . . feeding?"

"I don't like fast food," he said. I blinked. He sighed. "That was a joke. It's not as easy as just picking a person out of a crowd and guzzling, Fran. I have to be careful about whom I choose."

"Oh, because of disease and stuff? HIV?"

"No, I'm immune to disease. I'm referring to the fact that most people would notice if their wife or sister or daughter suddenly showed up woozy and suffering from a significant blood loss. It takes longer to find several people who can provide me the amount of blood I need without leaving them with a noticeable loss."

"Huh. I hadn't thought of that." I bit my lip and eyed his arm. The red marks still looked like they hurt, and I knew what sort of pain he held inside him. Since I had caused him pain, I figured it was up to me to sacrifice a little blood. Besides, there was something almost . . . *intriguing* about the thought of giving him my blood. "How about me?"

His eyebrows went up. "What?"

"You could have a little snack."

"Snack?" He looked like I had a boob sprouting out of my forehead.

"Yeah, you know, bite. Nibble. *Sink fang.* Not enough to make me woozy, but enough to tide you over until you can find someone else to . . . um . . . eat." Just in case you're wondering, this officially qualified as the strangest conversation I'd ever had.

Ben ran his hand through his hair again. I liked the way his arm muscles moved, but I tried not to let him see me admiring them. I'm really not looking for a boyfriend. Okay, the truth is, I wouldn't know what to do with one if I had him, but I decided it was better not to dwell on that.

"Fran, I can't have your blood."

"You can't?" Because he was mad at me? So mad he would rather sit there so hungry it hurt rather than sip a little Fran? "Oh. Okay. No problem. Forget I mentioned it."

He rubbed his face. "It's not because I don't want to—there's nothing I'd like more than to bind us together—but that's exactly what it would mean: we would be bound together for the rest of our lives, which, incidentally, would be measured in centuries rather than decades."

I stood at the door, part of me wanting to run screaming from the room, the other part wanting to stay and talk to him. He *looked* so normal. . . . "It would?"

He sighed and pulled the blanket up his chest a bit. "A Dark One who joins with his Beloved by taking her blood cannot feed from anyone else. They are bound to each other, together, for eternity, giving each other life."

"Oh, you mean you'd have to . . ." I made claw fingers and gestured toward my neck with them.

He nodded.

"Right, so snacking is out. I like you and all, but I don't think I want to spend eternity with you. You don't . . . uh . . . mind me saying that, do you? You're not still mad at me?"

He frowned. He even frowned cute. Maybe I should re-think this whole no boyfriend thing. "I'm not mad at you, Fran. Why would you think I was?"

I waved a hand around vaguely. "You didn't answer me earlier, and I woke you up and all. . . ."

"I didn't answer you?"

"Yeah, after I left Absinthe, I did the weirdo psychic mind-meld thingy with you to thank you, but you didn't answer. I figured you were PO'd at me."

He yawned into his hand. "Do it now."

"Huh?"

"Try the weirdo psychic mind-meld thingy now."

"Ah." *Like this?*

He just looked at me.

Helloooooooo? Ben? Anyone in there?

"Well?"

"You're not answering. If you're not going to answer you could at least have voice mail or something."

One corner of his mouth quirked up. "Fran, what was the last thing you did before you left Absinthe?"

I gave him moue lips. "You know, you told me to do it! I imagined I was in a sealed room where nothing could get into my mind."

"And nothing could get out?"

I blinked at him for a second, then grinned. "Oh. I didn't think of that. How do I unseal my mind?"

"You imagined yourself protected in the room; just visualize that protection gone."

I chewed on my lip. "Will I be able to get it back again? I don't think Absinthe is one to give up too easily. In fact, I don't know what's stopping her from reading everyone's mind who works here." And incidentally figuring out for herself who stole the money.

He yawned again. "You can protect yourself whenever you need to. Everyone can; Absinthe can't read anyone's mind who has protected it. The first thing someone with a psychic ability learns is how to protect their mind from invasion. Didn't your mother teach you that?"

"Um . . . no." I pictured myself opening a door to the stainless-steel room and stepping outside it. *Thanks, Ben.*

"You're welcome. Is there anything else?"

"No. I'm sorry I woke you, twice. And sorry about the arm. And the whole Beloved thing. I don't imagine you're terribly happy about it, either."

His eyes glittered blackly at me as he pulled the blanket up to his neck.

"Will you take me for a ride tonight? Mom says I can as long as I'm back by ten. I know that doesn't give you a lot of time after the sun goes down, but —"

"I'll see you at nine."

I nodded and waited until he pulled the blanket over his head before opening the door. I left a note for Imogen on her table, then hurried out, feeling pretty good about things. Ben wasn't mad at me, and had shown me how to beat Absinthe at her own game. Mom was in a relatively happy mood with me after I agreed to do what she wanted. Tesla looked happier at his new life—the vet had given him a clean bill of health—and he even did his funny little dance-in-place step when Soren and I led him and Bruno out and put chain hobbles around their front feet so they could graze loose in the meadow without running off.

Sure, I still had all that Nancy Drewing to do, but all in all, life was starting to look up.

CHAPTER SIX

My life sucks bullfrogs. No, seriously, I mean it.

Oh, okay, maybe it's not *that* bad. But if you found yourself having to talk to a guy who not only looked like Elvis Presley, and sounded like Elvis Presley, but who actually thought he *was* Elvis Presley, wouldn't your day be a bit on the bullfrog-sucking side? Yeah. I thought so.

"Hey, there, little lady. What can the big man do for you, uh-huh?"

See? Sucky.

"Hi, Elvis. I wondered if I could talk to you for a couple of minutes."

He did a little hip shake as he combed his big black do in front of the floor mirror he always set up outside of his trailer. Elvis was thin, a little shorter than me, and had lots and lots of thick black hair that he greased back into a puffy-fronted fifties hairdo. I can't believe guys actually wore their hair like that, but Mom says her dad used to, which is going to make me a little weird about Grandpa when I see him again.

"Sure ya can." He did another hip shake. Elvis is very big on his hip shakes. "Pull up a chair and we'll jaw awhile."

"I want you to tell me a little bit about demons."

He stopped in mid–hip shake, and turned around to look at me. "Demons? Now what would a little filly like you want with a big, bad ol' demon?"

Elvis is the resident demonologist. He claims he doesn't actually raise them (which I guess is major bad news), but Mom says there's something about his aura she doesn't trust. Technically Elvis is supposed to counsel people who think they're being plagued by a demon, and provide protective talismans against further demon attacks. I guess he does a roaring trade among businessmen.

"Well, I want to know what sort of things a demon can do for you. If you raised one, that is."

Elvis scowled and turned back to the mirror. "Your mama tell you to ask me that?"

"No, she doesn't know I'm talking to you. In fact, she'd be pretty ticked off if she knew I was. She doesn't like anything to do with the dark powers."

He snorted and stepped back to admire himself in the mirror. "Nothin' wrong with the dark powers as long as you know how to handle them." He turned and pointed his comb at me. "Demons ain't for little girls to play with, though. It takes a strong person to handle 'em."

I only *just* kept from rolling my eyes at the "little girl" comment. I'm three inches taller than him! "Can you make them do whatever you want?"

Elvis slipped on a leather jacket despite the fact that it was warm out. He does a trick during Kurt and Karl's Malevolent Magick show where they materialize him in full Elvis regalia right into a glass box on the middle of the stage. Soren says he thinks it's an illusion, not real magic, but I can't figure out how they do it if it's not real. "Demons? Course you can, assuming you're strong enough. If you aren't, you'll be demon chow."

He made snapping sounds like he was eating someone up.

"Are there any limits to what you can get a demon to do?"

"Limits?" He lit a cigarette and offered me one. I shook my head. "What kind of limits?"

"Like . . . can they go through walls? Say, into the box that you materialize into?"

He snorted and blew smoke out his nose (I hate that). "Honey, there ain't nothin' that can keep a demon out from someplace it wants into, 'cept if you were to draw a bunch of wards. Or if the walls were made of steel. They *hate* steel. Burns 'em."

"Oh. Okay. Well, thanks a lot, Elvis. I'd better be on my way. Have to help Mom set up."

"You're not planning on raisin' yourself a demon, now, are you?"

I held up my hand, oath style. "Nope. Wouldn't know how if I wanted to."

"Good. Demons should be left to those who know how to handle 'em." He turned to give himself one last look in the mirror. I reached out with my left hand (which just had the lace glove on, no latex underneath it) and gently touched his back. Latex and animal hide were the only things that could tamp down on my ability to feel things when I touched people, but I really hated the thought of filling my mind with Elvis. I was sure the dimmed version would tell me enough.

I snatched my hand back, smiling wildly as he turned around toward me. "Thanks! See you later."

Or never, if I got my wish. I had the worst desire to go take a shower, to wash out of my mind the lewd images and thoughts about Imogen that filled Elvis's. If they had such a thing as brain shampoo, I'd be buying a truckload of it.

"What a pervert," I said as I headed toward Imogen's tent. I was going to be sure to tell her to watch out for him—the things he was thinking about her just weren't healthy. "But at least he's a pervert who couldn't get a demon to steal the money for him. Not from a steel-lined safe."

Imogen's tent was empty. She'd been gone all day, probably shopping in town (she loved to shop), but it wasn't like her to be away so close to opening. I glanced across the meadow. I'd moved Tesla to the small section behind the portable toilets so he could graze out of the way of the Fairegoers. Soren was brushing Bruno, getting him ready for his appearance in Peter's magic act. The sun was still barely visible through the trees, long amber and pink fingers stretching across a deepening sky. In another half hour it would be dark, and the GothFaire would spring to life. Hundreds of people would tramp through the Faire, laughing, shrieking, having body parts pierced, communicating with their dead loved ones, playing with torture devices . . . you know, the usual evening out.

I went over the mental list of people who had touched the safe. Elvis, my prime suspect, was a no-go. Imogen and Mom, I was sure, were just coincidence. Peter had no reason to rob himself (motive, the detectives call it), and Soren probably also had a legitimate reason to be putting something into the safe. Which left Karl.

I looked down the long center aisle to where Kurt and Karl were wheeling their props into the main tent. I stopped by one of the booths to get a wurst and a big pretzel, scarfing the wurst down as I walked toward the main tent.

"Hey, Soren," I said, pausing by the horse trailer. He was rubbing shiny stuff onto Bruno's hooves to make them pretty. I held out the pretzel.

"Thanks," he said, wiping his hands onto his rumpled shorts before taking it. "You want me to feed Tesla with Bruno?"

I licked the last of the wurst juice off my fingers, frowning just a little. "That would be really nice of you, but you don't have to do it."

He grinned and chomped off a big bite of pretzel.

I was instantly suspicious. "Okay, how come you're being nice?"

He glanced around, his grin deepening, "*Tante* told me you're supposed to be figuring out who has been stealing the money. I thought you might be *on the case.*"

"You watch way too much American TV," I said, and pulled on both sets of my gloves. "Speaking of that, have you noticed anything suspicious about the safe?"

"Suspicious?" Little bits of dough flew out as he talked around his mouthful of pretzel. "What is suspicious about a safe?"

I did a little sideways head bob. "I don't know . . . someone hanging around it who shouldn't be, someone in the trailer when your aunt or dad puts money away, anyone who knows the combination, that sort of thing."

He looked around quickly, then leaned in, tapping his chest. "I know the combination."

I raised my eyebrows. "You do?"

"Yes, Papa wrote it down on a piece of paper because he

was always forgetting it. He left the paper in the tent one day. I picked it up."

My mouth hung open just a little bit until I realized that and got a grip on myself. "You mean to say that your dad left the combination to the safe out in the open where anyone could see it?"

"Not out in the open, no. It was in the tent a few weeks ago, when we were in Stuttgart, remember? It was on the dove case with some notes about towns we were going to. The only people who could have seen it were—"

"Anyone connected with the Faire, and that includes the band who ran out in the night. Jeezumcrow, Soren, anyone could be opening the safe! Did you tell Peter that you found the combination?"

He shook his head and stuffed the last of the pretzel into his mouth. "I put it back in the desk, so he wouldn't know it was gone. But I saw the number on it. I remember."

I looked at him, really looked, the way Mom says you should look at people, to see past their outer surface and into their soul. I've never been able to see into souls, but she says it just takes patience and practice. I tried now. I cleared my mind of all the suspicions and worries and other stuff that was polluting my thoughts, and looked at Soren.

I saw nothing. So much for Mom's way.

"Cow cookies," I snarled, and peeled off my gloves, touching his arm. He looked surprised at that, but I didn't pay attention. I was too busy trying to beat off all the things going on in his mind. Images of his dad smiling and laughing battled with Peter snapping at him, telling him he wasn't trying, that he would never be anything but an illusionist if he didn't put his mind to his work. There were also quick flashes of Absinthe yelling at

Peter, pleasurable moments of time when Soren worked with the animals, taking care of Bruno, feeding the doves, even petting Davide. Most surprising of all, there were also images of me in his mind, confusing images that didn't make any sense because they were overlaid with a mixture of frustration and pleasure.

There was nothing of the quiet desperation I felt on the safe, however.

"Are you okay? You look funny, like you're mad and happy at the same time."

I pulled my hand from his arm and gave him a half smile. "Yeah, I'm okay. Just trying something."

He looked interested. "An experiment? A detective experiment?" His eyes opened wide. "Am I a . . . a . . . what did they call it . . . a perp?"

"Man, you really *are* watching too much American TV." I laughed, glad for a chance to shake the creepy feeling I always got when I peeked into people's minds. "No, you're not a perp. Did you mean what you said?"

He dug through a canvas satchel and pulled out two apples, offering me one. I shook my head. "About what?"

"About bringing Tesla in for me. I have something to do at nine, so if you wouldn't mind doing it, I'd really appreciate it."

He leaned close and asked in a hoarse whisper, "Are you going to be giving everyone the third degree?"

I whapped him on the arm with my elbow. "No, stupid, I'm . . . I'm going to meet . . . I'm going to . . . um . . ."

He just looked at me as I stumbled over my tongue.

"Ben's going to take me for a motorcycle ride, that's all. It's nothing, really."

He froze, the apple halfway to his mouth as his eyes got small. "You've got a date with Benedikt?"

"It's not a date; it's just a ride on his motorcycle."

Soren blinked. "Did Miranda say you could go? I thought you said she didn't want you being with him?"

"She did, but she changed her mind, and before you say anything else, you can just stop, because it's not what you think."

"You don't know what I'm thinking," he said quietly.

"You'd be surprised," I muttered. "Thanks for taking care of Tesla tonight. I owe you. I'll see you later, 'kay?"

I hurried off before he could say anything else. It occurred to me that although I wasn't going on a date or anything, I didn't want Ben to see me in the same old grubby tee and jeans that Tesla had slobbered over. Mom was still in the trailer, just getting ready to go do her witch stuff. She stayed long enough to give me yet another lecture about going out with Ben (she insisted on thinking of this as a date, which it clearly wasn't, but no one else but me seemed to realize that), pressing her most powerful amulet into my hand.

"Let me see you put it on."

"Mom! I don't need it. Ben's not going to do anything to me. He's nice. He doesn't want to do anything to hurt me."

"He's a boy; that's enough. Put it on."

I rolled my eyes and slipped the chain over my head. "There. Are you happy now? I look like a total geek."

My mother's most powerful amulet consisted of the dried-up, leathery, nasty-looking leg of a chicken. She got it off a friend of hers who was a voodoo priestess. Mom said it had incredible powers of protection. I was sure it did. Anyone who got a good close look at the gross chicken foot would run away from the person wearing it.

"You just keep that on. And don't forget, I want to see you in front of my tent promptly at ten."

"I know, I know. I'm not a kid anymore, Mom."

"You're not the adult you think you are, either." She scooped up Davide, then paused at the door, coming back into the room to kiss me on the forehead. "Have a nice time. But not too nice."

I gave her a little hug, just enough to show her I loved her without either of us getting all mushy, patted Davide on his head (which he hates), and turned back to the three drawers that held my clothes.

"I wish I had some girl clothes," I muttered as I went through my things. "Not that this is a date or anything, but still, I wish I had . . ."

A vision popped into my head. Not the kind of vision I get from touching things, but a memory of the first couple of days we were in Germany. We'd just arrived, and Mom had tried to cheer me up by taking me shopping. We each bought soft, light-weight gauze broomstick skirts, Mom's in peach colors, mine in dark blues and purples, along with matching silk peasant shirts. She joked at the time that we could dress up as Gypsies for Halloween. *Those* were girl clothes, and best of all, I didn't look quite so linebacker in them.

Fifteen minutes later, right on the dot of nine, I emerged from the trailer, twitching my skirt to make sure it wasn't tucked up in the waistband, feeling a bit obvious in my girl clothes. There was also the fact that I had a chicken claw under my shirt. . . .

I took three steps before someone loomed up out of the darkness. I shrieked and jumped a foot in the air.

"It's just me," Ben said.

"Well, give me a heart attack, why don't you?" I gasped, clutching at my heart. He moved out of the shadow, into the pool of light cast by one of the nearby lamps. "Oh, I'm so glad you think it's funny. I just bet you won't be laughing when you have to explain my dead body to my mom."

His smile widened. "I haven't seen you in a dress before. You look lovely."

I tugged the neckline of the peasant shirt up, more than a little uncomfortable with the way he was looking at me. It was admiring. Don't get me wrong; I want to be admired, but it just didn't seem right that a guy who looked like him should be giving that look to someone like me. "Yeah, well, I'm a girl. Sometimes I wear girl stuff."

He held out his hand. I hesitated only a few seconds before I took it. We started walking toward the car area. "I'm glad you do, although I hope you won't be too cold riding in a skirt."

I stopped. "Oh. I hadn't thought of that. Maybe I should change—"

He tugged me forward. "No need. I'll make sure you're warm."

I walked a few feet, waiting until we were past a group of people who were laughing as they shoved one another toward the ticket booth. "Um, Ben? You're not still . . . uh . . . hungry, are you?"

He paused, looking down at me. I couldn't see his face, since it was in shadow, but the lamplight shone on his hair, making it black and glossy as ebony. He had it pulled back in a ponytail again, and wore another silk shirt (this one emerald green) and black jeans.

In other words, he was gorgeous as usual. A couple of girls who were giggling at each other stopped to look at him. He ignored them, shifting slightly until I could see he was smiling down at me. "Would it make you feel better to know that I've had dinner?"

I smiled back at him. "Yes, it would."

"Really?" he asked, letting go of my hand to pull his motor-cycle upright. "I will take that as a positive sign."

"Of what?"

He swung a leg over the motorcycle. "Our future. Climb on; we don't have a lot of time if I have to have you back by ten."

I decided to let the "our future" comment go and grabbed his shoulder to steady myself as I got on behind him, tucking my skirt up under my legs so it wouldn't get caught in the wheels.

"No helmets?" I asked.

"Do you want one?"

"Mom would probably have a hissy knowing I went out without one . . ."

He glanced over his shoulder at me, one eyebrow cocked in question.

"It's not against the law, is it?"

"Not here, no. If you were riding with anyone else, I'd say you should wear one, but I will see to it that you come to no harm." I weighed Mom's potential anger, and decided that just this once, I'd trust Ben. After all, I *was* wearing the horrible protection amulet. "Okay."

"Put your arms around me," he said, still looking over his shoulder at me.

"Uh . . ." I said, hesitating, wondering if I should show him the amulet in case he got any funny ideas.

"It's safer that way. I wouldn't want you to fall off." He looked like he wanted to laugh at me, so I leaned into his back, wrapping my arms around his middle. He started the motor-cycle, told me to keep my feet up, and off we went. My head rested against his shoulder, his hair right there under my nose.

He smelled good, kind of spicy, not like the aftershave my dad uses that makes me sneeze, but nice. He smelled . . . Ben-ish. I smiled into the back of his neck, my hair whipping back as we bounced off the grass and onto the smooth road, the motor revving as we zoomed into the yawning blackness of the night.

CHAPTER SEVEN

"**D**o you . . . to try . . . back?"

The wind snatched Ben's words away before I could hear them.

"What?" I yelled into his ear.

He waited until he was on a straight stretch of road, then turned his head toward me. "I asked you if you wanted to try driving before we have to go back."

"Really? You'd let me? Sure! I'd love to!"

Ben pulled over to the side of the road, holding the motorcycle steady while I slid off the back. We'd been zooming around the countryside for about a half hour, down long, curvy roads, through a couple of towns, and past a big lake. We were out in the middle of the countryside now, in a rural area where there were no streetlights and only a few houses. Conversation had been limited to Ben asking me a couple of times if I was too cold, and yelling the town names as we approached them. Other than that we just rode through the night, me pressed against the warmth of his back, the rumble of the motorcycle beneath us, and the rush of the wind our buffers against the rest of the world.

Ben slid backward on the seat so I could sit in front of him. He showed me how to use the throttle and clutch on the handlebars, how to brake, where the gearshift was, wrapping it up with a quick lesson in motorcycle physics before allowing me to take charge.

"This is very cool," I said as I settled back against his chest. It was really intimate being pressed up against him like that, with his legs hugging mine, but it was nice intimate, not at all like a guy grabbing your boob or something icky like that. I pursed my lips as I looked down at myself. "Don't look."

"What?"

"Don't look." I had tucked my skirt under my legs, but realized that without Ben blocking the wind, the lightweight material would soon flutter up around me, probably catching in the wheels and killing us both. Or at least me. I rose up, reached between my legs to grab the bottom of the back of my skirt, pulling it forward and tucking it up into my waistband so I was wearing my skirt Gandhi-style. I pushed the stray bits firmly under my legs and sat down. Ben pulled me back against his body (which was really nice, but I had to remind my inner Fran twice that this wasn't a date and she wasn't supposed to go gaga over him), wrapping his arms around my waist in a way that made me feel protected even though he was at my back. I gently let out the clutch, and we were off.

I suppose the best things that can be said about my motorcycle skills are that A) I didn't crash us, and B) I didn't get any bugs in my teeth. I drove along for a while kind of stop-and-start-ish, managed to kill the engine once, and almost tipped us over when I went off the road into the dirt. There was one really fun moment, though. We were on a stretch of road that ran past a winery, a long straight road. The moon was rising, so I could see that there were no cars coming toward us.

"I want to go really fast," I yelled back to Ben. "But we'll go off into the dirt if I do it."

"Lean back," he said, his voice nice and warm against my cold ear.

He let go of my waist and grabbed the handlebars, one arm on either side of me, his foot sliding under mine to the gearshift. The bike bucked beneath us as the engine roared into supersonic mode. All of a sudden we were flying down the road, going so fast I couldn't breathe, almost couldn't see for the wind-whipped tears that snaked from the outer edges of my eyes, the wind molding my shirt to my front like a pair of hands stroking my skin. Our shadows danced blackly along the shoulder of the road, gone in the flick of an eye. It was magical, as if there were nothing in the world but Ben and me and the motorcycle, and an endlessly long black road. I threw my hands into the air and laughed with the sheer joy of going so fast the air was stripped from my lungs.

Ben chuckled in my ear, his lips warm as they nuzzled me, sending a little shimmer of heat down my neck. He slowed down as he came to a sweeping curve at the end of the road, letting me take the controls again. "I've created a monster, I think."

My skin felt all prickly where he had touched me, but it was a good prickly, a nice prickly. I dragged my mind away from that feeling. No sense in going *there*. "No, but I want a motorcycle now. This is just too fun."

It was also really cold up front despite it being a warm night out, so after about fifteen minutes of my being a biker chick, I agreed to Ben's suggestion that he drive again. We rode back to the Faire without saying anything else, but I couldn't shake the prickly feeling his touch had given me. All of a sudden I wanted to give something back to him for such a wonderful evening.

He parked the bike alongside the far edge of the parking ground, waiting for me to dismount before he turned off the engine. I stood beside the bike, glancing around quickly. We were in the shadows cast by a nearby stand of trees. The people streaming past us didn't even give us a second glance, focused as they were on the bright lights of the Faire.

My stomach twirled around on itself. I wanted to do this, really wanted it, but it was also kind of scary. "Ben?"

"Hmm?" He pocketed his keys and turned to me.

My stomach started turning somersaults. I stepped forward, put my hands on his shoulders, and brushed my lips against his.

He froze, his hands at his sides. I couldn't see his eyes, but I assumed they were black as the sky above. "What was that?"

I let go of his shoulders and stepped back. "It was a kiss."

"It was?" I knew, I just *knew* by the tone of his voice that one of his eyebrows was raised in question. I also knew that a guy like him—so gorgeous, not to mention at least three hundred years old—had probably kissed a thousand women, all of them better kissers than me. I was certain the French Revolution babe with the legs was. I stepped back another step, feeling positively sick to my stomach now. *Stupid Fran! Stupid, horrible-kisser Fran!*

"Fran?"

I held up my hands and took a step to the side. "It's okay; you don't have to say it. I'm sorry. I won't do it again."

He took my hands, placing them on his chest, his palms

warm against the back of my hands as I was pulled gently up against his front. "Now you make me sad. That wasn't a kiss, Fran."

I couldn't look at him. Even if I could see him, I didn't want to look at his eyes. I looked at his earlobe instead, the one with the diamond in it. "I said I'm sorry. You don't have to rub it in that I'm so bad—"

"You're not bad, just inexperienced. Would you like me to kiss you?"

"No," I said, feeling all stubborn and even more stupid than ever. Now he pitied me because I didn't know how to kiss properly. I hate being pitied almost as much as I hate being called a freak.

"All right. How about you kiss me again? This time, don't just brush your lips over mine; keep them there while you say, 'Mississippi.'"

"You're laughing at me."

He let go of my hands on his chest, and slid them around my waist, pulling me closer until his breath feathered across my face as he spoke. "I can assure you that the last thing I want to do now is laugh. Kiss me, Fran. Please."

It was the "please" that did it. I stopped looking at his earlobe, raising my chin a little so my mouth was a hairbreadth from his. "Mississippi," I said, my lips going all warm and soft at the touch of his.

"Again," he whispered.

"Mississippi," I breathed, this time allowing my lips to touch his the whole time I said the word.

"Once more," he said, his voice low and smooth, like black satin.

Mississippi, I thought as I kissed him, really kissed him, my arms sliding up around his shoulders, catching in his hair. I tugged on the leather thong he used to tie back his ponytail, his hair spilling like cool silk over my fingers as his lips moved beneath mine, his mouth opening a little, just enough to suck at my lower lip.

I pulled back from him, slowly, my lips clinging to his like they didn't want to leave (smart lips), my hands trailing over his shoulders and down his chest until they dropped down at my sides, suddenly empty and cold. My brain—what there was of it—ran around like a hamster on a wheel, trying to think of something to say that wasn't, "Holy cow! Do you know how to kiss!"

"Um," I said, then wanted to die. *Um? Come on, Fran; you can do better than that!* "Did you know that your hair is longer than mine?"

He stared at me for a minute, then tipped his head back and shouted with laughter. I turned bright red, I just know I did, because my cheeks went all hot; then suddenly he hugged me, very hard, and let me go.

The hug made me feel better. My hands were on his arms while he hugged me, and I couldn't feel any sense of his mocking me. There was amusement, and pleasure, and a really warm, tingly feeling that I didn't want to look at too closely, but there wasn't any sign he was making fun of me. I relaxed. "I hope you're laughing with me, not at me, 'cause if you're not, you're going to scar me for life and I'll never be able to kiss anyone again without wondering if I totally suck at it."

He took my hand and squeezed it, pulling me toward the Faire. "You don't suck at kissing, Fran. I was laughing because you're such a delight."

A delight. *Hmm.* I thought about that for a couple of minutes as we walked toward my mother's tent, my hand in his, my insides all warm and glowy. Someone thought I was a delight. Made a nice change from freak.

I waved at Mom as she explained a spell to a customer. She looked at her watch, pursing her lips at me. I mouthed, *Sorry!* to her (we were ten minutes late) and pretended I didn't notice her scandalized look when she saw me holding Ben's hand.

"I have to talk to Imogen when she's not busy," I told Ben as we wandered down the center aisle. We stopped to check on Tesla, who was having a snooze, one back leg cocked up on the edge of his other hoof. I patted him, and turned back to Ben. "Thank you for the ride and . . . uh . . . everything."

He smiled at me; then his eyes shifted to Tesla, who woke up enough to realize that potential treat givers were present, and thus they should be snuffled to see if either had an apple or carrot on their person. We didn't, but I scratched his ears.

"Have you noticed this?" Ben took my hand, using my forefinger to trace an L shape on Tesla's cheek.

"Huh," I said, peering closely at Tesla's coat, my fingers feeling again for the slight thickening. It *was* an L. "What is it?"

"It's a brand."

I wrinkled my nose. "Ew. Why would someone brand him on his face?"

Ben just looked at me for a few seconds, then finally said, "Tesla is a special horse."

"That's what Panna said."

"Panna?"

"The girl whose grandfather owned Tesla. She said that he always told her that Tesla was a special horse."

"He is special. Have you ever heard of a breed called Lipizzan?"

I shook my head. I liked horses, but didn't know too much about them. "Is that why someone put an L on his cheek? Because he's a Lipizzan?"

"Something like that."

"What about the odd-shaped scar on his neck?"

"It's another brand. What did you want to see Imogen about?"

"You're pretty good at changing subjects, aren't you?" I patted Tesla's black nose and started back toward the main fairway. "Are you rich?"

He raised both of his eyebrows. "You're not so bad at subject changing, either. Do you need a loan?"

"No. I just want to know if you've got lots of money. I mean, you mentioned having servants a long time ago. I didn't know if that meant you'd run out, or if you're loaded."

"I think the word is comfortable."

"Oh." I knew what that meant. It was a polite word for rich. "Is Imogen comfortable, too?"

"I would imagine so. Why do you want to know?"

"She shops a lot."

He stopped, putting a hand on my wrist to stop me. "Why the questions, Fran?"

"I just wanted to know if she had oodles of money lying around to shop with, or if she . . ."

"If she what?"

I hesitated. I'd just kissed the guy; I couldn't very well blurt out that I thought his sister might be dipping into Absinthe and Peter's safe to fund her shopping trips. "If she needed some."

"I'm sure if you ask her, she'll tell you."

"Yeah, that's what I thought. I suppose I had better run

along. I'm supposed to be learning how to read palms, not that I want to, but Mom says I have to in order to pay for Tesla."

He looked curious. "Do you always do everything your mother says?"

I laughed. "Not even close. But I have to about this, or else I have to find Tesla a new home." I hesitated to tell him more, to explain how confusing it all was—part of me wanting to go home, back to the normal life I had carefully built; but the other part of me, a Fran I didn't know existed, suddenly popped up and said she wanted to keep Tesla, and to stay where Ben was liable to be.

I told that Fran she had things mixed up, and that nothing was worth being a weirdo touchy-feely girl, but she pointed out that I was a weirdo touchy-feely girl no matter where I went, so why shouldn't I have a little fun?

I hate it when I argue with myself. I *never* win.

"I'll see you around, huh? You're going to be here for a little while longer?"

He did the brushing-my-hair-behind-my-ear thing again. "Yes, Imogen has asked me to extend my visit. I'll be here for a bit more."

"Good." A big weight I didn't know was squashing me lifted. I gave him a little smile, deciding that now was as good a time as any to ask him what I wanted to know. "Um . . . can you read minds?"

He didn't even blink at the question; he just answered it. "Not unless I have a bond with the person whose mind I wish to merge with."

"Bond? Oh, you mean . . ." I made slurping noises.

A little teeny-tiny smile curled the edges of his mouth. "Not necessarily. A bond of blood sometimes will be strong enough that I can communicate with the person, but the most powerful connections are between people who have some sort of emotional bond. With trust comes strength."

"Oh, so that's why you can talk to me in my head?"

"You are my Beloved. We are genetically engineered to be able to communicate without words."

"Except when I don't want you to." I thought for a moment. "If I do the mind-protection thing, could you get through it? I mean, could you force your way into my mind because of this connection we have?"

He didn't say anything. With that silence came a sudden understanding.

"You can't lie to me, can you? That's one of the Dark One rules, isn't it?"

His eyes weren't black, as I expected. The gold bits glittered brightly. "Yes, it's one of the rules."

"So you could force your way into my mind, but you never would because you know it would really cheese me off?"

He looked a bit annoyed. "It goes deeper than that, but that is the basic idea, yes."

"Wow. This is pretty powerful stuff. You'd let me kill you— you can't lie to me . . . Is there anything else? I mean, do I have, like, absolute power over you?"

He gave me a really weak smile, kind of like he didn't want to, but couldn't help himself. "There's a lot more, and no, I'm not going to tell it to you. Not until the time comes that you are ready to hear it."

I couldn't help myself. I knew I shouldn't be encouraging this, but I just couldn't help myself. "When will that be?"

"I have no idea." His face was unmoving, the wind ruffling his long hair around his shoulders.

"Oh." I wanted to tell him that I didn't think things were ever going to work out between us, but I didn't. Some part of me, some tiny little part, wanted me to work things out. It kept me silent.

"What are you up to?" he asked. "Whose mind do you want to read? And what does it have to do with Imogen and money?"

I was a little surprised he didn't know what Mom and Absinthe had cornered me into doing. Soren knew, and although I doubted anyone else did, I was pretty sure either Mom or Absinthe would tell Imogen. For some reason—probably one of those Moravian things—Imogen always seemed to know the latest gossip. But apparently she hadn't told her brother about the thefts.

That was interesting.

It was also icky. I hated feeling suspicious of Imogen. She and Soren were my only friends here.

And Ben. But he wasn't really a friend; he was a Dark One who needed me to bring the light back into his life. . . .

"It's just a little project I'm doing," I finally answered, not wanting to tell him the truth of my suspicions.

"What sort of a project?"

"Nothing you need to worry about. I can handle it, no problem."

I started to walk past him toward Imogen's tent, but he stopped me again. "Fran . . ." His forehead was all wrinkled up in a frown. "If you get into trouble, any trouble, you know I will help you."

"Like with Absinthe? Yeah. I know. And thank you."

"No, not just like the episode with Absinthe. Any trouble—you know that I will help you no matter what the problem. You just have to ask me."

"What makes you think I can't deal with my own problems?" That warm, glowy feeling inside me fizzled out into annoyance. "You think that just because I'm a girl I need to be bailed out of every situation, right? Well, think again, Benedikt Czerny. This is the twenty-first century. Women don't need guys to do everything for them anymore."

His frown tried to match mine, but I'm the queen of frowns. "I didn't say you couldn't. I simply meant that there are some things that are better left to me. It doesn't lessen your strength to admit that there are some things you can't do."

"Yeah?" I poked him in the chest, just because I knew it would annoy him. How dared he think I couldn't handle my own problems? Patronizing me, that was what he was doing, and I hate being patronized almost as much as I hate to be pitied or thought of as a freak. Patronizing is number three on my list of things I really, really dislike. "You've got that 'I'm so macho, couldn't you just die' look on your face, so you're not fooling me one single bit."

"All I said was that—"

"I know what you said; I'm not stupid! You said if I was too wimpy to deal with my own life, you'd come along like some big, brave vamp knight and rescue my pathetic butt. Ha! I have news for you—my butt doesn't need rescuing. I can do anything you can do. Well . . . with the exception of peeing standing up. And drinking blood. I don't think I could do that; it's just too icky. And the healing thing. And warding stuff, but I could do that if someone taught me how, so that really shouldn't count."

"Fran—"

"Good night, Ben."

Without staying to hear any more of his macho bull, I headed off down the aisle that was growing more and more packed with people every minute. The magic acts were popular, but it was the bands that really brought the crowds out, and as Absinthe had brought with her a German band that had local fans, the crowds were even thicker than normal. I wound my way through them, skimmed around the line of people waiting for Imogen, and presented myself to her, saying, "Peter says you're supposed to show me how to read palms."

She looked a bit surprised at that, glancing at my hands. I turned my back on the people and tugged my gloves out from where I had tucked them into my pocket, pulling them on and taking the chair that Imogen indicated. She was reading a fat man's rune stones, but I figured it wouldn't hurt me to sit and watch how she did her readings.

"How did your ride go?" she asked in between customers.

"Fine. Has your brother always been so pigheaded?"

"Pigheaded?" Her eyebrows rose. "Benedikt?"

Two guys and a girl took the seats across the table from us, arguing about who wanted to go first.

"It doesn't matter." I waved aside my comment.

"Oh, but I think it does," she said, giving me one of her mischievous grins before turning to the threesome and asking who wanted what.

I sat with her for almost two hours, taking a little break to get some water and to give my mother a chance to run and change for her invocation hour. Imogen showed me all the pertinent points on the palms of those people who came to have her read them, telling me how to interpret the various lumps, lines, bulges, and assorted other hand stuff. It was okay, but to tell the truth, I didn't quite buy it. I guess that was because I knew I could tell a whole lot more about the person just by touching my bare fingers to their palm than by interpreting a big mound of Mars to mean they were particularly argumentative.

I didn't have a chance to talk to her alone until just as the new band was about to start. All of the tents except the piercing one closed down then. Most of the Faire people went in and watched the band, joining in the dancing and stuff. Peter thought it was good for business to have everyone mingling, and said it made for repeat customers. Imogen always went to see the bands, and almost always spent the two hours the band was on dancing with one guy or another, dodging Elvis as he tried to convince her to dance only with him. I usually hung around outside, sometimes talking to Soren, sometimes to Tallulah the medium (she hated music of any sort), sometimes just being by myself.

I waited until Imogen finished with her last customer. She glanced toward the big tent as the loudspeaker crackled into life when Peter announced the band.

"Here, take this," Imogen said, shoving her money box at me. It was crammed full of forints and euros.

"What do you want me to do with it?" I asked, wondering if she had skimmed some off the top for her shopping trips, then immediately felt guilty for even thinking that about someone who was my friend.

"Give it to Peter for me, please. I so want to hear this Picking Scabs."

That was the name of the band, Picking Scabs. I know. It's beyond me, too. I suppose it could be worse. It could be Pickled Scabs.

I gnawed my lip a bit. "Aren't you supposed to count it up and stuff, so you get your fair share?"

"You can do it for me, can't you? Please, Fran?" She stuffed her rune stones in a big leather satchel and gave me a brilliant grin.

"Wait, Imogen. I wanted to ask you . . . uh . . ."

"Yes?" She stood tapping her foot impatiently, her eyes watching all the people streaming into the big tent as the screech of feedback echoed throughout the Faire. The band was evidently about to start.

"Did you go shopping today? I looked for you, but didn't see you."

"Yes, I went into Sopron." That was a big city about ten kilometers down the road. "Was that all you wanted?"

"No. Um. What did you buy?"

She looked at me like my head had turned into a monkey. "Clothes."

"A lot? I mean, did you find a lot of good bargains?"

She laughed her tinkly little laugh that reminded me of a stream burbling. "Fran, I never buy bargains. Those are for the peasants."

She traced a quick ward above my head, and dashed off toward the big tent. I sighed. So much for my detective skills. I'd been questioning people all day and was no further than when I started. Except now I knew that possibly everyone connected to the Faire could have had a shot at the safe . . . but I had felt only seven people on the safe's handle. It didn't make sense. It just didn't make sense.

I spent ten minutes counting Imogen's take, writing up the info on her slip and tucking it neatly into the box. Then I went to hunt down Peter.

"Hey, Peter. Imogen gave me this to give to you. I counted the money and wrote it on the slip."

"What?"

Peter was at the back of the tent with Teodor the security guy/bouncer who kept an eye on everyone. Peter's little balding head was bopping along with the music, which was loud, loud, and then more loud. The bass positively throbbed in my teeth, it was so loud. The lead singer screamed in German into the microphone. I always crank my headphones up when I'm listening to music—loud is definitely better than soft—but this was ridiculous! The sound screeching from the big amps was so pervasive it filled everything, every space, both inside the tent and inside the people. I felt it crawling around the edges of my brain and knew then that Absinthe had managed to find a band that knew some sort of magic. Probably they cast a spell to make the audience adore them—Imogen said that was pretty standard stuff.

I repeated my words, bellowing them about four inches from his ear. It was barely enough to be heard. He nodded and took the cash box, tucking it under his arm to applaud as the music stopped.

I didn't want to touch him. I had touched more people in the last day than I had in a month, and I wanted my brain back to myself. I spent a few seconds being mad that my mother had manipulated me into the position of having to do the thing I hated most, but then my inner Fran pointed out that I had offered to do it in exchange for something I wanted.

I hate it when my brain does that sort of thing.

The next song started. I decided there was no way I could possibly come right out and ask Peter if he was stealing from himself for some purpose I couldn't begin to imagine, gritted my teeth, and peeled off the glove from my left hand, edging my way closer to him. He was bouncing and bopping around in that "I'm cool and I can dance" way that adults think make them look like they know how to dance (which they don't). I let my hand brush against him a couple of times, turning so it was my palm that touched his arm. He never even noticed when I backed away.

I noticed, though. I backed into Ben.

"Hi," I yelled, trying to be nonchalant, like I didn't care whether he was there or not, but failing when he grinned at me. I couldn't resist his grins. They made me go all warm and puddly inside.

"Dance?" he yelled back, and tipped his head toward the mass of people dancing like crazy in the main area of the tent.

"Sure."

He grabbed my hand, looked down, and, without even asking me, peeled off my gloves and stuffed them in his back pocket. He held out his hand for the other gloves. I gave them to him. He pushed us through the crowd until we were in the middle of the pack. There must have been three hundred people jammed into that tent, all dancing like mad. Ben kept a hand on me as we joined in, but it was hard going, since every two seconds someone's elbow bumped me, or leg jostled me, or arm hit my back, or hair swung out.

"This is like dancing in a can of sardines," I yelled in Ben's ear.

"Do you want to leave?" he yelled in mine.

"Not now. Maybe in a bit."

I swear, someone in the band was using magic, because everything started to get better. Ben smiled, and somehow managed to keep us moving so hardly anyone smacked into us. I kept my hands on his arms, and gave myself up to the moment. The music didn't seem nearly so harsh and annoying, and started to make sense. Along the fringes of the dance area I could see Mom dancing with a laughing Peter. Imogen had evidently given Elvis the go-ahead, because they were dancing near us, Imogen looking a little bored, Elvis all but drooling on her. Even Soren was dancing, with a girl, yet! I smiled at him and swung around when Ben turned us, just barely avoiding Kurt's long hair as he did a little twirl with a tall blond woman.

"Everyone's here," I yelled happily to Ben, feeling for once like I was truly a part of a group, nothing special, just me, just one little cog in a great big wheel.

"They have to be; the lead singer's using a glamour," he answered. "It makes people want to dance. Can't you feel it?"

"Yeah, but I don't mind. Hey, look, there's Absinthe." He looked where I pointed. I've never seen Absinthe even near the tent when the bands played, but there she was, her spiky pink hair bobbing up and down as she danced with Karl.

"I'm so happy," I said, and threw my hands up as Ben laughed with me, grabbing my waist to spin me around. "Everything's so wonderful!"

I realized my mistake the second my fingers came in contact with the bodies surrounding me. Images, thoughts, hopes, desires, sadness, sickness, sorrow . . . As Ben spun me around, a hundred thoughts filled my mind. I pulled my arms back in, but not before I touched someone.

Someone bad.

Someone evil.

Someone who was planning on killing the laughing, handsome man who held me in his arms.

CHAPTER EIGHT

"Are you all right?"

"Yeah. You can let go of my head now."

I sat up slowly, as if I had been feeling dizzy and was liable to pass out at any moment. I wasn't the least bit dizzy, but I was *very* sick to my stomach.

Someone wants to kill Ben!

Ben squatted next to the chair he'd led me to when I pretended to collapse inside the tent. I took a few deep breaths of fresh air, air not polluted by hundreds of bodies, and looked around me. We were outside Tallulah's tent, which was the farthest point away from the main tent. The music was a dull throb in the back of my head, like a headache that wouldn't go away. I didn't remember walking all the way here, and wondered if Ben had carried me. Wouldn't I remember that?

Someone wants to kill Ben!

I shook my head and closed my eyes again. Thinking was too hard to do with the music pounding away in my brain.

"Is she better? Does she want water?"

Someone wants to kill Ben!

"Shut up," I growled to the shrieking inner Fran.

"Did she just tell me to shut up?"

"I'm not sure. It sounded like it."

A shadow fell between us, on top of my hands, which were clutching Ben's as if I had been drowning. It must be Tallulah. She hated the bands; she always stayed away from the tent when one was playing.

"Someone wants to kill you." I didn't think I had said the words, but I did. It was my voice, and Ben's fingers tightened around mine.

"Someone always wants to kill me," Tallulah said very matter-of-factly. "That's no reason to tell me to shut up. It's because I can contact those who have passed on, and tell things the living don't always want made public. Once, a lady in Amsterdam who had suffocated her elderly father tried to kill me with a hatpin. A hatpin! Naturally, I knew she was coming. Sir Edward told me." Sir Edward is Tallulah's boyfriend. He's dead, but they still hang out together.

"I don't think that Fran is talking about you," Ben said, not looking in the least bit surprised or worried or freaked or any of the ways I would feel if I were told that someone wanted me deader than a squashed bug. He was just looking at me, a little concerned, true, but his eyes were back to honey oak with gold flecks.

I glanced up at Tallulah and gave her a feeble smile. "I wasn't telling you to shut up, and I'm glad you have Sir Edward so you'll know whenever someone wants to off you, but Ben's right. This is about him, not you."

"Someone wants to kill Ben?" Tallulah stepped back and stared at him. Mom says Tallulah is related to a Gypsy queen, and I have to admit, she looks like it. Her skin is the color of a double-tall latte, but her eyes are bright, bright blue. She has long black hair with a big white streak on one side, and she always wears her hair in a big blobby bun on the back of her neck. She's older than Mom, but it's hard to tell just how old she is, because there's not a single wrinkle on her face, and even Mom has a couple of lines around her eyes. "Why would anyone wish to kill Ben?"

They both looked at me. "Don't stare at me like that; I don't know why. I don't even know who it was; there were too many people pushed up around us. All I felt was someone wanted Ben sta . . . um . . . dead."

I know what you're thinking. There I was a few hours after telling Ben I could handle my own problems without his assistance, thank you very much, and what did I do? I spilled everything. The thing is, I'm not stupid. I know I can handle my own stuff—dealing with Mom's demands, pinning down the likeliest person to have taken the money—but this was different. This was Ben's life at stake. (Ow! Pun not intended.) He needed to hear it so he could get the heck out of Dodge before the staker got to him.

My hands shook in his. I knew he felt them shaking, but he didn't say anything. He just gave my fingers a little squeeze, then let go of my hands and stood up, pulling my gloves out of his back pockets. I put them on, mentally swearing an oath that I was never going to take them off again.

Yeah, okay, I knew it was an oath I wasn't going to keep, but it felt good there for about ten seconds.

"Can you walk, or do you want me to carry you again?"

Rats! He *had* carried me to Tallulah's and I had been too weirded out to notice it. "I can walk. I'm okay, just a little freaked. Thanks for letting me sit here, Tallulah."

"You know you're always welcome, Fran." She gave Ben a long look as I got to my feet. "I believe I shall contact Sir Edward and ask him what he knows about this."

Ben made a graceful bow to her. She inclined her head, and for a moment I could see why people thought she was related to royalty. I waggled my fingers at her and started off toward our trailer, Ben at my side. He didn't try to hold my hand, which was okay, except I kind of wanted him to.

"You want to tell me what happened? What really happened, not the Tallulah version. Everything, from the time you walked into the tent to when you felt sick."

I chewed my lip, deciding on a little judicious editing. "I didn't feel anything other than the glamour, and I didn't even feel that at first. To tell you the truth, I thought the music was kind of bad."

A smile flickered across his face. "It *was* bad. Hence the need for the glamour."

A glamour, for those of you not hip to the latest magic lingo, is a form of magic used to change the perception about something, usually from bad to good—in other words, someone in the band was using a glamour to make everyone think they were wonderful, giving them the overpowering desire to dance to their music. Lots of people can do glamours—witches, demon lords, vamps . . . It really is pretty common stuff. I'd just never experienced it before, since I'd always stayed away from Mom's weirdo friends.

"Then you asked me to dance, and everything started to be fun." I slid a glance at him to see if he thought I was enjoying myself because I was dancing with him as opposed to the glamour starting to affect me, but we were walking behind Elvis's trailer, and Ben was in the shadow. "And then the next thing I knew, I was being swamped by people's minds. Then I touched him."

Ben stopped. "Him? It was a man?"

I stopped, too, chewing my lip as I tried to remember (okay, so chewing my lip is a little nervous habit I have; I never said I was perfect). I closed my eyes and sorted through the emotions I remembered feeling. With the exception of the girl who was worried because she thought she was pregnant, it was impossible to tag the fleeting images by the person's gender. "I'm sorry; I can't tell. It was over so quickly, just a flash in my mind of someone who was filled with thoughts of staking you. Someone cold and black and"—I shivered and rubbed my arms—"extremely evil inside. Whoever it is, Ben, they mean business. You need to be careful, because this person really wants you dead."

"Hmm."

He started walking again. I followed, rolling my eyes. He was back to his tough-guy macho routine.

"You know, I read a lot of mysteries," I said.

"Do you?"

"Yeah, so I know all about someone wanting someone else dead, and detectives in the books always say that the who isn't important; it's the why. If you know why someone wants you dead, it'll tell you who it is. So who wants to see you staked?"

He waited for me to catch up to him, then walked beside me with absolutely no expression on his face. "Quite a few people, I imagine."

I goggled at him (something I'm not proud of, but hey, it had been a stressful day). "You're joking. Why would someone want you dead? You haven't, like, accidentally killed someone when you were having dinner, have you?" I couldn't imagine Ben doing something bad enough to make someone want to kill him. I'd been inside his mind; I knew what sort of person he was — tormented, in a lot of pain, yes, but he wasn't bad. He didn't like to hurt people.

"I'm a Moravian Dark One. Many people think we're the evil creatures of vampire legend, preying on the innocent, changing people to our own kind, damning them to eternal hell. Most vampire hunters don't bother to find out what we are; they lump us in with demons, ghouls, and the like. Such people kill us simply because we *are*, Fran. They don't need any other reason."

"But that's wrong! You're not evil; you're just a little different from anyone else. For that matter, I'm different, but I don't see anyone trying to knock me off."

He didn't say anything to that. I was starting to figure him out — what he didn't say was often as important as what he did. "You know, this thing where you can't lie to me makes me nervous. Does your not saying anything mean that you think someone is trying to kill me?"

He put his hand on my shoulder. I had to point out to my inner Fran that it was just a nice, comforting gesture, not a romantic one. "No, I don't. But your mother is a witch; you must know the history of witches through the ages."

"Yeah, I know about witch hunts and all that, but people don't do that anymore."

His silence filled the air between us.

"They do?"

"In some places, yes. But you have nothing to worry about. Your mother protects you, as does your own desire to blend in, and . . ."

"And what?"

He didn't say anything, but he pulled his arm off my shoulder. I had an idea of what he was going to say, and I didn't want to hear it. I didn't even want to think it, because then I'd get mad at him and his macho attitude.

So I didn't say anything either, and we both walked along in silence until Ben broke it. "Will you be all right alone until your mother comes back?"

"Sure, I stay by myself all the time." And usually I enjoyed being left alone, but tonight I wanted Ben to stay. I tried to think up a reason to keep him with me. "Are you hungry? Would you like a cup of tea? We have— Oh." I am *so stupid! Duh, Fran, he's a vampire; you were just talking about that.* "I'm sorry; sometimes I forget that you're a . . . Sometimes I forget."

I hurried forward, trying to pretend I didn't have a mouth as big as Colorado.

"Thank you, Fran."

"For what?" I asked miserably. "Putting my foot in my mouth . . . *again?*"

"For not letting it matter to you what I am."

I shrugged, but allowed the warm glow of his words to beat back some of the freaked-out feeling inside me. "I've never understood why people blame someone for what they were born being. It's not like they have any choice, is it? I mean, I don't have a choice about being a psychometrist any more than you have a choice about being a Dark One. We just are. So why get bent out of shape over something we can't change? My mom always says it's not who you are, but what you do that matters."

"Such words of wisdom from a girl who thinks of herself as a freak."

I glanced at him to make sure he wasn't laughing at me. He wasn't. "Yeah, well, it's not so much that I think I'm a freak, but other people do, and, you know, it gets old really fast being different from everyone else."

"Tell me about it," he said, stopping in front of our trailer. "You've lived with being different for only four years; I've lived with it for three hundred and twelve."

"Wow, you really are old," I said, awed by the thought of living so long.

He smiled, then leaned forward and gave me a little tiny kiss, probably an Iowa's worth of a kiss. "Yeah, I'm old, but not so old that I don't know a good thing when I see it. Go on in. I'll catch up with you tomorrow night."

It took me a couple of seconds to shut the inner Fran up (she was squealing over the kiss). "Where are you going? Back to the main tent? You're not going to go back there with the psycho who wants to stake you, are you?"

"I'm not afraid, Fran."

I stared at him, my eyes all big and googly. "Well, you should be! Ben, I'm not joking when I say the person who wants you dead is bad, really bad. Grade-A evil, in fact. You don't want to mess with him or her, whoever it is. Trust me; this person's thoughts were lovingly dwelling on the joy of watching you die a horrible, painful death."

He tucked a strand of my hair behind my ears. "Go inside, Fran. I'll be all right."

"Argh!" I yelled, wanting to strangle him and shake him and kiss him all at once. "You are the most frustrating guy in the whole wide world! Fine! Go back and get yourself killed. See if I care!"

I stomped up the stairs, slamming the door to the trailer behind me. Davide looked up as I threw my bag onto the chair and stormed down the narrow aisle. "Stupid Ben. Stupid, stupid, stupid Ben. Oh, he's so friggin' tough, no one can kill him. Ha! Well, who needs him? I sure don't. If he wants to get himself killed, that's just peachy keen with me. Just means I don't ever have to redeem his soul, however you do *that*. He doesn't matter to me, not one little bit. Him and his long hair and his nummy body and the motorcycle and that wonderful way he kisses — none of it matters! Not one stupid iota!"

Davide made a face that looked remarkably like he was pursing his lips at me.

"And you can just stop looking at me like that! It's not my problem!"

I swear he raised his eyebrows at me.

I pointed my finger at him. "Not one word from you, cat. I tried to warn him. I told him flat-out that he was stupid to tangle with whoever it is who wants him dead, but he's all 'I'm a Dark One. I can do anything' to me. Dark One—*Dork One* is more like it."

Okay, so that was unfair—there was nothing dorky about Ben—but I wasn't about to admit that to a cat.

Davide stood up, arched his back in a stretch, then sat down and curled his tail around his feet while he gave me a yellow-eyed look that spoke louder than words.

"I did everything I could!" I said, yanking the closet open to get my pillow and blanket. "There's nothing else I can do!"

He just kept staring at me. I peeled off my gloves and threw them on the floor. "*Gah!* All right! Stop it! I'll go save Ben's butt. Are you happy? Everyone will probably find out about me because of this, and then someone will do a witch hunt on me, and I'll end up dead, and *then* who'll give you the good tuna, huh? It's on your head now, buster!"

I snatched up my keys and stomped out of the trailer, muttering to myself as I headed toward the loud pulse of music. This far out, the glamour was too diluted to work, and my original opinion about the band was justified. They really did suck.

The area outside of the tent was absolutely devoid of people, which was unusual even when a band was playing. Usually people wandered out to use the portable toilets, or to have a smoke, but not tonight. There wasn't a single person to be seen all the way down the main aisle; all the smaller tents were black and closed up. Even Tallulah's was shut down. A few chip wrappers and empty cups were kicked along the ground by the slight breeze, but other than that, nothing moved.

It was really very eerie.

I slipped into the back of the main tent, pressing against the canvas wall, trying to keep myself out of the way of the people, and as far away from the power of the glamour as was possible. What I really needed was a way to—

"Imogen!"

A few feet away Imogen stood swaying to the music, Elvis and another guy arguing violently next to her. That was a common enough sight—Elvis got really jealous when Imogen danced with other guys. Usually she ignored him. "Imogen!"

She turned and smiled at me. I motioned her over. "You're just the person I want to see."

"Isn't that sweet of you, Fran! Why aren't you dancing?"

I waved her question away. Already I could feel the glamour working, making me want to drop everything and join in the happy dancing throng. "No time for that. Is there a ward that can protect you from a glamour?"

She smiled at the guy who was now threatening the much smaller Elvis with two big fists. "I hope he knocks him out; Elvis has been so persistent tonight. Yes, of course there is a ward; there is a protection ward for everything."

"Can you show me how to do it? If it's not a Moravian secret, that is. Something I could use specifically against this glamour?" My toes started tapping against my will. My legs wanted me to plunge into the crowd.

She turned to me with a slight frown between her brows. "Why would you want to be protected against this glamour? It's not a harmful one, and the band sounds much better with it."

"Please, Imogen, I don't have time to explain. Could you just show me the ward?"

She gave me a curious look, then turned so her body was blocking the view of anyone who might glance our way. I had a hard time paying attention to her instructions; the music was so persuasive that everything in me cried out to go dance, to have fun, to let it fill me and wipe away all my worries.

She drew the ward on me, then showed me how to draw it. The thing with wards is not actually in drawing the symbol correctly; it's the belief you put behind it. That's the way it is with all magic—believe, and it works. Doubt, and the power of the magic weakens. I had no doubt of my own abilities—such as they were—which helped me draw the ward. The second my finger traced the last curve, the symbol glowed into life in the air in front of me, a bright gold shimmering that immediately dissolved. The feeling of protection remained, however.

I had done it! I had drawn a ward, and it worked! "Ugh!"

I yelled, and clapped my hands over my ears, "Man, they are so bad!"

Imogen laughed and turned back to the music, holding out her hands for the guy who stood over the crumpled form of Elvis. Evidently the guy had heard Imogen's wish, because he rubbed his knuckles before taking Imogen's hands and dancing off with her. I went over and prodded Elvis with my toes, but he didn't move. His chest rose and fell, though, so I knew he wasn't dead, just knocked out. "Sorry. I have more important things to do," I told him as I turned toward the dancing crowd, skirting along the edges as I looked for Ben. For a moment my ward flared to life, an ugly black, but just as quickly the image of it dissolved. I figured whoever was making the glamour had added a little power to it, but as long as my ward held, it didn't concern me.

I hesitated as I watched everyone dancing, hating what I had to do, my mind squirreling frantically for another option, but there was none. Ben thought he could take on the person who wanted him dead, but I knew the truth. Whoever it was, man or woman, was cold with desperation, wholly committed body and soul to seeing Ben dead. You don't get that sort of determination in your average vampire hunter. At least, I didn't think you did.

"No pain, no gain," I told myself and, taking a deep breath, plunged into the crowd. I let my hands touch everyone, not trying to guide them, just allowing myself to be jostled around randomly. People, images, objects, emotions, moments in time, thoughts, wishes, fears—everything that people carry around in their subconscious filled my brain until I thought my head was going to burst, pain lancing through my entire body with the effort to hold it all. I couldn't breathe; there were so many people pressing in on me, filling me, so many of them they pushed me aside and took over. There was nothing left of me, not one little bit left; it was all them. Just as I was sure my mind was fracturing, at the exact moment when I knew I was stepping over the line of sanity to insanity, blackness filled me, a soft, warm, velvet blackness. It shut out the voices, the images, the people who filled me. The blackness covered me, protecting me in a soft cocoon, slowly separating me from the crowd until I slipped into a long, dark, inky pool that seemed to welcome me with a warm embrace and a whisper that all would be well.

CHAPTER NINE

"Hey," Soren said.

"Hey. Oooh, almond croissants?"

He nodded and plopped down beside me, waiting patiently for me to return the paper bag I'd snatched out of his hands. There were two things I really liked about being in Europe — castles (very cool), and the way everybody went to the local bakery every morning to get fresh-baked stuff. The bread was good, but the almond croissants . . .

"Mmm," I said blissfully, allowing the featherlight flakes of croissant to melt on my tongue. "It's probably got a gazillion calories, but man, this is good."

Soren tore off one of the two curved arms of a croissant and popped it in his mouth, chewing as he squinted into the morning sun. Bruno and Tesla grazed in front of us, throwing elongated, wavering shadows as they moved slowly across the edge of the meadow, chomping happily at the grass, their tails keeping a lazy rhythm as they switched at flies. I love this time of the morning. It isn't late enough to be really hot, but it's warm enough to make your spirits soar. A couple of blue-green drag-onflies skimmed low over the grass, then headed off toward the trees, where a thin stream trickled.

"How do you feel?" Soren finally asked.

I finished my croissant before answering, wrapping my arms around my legs and propping my chin on my knees as I sucked the last sweet, almondy bits of croissant from my teeth. "I'm fine; why do you ask?"

"Why do I ask? You had some sort of panic attack last night and had to be carried out of the main tent. You don't normally do that. I thought you might be sick or something."

"Carried?" I rested my cheek on my knee and looked at Soren. His nose was peeling from a sunburn he'd gotten a few days ago. "Who carried me?"

He picked at the grass, throwing a handful at the horses. "Benedikt."

Drat with bullfrogs on it. Twice Ben had carried me, and both times I'd been too out of it to notice. I looked back at the horses. "Dr. Bitner said I could ride Tesla if I wanted, as long as I didn't take him out on the road, 'cause he doesn't have any shoes, and I shouldn't push him too far. He said I should start slow, and build his stamina up, but that he was so old he'd never really be able to be ridden a lot."

Soren slid me a sidelong glance. "Why are you changing the subject?"

"That's what people do when they don't want to talk about something."

He thought about that for a minute, then asked (just like I knew he would), "Why don't you want to talk about what happened last night?"

I picked a buttercup and held it under his chin. He batted it away. "If I tell you what happened last night, will you show me how to ride?"

He looked at Tesla. "Bareback?"

"I don't have a saddle."

"You don't have a bridle, either."

I shrugged. "Can't I use the nylon lead rope and his halter?"

He shrugged, too. "It won't have a . . . what do you call it . . ." He made a gesture across his mouth.

"Bit?"

"Yes, bit. But I will show you if you tell me what happened."

"If I tell you, you have to swear not to tell anyone. Not your father, or anyone. Got that?"

His eyes widened. "Is it something to do with the theft?"

"No. Yes. No, not really. It's something to do with me. Do you swear?"

"*Ich schwöre.*" He spat on his hand and held it out for me to shake. *Ew*. I grabbed the very tips of his fingers and shook there. "What happened?"

"You won't believe me if I just tell you. What do you have in your pockets?"

He looked surprised, a little puzzled frown pulling his eyebrows together, but he stuck a hand into his shorts pocket and pulled out the contents. There was a small blue plastic comb, a few coins, string, a used bandage, a set of keys, and a tube of lip balm. I peeled my gloves off and plucked the keys from his hand.

"You've never shown me these keys before, have you?"

He shook his head.

"Right." I separated one key from the rest and held it up, allowing the images the key conveyed to tell me about its use.

"This key is to the big wooden chest your dad keeps his props in. The big props."

Soren's eyes widened as he looked at the key; then he nodded. I picked out a second key. "Trailer." His eyes widened even further. I held up a tiny little key. "This is to a violin case. I didn't know you played the violin."

His jaw dropped. "No one knows except Papa and *Tante*. How do you do that?"

I help up another key. "This one unlocks the big box you keep the doves in. What's it called—a dovecote? Whatever, this key is new. You haven't had it long."

I thought his eyes were going to pop out of his head, so I wrapped up my show, setting the keys gently into his hand. "It's nothing special, Soren. I can feel things by touching them, that's all."

"That's all? It is too special; it's very special!" He looked down at my hands like they were painted purple or something. I pulled my gloves back on. The sun was still shining, but all of a sudden I felt like a cloud had passed overhead. "I can't believe you can do that. Is that why you wear gloves? Can you do it with people, too? Can you read my mind if you touch me? Can you tell everything I'm thinking?"

I got up and walked over to Tesla, who paid absolutely no attention to me, having checked me over for apples earlier (I had carrots, which he graciously accepted). Tesla and Ben seemed to be the only ones who didn't care about my curse. How sad is that? "If I touched you with my bare hand, yes, I could tell what you're thinking, Kind of. More like what strong emotions you're feeling at the time."

Soren sucked in his breath, looking at me as if I were dancing naked. Upside down. I threw my arms out, annoyed that he of all people should make a big deal about a little difference. "I'm still the same person I was a few minutes ago, Soren! You didn't think I was weird then!"

"I didn't say I think you are weird," he said slowly.

"You don't have to say it; that look says it all. I've seen it before, you know. Everyone who finds out about this has that same look, the 'Fran is a freak' look. I thought you would understand what it was like to be born with something you can't do anything about. It's nothing different from you being born with one leg shorter than the other."

His face turned red as he looked down at his leg.

"My leg can't tell me what you're thinking."

"And my hands can—yeah, so? I can't turn it off, Soren. I just have to live with it. I thought you'd understand. Now I'm sorry I told you."

I turned away from him, leaning on Tesla's side, tracing my fingers over the scar on his shoulder, blinking furiously so Soren wouldn't see me cry.

"Fran?"

I twisted the ends of Tesla's mane into a braid, sick that I'd ruined my friendship with Soren. "What?"

"I don't think you're weird. I think . . . I think it's cool."

"It's not cool; it's a curse," I mumbled down at my hands. Tesla's white mane was tangled between my fingers. That was what my life had turned into, a tangle. I was tangled up with Mom and the Faire, tangled up with Ben, tangled with Soren and Imogen, tangled with Tesla. . . .

"I don't think so." Soren came around to the other side of Tesla. "I really do think it's neat. I'm sorry if I made you feel bad."

I twitched a shoulder. "I'm used to it."

He looked down at my hands. "Can you do it with animals?"

"Tell what they're feeling? No. I think it's because they think differently. The only things I pick up on are human emotions and stuff like that."

"Oh." He looked thoughtful for a few minutes. "Still, I bet that could be useful."

"Useful!" I snorted. "Yeah, if you want everyone to jump back every time you come near them because they're afraid to let you touch them, then it's useful. Otherwise it's a curse, like I said."

"That's why Miranda wanted you to find out who's stealing our money, isn't it? She wants you to touch everyone and see who is the thief?"

I combed through Tesla's mane with my fingers. "Something like that, yeah."

His eyes widened again. "You touched me the other day, I remember! You touched me with your bare hand. Were you reading me then?"

I chewed on my lip and tried to think of a polite way to tell him that there was a short time when I thought he might be a suspect. "Well . . . I had to eliminate everyone who touched the safe—"

"Was I a suspect? You thought I was a suspect? Cool!"

I rolled my eyes, bending to check that Tesla's hobble was on correctly. The leather cuffs around his front feet weren't tight, and the chain that connected them was long enough to let him graze without giving him the full range of his normal stride. "You are the only person I know who thinks it's cool to be a suspect."

"I've never been a suspect before," he explained, limping after me as I walked back toward the Faire. "I wish you had told me. I would have liked to write it in my journal."

"You can write it in there now."

"Am I still a suspect?"

I stopped and waited for him to catch up to me. "No, of course not. You checked out."

"I checked out," he said in an awe-filled voice. "That's cool, too."

"Whatever."

We walked down the long length of the Faire, swallows wheeling and diving ahead of us as they did their aerobatic act between the tents. "What happened after Ben carried you home?"

"I don't know."

He pursed his lips. "You don't know?"

"Nope. I was out. I don't remember anything except waking up this morning."

"What did Miranda say?"

"Zzzzzz."

"What?" Soren stopped to gawk at me.

I smiled. "She was asleep when I got up this morning. I assume that Ben hauled me back to the trailer, and Mom tucked me in. That's all."

"Oh." He looked a bit disappointed by that and evidently decided to go after something more promising. "Who is a suspect? Who do you think stole the money?"

I stopped at the fringe between the Faire and the trailers. It was still too early for most of the people to be up, but a few bleary-eyed people staggered out of their cars with cups of coffee and bags of baked goods clutched in their hands, heading for their trailers. "I don't know. Seven people touched the safe, and of those seven, almost all of them check out."

"Almost all?"

"I haven't talked to the last couple of people."

"Oh. He sucked the inside of his cheek for a moment as we watched Absinthe, a lurid-pink scarf that clashed with her hair tied around her head, and a pair of black glasses hiding her eyes, slip out the door of Kurt and Karl's trailer. She went straight for her trailer.

"That was interesting," I said.

He made a face. "Not really. So, last night, when you had your attack —"

"It wasn't an attack," I interrupted. I mean, sheesh, I felt weird enough; I didn't need people thinking I had attacks, too!

"Okay, when whatever happened to you happened, that was because . . ." His nose scrunched up. "Why *did* it happen?"

I kicked at a rock, prying it out of the sod so I could toss it into the garbage can nearby. "I think it was overload. I've never touched more than a couple of people a day, and in there, I was touching hundreds. I felt like I was being crushed by them, like I was just an empty shell. It was awful."

"Ben touched you."

"Yeah."

Soren turned blue eyes full of accusation on me. "He knows, doesn't he? You told him, but you didn't tell me."

I tried for a supportive smile. I don't think I succeeded. "I told you now; that's gotta count for something."

"You didn't trust me, and you trusted him. You only just met him!"

"Come on," I said, tugging him toward the trailer Absinthe had just left.

"You like him more than me, don't you?"

"Oh, for Pete's sake . . ." I stopped and shook him. "This isn't a contest, okay? Ben knows because . . . because . . . because he just knows! I didn't tell him; he figured it out himself."

"You didn't tell him?" Soren's eyes were narrowed; he was suspicious despite obviously wanting to believe me.

"I didn't tell him; he guessed. Feel better? Good. Now come on; I need some help."

"Help with what?"

"I need to touch Karl."

Soren's eyes bugged out again. I smacked him on the arm.

"Not that kind of touch, stupid! I need to *touch* him. He's one of the people who used the safe. I need to see if he feels cold and desperate inside."

Cold. Desperate. Just like the person who wanted Ben dead. I sucked in my breath and thought about that for a moment. Could it be? Could the thief be the same person who wanted Ben staked? Why?

"Fran? You okay? You're not going to have another attack, are you?"

I made mean eyes at him. "I do not have attacks!"

"Okay, but you're scaring me. Your eyes went all funny. What's the matter?"

"Nothing. I just need to think for a minute." I looked around, then grabbed Soren's hand, dragging him over to a couple of plastic crates that were stacked behind Elvis's trailer, out of sight of the rest of the trailers. "Sit."

He sat. He also watched me as I paced back and forth, trying to figure it all out. "I'm going to do this the way the detectives do it in books."

Soren dug a small, grubby notebook out of his pocket. "I'll be your trusted sidekick."

I stopped pacing to give him a look.

"What? That's not right?"

"We're not in a Western, Soren. This is serious."

"You're the boss." He looked thrilled. I felt peeved.

"Point one," I said, resuming pacing and ticking each item off on my finger. "Someone stole the Faire money, not once but three times in the last ten days."

"Yes." Soren bent over his notebook, his tongue peeking out as he wrote with a broken pencil.

"Point two: Seven people touched the safe—your father and aunt, you, Imogen, my mother, Elvis, and Karl."

"Hey!" Soren looked up. "Elvis! I bet it's him."

"You're jumping ahead. Trusty sidekicks never jump ahead."

His lips made an O. "Sorry."

"Point three: It doesn't make sense for either Absinthe or Peter to steal from themselves and make a big stink about it."

"Big stink," Soren repeated as he wrote.

"Point four: Elvis is a demonologist. Demons can get into anything if they are so ordered."

"Yeah," Soren said, his eyes lighting up.

"Except something made of steel," I added. His face fell.

"Oh. The safe is made of steel."

"Exactly. So unfortunately, although I'd like the suspect to be Elvis, I just don't see how he could use a demon to switch the money with the bits of newspaper that your aunt found."

He sighed noisily. "I can't either."

"Point five: Your dad left the combination to the safe lying around where anyone could see it, but only seven people touched the safe, so that eliminates everyone else."

Soren looked thoughtful, sucking on the end of the broken pencil. "That leaves Imogen, Miranda, and Karl."

"Exactly. And since Ben says Imogen doesn't need money, and I know my mom wouldn't steal anything. That leaves—"

"Karl!"

"Someone my name in vain is taking?"

Soren jumped up and I whirled around to see Karl dressed in a tank top, jogging shorts, and tennis shoes. Karl didn't speak English as well as the rest of the Faire people, but to give him credit, he spoke it better than I spoke German.

"Oh, hi, Karl. Uh . . ." I slipped my gloves off of my hand as I held it behind my back. Soren, who stood behind me, suddenly rushed forward.

"Karl, I was trying to show Fran the trick you do with the coin—you know, the one where you make it come out of someone's nose? I can't do it as well as you. Would you show it to her?"

I blinked for a second, then nodded my head. "Yes, would you, please? I'd love to learn some magic."

Karl didn't look like he believed either of us, but he obligingly pulled a coin out of Soren's ear, my eyebrow, and his own elbow.

"Wow, that's really cool; can I try it?" I asked, holding out my bare hand.

Karl gave me the coin, his fingers brushing my hand as he dropped it onto my palm. "It's not a difficult trick, but much practice it takes."

I made a couple of fumbled passes with the coin, then gave up with a laugh, handing it back to him. "Guess I'm not cut out to be a magician. Thanks anyway. Happy jogging." I let my fingers touch his hand for a second longer than was necessary, then waved as he trotted off toward the road.

"Well?" Soren asked as soon as Karl was out of hearing.

I sat down on the crate. "We can cross him off. He didn't feel at all guilty."

Soren looked up as his father called for him. "I have to go."

I waved him off. "That's okay, I've got some stuff to do for my mom. I'll see you later."

"Yes, later. I am to show you how to ride, don't forget." He stuffed the notebook in his pocket. "And we'll work on this, too. We will come up with other points; don't worry."

I let him run off without telling him that I wasn't worried in the least. I already knew of one more.

Point six: Someone who was on the dance floor last night would have given his or her soul to see Ben dead, and my gut instinct told me that that person and the thief were one and the same . . . and there were only two names left on my list of suspects.

Imogen and my mother.

CHAPTER TEN

This was our last day outside of Kapuvár. The next morning we'd pack everything up, and head off for Budapest, where we'd stay for ten days. Although my mom and I had only been with the Faire for a month, I'd decided I liked playing the smaller towns better than the bigger ones. The smaller ones gave me more freedom to wander around, exploring the town and countryside. In the big towns, like Stuttgart and Cologne, Mom got a little weird about me wandering around alone, which meant I couldn't go see any castles or the other cool stuff (torture museums—'nuff said) without waiting for her to have the time to take me.

There were also a lot more people in the big cities than in the towns. You'd think a lot of people would make for a good place to disappear in, but I'd found that even in a really busy square in Frankfurt or Cologne, surrounded by hundreds of people walking, laughing, talking, kissing . . . even plunked down in the middle of that, I still felt different. I wasn't one of them. I didn't blend in.

"Bullfrogs with big fat warts," I swore as I kicked at the

plastic crate behind Elvis's trailer, then went off to see if Imogen was up.

I tapped on the aluminum side of her door and stuck my head in. "You up?"

"Fran! Yes, I'm up. How are you feeling?"

I climbed up the couple of steps into the trailer and sat in the swivel chair across a small round table from her. She was drinking a latte and toying with the remains of a sticky roll.

"Fine." I glanced at the closed door to her bedroom. "Mom wasn't up this morning, but Soren said Ben hauled me out of the main tent last night?"

She sipped at her latte, her face smooth and unreadable. "Yes, he did."

I nodded. I thought the warm blackness that had cloaked me from everyone else had a Ben sort of feel to it. "Did you have fun last night? You looked like the glamour was working overtime on you."

She sighed happily. "It was so wonderful, wasn't it? And Jan—he was the one with all the yummy muscles—was a delight. He has many fine qualities. We went to a club in town after the band ended."

I couldn't help but grin at the wicked look in her eyes. "Sounds like you had even more fun than I imagined. I'm glad you and Jan had a good time. I kind of thought you would after he decked Elvis."

She giggled. "Wasn't that terrible? I should feel sorry about that, but I couldn't help being delighted that Jan knocked him out. Elvis is such a pest about me seeing anyone else, and he's gotten so much worse in the last few weeks."

"He's in looooove," I drawled, making big love-struck cow eyes at her.

"Lust is more like it. I don't think he knows the meaning of the word 'love.'" Imogen set her cup down and gave me an encouraging smile. "Enough about me. You want to tell me about what happened?"

"Last night?" I chewed on my lower lip, trying to think of a way to touch her without her realizing what I was doing, subsequently getting her undies in a bunch because she was officially on my list of suspects. "Um."

She put her hand on my wrist and gave it a little friendly squeeze. "Fran, you don't have to tell me if you don't want to. Friends don't force their friends into divulging secrets."

Friends also don't put their friends on the top of a list of suspected thieves. I squirmed in the chair.

"It's just that I'm worried. Benedikt was very concerned last night; he said you were in a fugue state, and that you'd had some sort of a psychic trauma. I just want you to know that I'm here for you if you need me. We both are. Benedikt cares for you very much, you know."

"Yeah, well, he kind of has to, me being his Beloved and all," I said, utterly and completely miserable. How could I possibly think the thief was Imogen? She was my friend! I liked her. I trusted her. I believed in her.

"Did last night have something to do with your investigation?"

I made another one of those moue faces. "I figured you'd hear about that."

Her eyebrows raised slightly. "Of course I heard about that; I hear about everything. It is true that you agreed to find out who the thief is?"

I nodded, toying with the fingers of my gloves.

"And you're doing that by reading people's intentions when you touch them?"

"Some people," I admitted to my fingers. I hated this, but my back was up against the wall. The only other person on my list was my mother, and I knew, I *knew* she wasn't a thief. Besides the fact that she'd never steal, she wanted the Faire to succeed too badly to do anything to endanger it.

"How many?"

"Seven. Seven people touched the safe." I looked up, trying to dig out my courage from where it had crawled behind my stomach. "Seven people . . . including you."

"Me?" Her eyebrows really went up at that. She looked completely surprised. "I can't imagine when I— Oh, yes. I asked Peter to put something in the safe for me a few weeks ago, and he had me do it."

I blinked a couple of times. It sounded plausible, but at the same time, it sounded awfully darn convenient. "He did? What . . . uh . . . what was it . . . ?"

She smiled. "It was my will."

"Your what?"

"My will. A dispensation of my worldly goods."

"I know what a will is, but geez, Imogen, you're immortal! You're not going to die."

"I can be killed," she said, the faint smile that had been lingering around her lips fading as she traced a finger around the edge of the big latte cup.

"You mean someone wants to kill you, too?"

Okay, the words slipped out without my thinking about them, but as soon as I said them, a weight lifted off my shoulders. Thus far everyone who knew about my curse—Ben,

Mom, Imogen, and Soren—thought I had gone back into the main tent last night to find the thief, but the truth was, I had gone specifically to find the person who wanted Ben dead. It was just a hunch that the two people were one and the same.

"Too? What do you mean, 'too'?"

I glanced at the closed door behind her. She froze, her eyes going dark. "Benedikt," she whispered.

"Yeah. That's what I was doing last night. Earlier, when Ben and I were dancing, I felt someone. Someone who was thinking about how much he or she was going to enjoy staking him. Someone really bad."

"Who?" she asked, her voice deep and rough. Her eyes had gone absolutely black now, a shiny, flat black.

"I don't know," I answered, peeling off one set of my gloves. "I wish I knew, I really do, because whoever it is is one sick person."

She looked at the discarded glove on her table, then raised her eyes to mine. The pain in hers was so great, it tainted the air between us. "You wish to touch me. You believe I am guilty."

"Not in wanting Ben dead, no. And not as the thief; it's just that . . . Oh, bullfrogs! I don't know what's what anymore, Imogen. As far as I can tell, no one has stolen the money, but I believe Absinthe and Peter—they don't have it. Which means someone has taken it, either the way a normal thief would, or by . . ."

"Psychic means," she finished, closing her eyes for a moment. She held out her hand. "I understand. You must do this, if only for your own satisfaction."

"I'm really sorry," I said, hating to eavesdrop on her thoughts. "I'll be quick."

My fingers rested on the pulse point of her wrist. Instantly

I was swamped with fear—fear for Ben, fear that the old horrors had started again, fear that she would have to make yet another new life for herself, fear that she would be left alone. Mingled into that was worry about me not accepting who I was, and the role I had to play in Ben's life.

I pulled my fingers back, more than a little shaken by the peek inside her head. "I'm sorry," I said again.

She gave me a smile, a real smile, one filled with understanding and forgiveness, so bright it made the inside of the trailer light up. "It is forgotten. Now, tell me everything about this person you touched. Don't leave anything out."

I didn't. I spilled my guts for a good half hour, telling her everything, from Absinthe's trying to break into my mind, to everyone I had touched, to the dance with Ben . . . It was like she used one of those truth drugs on me, only I *wanted* to tell her everything.

"That's it," I said, wrapping everything up with my few minutes spent with Karl. "That's everyone on my list. I've touched them all, and none of them is the thief. If I can't even find one lousy thief, how am I supposed to find a potential murderer?"

"You didn't touch everyone on the list," Imogen said, her eyes firm on mine. They were back to their original blue, just as blue as the sky outside. "There is one you have not read."

"My mom? I did touch her; I touched her a couple of days ago to find her keys. I would know if she was thinking about taking money—"

"Not your mother . . . Absinthe."

I made a face. "Yeah, well, I eliminated her because it doesn't make any sense for her to make a stink about the money missing. Peter doesn't do the accounts; she does, so he would never have known it had gone missing if she hadn't said something.

Besides, I don't think it would be a good idea to touch her. She almost got into my head. . . . If I were touching her while she tried that, I don't think I could keep her out."

"There are ways," she murmured.

"Really? Has she tried it with you?" I couldn't help but be curious. Imogen always seemed so in control, so strong, it was kind of a surprise to know that Absinthe had tried her party tricks on her as well.

"She tries at least once a month." She laughed.

"Really? But . . . you said she already knows about you. Why would she want to get into your head?"

"I have no idea, probably power. She knows who I am, yes, but with that comes the knowledge that should she anger me, I have the means to bring about her destruction."

"You can do that?" I sat in openmouthed surprise. "Then why . . . why . . ."

"Why do I work for the Faire rather than living in a penthouse apartment surrounded by beautiful people and clothes and things, and lots of money?"

I nodded. If someone handed me life on a silver platter, I sure as shooting knew what I'd do with it.

"I've lived that life, Fran. It's amusing for about ten minutes; then the artificiality of it tarnishes everything. I find that real life, life among mortals, is the only thing that brings me satisfaction. It has brought me such friends as you, after all, and I wouldn't trade your friendship for the most expensive of lifestyles."

"Geez, Imogen," I said, frowning at my fingers, blinking really fast so she wouldn't see the tears. "Just make me cry, why don't you! And after I treated you like a suspect and all . . ."

"You did your job; don't kick yourself for that. Now come, let us put our heads together about this animal who wishes to see Benedikt dead. Tell me again about what you felt when you touched the person."

We spent the next twenty minutes talking over everything I guessed about the person (not much) and everything I had felt in the brief moment of contact (even less). An idea was growing in the back of my mind, just a little niggle of an idea, but the more I tried to look at it, the more it slipped away from me. I gave up on it and turned my attention to stuff I could deal with. We discussed the problem of Absinthe, Imogen insisting that I was going to have to touch her, me swearing to high heaven that I'd rather die than let her know the truth about me.

"She can't hurt you if your mother and I stand behind you—"

"She can, too! Mom'll do anything to stay with the Faire, and that includes selling me into indentured bondage. I don't trust Absinthe one little bit—if she finds out about me, she'll have me doing Fran the Touch Freak acts so fast your head'll spin."

Imogen stood up. "Let us go wake up Benedikt. He will have some ideas, and since you said you warned him about the attempt on his life, he might have discovered something last night that can help you."

I stood up slowly, not wanting to follow her as she started closing the blinds on the windows. I couldn't deny that he had saved my butt when I was overwhelmed with everyone the night before, but I had my pride. I wasn't going to go running to him every time I had a sticky situation to work out.

"Fran?"

"You know, he probably needs his beauty sleep after last

night. And speaking of that, I've got to run along. Since it's our last night here, Mom is holding a circle, and I'm supposed to help her set up for it. She's probably up by now."

"But Fran—what about the investigation? What about Benedikt?"

I paused at the door. "I won't forget; don't worry. I like Ben; I don't want to see him staked. I think . . ." I bit off what I was going to say. There was no way I could put into words the thought bouncing around the back of my head when I couldn't even get a good look at it. "I'll think on it for a while, okay? You, too. If you come up with anything, let me know. I'll see you later."

"You'll see me in an hour, or have you forgotten the children's show?"

"Poop on a stick," I swore. I *had* forgotten. Peter made it a policy that at the end of every stint in towns with a hospital, some of the Faire folk spent a few hours doing magic and illusions for the sick children. He said it was a good way to promote goodwill and all that, but the truth was that Peter was an old softy, and he just liked cheering up sick kids. "Do you really need me? You can read palms by yourself—"

"You are my apprentice," she pointed out. "That means you have to come with me. It will be for only a few hours, Fran, and we might learn something. Everyone on your list will be there."

There was that. I'd never been on one of the hospital visits, since the thought of sick people gave me the willies, but Mom had gone every time. "Okay. I'll be ready. See you then."

The next hour went pretty quickly. I helped my mother draw a circle on the floor in her tent, setting up the flowers and invocation candles, all while avoiding her questions about what happened last night. She didn't ask very many, which made me believe she and Ben had had a little talk about me while I was passed out, something that made me feel all hot and uncomfortable when I thought about it, so I didn't.

Mom and Imogen and I all rode into town together, following the other cars to a big, ugly green hospital. I kept my hands to myself, afraid of what might be able to seep through the protection of the gloves if I touched anything.

The show for the kids was actually pretty fun. It was all illusion, with just one notable bit of magic that absolutely stopped the show. The kids and nurses and doctors filled one of the big wards, kids in wheelchairs, on regular chairs, propped up on the beds, some even sitting on the floor on big pillows. I figured everyone would be moaning and groaning and near death, but the ward was painted blue and yellow, with brightly colored butterflies scattered around the room. The kids themselves looked pretty cheerful, some of them wearing caps to cover bald heads, others wearing face masks, some in weird contraptions, almost all of them with IVs hooked up to them, but every single one of them had a smile when the show started. I began to see why everyone looked forward to Peter's hospital trips.

Karl and Kurt did a few flashy illusions that had the kids wowed—stuff like turning birdcages with canaries into a big pink rabbit (the rabbit's name was Gertrude, in case you were wondering), making showers of confetti fly out of the unlikeliest of places, pouring milk into some of the kids' hats, only to turn them inside out and show they were dry, that sort of stuff. Mom taught everyone flower-growing spells, and passed out little vials of happiness. Elvis did some card tricks, including one in which he was put into a straitjacket so he couldn't manipulate the cards, and yet he still managed to produce the cards three volunteers had hidden. I felt a little bad about not helping Elvis last night after seeing him do the card tricks — he had a huge bruise under one eye where Jan had socked him. To tell the truth, I was a bit surprised he was part of the show, since I hadn't known he did magic, but the adoring looks he was throwing Imogen explained a lot. No doubt he was there to impress her.

Imogen and I read a few palms, me with my gloves on, trying to do my best to sound upbeat and positive about kids who probably wouldn't have a long life ahead of them. Imogen did a lot better job than me — the kids she read for were laughing by the time she was finished with them.

Peter and Soren's act was the finale of the show, and although most of it was illusion, the last bit Peter did was my favorite example of pure, unadulterated magic. Every time I saw it, it gave me goose bumps, raising the hair on the back of my neck with its simplicity.

"What do I have here?" Peter asked, holding up two eggs, translating his words to Hungarian.

"*Tojások!*" the children cried. "Eggs!"

"Who wants to write their names on the eggs?"

Two dozen hands went up. Soren and Peter walked around, letting a few of the kids sign the eggs with different-colored markers.

"And what happens when you break eggs into a bowl?" Peter cracked both eggs into a clear glass bowl, carefully setting the shells aside. He held the bowl up so everyone could see it, walking along the front row allowing people to look.

"Now, I have here a magic fork! It is magic because it can turn both forward" — he made a clockwise circle with the fork — "and backward."

The fork made a counterclockwise circle.

"When I put the magic fork into the eggs, it scrambles them!"

I rubbed my arms, feeling the goose bumps start. The children watched as Peter whisked the eggs with the fork, giving his standard patter about how magic comes from within each of us, a power that everyone has, but few know how to unlock. Most of the children watched with rapt looks on their faces; a few rolled their eyes as if they knew what would happen.

I smiled to myself. They had *no* idea.

Peter whipped the eggs into an eggy yellow froth, then gave the bowl to Soren to pass around. "What do you get when you beat eggs?" he asked the crowd.

"Scrambled eggs!" the kids yelled back.

"That's right. Has everyone seen? Yes? The eggs are scrambled?"

"Yes," everyone shouted, even the doctors and nurses.

I smiled at Soren. He grinned back at me.

"Ah, but you forget, this is a magic fork! It can work forward . . . and backward."

Peter put the fork in the bowl and began to beat the eggs again . . . in the opposite direction. I rubbed the goose bumps on my arms, watching the kids' eyes grow wider and wider as the eggs began to unscramble themselves. It was magic, pure and simple, and it was wonderful. I understood now why magicians did what they did—the astonishment on the audience's faces was a wonderful thing to behold.

Peter pulled his fork from the bowl, holding it up so everyone could see the two perfectly whole eggs in it. "And now I give the eggs a tap with the magic fork. . . ." Using the two eggshells, he scooped up one whole egg, tapped it with the fork, and handed it to a child he beckoned forward. The kid stared at it with huge eyes while Peter reshelled the second egg, passing that around, too. I knew what everyone who examined the eggs would find—two perfectly whole eggs, signed with the names of the audience. There was no trick, no illusion, no exchange of broken eggs for whole—they were the same eggs, the exact same eggs, broken, scrambled, unscrambled, made whole again.

Magic, huh? Yeah. It's pretty cool.

It's also a heck of a showstopper. Everyone was talking excitedly when we packed up to leave. I know the kids had a good time, but what surprised me was how much fun I had. There I was surrounded by a bunch of children who were just as different as I was, only they were dying because of their differences, and yet none of them asked anyone to use magic to make them better; none of them asked Mom to make the pain go away, or the cancer to disappear, or their blood cells to go back the way they should be. They just laughed and enjoyed, and accepted everything offered.

Mom and Imogen chatted on the way back to the Faire. I let them, trying to figure out what it was that was rattling around the back of my brain. It was something important, something that I saw, but missed seeing, if you know what I mean. Something to do with what was going on, but I couldn't figure out how, or who it concerned, or even why it mattered. It just . . . was.

CHAPTER ELEVEN

I tried to pin down the thought later that day, but the last day is always a busy time, usually the busiest night of our stay.

"Hey!" Soren called to me just after lunch. He held up a bridle. "Want to go riding?"

I glanced over at my mother. She was making good-luck amulets. "Do you need me?"

"No, go have some fun. You've worked hard this morning."

I jumped up. She stopped me with a hand on my wrist. "Franny, I want to . . . I want to thank you."

"For what?"

"For joining in. For being part of the Faire. I know you like to think yourself aloof from everyone, but your participation in our new life has meant a lot to me. So . . . thank you."

I mumbled something and escaped, wondering how she could be such a smart witch, and so clueless about me. "I was blackmailed into joining in," I grumbled as I ran out to where Soren was putting a bridle on Bruno. "It's not like I had a choice or anything."

"A choice about what?" he asked as I picked up the bridle he set near Tesla.

"Nothing, doesn't matter. How does this thing work?"

He showed me how to put the bridle on. Tesla wasn't particularly interested in the whole idea, but Soren showed me how to find the spot on Tesla's jaw that I could press to make him open his mouth so I could slide the bit in. We adjusted the straps until the bridle fit; then I jumped onto a rock and climbed onto Tesla's back while Soren held him steady.

"Whoa, big horse," I said, my inner thigh muscles immediately screaming a protest at having to straddle his broad back.

Tesla decided enough was enough; grazing was much more important than standing around with a human on his back. The reins jerked out of my hands, sliding up his neck to his ears as he lowered his head to the ground. I leaned forward to get them, and promptly fell off.

Tesla ignored me.

"You!" I pointed to Soren, who was sitting comfortably on Bruno's back. "Stop laughing. You!" I pointed to Tesla. "Prepare to be ridden. This is war, horse."

It took me three tries, but at last I hoisted myself onto Tesla's back. He wasn't terribly happy about leaving all that lovely grass just waiting to be eaten, but with a few hollered instructions from Soren, we were soon trotting around the big open part of the meadow, where later the cars would park.

"This . . . ow . . . this is . . . *ow* . . . this is a little hard on the . . . ow . . . teeth," I said once I felt safe enough to stop clutching Tesla's mane. "It's a . . . *ow!* . . . bit hard on the thighs, too."

"That's why you need a saddle," Soren said, although I noticed he wasn't grimacing like I was. "Then you can post."

"Post what?"

"Post—it's the way you move to the horse's trot. Makes it easier on your bum."

"Oh. Good. My bum could use easier." I squirmed around a little on Tesla's back, trying to find a comfortable position, my legs tightening on him as I tried to shift off his hard backbone. All of a sudden his head came up and his neck arched as he shifted into another gear. I know, I know—horses don't have gears, but he went from moving like he was on a road filled with potholes to one that was newly paved. His trot smoothed out so I was hardly jarred at all as he kind of floated along the ground with long, sweeping strides. I kept my legs tight around his sides, unsure of what had happened, but appreciating the new gait.

"What are you doing?" Soren yelled. I looked back. He was stopped, his mouth hanging open in surprise.

"Darned if I know," I yelled back, and eased up on the reins. "Whatever it is, I like it!"

Tesla did the smooth, flowing trot in a big wide circle around Soren and Bruno, then stumbled over a hole, regained his feet, and came to an abrupt stop as he did so.

I, of course, promptly fell off again.

"How did you do that?" Soren asked as he rode up. I stood up, rubbing my butt. Just my luck—I had landed right on a rock. "How did you make him move like that?"

I grabbed the reins and started walking back toward the small area where the horses grazed. "I told you, I don't know. It's something Tesla did by himself."

"I've seen that before," Soren said, more to himself than to me. "On TV. Horse trials. Dressage, it's called."

"Whatever. I think I've had enough riding for— Oh, hey,

look, it's Panna! That's the girl whose grandfather owned Tesla," I explained to Soren.

I led Tesla over to Panna, who greeted him with teary eyes. (No surprise there; I had her number now. She was a puddler—the type who puddled up at anything.) "Hi, Panna. I was starting to think you wouldn't be able to come by."

"Hello, Fran. Hello, Tesla. You were riding him."

"You saw us? Yeah, we were trotting. The vet said that a little exercise is good for him, as long as I didn't push him too far. This is my friend Soren."

Soren said hi, then took Bruno off to be groomed for the evening's show. Panna patted Tesla, gave him an apple, and chatted happily about how her grandfather used to let her ride him when she was a little girl.

"You want to ride him for a little bit? I don't think he'd mind. We didn't do too much."

She smoothed down her cute blue-and-white sundress. "No, thank you. I am not dressed for the riding."

I looked down at my scruffy cutoff shorts and faded purple T-shirt with horse slobber on it, and decided it was better if I didn't say anything.

"Tesla looks happy, doesn't he?" She moved around to stroke his velvety-soft nose, giggling when his whiskers tickled her hands. "I am so glad you bought him. He will be happy with you."

"I think so. I hope so. He's eating enough, and the vet says he's in good shape. Hey, while I'm thinking of it, what did your grandfather tell you about Tesla?"

She stroked the long curve of his neck. Tesla, I had come to realize, was a big ham who ate up attention like that. He'd nod his head whenever someone stopped petting him, watching you with those big, huge brown eyes that always seemed to be secretly laughing. "What did Grandfather tell me? Nothing other than that Tesla was special, very special."

I flicked a piece of grass off his mane. "Special, how? Special, smart? Special, fast like a racehorse?"

Her shoulders rose and fell in a shrug. "Grandfather did not say. He just said *alkalmi*. Special."

"Huh." I traced the L on Tesla's cheek. "Do you know what a Lipizzan is?"

She shook her head.

"Hmm. I don't know anything about them, either, other than that a friend of mine thinks Tesla is one. Guess I'll have to ask him just what one is."

Panna chatted for a little longer, then waved when a girl a little older than me called for her. "That's my sister, Jolan. She's coming to the Faire tonight, but says I can't because I'm too young. I don't think I'm too young, do you?"

"How old are you?"

"Thirteen."

"Um . . ." I thought of the piercing tent, the dungeon room, the people crammed together dancing under the influence of the glamour. I might be only sixteen, but I sure felt a gazillion years older than her. "You know, it might be better if you waited until we come back next year."

She made a little pout, but didn't have time to argue. Instead she pressed a slip of paper into my hand. "It is my address. You will write to me. I like to have a pen pal with you."

"Sure thing," I said. "I'll let you know how Tesla's doing, okay?"

"Okay," she said; then her eyes filled with tears (again) and she hugged Tesla, hugged me, and ran off wiping her eyes.

I spent the next hour grooming Tesla, ate a quick dinner with Mom, Peter, Soren, and Imogen, then changed into my Gypsy wear for the evening. Imogen said I looked very mysterious in the skirt and blouse, and that people who had me read their palms would be more inclined to believe me if I looked the part.

"That's stupid," I groused as I accepted the book on palmistry that she'd forced on me. "I could do an absolutely perfect reading wearing my jammies and bathrobe as long I was touching them, but no one will believe me unless I look like Esmeralda the Gypsy Vixen?"

"Not Esmeralda," Imogen said as she tipped her head and eyed me when I presented my Gypsy-clad self to her for inspection. "Francesca the enigmatic. With your lovely dark hair and eyes, you very much look the part. The customers will adore you."

"Yeah, right," I said, not believing a word. I glanced toward the windows. The sun was going down, the sky streaked with the familiar peach and orange and brilliant red. "So . . . um . . . when does Ben get up?"

She smiled a "you like my brother, don't you?" smile at me. "If we closed the blinds, he could come out of the bedroom now. Would you like me to see if he's awake?"

"Naw," I said. "It's not important. Maybe I'll see him later."

"Don't forget the book!"

I made a face but grabbed it, waving as I toddled out the door. Mom wanted to introduce me to some of her Wiccan friends, so I made a brief appearance in our trailer, where everyone was gathered for precircle munchies. Mom held circles about once a month and often on the last night we were in a town, when she knew there would be a lot of witches to form a circle powerful enough to have an effect.

Okay, word to those of you who are at this very moment freaking out—just like everything else in this world, there are good witches and bad ones. Some call themselves Wiccans; some call themselves priestesses of the Goddess. They're all basically the same—witches. My mother, of course, practiced good magic—earth magic, they call it. Pagans are very big on that sort of thing. When she and her fellow witches/Wiccans/whatever get together, they hold circles to practice their magic. A witch by herself can do limited magic, but a circle . . . Well, let me just say that you don't ever want to go up against a circle if you've done something bad. There was a guy in Oregon, one of those religious-rights guys who thought all witches were bad and should be put in jail (or worse), who started physically attacking local witches. Mom and her gang formed a circle and took care of him pretty quickly.

I heard he still walks backward, seven months later.

So I did the meet-and-greet thing, smiled at all the Hungarian witches, and took myself off before they all wanted to start doing blessings on me (Mom's group is very big on blessings). As I was leaving, one of the witches—an older woman with tiny gray curls and really big, chunky jewelry—suddenly tensed and sniffed the air just like one of those hunting dogs does when it sees a bird.

She rattled off something to Mom, who looked confused. Mom's friend Zizi, who'd come in from Germany, translated for her. "She says she smells something foul."

"That would be Davide. He gets gas when he eats too much fish," I said.

Davide shot me a look that would have killed a normal person.

Everyone else ignored my little joke. The big jewelry woman

said something else. Zizi's eyes got big as everyone in the trailer fell silent. "Bella says what she smells is unclean."

Unclean? I don't think she was talking about someone missing their morning shower. I glanced at Mom. She was looking very worried. "Unclean how, Zizi? Unclean as in impure, or unclean as in"—Mom waved her hand around—"damned?"

Bella made a show of sniffing the air again. *"Kárhozott,"* she said.

Everyone gasped.

"Damned," Zizi whispered.

"Erp," I said. And meant it.

"What are you doing?"

I stopped sniffing the air and turned. Ben was leaning against one of the posts holding the main tent up. "Trying to find something damned. You look gorgeous, as usual. You've probably never have a bad hair day in your whole life, have you? I bet you've never even had pimples. You're too handsome for pimples; they're probably afraid to come near you."

One ebony eyebrow zoomed upward. "Thank you. I think. You look . . . nice."

I crossed my arms. I looked as good as I was going to get, and we both knew it. "Nice? Just nice? I was lovely the other night."

"Yes, you were, but then I'd never seen you in 'girl stuff' before, and now I have."

My nostrils—of their own accord, I'll have you know— flared in anger. "Well, too bad, so sad; this is it as far as my girl stuff goes."

He smiled one of his wicked smiles, the one that makes me

forget that I don't want a boyfriend, especially one who thinks of relationships in terms of centuries. "I have something for you."

I looked at what he held out to me. "That's a ring."

"It is."

"It's pretty."

"I like it. I hope you will, too."

I took a step forward and peered into his hand. "What kind of a stone is that?"

"A ruby."

"Oh. Those are kind of expensive, aren't they?"

His hand never wavered. The ring sitting on his palm glowed a warm red at me. The stone was set into a dark gold band, words in a fancy script wrapping around it.

"That's the same as the tattoo you have."

"Yes, it is. Are you going to take it?"

I kept my arms crossed and considered him. "That depends. It looks old. Did it belong to someone else?"

"Yes. My mother. I want you to have it, Fran. The ring won't give you any pain, I promise you."

Of its own volition, my hand reached out to take it. It was heavy and warm, a soothing warmth. A woman's face flashed before my eyes, her hair dark like Ben's, a laughing woman, a happy woman. "Your mother was pretty."

"I thought she was."

I kept my eyes on his, the ring pulsing with remembered life in my hand. "She loved your father very much."

He said nothing, just watched me.

"But she died. I thought Moravians were immortal?"

"They are. My mother wasn't a Moravian."

I glanced down at the ring. I liked it. It was nice. He was

right: touching it didn't bring me any pain. "She wasn't your father's Beloved?"

"If she was, I wouldn't be what I am."

"Huh?"

He stepped forward, taking the ring from my left hand, sliding it over my thumb, then over my forefinger, then over my middle finger, where he left it. The ring grew warmer for a second, then tightened around my finger until it fit securely. "*Now* you look lovely. Dark Ones who find their Beloveds are redeemed. Their sons aren't born bearing the sin of their fathers."

"Oh, I see. But your mom loved your dad. How could she do that if she wasn't his Beloved?"

A flash of pain darkened his eyes for a second. "I couldn't tell you why; I know only what was. She loved him. And she was happy with him. She would want you to have this ring."

I looked down at my hand where the ring sat. It felt right, like it was meant to be there. "This doesn't mean we're engaged or anything, right? That weird finger thing you just did isn't some strange Moravian ceremony, is it? 'Cause if it is, I can't keep it."

"No, it doesn't mean we're engaged."

You'll notice he didn't answer my second question. I noticed, too. "It doesn't mean we're dating?"

"Nor dating."

"A friendship ring, that's all it is, right?"

He tucked my hair behind my ear. I decided not to push the point. He leaned forward, just a smidge, just a tiny little lean forward.

"Are you going to kiss me?" I asked, unable to keep my mouth from blurting out everything I thought.

"Do you want me to?" he asked, his breath fanning my face.

My inner Fran started turning cartwheels of joy. I told her to take a Valium and call me in the morning. "Yes. No. I'm not sure. What was the question?"

He leaned forward another smidge. Inner Fran threw a party, complete with balloon animals and ice-cream sundaes.

His lips were warm and soft on mine, teasing me, begging me to accept them, to caress them, to yield to their seductive heat. He kissed me until my head started to swim; then when he was done kissing me, he held me up while I tried to get my legs to support me.

"Boy, you sure can learn a lot about kissing in three hundred and twelve years," I said once I got my breath back.

He smiled. It was one of those smug male smiles, but I let him get away with it. Any guy who kissed like he did deserved to be a little bit smug.

"What happens to your fangs?" I asked. "Oh, geez, I didn't say that out loud, did I?"

His lips quirked. "Yes, you did."

"I'm sorry. I'm an idiot today. You'll have to forgive me; I'm not normally such a boob." I glanced up at him. "Um. What does happen to them?"

"What happens to them when?"

"You know, when you're not using them. Do they fold back like a snake's? Do they pop up into your gums? Do they grow when you need them?"

"Does it really matter?"

"No, I suppose not. I just kind of wondered."

"When I need them, they're there. Does that answer your question?"

"Not really, no, but I suppose it would be rude to push it, huh?"

His look said it would. "I have a question for you: what were you trying to accomplish last night?"

"In the crowd, you mean?" He nodded. I took a couple of steps away, just because inner Fran gets all swoony when she is too close to him. "Ah. I kind of figured you'd ask about that. You got a few minutes?"

"As many as you need."

I told him about the deal I had made with my mother and Absinthe. I didn't, however, explicitly tell him I was thief hunting in the main tent. I decided that if he couldn't lie to me, it wasn't nice of me to lie to him. So I just *implied* that I was thief hunting.

Unfortunately, Ben wasn't stupid. "You were looking for the thief when you returned to the main tent last night?"

I tried on his silence policy to see how it felt.

"Fran, what were you doing in the main tent last night?"

Guess I didn't do it quite right. I gave a little sigh. "I think the thief and person who wants to kill you are the same person. I was looking for him. Or her. Whichever."

His eyes went absolutely black—not a shiny black like when he kisses me, but a majorly annoyed, ticked-off, so-black-no-light-escaped-from-them black. "You were trying to find the person who wants me dead."

I turned my back on him and strolled off a few steps, looking up at the stars like I didn't have a really pissed-off vampire behind me. "Maybe."

The pissed-off vampire was in front of me all of a sudden, moving so fast I couldn't see him, his hands hard on my arms. "You are *not* to protect me, Fran. That's my duty."

I squirmed out of his grip. "Look, you may think there's something between us, but there's not. And if there were, I didn't agree to it—got that? So you can just cut out all of this macho bull about big strong you protecting weak little me. In case you haven't noticed, I'm neither little nor weak. I can solve my own problems. I can take care of myself."

"You don't know what you're talking about—" he started to say.

I interrupted him. "Oh, so now I'm stupid as well as being weak? Thanks, Ben. No, really, thanks bunches."

I turned and walked in the other direction. His voice stung my back like a lash, making me stop. "You *are* weak, Fran, weak when it comes to the dark powers and those who use them. You have *no* concept of how dangerous this person is. Whether or not you like it, we are bound together, and I will protect you as best I can, and that includes making you stop this investigation into the thefts."

"Ha!" I marched back to where he stood all stiff and glowering. One part of my mind—the inner-Fran part—was swooning to herself about how powerful and deadly he looked; the other part—the sane part—commented to itself that it was odd that no matter how menacing Ben was, I felt perfectly safe with him. "You can't make me stop anything, fang boy! I made a deal with my mother and Absinthe to investigate, and that's just what I'm going to do."

"You'll get yourself killed . . . or worse."

"There's nothing worse than death, except maybe having to go through the tenth grade again."

He didn't even bat an eyelash at my joke. *Men!*

"You have no idea of the dangers in this world, Fran. You don't even have the most basic, rudimentary protection skills, skills your mother should have taught you."

I shoved his shoulder. He didn't budge, not an inch. It was like he was made of rock or something. "No one picks on my mom but me; got that? She hasn't done anything wrong."

His eyes all but spat black at me. "She didn't even teach you how to guard your mind against others! That is the most basic skill, and yet you didn't know it. You know no protection wards, no ways to keep yourself from harm when facing someone more powerful than you—"

"Mom doesn't know how to do wards! She asked Imogen about them, but *your* sister wouldn't tell her how to do it. How can she teach me something that she doesn't know?" Now he was really ticking me off. I admit I was curious about Mom's not telling me how to guard my mind, but she probably didn't know there was such a thing.

"Then *I'll* show you!" he yelled at me.

"Fine!" I bellowed back at him.

We both stood there glaring at each other, breathing a little hard because of our fight.

He closed his eyes for a second, then opened them. The weren't quite as black as they were before. He touched my cheek, just a little butterfly touch, but I felt it all the way to my toes. "I can't lose you, Fran. If anything happened to you—"

I smacked his hand away. "What's the ward, tough guy?"

He showed me. When you draw a ward, you follow a basic pattern, but each person makes a little change to it, something unique that only he or she knows. Ben watched me draw the basic ward, then told me to add something else, another little bit that was all my own. I tried a few curves, a few extra swoops in the middle. He made me do the customized ward over and over again until I had it memorized.

My inner Fran pointed out that the customized bit was his name, written in cursive. I told her to get a life.

"Try it again," he snapped, still obviously peeved with me. That was fine with me, because I was still annoyed with his Mr. Protecto attitude. "You're still not doing it right."

"I am so! I'm drawing it the exact same way!"

"You have to believe in the power of the ward, in your ability to draw it. Without that you're just waving your finger around in the air."

I felt like screaming at him. Goddess above, was there anyone so annoying as a pushy vamp? "I'm trying, okay! So get off my back!"

"Do it again!" he snarled.

"Fine, I will. And then you know what? I am *so* leaving you! I never want to see you again — got that? *Never!*" I threw everything I had at the ward, all my emotions, all my thoughts, all my will, every last bit of desire I felt to go home and crawl back into my nice, safe little world. As I traced the last symbol, the last curve, the ward flared to life in the air between us, an intricate gold pattern that slowly dissolved particle by particle into nothing.

The ward was drawn. I was protected.

"Happy?" I snapped.

"Not even remotely," he growled.

"Noogies of toughness," I said through my teeth, and walked away.

"Where are you going?" he yelled after me.

"To do my job!" I yelled back, and stormed off toward the bright lights of the Faire.

CHAPTER TWELVE

Yeah, okay, so you saw through my big act. The truth was, I was so angry at Ben and his "you will stop investigating this because you are a girl, and I am a vamp" attitude, I ran off without asking for his help, which I had finally decided I would do, because honestly, what is the good in having a tame vampire around unless you put him to use once in a while?

So there I was, marching down the length of the Faire looking really mean and all, when inside I was wondering just how the heck I was going to tackle Absinthe without a little help from my friends (namely Ben). I was so focused on yelling at myself—and thinking of at least a dozen really cool responses to Ben's snarky comments—that I ran right into Imogen before I saw her.

"Fran, I'm sorry; I didn't see you." Evidently I wasn't the only one walking around all introspective. Imogen looked mad enough to kill, her blue eyes all sparkly with anger. She held a crumpled-up bit of paper in her hand. "Have you seen Benedikt?"

"Yeah, just a few minutes ago, over by the main tent. What's the matter? You look really cheesed about something."

"I *am* cheesed; I am so very cheesed you could call me Gouda." She shoved the paper into my hands. "Read that. Have you ever read anything so ridiculous in your life? The nerve of him!"

I smoothed out the paper and read the short typewritten note. *My beloved Imogen,* it started. I glanced down to see who had signed it (Elvis), then looked up. "Um . . . do you really want me to read your love letter?"

"It's not a love letter," she said, grinding her teeth over the words.

Ouch. I read the letter aloud. "'My beloved Imogen, long have I waited for you to realize that I am the one man life has fated for you, but time and time again you insist on flaunting your infidelities before me. This will end, tonight, once and for all. You will meet me at the bus stop to Kapuvár at midnight.' The bus stop? Oh, the one down the road from here. That's close to where I found Tesla. 'From there we will go into town and be married at once. You are mine, Imogen, and I no longer intend to share your charms. Your devoted Elvis.' Boy, what a maroon. What is it with these guys and their bossy ways?"

"He is insane. That is what he is, insane! I am *not* his, and he is *not* the man fated for me, and I will have Benedikt tell him so in a way that will guarantee that Elvis will not bother me again."

I looked down at the paper in my bare hand. The letter was typewritten, so it didn't hold as much emotion as one that was handwritten might, but even so I could feel Elvis's determination to have Imogen. I gave it back to her. "Yeah, well, I suppose Ben could put the fear of the Goddess into Elvis."

"It is not the Goddess that Elvis shall be fearing when Benedikt is finished with him," Imogen said dramatically, shaking back her mane of blond hair. She looked different somehow, more intense, more . . . just more. I guess it was because I'd never truly seen her angry before that I was impressed by her fury. "I shall send him to this little rendezvous. My brother is very protective of those he loves. Elvis will soon learn just how unwise it is to cross a Moravian."

I pursed my lips as she thanked me, and strode off down the long aisle, her hair streaming behind her, righteous indignation pouring from her in waves. I almost felt sorry for Elvis . . . almost.

"Like you have any sympathy to spare for anyone else when you've got the mother of all mind readers to grill?" I asked myself, then reluctantly turned toward the small kiosk where I knew Absinthe would be setting up for ticket sales.

I found her just leaving the kiosk, giving Tess, the ticket girl, some last-minute instructions. I watched her for a minute, trying to steel my nerves to touch her. I put my lace gloves on over my bare hands so she wouldn't notice anything different about me, reminding myself that I was protected by my ward and could keep Absinthe out of my head (I hoped) if she tried to get in. I had faith in the ward—I knew Ben wouldn't lead me astray with it—but am not too ashamed to admit that my faith in my mental No Trespassing sign was a bit shaky when it came to being physically in contact with Absinthe.

"You can do this, Fran," I whispered to myself, moving out of the shadow so Absinthe would see me when she turned around. "It's just one person, one last person. She can't hurt you."

Absinthe turned and started toward me. Inner Fran screamed and urged me to run away. Outer Fran forced a smile and tried to look like she wasn't going to barf. "Hi, Absinthe. I have a quick question for you, if you've got a mo'."

"A mo'?" She stopped, frowning as she scanned beyond me. She normally made the rounds just before the Faire opened to make sure everyone was where they were supposed to be.

"Moment."

"Ah. Are you not assisting Imogen vith the reading of the palms? Vy is it you are not at her tent?"

"There's still fifteen minutes." I chewed on my lip for a second, sizing Absinthe up. Really, she was a tiny thing, tinier than Imogen, but you forgot about that because her personality was so big, if you know what I mean. Her spiky pink hair helped, too. Besides, there's nothing like the knowledge that someone can bring you to your knees with just a flex of their psychic powers to make you respect them. I tried once more to pin down the fleeting feeling that I had seen something today that was important, something that I should have noticed, something someone said or did, but there were too many vague "somethings" to be of any help. I took a deep breath. "It's about the safe. You said that the morning after it was stolen the door was locked? You're sure it wasn't propped open?"

"No, it vas closed. Vat sort of a fool are you thinking I am?"

"Sorry. I didn't mean to imply anything; I just thought I'd better check."

"You have found nothing, *ja?*" She *tsk*ed, and started to walk past me. "That is because it vas that Josef who is the thief. I vill find him, you vill see, and ven I do —"

Desperate to touch her before she walked off, I said loudly, "Oh, you have a big bug on you," just as I brushed my hand across her shoulder.

She stopped and spun around, her eyes wide and almost glowing. "You." She gasped. I snatched my hand back, mentally slamming shut the stainless-steel doors of my sealed room, just barely closing my mind to her before she got in. I could feel her nudging around the edges, pushing at the walls, trying to find a way in, but I kept the mental image of my sealed room solid, and thank the Goddess, both it and the ward worked.

She swayed for a moment as if she were suddenly weak; then her chin snapped up and she leveled a pale blue gaze at me that made me take a couple of steps back. "I am not finished with you," she hissed, turning on her heel to stomp off.

"Holy moly," I breathed, rubbing my arms. They were all goose bumpy, like they got around real magic, only these weren't goose bumps of fun. They were scared-silly goose bumps.

Imogen ran past, stopped to have a word with Absinthe, then beckoned me toward her tent. I followed more slowly, trying to fit together everything I knew. Absinthe wasn't the thief. She had more power than I had imagined, but she wasn't a thief. She honestly thought Josef, the lead guitarist, had taken it. Which meant I had seven suspects, all of whom *weren't* the thief. In other words, I was back to square one.

We were busy for the next three hours, just as I knew we would be. Last nights are always packed, since the Faire comes around only every year to year and a half. I more or less handled all the palm reading (with both sets of gloves on, in case you were wondering) while Imogen read runes. I didn't even have time to ask Imogen whether she found Ben, and what he thought of Elvis's letter, let alone try to figure out what I was going to do about my failed investigation.

Just before midnight it started to rain bullfrogs. And no, I'm not speaking metaphorically.

"What the . . . That's a frog," Imogen said as a big lumpy green-and-yellow frog jumped onto her table, blinked at her a couple of times, then jumped off.

"Not just a frog, a bullfrog," I said, then stood up and hurried toward the front of the tent when I heard shrieking. People were yelling and holding things over their heads as they raced for cover. "Bullfrogs aren't good. I'm going to go check on my mom. I'll be back in a minute."

I raced out of the tent, trying to avoid bumping into people or stepping on the frogs that were falling out of the sky. Luckily the frogs were pretty quick on their feet, because I didn't see any of them smooshed as people ran through them. I saw a lot of them bounce when they hit the ground, though, and I have to say, they looked as surprised to see me as I was to see them.

"Mom? It's raining bullfrogs!" I yelled as pushed past the people who were hiding under the opening of the tent. Because of the circle, the rest of the tent had been emptied of its usual table, chairs, etc. My mother and the rest of the witches had closed the circle and were all standing with their eyes closed, swaying slightly as someone chanted the invocation to the Goddess . . . standard circle stuff. I knew better than to cross into the circle (I did that once—it took three weeks before my eyebrows grew back), so I skirted around the circle until I could tug on the back of Mom's dress.

"Bullfrogs," I whispered. She opened one eye and let it glare at me.

"No, seriously, it's raining bullfrogs. Outside."

"It is a plague," the woman standing next to her said without opening her eyes.

"It is?"

"I know about the frogs, Fran," Mom whispered, shooting me away. "Now go on; we're trying to focus our energy on identifying the unholy one that has brought them here."

Wonderful. Something unholy was causing bullfrogs to rain down on the Faire. Could my life *get* any stranger?

A man in a blue-and-red-sequined jumpsuit with a gold lamé shoulder cape walked by, pausing to do a hip shake when he saw me.

Well, I guess that answered my question.

"Hey, there, little lady. You're looking mighty fine to the King, yes, you are. Would you be looking for someone to dance with?"

"Um . . . no, not really. Have you . . . uh . . . noticed the frogs, Elvis?"

He looked around him. "Now that you mention it, there are an awful lot of the little buggers. Loud things, frogs. Don't like 'em, uh-huh."

Evidently the rain of bullfrogs was ending, because only one or two more fell. The last few on the ground hopped around with loud croaks, heading off into the darkness. I hoped they all found the stream before they got squashed by cars.

"Right. Well, if you'll excuse me." I started past Elvis back toward Imogen's tent, then paused, twisting the ring Ben had given me, something making my inner Fran stand up and shout.

"Suit yourself," Elvis said as he headed toward the main tent. I glanced at my watch. It was two minutes to midnight. How could Elvis be here if he intended to meet Imogen in two minutes at a bus stop almost a kilometer down the road? And where was Ben?

"Hey, Elvis?" I ran after him, careful not to touch him when he swung around toward me. "Are you going to watch the band?"

"Sure am, little filly. You want to dance with me after all?"

"No, I can't; I have something to do. I just thought . . .

uh . . . I thought Imogen said she was meeting you some-where. Somewhere else." Lame, yes, but it was the best I could do, given the circumstances.

He looked puzzled, and scratched his big, poofy black do. "Meet Imogen? Nope, don't have any plans to go anywhere else, just the main tent. I'll see her there. You sure you don't wanna dance with the King?" He did a few swivel-hip moves. "I'm pretty good!"

"No, thanks, I've got something to do. See you."

Other than the psychometric thing, I've never been psychic — not ever, nothing, *nada*. But all of a sudden, as Elvis walked off to the main tent, I knew that something was terribly, horribly, mas-sively wrong. Little tiny bits of things started to come together in my brain, just like a jigsaw puzzle.

Elvis wrote that note to Imogen; I knew it. I felt it.

Elvis was obsessed with her; everyone knew that. I had felt it, too.

Elvis probably wouldn't like a brother who had the power to make him leave Imogen alone. He might even go so far as to want to hurt that brother.

Elvis was a demonologist. Demons were bad news, impure beings, unholy. *Damned*. Their appearance was usually heralded by a physical manifestation, something like . . .

"Bullfrogs!" I raced back toward Imogen's booth. She was putting everything into her bag, chatting casually with a linger-ing customer.

"Where's Ben?" I yelled as soon as I got within shouting distance.

"Benedikt?" Imogen glanced toward the guy who was chat-ting with her. "He's gone to take care of the little matter I men-tioned earlier."

"It's a trap," I yelled, and veered off to the left. "Elvis is here, but it's raining bullfrogs."

She frowned as I dashed by her. "Fran, what are you talking—"

"Demon!" I yelled over my shoulder, and raced around the nearest trailer to where Tesla and Bruno were hobbled. My fingers shook, slipping off the leather buckles as I tried to un-hook the hobble. Tesla nosed my head as I bent over his feet. I ripped my gloves off, tearing at the leather straps until they gave way.

"Come on, old boy, we have to go warn Ben that it's a trap." I snapped the lead rope onto Tesla's halter, swinging it over his neck to tie it into a kind of bridle. I led him over to a crate, lunging onto his back. "C'mon, c'mon, c'mon," I urged, tapping him with my heels like Soren had taught me.

Tesla trotted through the trailers, weaving through the long black shadows cast in the light of the big lamps until suddenly we were past the edge of the Faire. A long, sloping length of ground stretched toward the road. I wrapped Tesla's mane around my hands and dug my heels in, shouting encourage-ment. He took off, his speed surprising me. I guess he wasn't as old as everyone thought.

The ride to the bus stop is a bit of a nightmare in my memory—although the moon was out, there wasn't a lot of light to see by, and cars were heading toward the Faire, not away from it, so that their headlights blinded us. I remem-bered that the vet said I couldn't ride Tesla on the pavement until he had shoes, so I kept him to the soft grass shoulder. Even so, he stumbled in the dark a couple of times. I leaned low over his neck, both hands tangled in his mane as he galloped

along, his breath growing louder and louder until it matched
the refrain of *Please be all right, please be all right* that was chant-
ing in my head. We took a couple of shortcuts through some
front yards, but I don't think we trampled too many flower
beds. We raced past cars, dogs, houses, other horses . . . All of
it was a blur as Tesla's legs pounded the ground in a rhythm
that was etched into my brain. *Please be all right, please be all
right. . . .*

By the time we rounded the corner a short distance away
from the stop, Tesla was sounding like a freight train, his breathing a winded roar. My hands were cramped from clinging to his
lead rope and mane, my legs shaking with fear and strain as
they clung to his heaving sides. Up ahead on the road, next to
a big open pasture, a lone streetlamp lit a wooden sign marked
with an A (for *autobus*).

"Ben?" I yelled, pulling back on the makeshift reins. Tesla
slowed down to a painful trot, then stopped, his head hanging
down. "Ben? Are you here?"

There was nothing to be seen, no Ben, no cars, no houses
even. Just a lonely stretch of road with a bus stop sign. Maybe
I was wrong; maybe I'd gotten everything wrong. Maybe Elvis
wasn't the one who wanted Ben dead—

Tesla gave an ugly scream, a sound I hope I never hear
again, his front end rising up in the classic horse-standing-on-
back-legs pose you see in statues. I yelped and grabbed his
neck, wrapping my arms around it as his front legs slashed out,
but I lost my grip anyway and ended up going sideways, off
Tesla and onto the ground next to him.

In front of us, a black, horrible shadow gathered itself, then
formed into a man. That is, it looked like a man—it had two

eyes, two ears, a nose and mouth, all that stuff—but I had to blink a couple of times as I got to my feet to make sure I was seeing what I thought I was seeing. As soon as the stench hit me, I knew it for what it was.

Demon.

"Holy cow," I breathed, then jumped to attention as the demon turned toward us. My ward suddenly glowed to life, but not gold like when I drew it; this time it was black, a heavy, ominous black that seemed to scream into the night.

The demon shrieked and jumped back as if it had been stung. Two bullfrogs fell from the sky. The demon snarled something that just *felt* bad, and turned its eyes to Tesla, who was snorting like mad, alternating pawing at the ground and rising up to slash the air with his front feet. The demon didn't seem to like Tesla, either, and backed up a couple more steps.

Okay, now here's the thing—I know nothing about demons, not one single thing. Except that they're bad news. But here I had one standing there more or less looking me in the face, and I didn't have the slightest clue about what to do to stop it, or how to make it tell me what it had done to Ben, or even how to destroy it. I was helpless, clueless, and for the first time in my life, I wished I had paid attention when Mom tried to teach me all of her witchy stuff.

I wanted to run screaming into the night, but Ben's life was at stake. I had made a big deal about being able to take care of my problems, so I figured I'd better do just that. "What have you done with the Dark One?" I yelled at the demon.

It laughed at me, a nasty, hissing sort of laugh that had two more bullfrogs and a surprised-looking snake falling from the sky. "You have no power over me, mortal."

Its voice was awful, like an amplified screech of fingernails on a blackboard. Tesla rose up again, his front hooves slashing through the air. The demon jumped backward.

When in doubt, freak 'em out. I threw my left hand into the air like Mom does when she's calling on the spirits. "I am Francesca. I wield a far greater power than you will ever know, demon. Answer me—what have you done to the Dark One you were sent to destroy?"

It snickered again (more snakes and a couple of what I think were eels dropped onto the ground behind it), slowly walking a big circle around me and Tesla. My ward flared black again, and I turned to keep it between me and the demon. "You wield no power, mortal. I do not fear you. The one you seek is beyond your help." It nodded its head toward the field behind me. "Go and find him if you like; my work is finished."

While it was speaking I was aware of the two round lights from a car coming from the Faire growing brighter and brighter. The demon's back was to the car, though, and evidently it was too busy taunting me to hear the engine until it was too late. As the headlights finally hit it, it spun around. The car didn't even slow down; it just ran the demon over. I jumped for the pasture, yanking Tesla off the shoulder. Although I heard the car squeal to a stop, I didn't hesitate. I ran out into the blackness of the field, guided by a horrible pain in my heart to where I knew Ben was lying dead.

I had killed him. If only I had figured out what was going on before it was too late . . . but I hadn't, and now he was dead. Gone. I'd never see him again.

I almost stepped on him because I couldn't see through the tears. His body was crumpled up next to a small shrub, his jacket half off, a huge, bloody, gaping hole in his chest. "Oh, Goddess, no!" I yelled, and grabbed Ben's head, holding him with one arm as I tried to slow the bleeding in his chest. "Please, no, oh, Ben, no!"

The demon shrieked again, an angry shriek, one that promised pain and retribution and all sorts of revenge that I couldn't even imagine. I ignored it. "Ben, please don't die. Please. I'm so sorry for what I said. I won't leave you; I swear it."

A white shape blurred at the edge of my vision. I looked up, expecting to see Tesla, but it was Imogen. Tears blurred my eyes as I clutched Ben's lifeless body. "He's dead, Imogen. The demon killed him and it's all my fault. I should have known it was Elvis. I should have known what was happening. He's dead because of me."

"He's not dead," Imogen said, falling to her knees beside us. "I would know if he were dead, and he's not." She put her hands over the huge hole in his chest, the one that blood was still sluggishly dripping out of. "You have to help him, Fran. I can't heal him and anchor him at the same time. You have to help."

"Help him? Help him how? I don't know what to do about a demon—"

"Don't worry about that; I broke its legs and pierced its heart with silver. It won't be going very far."

It stared at my hands, which were covered in Ben's blood, hearing the words, but not understanding them. "How . . . how do I help Ben?"

"You're his Beloved; you're the only one who can reach him. Merge with him, join your mind to his, and hold on to him, bring him back to us. Don't let him go."

"I don't know how to merge with him! I've never done anything like this! I don't know what to do."

"Only you can do it, Fran. Only you." Tears streaked down her face as she closed her eyes, murmuring words over him in a language I didn't understand, I looked down at Ben's face, that handsome, wonderful face, and knew that if I did what Imogen wanted, it would bind me to Ben in a way that would never leave me free from him. I wouldn't just be Fran the weirdo who could tell things by touching them; I'd be Fran the Beloved, and if I thought I'd had a hard time fitting in before, I imagined being the immortal girlfriend of a vampire would just about make blending into the crowd impossible. It was Ben or me; the decision was that simple.

I put my hands on either side of his face and mentally opened up the door to my safe room.

Ben? Are you there? It's me, Fran. Imogen's here, too. She's trying to fix the hole in your chest so you won't die. I don't want you to die, Ben. Can you hear me?

There was silence. No sense of him filled my head. It was like he wasn't there.

Ben?

"He's not answering," I said, not caring that the tears were rolling down my face, too. "He's not there."

"He's there; you just have to find him," Imogen said, lifting her head. Her eyes were filled with so much pain that it hurt to look at her. "Please, Fran. Please save my brother."

I can't, my inner Fran cried out. *I'm just me; I can't do any of this. I don't have any power, not really, nothing useful. I can't save him!*

You already have, a soft voice echoed in my head.

I sobbed his name out loud. *You're not dead? Please, Ben, tell me you're not dead.*

I'm not dead, Fran. I won't leave you, not now, not ever. We belong to each other.

I sobbed over him as his chest rose, his lungs wheezing as he dragged air into them. *There you go again, getting all pushy with me. I haven't said I want you, let alone belong to you.* I wiped my eyes on my sleeve as I bent over his face. His lips twitched.

Ah, Fran, what would I do without you?

Probably date a bunch of really pretty girls with no brains who oohed and aahed over your gorgeous self and very cool motorcycle, and didn't appreciate you at all for your ability to have a hole punched through your chest and still be able to make all sorts of he-man-type comments.

Probably. I guess it's good I have you.

"I guess it is," I said, and pressed a little kiss to his lips.

CHAPTER THIRTEEN

"This is all your fault."

Whump!

"It most certainly isn't!"

Thud!

"Yes, it is. You're his older sister; if you hadn't let him brainwash you into thinking that you couldn't do things by yourself" — *Whack! Screech* — "he wouldn't be so Mr. 'I'm the Dark One; I will fix everything' with everyone, and we wouldn't be here now, having to beat up a demon."

Slam!

"That is totally unjustified!" Imogen lowered one end of the board she was using to beat the demon on the head, and glared at me. "I never said I couldn't do things myself; it's just easier to have Benedikt take care of them for me. He knows perfectly well that I could have taken care of Elvis if I wanted to."

The demon started to snarl out a curse that would damn us both to hell as it lunged for Imogen, its hands dripping from where it had attacked Ben. I walloped it on the back with the tire iron I'd pulled from Imogen's trunk. "Oh, yeah, right. I am *so* not believing that."

The demon spun around and jumped at me, a wicked knife suddenly appearing in its hand. I gave myself a quick mental lecture about not paying attention and jumped out of the way just as it swung the knife toward me. Imogen did a fabulous martial arts kick that sent the knife spinning helplessly away. The demon screeched again. "I could have! I just thought it was more expedient to have Benedikt do it. He enjoys doing those sorts of things."

"Expedient?" The demon jerked the tire iron out of my hands, throwing me into the car parked nearby. I shook the stars from my eyes as it hurled itself at Imogen. Without waiting for common sense to kick in, I threw myself on its back, and slapped my hands over its eyes. It hurled oaths at me, invoking the name of its demon lord as Imogen avoided the spikey end of the tire iron. She walloped it across the knees with a board, yelling at me to get out of the way. The demon crumpled up into a little ball. "How expedient is it for your brother to be lying in the field over there with more than half of his blood drained out of his body?"

"Correction," a tired voice said behind me. Ben limped into the circle of light cast by the streetlamp, one hand over his chest. The wound no longer dripped blood, but he looked awful. "I'm no longer lying in the field. I'm here to get rid of the demon. Stand aside, both of you."

I made a face at Imogen. She raised her eyebrows at me. "Oh, very well, I will take a modest amount of the blame for his being the way he is, but not"—she swung at the demon with her hunk of wood, connecting with its shoulders. It screamed and tried to cut her with a broken piece of glass it picked up from the side of the road. I kicked the glass from its hands, my whole body hurting from the battle. The demon finally must have had enough, though, because it just lay there on the ground, a quivering, stinking mass of evil intentions and demonic power—"not for everything. Dark Ones are naturally arrogant. You're just going to have to deal with that particular trait as best you can."

"Imogen! Fran!" Ben snarled, or tried to snarl. It came out kind of a really mean whimper. "You must leave, both of you. I will deal with this situation."

I stopped glaring down at the demon long enough to push Ben up against the hood of Imogen's car. "Sit down before you pass out."

"I will not allow you—"

"Will you just let us take care of this, please?" I waved toward where Imogen was jumping up and down to avoid one last attack by the demon. "If you'll notice, we're doing a pretty good job of taking care of ourselves—and you."

"Fran does have a point, little brother. We are quite capable of taking care of this evil one, although I do appreciate your desire to protect us." She whomped the demon upside the head with the board. It fell over, moaning and twitching a couple of times before it finally gave up trying to kill us.

"Fran doesn't know what she's talking about," Ben said, pushing himself away from the car. "She's never even seen a demon before, let alone know how to fight one."

"I know now," I said, setting down the tire iron I had reclaimed to tick off the items on my fingers. "I know that demons don't like steel. It burns them."

"Steel?" Imogen drew a ward over the demon that made it arch up backward, scream twice, then disappear into a plume of really nasty-smelling black smoke. She dusted off her hands and walked toward us. "Not steel—silver."

"But Elvis told me . . . Oh. He lied."

She brushed her hair back over her shoulder and smiled at us both. She didn't look at all like someone who had just beaten a demon to a pulp. "I suspect he's lied about a great many things."

"Hmm. I guess that means he's the thief, too." Something nudged my mind, a thought that wanted attention, but I had something more important to do.

"Go on, Fran. I think Benedikt needs to hear just how much you've learned."

"Oh." I smiled back at her. "Well, let's see . . . there's also the fact that when a demon takes a human form, it's bound by the strengths and weaknesses of that form, so if you can run it down with a car and break its legs—"

"And drive a dagger of pure silver through its heart—I'm afraid that did more damage than the car, Fran."

"—and drive a dagger of pure silver through its heart, you will disable the demon enough to allow you to beat it up."

"Even then you have to weaken the body significantly so the demon is forced to leave it and return to the fiery pit from which it came."

"Right." I nodded and turned to face Ben. "So see? We didn't need you. We defeated the demon all on our own. *We* saved *you*."

"That's not how it's supposed to work," he said, frowning at me.

"It's 2005, not 1705," I said, patting him on the shoulder. "Learn to deal with it."

✺

We didn't get back to the Faire for another half hour. Ben had to replace some of the blood he'd lost. I worried that he was going to need me to play blood donor—and I wasn't sure how I was going to explain to him that although I didn't want him to die, I wasn't sure I wanted to be bound to him for all eternity, either—but luckily Imogen offered him her wrist. It was the first time I'd seen Ben . . . *drinking*. His teeth flashed as he bit her wrist, giving me a brief, momentary glimpse of two long canine teeth before his mouth closed over her flesh.

"Wow," I said, watching him, feeling like an intruder on something private, and yet unable to look away. "That's pretty wild. Does it . . . uh . . . hurt?"

"No," Imogen said, stroking Ben's hair with her free hand. She kissed the top of his head. "It brings me pleasure to give him life. Just as it will you someday."

Uh . . . not going to go there.

While Ben sucked down some much-needed blood, I went out to round up Tesla, who was happily grazing now that the demon was gone. "You were pretty impressive there for an old guy," I said, patting him on the neck. He walked along quietly, nuzzling me now and again as if he hoped an apple might magically appear. "You can have two when we get back home," I promised.

We had a brief skirmish when Ben, looking a bit better, insisted that I ride back with Imogen in her car while he led Tesla, but in the end I settled the matter by scrambling onto Tesla's back and nudging him off toward the Faire while Ben was still tossing out orders.

He caught up with me a few feet later. Imogen's car zipped by us, giving me enough light to see the furious scowl on Ben's face. "Maybe you should ride and I should walk. You're the one who's been injured."

His hand clamped down on my leg. "Stay where you are. I can walk."

He was moving a bit easier now, no longer hunched over like his chest was hurting him. I remembered how quickly he'd healed his blisters, but even so, the size of the hole that had been punched through him was awfully big. I let Tesla amble along at a slow pace, glancing down at the man who walked silently beside me.

"Do I get to see your fangs?"

"No."

He didn't even look at me when he said it. What a poop. "How come?"

"You don't have a need to see them."

"I saved your life; that should count for something. I want to see your fangs."

"I did not need you to save me. I would have recovered on my own. I would have defeated the demon."

I snorted. "That's not what Imogen says."

He walked along, scowling, but silent.

"I bet Imogen's seen your fangs."

Tesla dropped his head to graze. I slipped off his back and touched Ben's arm. "I bet all your other girlfriends have seen your fangs."

"They have not." Ben turned to me, his black brows drawn together. His hair was loose, a dark curtain of silk around his face, his eyes a beautiful oak with tiny sparkly gold bits. "I do not make it a habit to show . . . *other* girlfriends?"

I smiled and slid my hands over his shoulders, into the cool length of his hair. "I thought maybe since I saved your life and all, we might try this boyfriend/ girlfriend thing for a bit. Just to see how it feels."

His arms went around my back, pulling me toward him. I leaned against him very, very gently, not wanting to harm his healing wound. "You're going to drive me mad, aren't you? You're going to torment me for years while you try to decide whether or not you wish to fulfill your destiny with me."

"Maybe," I said, smiling against his lips. "Are you going to show me your fangs?"

"No," he said, his breath warm against my mouth. "I'll let you feel them."

His lips moved over mine, encouraging me to investigate. I did, hesitantly, unsure whether or not I really wanted what he offered, but in the end I allowed him to tease me into tasting him. The tip of my tongue slid over his front teeth, curling under to feel the points of two long, very sharp canine teeth.

Elvis disappeared. When Ben and I walked Tesla back to the Faire, it was business as usual . . . with the exception of Mom and her gang running around trying to force amulets on everyone. We dragged Absinthe and Peter (and Soren) from the band tent, collecting everyone in Mom's tent to give an update on what happened.

"I think Elvis is your thief," I told Absinthe and Peter. "I'm not sure, but I think he did it as a way to get Imogen."

Imogen frowned. "Why on earth would he think driving the Faire into the ground would win my favor?"

"Well . . ." I chewed on my lip and glanced at Ben. He sat in the shadows, a large, black shape that oddly enough exuded comfort and support. He had faith in me, even when I didn't. That gave my mental processes a little boost. "I think his plan was to push the Faire into a desperate situation, then offer to buy it himself with the money he'd stolen."

Imogen snorted.

"I know, it doesn't make a lot of sense to me, either, but he was desperate to have you. I think he felt in some weird way that if he owned the Faire, he'd own you, too."

"But how did he take the money, eh? How did he get into the safe without my knowing it?" Absinthe asked.

I took a deep breath. Mom and the other witches were sitting on the ground, clutching their amulets. Mom gave me an encouraging smile. It was kind of weird being the focus of so many people's attention, but at the same time, it felt good. Kind of like they accepted me, as though they valued what I had to say. It wasn't the same as when I tried to blend in at school, but it was . . . all right. Good, even.

"He didn't get into your safe," I said, the final pieces of the puzzle sliding into place. The thing that had been bothering me all day finally came into focus. I turned to Peter. "You must have known that Elvis knew magic, right?"

"He knew sleight of hand." Peter shrugged. "Close magic, yes. Card tricks."

"Substituting one thing for another as part of a trick, right? That's what he did today at the hospital."

"Yes, that is what sleight of hand is."

I turned to Absinthe. "How would you put the money away for the night? That is, what would you do before you put it into the safe?"

Absinthe's eyes narrowed. She still looked at me suspiciously, but ever since I'd come walking back into the Faire with Ben's arm around me, she'd given me a wide berth. "I took the money from Peter and counted it, tallying it against the slips from each employee."

"Where would you count it?"

"In my trailer."

I glanced at Ben. He smiled.

"While you did that, were you alone?"

Her frown grew blacker. "No, sometimes Karl would help, sometimes . . ."

"Elvis?" I asked when she stopped.

She said something that even in German I understood. "That pig! I will roast his guts! I will cut out his heart and eat it! He stole from me!"

"Sleight of hand," I said to Soren, who looked puzzled. "Elvis was a master at taking an item and switching it with another one. I bet he had some of those money pouches all made up with newspaper, so all he had to do was switch them when Absinthe was looking the other way. Then she'd tuck them away in the safe, never knowing that she'd been robbed."

It was Peter's turn to swear. Everyone left a few minutes after that, Absinthe promising dark vengeance on Elvis's guts, Peter muttering about calling the police, Mom and her gang to hold another emergency circle to see if they couldn't bring down Elvis, or at least blight him with boils or a really nasty rash.

Soren gave me a pitiful look just before he followed his dad out of the tent. "You were supposed to let me help you find out who was the thief. I'm your sidekick."

"Sorry—it just kind of happened. Next time you can be the detective and I'll be the sidekick."

He glanced at Ben, then shrugged and limped off after Peter.

"Tomorrow we shall be on our way to Budapest, where I will be able to shop until I drop." Imogen slid off the table she was sitting on, stretched, and blew a kiss to Ben. "I will need a new silver dagger. I shall buy you one as well, Fran. Thank you for what you did. I believe I will go and see if Jan is still here. He has many qualities I have not yet investigated. . . ."

She drifted off. I looked at Ben, gnawing on my lip. I'd kissed a vampire, survived Absinthe's attempt to get into my mind, and helped beat up a demon—surely I could do this, too. "So, um . . . are you . . . uh . . . you know, going to be hanging around with us in Budapest, or do you have to do stuff somewhere else?"

He stood up and cupped my jaw in his hands, pressing his lips to my forehead. Mom gasped in the background. "I must go hunt down Elvis, but once I have found him, I will return."

He stared into my eyes for a second, then left. Just walked out of there and left. I stood there with my jaw hanging around my knees for a moment, then realized what he'd done.

That rat!

I ran out of the tent, grabbing the back of his shirt as he strode down the center aisle. He ignored my tugging and marched onward. "Hey! Didn't we just have a talk about you being all macho and feeling like you have to save Imogen and me all the time? No one says you need to hunt down Elvis; Peter is going to call the police—"

"I am a Dark One. He is a threat to Imogen, and now that you have identified him as the thief, he is a threat to you. I cannot tolerate that threat."

"Do you know what you are? You're just a great, big chauvinist pig; that's what you are. My mother's told me about guys like you."

"You will not argue with me about this—"

"I will so argue about this, and don't you tell me what to do. I'm in charge of my life, not you—"

"You will stay with your mother and Imogen, and you will not endanger yourself again—"

"I never was in danger, you pigheaded boob! I had the ward to protect me. You were the one lying on the field with his guts spread out all over—"

"I am a Dark One. You are my Beloved. It is my right to protect you—"

"'I am a Dark One; I am a Dark One. . . .' Of all the hooey! You are so full of it. You know what? My *next* boyfriend is going to think I can do anything. He's going to worship the ground I walk on."

"I worship you—"

"Ha!"

"I do!"

"Double ha with frogs on it!"

You know, I have to admit, I'm kind of looking forward to the rest of the summer. I may still be Fran the Freak Queen, and I may still not fit in anywhere but with a bunch of fellow freaks, but somehow that doesn't seem quite as bad as it used to be.

Who knows, I may just survive this year after all. Stranger things have happened.

Circus of the Darned

CHAPTER ONE

"Good morning, Fran."

"Morning, Tallulah. How's Sir Edward?"

Tallulah smiled a sad smile. "Still dead, alas."

I nodded, not surprised at all by her answer. According to what Tallulah, a medium of Gypsy ancestry, had told me a couple of months before, Sir Edward had been dead for a few hundred years. It didn't stop him from being her boyfriend, but I didn't have the nerve to ask just what sort of a relationship was possible with a ghost.

I wandered down the line of trailers that housed the members of the GothFaire, musing on the fact that in a short time, I'd come pretty far.

"*Guten morgen,* Francesca."

"Morning, Kurt." It was hard to believe, but just two months ago, Mom had to drag me kicking and screaming to Europe to spend the next six months with her while my father had time to "get to know" his new trophy wife. What was harder to believe was that I would find an odd sense of companionship with members of the GothFaire . . . a stranger group of people I couldn't imagine.

"Ah, Fran. It is you." A slight woman with spiky pink hair appeared in the trailer's doorway behind the big, blond Kurt (according to Faire gossip, both Kurt and his brother Karl had a thing going with Absinthe).

"Sure is. Morning, Absinthe." I gave her a friendly smile that I didn't really mean, and hurried on my way before she could say anything else.

"Vait a moment! I vish to speaks with you . . ."

"Sorry—have to feed Tesla. Maybe later!" I called over my shoulder, silently swearing at the unhappy frown she fired off at me. The last thing I needed was to tick off the woman who ran the Faire, but no way was I going to let her pin me down again. Ever since she'd found out about my special power, she'd been after me to do a mind-reacting act . . . something I intended to avoid like the plague.

"*Tja,* Fran."

"*Hej, god morgon,*" I answered politely. I figured since we were in Sweden, I should at least learn a little of the language. Tibolt stood outside his trailer in a tank top and a pair of sweats and did some stretches before his morning run. I stopped, unable to keep my feet moving. "Um. *Hur mår du? Allt väl?*"

Tibolt smiled, and I swear, the birds started singing louder. From behind me, I heard a loud gasp, then the sound of feet racing toward us. "I am fine, everything is good, and your Swedish is improving greatly."

"*Tack,*" I thanked him, trying to stop the inner Fran from squeeing like she always did at the sight of Tibolt. "What are you guys planning for tonight's show?"

Beside me, Imogen came to a screeching halt, her hair rumpled, her face without even a smidgen of makeup, a paper cup of latte in her hand.

"Good morning, Fran," she said hurriedly without even looking at me. Since she was my best friend next to Soren and Ben, I didn't make a big deal about it. Besides, I knew she couldn't help it. All the women of the GothFaire seemed to be under the Tibolt spell, Imogen included. "Good morning, Tibolt. Isn't the day lovely?" she purred.

"Yes, it looks like the rain is gone at last. We should have a good turnout tonight." He turned to me, adding, "We are doing the sword swallowing, I believe."

"Oooh," Imogen said on a heavy breath, just like she was sighing with happiness.

"Speaking of that . . ." Tibolt's head tipped to the side for a moment as he considered me for a few seconds before nodding. "You are going to your mother's circle tonight, aren't you?"

"Yeah, she likes me to be there. Why?"

"Ah. Good." He glanced beyond us, distracted for a moment by the sight of one of the volunteers who worked the archaeology dig on the other side of the island. "What is going on there?"

Imogen didn't bother taking her eyes off Tibolt. "The dig people found an ancient grave early this morning, according to Peter. Have I told you how very much I admire your ability to sword-swallow?"

"Hmm?" He frowned as he looked across the big meadow and part of the beach that GothFaire and Circus of the Darned rented for the shows. We were near the causeway that connected the island to the mainland, which made it easy for people to attend the Faire. "I wonder if he is near. I feel his presence . . ."

"Whose presence?" I asked, rubbing the slight goose bumps that had suddenly appeared on my arms.

"No one important." He smiled ruefully. "I apologize, ladies. I was thinking out loud. Fran, if you don't mind, I have a favor to ask of you."

"Favor? Sure." I was flattered that he asked.

Beside me, Imogen tensed. "I would be delighted to help you any way at all," she said, looking hopeful.

Tibolt flashed a smile at her that came close to making her fall down in a dead faint. "I appreciate that, but only Fran can help me with this." He spilled a little of the smile on me, and my knees almost buckled. "It will be safe with you. You are not closed to the *Vikingahärta*."

I stiffened my knees and made a confused scrunchy face. "The what?"

Tibolt pulled a dark gold chain from beneath his shirt. On it hung an old-looking gold pendant made of three intertwined triangles. "The *Vikingahärta*. It means 'heart of the Viking' and is the name of this valknut."

"A *Vikingahärta* valknut?" I wondered if it was some sort of Swedish tongue twister.

He nodded and slipped the necklace over my head. The pendant hung below my breastbone, warm from his body heat. I got a strange little thrill that was partly from the pendant, partly from Tibolt being so close to me. "That is it exactly. A valknut is the knot of the slain, a symbol of eternity and the afterlife. You see the nine points on it?"

I touched the three triangles. The pendant felt nice, kind of tingly, like it hummed with power of its own. "Yeah "

"They represent the three Norns, the weavers of fates."

"Fate weavers. OK. Um . . . why are you giving me this?"

He smiled. Imogen sucked in her breath again. "I need it kept safe for me tonight. You can wear it under your shirt while you read palms. It won't interfere with your reading. In fact, it may even help you."

I touched the pendant again. Imogen made an envious sort of noise, so I held it up for her to touch, as well.

"It's lovely," she said, stroking one of the points. "Is it old?"

"Very. It was my grandfather's, and his before him on back for as many generations as my family has existed. And now, I must be on my morning run, or I will not have time to prepare the hallowed ground for the *blot*." He stretched both arms above his head. Imogen froze, clutching my arm, her eyes huge as she watched him.

"You're going to prepare a bloat?" I asked, glancing at Imogen. Her mouth hung open a little. I elbowed her until she closed it.

"Yes. A *blot* is a ritual sacrifice we in the Asatru make as an offering to the gods." Tibolt did two hamstring stretches that had Imogen gurgling, and me clutching the side of the trailer.

"Um," I said, desperate to distract myself from him. I knew the Asatru religion honored ancient Nordic gods. But I'd never heard of a *blot*. "Don't ritual sacrifices involve killing sweet little innocent animals?"

"In the old days, they did," he said, nodding as he did calf stretches. "But now we use mead instead of blood. It is much more pleasant that way. See you later." He took off before we could ask him how you ritually sacrificed a glass of wine with honey.

Imogen and I stood together, our eyes glued to the figure of the blond hottie as he trotted around the line of trailers and headed to the other side of the island, toward the ruins of a Viking fortress.

"He is the most gorgeous creature I have ever seen," Imogen said in an awestruck voice.

I dragged my eyes from the disappearing figure of Tibolt (which wasn't easy) to look at Imogen, and giggled at the googly-eyed look of utter besottedness on her face, even though I had a horrible suspicion I wore the very same expression. "Yeah, he's pretty all that and a bag of chips, but as Soren says, he's just a guy, you know?"

"Soren?" Imogen said, making a ladylike snort. Everything Imogen did was ladylike. Even now, having just gotten up and accepted the latte that Peter, Soren's father, had brought her, she looked gorgeous. Long curly blond hair, a fashion sense that made me feel like I was forever wearing a garbage bag, and delicate, pretty features would probably be enough to make me hate her on sight if she had been a normal person, but Imogen was anything but normal.

Which more or less described everyone here at the Faire.

"Yeah, I know, he's only a kid, but sometimes he sees stuff better than other people."

She released my wrist, smiled, and patted me on the shoulder. "Soren is only a year younger than you, Fran. That hardly makes him a little kid."

I lifted my chin and gave her one of my "I'm confident" smiles that I've been practicing when I'm alone in our trailer. "Yeah, but there's a big difference between fifteen and sixteen. I've killed a demon, and figured out who an international thief was. Not to mention that whole vampire business."

"Dark One," she corrected automatically, taking a sip of her latte as she turned back toward her trailer.

"Sorry, Dark One. Anyway, I doubt that I could have done

all that last year without having a major panic attack. Fifteen can be so, you know . . . *fifteen*."

"Mmm." She didn't look impressed. In fact, she changed the subject. "Speaking of Benedikt, he should be here soon."

I had started walking toward the field beyond the horse trailer, where Bruno, the horse that Peter used in his magic act, and Tesla, my bought-on-a-whim elderly horse, grazed. But at Imogen's words, I spun around. "What? You've heard from him? Where is he? What happened to him? Why did he leave so quickly, without any explanation, just a note saying there was something important he had to do, and he didn't know when he'd be back? And why didn't he tell one of us where he'd gone?"

Imogen shrugged and kept walking. "I haven't heard from him directly, but I can feel that he's near. I'm sure he'll answer all your questions once he returns." She gave me an amused glance over her shoulder. "You are, after all, his Beloved. He can't lie to you."

"Hrmph," I answered to no one in particular, heading back to where the horses grazed, pausing long enough to snatch up the nylon lead. "I'm beginning to believe that whole Beloved thing is more trouble than it's worth. If Ben really thought I was the only person on the face of the earth who could save his soul, you'd think he'd be a little more chatty about where he's been for the last three weeks, and what he's been doing, and why he hasn't called or sent a letter or anything."

Tesla wickered softly and shoved his big horsey nose against my stomach as I approached, looking for a treat. I undid the leather hobble that connected his front legs and kept him from wandering. Not that I seriously thought he'd run off. I had rescued him from a knacker while we were in Hungary, and though I didn't know much about his history, I knew he was too old to go far. But Peter insisted that the horses be hobbled while they were grazing at night. "Yeah, yeah, hold on a moment, will you? Here. Apple. It's the best I could do."

Tesla's gray whiskers tickled my palm as he snuffled the apple that lay across my hand. He decided to accept the offering, carefully plucking it off my hand, munching it happily while I snapped the lead on his halter, and led him toward the trailer. As we walked, I slipped my hand under his mane and touched the raised marking on his neck. Ben had said it was a brand and that all Lipizzans, a very special breed of horse, had them. Since Ben had lived for more than three hundred years, and learned a lot about horses during that time, I figured he had to know what he was talking about. "Although that doesn't mean he's not the most irritating guy in the world," I told Tesla as we halted behind the horse trailer. "Going off without a word to anyone like that . . ."

"Talking to yourself?" Soren limped around the trailer, two buckets of grain in his hands. I tied Tesla next to Bruno, a glossy white Andalusian, and made yet another mental promise to give Tesla a bath. It wasn't that Tesla was dirty, but next to Bruno's glossy coat he was more of a grayish color than pure white.

"No, I'm talking to Tesla."

Soren's eyebrows scrunched up as he handed me a bucket. "Same difference. I bet you were talking about *him* again."

I fed and watered Tesla, waiting until Soren was done pampering Bruno before grabbing his sleeve and tugging him toward the blue-and-gold trailer I shared with my mother. "Come on, my mom is cooking breakfast."

"Really? She's cooking?"

"Yeah, I know, a miracle, huh? Think I should call the newspapers or something?"

Soren snickered. We both waved at Mikaela and Ramon as they emerged from their Circus of the Darned RV looking sleepy.

"Why is she cooking?" Soren asked. "You didn't cast one of her own spells on her, did you?"

I laughed. "Mom is the witch, not me. I'm just . . ." I held up my gloved hands, the black lace outer gloves hiding the fact that beneath them I wore, a thin, flesh-colored pair of latex gloves. "She's making breakfast as penance."

"Ah," he said, nodding his head wisely. I fought to keep a smile from curling my lips. Soren was the only one near my age in the whole GothFaire, so we tended to hang out together a lot. Besides which, he was my friend. He helped me with Tesla, and he tried to teach me the magic tricks he was learning from his father, although I didn't seem to have his knack for it. "She lost her keys again?"

"Cell phone," I answered. "The new one she just bought to cover all of Europe."

"Ah," he said again, and this time I did grin. I thought he'd grin back, but instead he shot me a serious, half-wary look from beneath the thick brown lock of hair that hung over his forehead. "What did you say to Tesla?"

"What did I say . . . oh. Just now? Nothing important."

Soren sucked on his bottom lip for a moment, before saying quickly, "You were talking about *him*, weren't you?"

"Him who?" I asked, knowing exactly whom he was talking about.

"Benedikt." He rolled his eyes as he hurried alongside me. I slowed down a hair, remembering that he couldn't walk as fast as I could. "He's the only one who makes you get that look on your face."

"What look?" I touched my gloved fingertips to my face.

His brows pulled together in a frown. "The one you get around Benedikt—kind of dreamy, kind of annoyed."

I laughed out loud. I couldn't help myself—Soren's description of my expression just about perfectly described my reaction to Ben, vampire of my dreams. Or so he wanted to be. I still wasn't sure about the whole girlfriend to a Moravian Dark One thing. "I wish you'd lighten up on Ben, Soren. He's not really as bad as he looks."

"He has a motorcycle and long hair," Soren said darkly, his freckled, fair-skinned face going red with embarrassment. He refused to meet my eyes as I socked him gently on the arm. "And earrings and tattoos. And he makes you angry sometimes."

"A lot of people have long hair, motorcycles, earrings, tats, and make me angry," I said, caught between the desire to tell Soren the truth about Ben, and the urge to tell him there was nothing going on between us. Because of his physical defect (one leg was a few inches shorter than the other), Soren tended to be a bit touchy sometimes, especially concerning Ben. I don't quite know why he'd taken such an instant dislike to Ben, but I did my best to keep him from getting too bent out of shape. "He just happens to be one of them. And before you say it, I know he's dangerous, you don't trust him, and he means only trouble for me. Heard it before, got the T-shirt, Soren."

He made an angry sniffing noise as we rounded the long metal trailer that Mom had let me paint when we arrived at GothFaire two months before. Everyone's trailer had been customized to reflect their personality, and ours was, I thought, a particularly nice arrangement of gold stars and moons on a midnight blue background. I admired it for a moment before I realized that Soren wasn't saying anything.

I sighed to myself, knowing that I'd inadvertently offended him. "I'm sorry, Soren. I didn't mean to make you mad. I appreciate you being all concerned about Ben, but honest, there's no reason to be. We're just friends. And he's not going to do anything to hurt me. He can't—he's . . ." I closed my mouth over the words that would spill Ben's secret. As far as I knew, only two people in the GothFaire other than Imogen and I knew what she and Ben really were. I wasn't about to go blabbing around to everyone that they were part of an immortal race that most people thought of as vampires.

"I'm not mad," he said stiffly. "I don't care what you do."

I stopped Soren as he was about to walk past the door to our trailer, my hand on his arm. He looked down at my gloves, his eyes stormy. I gritted my teeth for a moment, then peeled off both the black lace glove and the latex one, gently touching my fingertips to his wrist. Instantly my head was filled with his emotions, anger roiling around with frustration, a smidgen of jealousy, and something soft and warm, a squidgy feeling of . . . I gasped and jerked my hand back. Soren's cheeks fired up even redder than they had become with just a few days in the strong Swedish sunlight, but his eyes didn't leave mine, almost belligerently daring me to say what I'd felt within him.

"Oh. I . . . uh . . ." I stammered, not knowing what to say. I slipped my gloves back on, waving toward the trailer door. "We'd better hurry to breakfast while Mom is still in the cooking mood."

He stiffened for a minute, and I thought he was going to say something, but instead he gave a sharp little nod and swung open the door to the trailer.

I blew out a breath I didn't realize I'd been holding and followed him, wondering how it was that just two months ago I'd wanted to blend into the crowd, praying that no one would notice that I was different from everyone else in my high school. Big, gawky, and uncomfortable around the kids in my school because of my weird talent, I had few friends and not much of a life. Now here I was traveling all over Europe with a job — palm reader in training — a horse that depended on me to earn his feed and vet bills, a drop-dead gorgeous vampire claiming I was the person he'd waited three hundred years for, and Soren crushing like mad on me.

Life is sometimes too weird for words.

CHAPTER TWO

"Oh, there you are. How did the readings go tonight, honey?"

I shrugged and slipped behind my mother into the booth, where she handed out spells and bottles of good luck, protective amulets of all varieties, and her big seller, love charms. "Same old, same old. Big and small mounds of Mars, lots of lines, a couple of scars, and one missing finger."

She gave me a warning look out of the corner of one eye as I picked up Davide, her fat black-and-white cat, and sat down in the chair he'd been occupying. Davide gave me a long look, his whiskers twitching irritably as I stroked his back. Mom handed over a bottle of good luck, warning the buyer to use it sparingly.

"Were you wearing your gloves?" she asked, once the buyer had trotted off. "Or did you really read palms?"

I lifted my chin. Mom had made a deal with Peter that I would read palms every night for four hours, in exchange for Tesla's food and other incidentals. Peter said once my apprenticeship to Imogen was up—I had another two months left on that—he'd also start paying me a salary in addition to the horsey things. "I did the readings the only way I know how."

She shook her head as she gathered up her things. "Franny, Franny, Franny . . . the God and Goddess gave you a gift. You should be proud of it, proud to use it to help people."

"I don't see how being able to feel people's emotions and thoughts is going to help anyone—"

"You were given that gift for a reason, honey," she said, just like I knew she would. We'd had this argument regularly since I was twelve, when my "gift" (*I* thought of it as a curse) manifested itself. "If you would just open yourself up to the path . . . oh, bullfrogs, I'm late. I'm off to get into my invocation things. We're short on happiness and insight, honey, so don't allow anyone to buy more than one of each."

I nodded, eyeing the colorful array of glass vials that Mom had set out to entice buyers. Unlike other people who hocked similar items, the stuff my mother made and sold actually worked. I know. I had a case of the giggles for three weeks straight last year after she accidently spilled a batch of happiness on me.

"Oh, there's a man looking for you," she called over her shoulder as she hurried off toward our trailer. She waved toward the end of the row of booths, where the main tent that held the magic shows was located. "I think he's somewhere down there."

"A man?" I asked, wondering if Ben had returned. But no, Mom knew Ben. Even if she didn't approve of him—and I sensed another "you're too young to have a boyfriend" lecture coming over her—she wouldn't refer to him as just a *man*. I wondered who could be looking for me, and why, but didn't have too long to ponder the question. Mom's booth was very popular no matter what country we were in because she used only positive magic.

"I'm sorry, but for curses, you'll have to visit the demonologist," I politely told a serious-looking young man. I held up an onyx-colored bottle decorated with a question mark charm. "The nastiest thing we have here is forgetfulness."

The man frowned even more. "Where is this demonologist?"

I pointed toward the right. Although it was almost eleven o'clock at night, it was still light out, kind of a twilight. Because we were so far north, the sun never completely set during the summer. The Swedes have something they call white nights — basically, it's light enough to read by, but not as bright as the midnight sun areas farther north in the Arctic Circle. "Black-and-white-striped awning on the left-hand side. His name is Armand. You can't miss him — he has a goatee and horns."

The man blinked at me.

"The horns are fake," I reassured him. "Just for effect." I waited before the guy left before adding, "At least I *think* they're fake."

You never really knew with the people around here.

I sold a few spells, had to argue with a lady who wanted to buy all three of the remaining bottles of inner beauty, and caught someone trying to do the five-finger discount on a packet of dried rose petals (one of the ingredients in the do-it-yourself love spell kit). I've always told Mom that she should keep something bad on hand for people who tried to rip her off, but she insists that we return cruelty with kindness, so instead of calling over Kurt (who, in addition to being a magician, also doubled as a security guy), I grabbed the girl's hand and sprinkled a little kindness on it, gritting my teeth the whole time.

"Have you seen Tib?" Mikaela asked when the shoplifting girl ran off rubbing her hand. She stopped in front of the booth, scanning the crowds.

"Not lately, but if you look for a group of drooling women, you're bound to find him," I answered, sucking in my lips in case I was slobbering just thinking about Tibolt.

Mikaela, her husband, Ramon, and Tibolt made up Circus of the Darned, a group that specialized in odd sideshow-type acts. C of D was traveling with us for a couple weeks, something they evidently did each year.

Mikaela made an annoyed sound, her short black hair sticking up like a porcupine's spines. She muttered something in Swedish, then said, "He is supposed to be checking the chain saws!"

"The chain saws? Oh, for your juggling bit. Yeah, well, you know Tibolt. Where he goes, so go a whole bunch of girls."

Mikaela, who just happened to be Tibolt's cousin, rolled her kohl-lined eyes. "Hrmph. When is your mother's circle?"

"In an hour. She always holds them at midnight. Something to do with the lineup of stars and stuff. Are you going to watch?"

"No, she has invited me to join."

My eyebrows raised up. Mom was usually very picky about inviting non-witches to participate in her circles. She normally tapped into the big Wiccan network that spread across Europe, using the local witches to form circles.

"Are you Wiccan?" I asked.

Her spiky hair trembled as she shook her head. "I am a high priestess of Ashtar."

"Wow. A high priestess who juggles running chain saws, spews fire, and swallows swords. Cool!"

She grinned at me for a minute. "It runs in my family. Tibolt is a mage, you know, but he will be at the *blot* tonight after our show."

"He's a mage?"

She nodded. "A practitioner of magic. He is fifth level."

I couldn't help wondering if he was working some sort of mojo that had all the girls fawning on him. I mean, yeah, he was gorgeous and all, but I had a seriously hot guy who believed that I was the key to his salvation, and yet even I couldn't resist staring at Tibolt.

"Uh . . . how many levels of mageness are there?"

"Seven. Oh, there he is—I will see you at the circle, yes?"

I sighed. "Probably. Mom likes me to watch. She thinks it's good for my inner spirit or something like that."

She mumbled something about that being true, then raced off toward the tall blond man who was being swarmed by a gaggle of females.

Ten minutes later I was relieved of booth duty, and went off to watch the end of Peter and Soren's magic act.

Normally the magic acts were over by ten P.M. so whatever Goth band was playing with us that week could set up and go live by eleven, but during the two weeks that Circus of the Darned teamed up with the Faire, there were no bands, and the magic acts alternated with C of D shows, which included a killer double sword–swallowing finale that made me hold my breath.

I slipped into the back of the main tent, standing at the rear to avoid getting in anyone's way. When you're almost six feet tall and built like a linebacker, you tend to block people's views. On the raised stage, Peter and Soren were turning a member of the audience into Bruno. That was an illusion, of course, not the real magic that Peter sometimes did, the kind that left my arms covered in goose bumps. I rubbed my arms just thinking about it, hoping that tonight he would feel inspired enough to perform one of his mind-boggling magic tricks.

". . . and with the magic words—what were they?" Peter waited for the crowd to shout back the magic words, which were never the same.

"Isosceles triangle!" the audience shouted in response.

I smiled. Peter told me two nights before that he was running out of magic words, and did I have any suggestions for words that had a nice alliteration. Evidently he was as desperate as he said, because I didn't think my suggestion sounded particularly magical or alliterative, but the crowd seemed to get a kick out of it.

"I say the magic words—*isosceles triangle*—and voilà! Jan has been turned into a wild stallion."

Soren whipped off the thin nylon covering the metal frame that hid Bruno from the audience's view. The horse charged down the stage, stopping at the edge to rear on his back legs and paw the air as if he were about to leap straight into the audience. People shrieked and threw themselves down, some laughing, some yelling exclamations at the thought of a dangerous horse loose.

It was all an act, of course. Bruno was very well trained, so well trained that I'd never seen him put a hoof wrong. I watched him paw the air, the sight of it triggering a memory of something Tesla had done a few weeks before, when a demon had attacked us.

Why do you look so puzzled? a soft voice asked next to me.

"What Bruno's doing . . . I think Tesla did the same thing. That move where he sits on his haunches and paws the air—"

It suddenly struck me that the voice I had heard had spoken directly into my mind. And there was only one person I knew who could do that.

Ben?

Right behind you.

I spun around to see Ben lounging in the doorway of the tent, wearing a cool Indiana Jones–type hat, and the same black leather motorcycle jacket I'd seen him in before. His arms were crossed over his chest, a kind of half-smile on his face as he watched me. My stomach did a funny little flip-flop as I smiled back at him. I forgot for a minute that I was mad at him for taking off without telling me, instead wanting to just look at him.

Tesla is a Lipizzan. I told you that.

Huh? I was a bit confused by why he was talking about Tesla for a moment. *Oh, yeah, you did. So?*

The move Bruno made is called a levade.

A le-what?

Levade. It's one of the airs above the ground.

I walked over to where Ben leaned against the doorframe. "Hi. What's an air above the ground?"

"A series of movements that Lipizzans are known for."

"OK. But Bruno isn't a Lipizzan."

"No, he isn't, but he's related to them. Andalusians are occasionally trained in the airs above the ground as well."

"Huh," I said, then socked him on the shoulder. Hard. "Where the horned bullfrogs have you been? And why haven't you called? Or sent me an e-mail or a letter or something? Why did you disappear like that, without a word to anyone? I thought you wanted to do the boyfriend thing with me?"

"What boyfriend thing would that be?" he asked, looking at my mouth. My stomach did three backflips in a row. "Are you talking about kissing? Did you want to practice on me some more?"

If my stomach had been in the Olympics, it would have won a medal for gymnastics. I stared at Ben's mouth, feeling incredibly squidgy, but at the same time, I couldn't look away. Ben was the world's best kisser—he'd had more than three hundred years to practice, so that was no surprise—but what *was* a surprise was how much I enjoyed his lessons.

Don't get me wrong, I've never had anything against guys. They're, you know, guys. Nice sometimes, sometimes not. But I've never really wanted to kiss one of them the way I wanted to kiss Ben.

"Fran? Do you want to kiss me?"

"Yeah," I answered, then remembered an episode of Ricki Lake that said guys like it when you play hard to get. Something about the thrill of the chase. "I mean, no. Maybe. Er . . . what was the question?"

He laughed and pulled me outside the tent, into the shadow of the ticket booth, his hands warm around my waist. *I prefer you enthusiastic and willing rather than hard to get. Say Mississippi.*

"I have a better place-name," I whispered against his lips. "It's the name of a town in Wales."

And that would be . . . ?

"Llanfairpwllgwyngyllgogerychwyrndrobwyllllantysiliogogogoch," I murmured, my lips against his in a way that made all my insides melt into a great big puddle.

He laughed into my head.

What, did I say it wrong? I memorized the pronunciation from a Web site.

I don't know if the pronunciation is correct or not; all I know is I like how you say it.

I let him kiss me then, *really* kiss me, because . . . well, he was good at it. And even though I was pissed at him, I wasn't so pissed I didn't want to kiss him, so I just kept whispering the Llanfairpwyll word (it's easier to pronounce than it looks).

"Miss Ghetti?" A soft voice followed by an embarrassed cough managed to work its way through my brain. "My apologies for disturbing you, but are you Miss Francesca Ghetti? The owner of the horse currently grazing in the meadow next to the fortress?"

Ben spun around and blocked my view of the man who spoke. "Who are you?"

I shoved his back, but he didn't move, so I edged my way around him, blushing like mad that someone had caught Ben and me lip wrestling. "Hi. I'm Fran."

"What do you want her for?" Ben asked.

I pinched his wrist, smiling at the man in front of me. He didn't look like a stalker or anything—he kind of looked like my father, tall, with faded red hair and dark brown eyes. "Can I help you with something? Were you looking for a palm reading?"

The man slid a look toward Ben before answering me. "Palm reading? No. Not unless . . . no. I am Lars Laufeyiarson. The young man taking care of the Andalusian gelding told me that the other horse belongs to you. Is that correct?"

"Tesla? Yeah, I guess he belongs to me."

His forehead wrinkled. "You guess? You are not certain? Are you not his legal owner?"

"Yes, I'm certain. My mom made me get a receipt from the guy I bought Tesla from before we left Hungary. I'm his legal owner. Why do you want to know? Tesla hasn't been loose, so I know he couldn't have done anything, or gotten into any trouble—"

"I wish to purchase him," the man said abruptly, sliding Ben another wary look. "I will pay you one thousand dollars American for him."

CHAPTER THREE

I swear my jaw just about hit my feet when Mr. Laufeyiarson offered a grand for Tesla. A thousand dollars! For a horse! *My* horse? Something was definitely not right.

"You want to pay a thousand *dollars* for Tesla?" I asked, thinking maybe he was offering me a thousand of some other currency, something that sounded big, but really only meant ten bucks.

Mr. Laufeyiarson nodded. "Yes, one thousand dollars American."

Maybe he had the wrong horse? Maybe he thought Bruno was Tesla? Bruno had to be worth a ton of money; he knew all sorts of moves and special tricks, but Tesla? Tesla was just an old horse who like to snuffle people for treats, and occassionally allowed me to ride him around a field at a slow pace. "I don't want to sound insulting, Mr. Laufeyiarson, but are you sure you're talking about Tesla, and not Bruno? He's Andalusian, and very valuable—"

He shook his head. "No, the Andalusian is a gelding. I'm interested in the Lipizzan stallion."

I slid a confused glance toward Ben. He stood next to me, his arms crossed over his chest, watching me with dark oak eyes with pretty, sparkly gold flecks. "Um . . . that's really nice of you, Mr. Laufeyiarson, but I don't think I could sell Tesla. I kind of promised a girl in Hungary that I'd take care of him."

"I understand. You have received another offer, yes? I will match the offer. How much do you want?" He pulled out a big leather wallet. My eyes bugged at the amount of money he had stuffed into it. "I brought fifteen hundred in cash, but if the offer was for more —"

"No!" I yelped, holding up a hand as he started digging out the wad of money. "There's been no other offer, honest. I just don't want to sell Tesla."

He frowned at me, a kind of puzzled look in his eyes that cleared as he looked at Ben. He said something in a language that wasn't English. Surprise flickered across Ben's face for a moment, and then he answered in the same language. A few seconds later, Mr. Laufeyiarson gave me a long, considering look, then inclined his head. "I see. I regret you could not accommodate me. If you change your mind, you may reach me at any time."

I looked down at the card he pushed into my hand before he walked off, leaving me to wonder just what was going on, what Ben had told him, and why he thought I would change my mind. Time for some answers.

"All right, what did all that mean?"

"All what?" Ben didn't wait for me to reply. He grabbed my hand and tugged me toward the area where the trailers were parked, stopping when we were hidden by shadows.

"All that he looked at you, and you looked at him, and you

both did that secret guy-talk thing that males do, and then Mr. Laufeyiarson left. Hey! You can't kiss me again!"

"I can't? Why not?" Ben pulled me into his arms and I stood for a moment, queen of indecision. Part of me—the girly part—wanted to swoon up against him and breathe in that wonderful Ben smell that was part leather jacket, part woodsy outdoors, but the other part of me—the brainy part—reminded the rest of me that he had disappeared for the past three weeks without any sort of an explanation, without even a good-bye.

"Because you already had your welcome-back kiss, and now it's time to start explaining a few things, like where you've been, and why you went away without saying anything to me or Imogen, and who Mr. Laufeyiarson was, and why would anyone want to pay a thousand dollars for an old gray horse?"

"Tesla's a Lipizzan. I told you he was valuable," Ben said, ignoring the more important questions. At least he let go of me so I could step back and get a little distance from him. "Obviously this man recognized his bloodlines, and thinks stud rights are worth the money despite the stallion's age."

"You didn't say Tesla was valuable," I said, frowning. Stud rights? Someone wanted Tesla to get busy with a mare? My old creaky Tesla who had to walk around for a couple of hours to work out the stiffness in his joints? Valuable? "Do you think he was, like . . . oh, I don't know, stolen or something? Maybe I should write to my friend in Hungary and ask her how her grandfather got him."

Ben shrugged. "I meant to look into Tesla's past while I was in Hungary, but I was . . . er . . . sidetracked."

"By what?" I asked, my attention immediately yanked away from the mystery of Tesla.

Ben just looked at me. I made an annoyed sound and stripped off both gloves of my right hand, scratching an ichy spot on the back of it before placing my palm against the patch of skin exposed above the neckline of his black T-shirt. Ben was one of the few people who could close off his mind to me so I wasn't overwhelmed with all sorts of emotions. Now all I felt was a deep, burning red hunger.

I sighed and pulled my hand back. I didn't really want to, but I knew if I continued to stand there touching him, I'd end up kissing him again, and I really wanted some answers. A little spot on the side of my head tickled. I scratched it and said, "You know, you don't have to shut off all your emotions. A few would be helpful."

Even in the darkness of the shadows I could see his teeth flash white in a quick grin. "If you knew everything, then there would be no mystery to keep you coming back to me."

My nose itched. I scratched it as I answered. "Any more mystery and I'm going to start thinking a less annoying boyfriend is the way to go. So you were in Hungary after we left?"

My cheek itched. Ben said nothing as I scratched my cheek.

"What exactly were you doing in Hungary? Something to do with this job you have that you won't tell me anything about?"

The back of my neck almost twitched it itched so badly. I scratched it with both hands, mentally cursing the fact that Ben couldn't lie to me. Not that I wanted him to lie, but I'd found out that it was more annoying to have him refuse to speak than to try to decide whether what he was saying was true.

"And what happened to your cross? You're not wearing it

anymore. You haven't suddenly gone all vampy about it, have you? You told me you could wear crosses and go into churches and all that stuff—has something changed?"

"No, nothing has changed," he said, his eyebrows pulling together as I reached behind me with both hands, yanked up the back of my shirt, and scratched like mad at a really itchy spot on my spine. "Have you picked up fleas from Tesla?"

"I don't have fleas!" I said, outraged, as I leaned against the trailer and rubbed my back on a protruding bit of metal. The itch wasn't appeased, but figured it couldn't hurt to try. "And neither does Tesla!"

"Then why are you hopping around like you are covered in itching powder?"

"It's my mother. It must be time for the circle to form. This is her subtle way of telling me she wants me."

His black eyebrows rose. "She torments you when she wants you?"

"It's just a simple itching spell," I said over my shoulder as I started toward the clearing beyond the Faire area where the circle was going to be held. "Nothing harmful, only really irritating until she stops it. You want to come to the circle?"

He shook his head. "Most witches don't care to have one born of the dark powers diluting their purity."

I debated telling him that Mom didn't think of him as evil just because he was a vampire, but seventeen different spots on me itched like mad, which meant my mother was upping the wattage in her spell. "Come on, no one will mind." I grabbed Ben's hand and hauled him after me as I jogged toward the flat area behind the main tent where my mother was holding her circle.

"Fran—" Ben dug in his heels and stopped.

"What? Oh, the sun! Sorry. Is it light enough to bother you?"

"Not so long as I remain covered," he answered, tugging his hat so it shaded his face.

"Good." I pulled on his hand. "Come on. Please? I missed you. I want to hear about what you've been doing, and tell you about all the interesting things I've been up to since we left Hungary."

He gave in, giving my hand a little squeeze before letting it go to wrap his arm around my waist. I went a little squidgy at that, but didn't have time to analyze just what that feeling meant—and what I should do about it—before we burst out into the circle.

"There you are," Mom started to say, stopping when she saw Ben with me. She held a sword in her hand, the sword she used to draw circles. The other ladies in the circle—there were five of them, including two members of GothFaire—gasped as a group, like they were shocked that Ben was there.

"I will leave," he said quietly.

I tightened my hold on his hand. "If you're not welcome, then I'm not staying."

"Fran . . ." Mom frowned for a moment, looking where I held Ben's hand hidden against my skirt so he wouldn't get sunburned, then to his face, thrown into shadow by the brim of his hat.

I don't want to make trouble, Fran. It's better if I leave.

You just got here! If you leave, I leave.

Mom sighed. "Very well, you may stay, Benedikt. But please do not interfere with the proceedings."

"We won't say a word," I promised, moving aside to stand

with the others. Mom had evidently just completed drawing the first circle, the one cast in the sight of the gods. She did that by drawing a circle on the ground with the sword.

Have you ever been to a Wiccan circle? I asked Ben as he scooted over behind me. I turned so I'd block him from the weak sunlight peeking over the horizon.

No. Dark Ones are generally considered tainted. What is your mother doing?

Mom held a sword at waist level and walked the boundaries of the first circle she'd drawn.

A circle is drawn in three passes—the first is in honor of the gods. She did that before we got here. This one is to honor nature. The third signifies the spiritual level of the circle.

Ah. Mom walked the third circle with the sword held over her head. *Interesting. I had imagined there would be some sort of invocation or words spoken.*

Oh, there will be, don't worry. She'll do the invocation to the God and Goddess after she welcomes everyone into the circle. See? She's getting the anointing oil now. Sometimes she uses flowers to welcome people to the circle, or honey, or even incense, but it looks like tonight is going to be oily-forehead night.

Oily forehead?

Desdemona, GothFaire's time-travel counselor, stepped forward into the circle. Mom anointed her on the forehead with a drop of oil. Desdemona bowed her head as if she was honoring my mother, but I saw her sneaking a peek at Ben. I moved a smidgen closer to him, doing my best to convince myself that I wasn't jealous.

I like it best when she uses wine to welcome everyone to the circle, I said, smiling into Ben's mind. He smiled back as I followed

Mikaela into the circle. A rich, pungent, spicy scent curled up as my mother touched my forehead and murmured a few words of what I knew was a blessing. I sniffed happily. She was using frankincense and myrrh oil, my favorite anointing oil. I took that as a sign that good things were going to happen, a thought that soured somewhat when I noticed Desdemona was still watching Ben.

Navy, a nice woman who was really, really preggers (she was the wife of Armand the demonologist), entered the circle next. She went to sit next to Mikaela and one of the local Wiccans. Mom hesitated a moment when Ben, the last person remaining, stepped into the circle. Everyone else held their breath for a moment, but once my mother decides to do something, she does it. She touched Ben on the forehead with the oil, saying the standard blessing.

Something within the circle changed at that moment, though, something I'd never felt before in a circle. It was like something had awakened from a long sleep. The pendant I wore beneath my shirt hummed to life, glowing with a warm heat.

Fran? What's wrong? Ben asked. I could feel his concern wrap around me like a soft velvet blanket.

Nothing, I said, trying to pinpoint what it was that felt different.

Something is bothering you. What is it?

I went to sit at the spot my mother indicated. Ben paused a minute when she pointed out to him a spot across the circle from me, but he went when I gave him a mental push. *Nothing. It's just this midnight sun thing, I think. It always throws me off. It's just weird being able to see everything in the middle of the night.*

You will tell me if you are unhappy about something, he said in his bossy voice.

I rolled my eyes at him. *I might have said I want to do the girl-friend thing with you, but that does not give you the right to push me around.*

Of course it does. You're my Beloved. It is my job to protect you from all evils.

OK, I admit—I went a bit girly at that. Not at his bossiness—that annoyed the crap out of me, and was something we had argued about a lot before he disappeared and we came to Sweden—but at the fact that Ben really did want to keep me safe from things. I would have argued that fact now, but my mother pulled out a handful of dried lavender branches, and started sweeping the circle.

This is a cleansing ritual, I told Ben as she moved along the circle, pausing to touch each person's feet with the lavender. *It's supposed to clean the circle of bad influences.*

Why is she touching our feet?

That's to clean you, too. It's all symbolic. Mom says a lot of witches use brooms for this, but she thinks that's way too stereotyped. She likes lavender instead.

"We will now begin the invocation to the God and Goddess," my mother announced, having completed the cleansing. "Normally I would now call the quarters, but because our Asatru brothers and sisters are holding a *blot* a short distance away, we do not wish to disturb their forces by drawing their attention away. Thus, we will content ourselves with inviting the Goddess and the God to join our circle."

Here comes the invocation part, I told Ben. *Inviting the Goddess into the circle is called "drawing down the moon." Doing the same for the male God is called "drawing down the sun."*

Hmm. Two gods only?

Yup. Male and female halves, basically.

My mother stood in the center of the circle, her eyes closed, her arms spread out as she spoke the invocation to the Goddess.

"Air, Water, Earth, Fire,

Elements of the stars conspire.

Goddess, mother of all, come to us!

Into the circle, right next to the bus."

I blinked in surprised. That wasn't the normal invocation. Evidently Mom realized something was wrong too because she opened her eyes and squinted at a nearby school bus that had been converted into a trailer for Desdemona. She shook her head, closed her eyes again, and centered herself.

"Keep us safe from curse or threat,

Just like a deodorant that guards from sweat."

Someone snickered. Mom had her eyes open again, frowning at nothing.

Er . . . that seems a rather incongruous invocation, Ben noted.

It's not right. Those aren't the correct words. For some reason, she's not saying it right, I answered. *Crapbeans. I wonder what's going on?*

I couldn't tell you.

"My apologies, sisters. Er, and brother," Mom said, shooting Ben a quick look. "I seem to be a bit . . . off tonight. I beg your indulgence."

"Of course, you have it," Desdemona said. She sat near me, which was good in one respect (I didn't like the way she kept shooting little glances at Ben), but for some reason, tonight her nearness made me feel edgy. I scooted a bit away from her, hoping no one would notice. Wiccans were very big on maintaining contact in a circle. To back away from someone was an insult.

Mom took a deep breath and gave it another shot.

"From sea and mountain, desert and trees,

By staff and sword and a mangy dog's fleas,

Heed our plea!"

Silence fell on the circle.

"Oh, dear," Navy said, leaning over to talk to one of the local Wiccans. "That's not right, is it?"

"Earth, Fire, Water, Air," Mom said grimly, her hands fisted as she started the invocation to the God.

"Elements of the stars conspire,

God, father of all, come to us!

Don't worry about being male, we'll make no fuss.

Guard us within from all threats beyond

I wonder if there are leeches in yonder pond?

By wand and cup and ball and bat

I just know these pants make my butt look fat.

Heed our plea!"

Desdemona burst out into laughter at the invocation. I wanted to giggle as well, but one look at the horror on my mother's face killed all thoughts of that. Clearly something was up to throw my mother so far off the track. I couldn't ask her what was wrong, though, because right at that moment, things got *really* weird.

"Goddess above—is that what I think it is?" Mikaela asked, pointing at me.

"Huh?" I asked, looking down at myself to see if I'd spilled something on me. Ben stood up, staring past me. I turned around to look and saw a thin, pretty woman with lots of long blond hair in the shadow of the tent behind me.

"It's a *huldra*," one of the local Wiccans said, her voice all hushed with awe. Or something.

"Is that a *tail*?" I asked as the stranger bent down to pick up something from the ground. I could have sworn there was a cow's tail popping out from under her long skirt.

"Yes, huldra have tails," Mikaela said, also getting to her feet. "They are spirits of the wood. A type of nymph, actually. They are supposedly harbingers of disaster, appearing briefly to warn of impending danger, then disappearing just as quickly—"

"Hey!" I yelled, jumping up as the woman snatched up the purse I'd set down in order to join the circle. "That's mine!"

"Franny, no! Do not break the circle—"

I knew it was bad to leave a circle before it had been formally unmade, but I couldn't just let the woman—spirit, nymph, whatever she was!—run off with my purse. It had all my money in it, for one thing, and for another, I just don't like people stealing from me. So I bolted after her as she raced past the main tent, heading straight for a small clump of scraggy trees that marked the boundary of the archaelogical dig.

You should never run after a being you do not know, Ben chastised, his dark shape leaping past me after the blond huldra.

You're so cute, I thought at him, puffing just a little as I jumped over a fallen tree trunk. Ben was faster than me (he had longer legs plus that whole immortal thing going for him), but I wasn't going to just stand around and let him be Mr. Manly and get my purse back. Anyone who had to the nerve to steal from me had to deal with *me*, not my boyfriend.

The archaeological dig was at the far edge of the island. It didn't look like much—a bunch of deep trenches and areas where square blocks of stone had been dug out and revealed, but evidently it was hot stuff archaeologically speaking. Right in the center of the dig, in a ragged rectangular spot framed with bits of stone that Imogen had told me was the long house (the main living place of the Vikings who built this area), Tibolt and his gang were having their *blot*, also in a circle. Because the trees surrounding the area made it dark, they'd lit a few torches and stuck them in the ground, the light cast by them making odd little flickering shadows on everyone as they did whatever it was they did during a *blot*.

I stopped for a minute to survey the situation. Imogen was there, as I knew she would be, looking like a goddess in a shimmering gold-and-white dress as she stood next to Tibolt. He was dressed in some sort of long black robe, I guess his mage wear. I didn't pay too much attention to what was going on in the *blot* circle because beyond them, the huldra dashed out from behind a tree, and went racing across the dig site toward an unpassable rocky area.

Fran, let me catch her, Ben said as his shadow flickered in and out amongst the trees. He was following the path the huldra made, but I could tell he wasn't going to catch her before she got to the rock cliff. I sprinted to my right, along the outer edge of the *blot*, hoping to intercept her.

"Fran!" Tibolt yelled, startling me for a second. "No, you must not be here!"

"Don't worry. I know better than to intrude on a circle," I answered him, flinging myself forward to scramble onto a loose pile of earth that had been excavated from one of the nearby pits. The huldra was heading straight for me, too busy watching Ben over her shoulder to notice me about to tackle her.

"No, Fran, you must leave—"

Suddenly, the huldra whipped her head around just as I was getting ready to spring and veered to avoid my tackle.

Instead, she jumped up onto the dirt mound with me, my purse clutched in one hand, the other outstretched like she was going to push me backward into the cleared area. The ground beneath my feet evidently objected to having two people on it, because it simply gave away beneath us, sending both the huldra and me falling backward into the excavation—and the *blot* circle.

My body broke the circle and I hit the ground hard, right at Imogen's feet. The huldra landed next to me. The impact had knocked the air out of both of us. A loud noise shook the ground like an earthquake. I ignored it as I threw myself on the huldra, yanking my purse from her hand. She snarled something at me in Swedish that I was willing to bet wasn't polite at all.

"*Luspudlar!*" I shot at her, the worst thing I'd learned to say so far (it meant lice-ridden poodle). I spat out a bit of earth, pushing my hair back from my eyes so I could add a glare that would teach her to mess with me. "No, son of a *luspudel* . . . holy bullfrogs!"

Around us, silence fell. Not a normal silence, the kind you get when a dozen or so people all decked out in robes and fringed dresses stand around the middle of the night sacrificing mead, but a heavy silence. A stunned silence. A silence that pretty much says, "Hey now! Something is seriously wrong here!"

Are you all right? Ben asked, sticking out a hand to pull me up.

Yeah. Or maybe not. Am I seeing what I think I'm seeing?

To the left, Tibolt sank to the ground, his head in his hands as he moaned something unintelligble.

That depends, Ben answered, his fingers tightening around mine. The huldra shrieked and ran off into the night. No one paid her any attention. *Are you talking about the* blot, *the fact that you scraped your wrist on a rock when you fell, or the Viking ghosts that just materialized around us?*

CHAPTER FOUR

"It is the valknut," Tibolt moaned as we all stood around, stunned. The *blot* people—about five of them—had broken the circular formation and were now huddled together in a group. Surrounding all of us were about a dozen men, all wearing basically nothing but leather and cloth leggings, each one carrying a really big sword. None had on a silly horned helmet (Mikaela told me later real Vikings didn't wear them), but I knew without anyone saying anything that we were looking at real Vikings—or rather, *dead* real Vikings. Viking ghosts, probably the guys who had died at this site.

To be honest, they looked as surprised to see us as we were to see them.

"I told you it had the power to raise the dead. That is why I gave it to you to wear tonight—to keep it from the power of the *blot*."

"Oh, the pendant?" I pulled it out of my shirt, absently noticing that it felt three times heavier than normal. "You said it had something to do with the Fates, not that it was going to do a Viking zombie sort of thing." The nearest Viking strolled over and peered at the pendant. Ben moved to stand next to me, a protective gesture that simultaneously warmed my heart and annoyed me. "Ah. *Vikingahärta*," the Viking said, nodding, then turned to his fellow ghosts and yelled something that had them all screaming like banshees.

"What the heck is that?" I asked, scooching closer to Ben. He wrapped an arm around my waist. I didn't protest at all, not with a dozen screaming Viking ghosts standing around.

"I think it's their war cry," Ben answered.

"They are happy to be resurrected," Tibolt said, finally looking up. "They are calling to Tyr, the god of war. It's all over now."

"All over? What is all over?" Imogen asked, looking worried. "I don't understand what has happened here. Why are there ghosts? What has Fran's necklace to do with it? And why are they shouting *'holle, holle'* at her?"

I was about to ask that last question myself. The Viking who had checked out the valknut was back in front of me, raising his sword in the air as he led a chant.

"Holle was the goddess of the dead," Tibolt said, getting to his feet. His shoulders sagged, like he was tired, and for the first time since I'd met him, he didn't seem to hold the same attraction for me. I wondered if his glamour, or whatever it was he'd been using, had worn off, or if the pendant had something to do with it. "She is the daughter of Loki. The valknut, combined with the power invoked by the *blot*, is what raised them. What has happened here is unfortunate—I had hoped to avoid this outcome, since he is near. But what's done is done."

"Um . . . where are you going?" I asked as he gathered up a small leather bag and started to walk away. The other *blot*-ters did likewise, although they also shot confused little looks between Tibolt and the Vikings. "Are you going to get something to put these ghosts back?"

"No," he answered without even turning his head. "I do not have the means to do that."

"Who does?" Ben called out after him. Imogen moved over to stand next to us, eyeing the Vikings as if they were aliens.

"The master," Tibolt said; then he and the *blot*ters disappeared into the woods, leaving the three of us surrounded by Viking ghosts.

"Master? What master?" Imogen asked, frowning slightly.

"Anyone who calls himself the master can't be good," Ben said, eyeing the ghosts. "But that's a moot point since he's not here, and we are. I suppose we should leave as well."

"And do what?" I asked, waving my hand toward them. "Just leave them here yelling and stuff? Ben, they're ghosts! The dig crew is going to get here in the morning and find ghosts wandering around their site. You think no one is going to notice that?"

He sighed, his mind a soft touch against mine. *It is none of our concern.*

Yes, it is. I'm evidently the one who brought them back.

"It was not intentional," he argued, pulling me after him as he started to leave the dig site.

"That doesn't matter. I still —"

"You are leaving, Holle?" a voice asked from behind us. We spun around, staring at the big Viking who had been next to me. "We just arrived. Why are you leaving us?"

"You speak English?" I asked, stunned, my feet coming to a halt.

"Of course. We have not much else to do over the centuries but watch the visitors and learn their languages." The Viking frowned. "I am Eirik Redblood. These are my men, my family, my brothers. Who do you wish for us to slaughter?"

"Slaughter?" I asked, the word coming out like a squeak. "No one!"

"Begone, spirit," Ben said, waving his hand toward Eirik. "We have no need of you in this place."

The Vikings all burst into laughter, a couple of them doubling over and wiping their eyes. Ben's eyebrows pulled together in a puzzled frown as he watched them. He lifted his hand toward them again, making the same waving gesture. "I command you to leave now."

That made the Vikings laugh even harder.

"Uh-oh," I said, peeking at Ben from the corner of my eye. He didn't look happy. *Was that little hand thingie supposed to do something?*

Yes.

Oops.

Eirik stalked over toward us, lifting his sword so the tip was almost touching Ben's throat. "You have no powers over us, Dark One. Not here, in the land that is soaked with our blood."

"OK. Time for us to leave, I think," I said, stepping backward carefully, tugging at the back of Ben's jacket. He didn't move, of course. "Um, Ben? Let's go."

"I will stay here until you and Imogen are safely away," he answered in his macho guy voice. I almost rolled my eyes, but didn't because there is a time and place for eye rolling, and doing it while a big, bad Viking ghost holds a sword to your boyfriend's neck isn't one of them.

Eirik's blue eyes eyes narrowed as he looked at me. "You know this Dark One, Holle?"

"My name isn't Holly, it's Fran, and yes, I know him. He's . . . er . . . he's my . . ."

His eyes narrowed further. "Does he hold you prisoner?"

"Stay back, Fran," Ben said, moving slightly to the side to block Eirik's view of me.

"No," I said on a sigh, answering both Ben and Eirik's question with one word as I let go of Ben's jacket and stood beside him. "No, he doesn't hold me prisoner, and no, I'm not going to stay back. Ben is my boyfriend, OK? Now please move your sword. It's making me really nervous."

To my surprise, Eirik did as I asked. "By your will, Holle. Who would you have us destroy, if not this Dark One? The female?"

Imogen, who had been watching everything, silently, gasped, her eyes flashing at him. "I would like to see you try!"

"Why do you keep asking me who I want destroyed?" I asked. "And why do you insist on calling me Holle? I'm not the goddess of death, or whoever Tibolt said she was. My name is Fran, I work for the GothFaire, and Ben and Imogen are my friends."

"You raised us, so we are yours to command, O mighty goddess Fran," Eirik said, dropping to one knee. "We are bound to you until you call the Valkyries to take us to Valhalla."

"Just when I thought my life couldn't get any weirder," I muttered.

"Other than the rude one who offered to kill me, I think they're rather charming," Imogen said, smiling at a half-naked Viking ghost. To my surprise, he smiled back at her.

Any ideas on what I should do to get rid of them? I asked Ben.

None, I'm afraid, he answered with a puzzled look on his face. *Ghosts are out of my range of experience. Most likely the best thing to do is ask them.* "How does Fran release you?" he asked Eirik.

Eirik's nostrils flared as he looked Ben over from head to toe. Ben wasn't as big and bulky as Eirik, but he wasn't a skinny little nothing, either. Beside me, all his muscles tensed like he was going to fling himself forward.

"You are mated to the goddess?" the Viking asked.

"Yes," Ben said without even a second's delay.

"Whoa! We are not mated!" I said, giving him a glare. "All I've done is kiss you!"

Eirik's eyes lit up as he took a step forward. "You are not mated to the Dark One? Good. I have always desired to rut with a goddess."

"Rut?" I asked, holding my ground even though Eirik took another step toward me, because I didn't let anyone intimidate me. Ben's arm tightened around my waist.

"Swive," Eirik said, with a smile that made it pretty darn clear just what he was talking about.

"Oh, *that* mated! Silly me! Yes, yes, we are. Ben and I, that is. We're *so* mated, like every night. Sometimes four or five times a night," I said, figuring more was better where that sort of thing was concerned. Ben I knew I could trust—with Eirik I wasn't really so sure.

"I'm not mated to anyone," Imogen said, smiling again at the Viking behind Eirik.

"Imogen!" Ben growled. "Behave yourself. They are ghosts."

"Yes, but such cute ones. Are you corporeal?" She walked forward and put her hand out toward the hottie Viking's chest. To my surprise, her hand didn't go whipping through him. Instead it stopped and rested on his bare chest. Imogen gave a little squeal of delight. "You are! How exciting!"

Ben swore under his breath. I pinched his hand to remind him that Imogen was not going to be happy if he made a fuss about whom she dated. "You didn't answer my question, Viking. How does Fran release you?"

Eirik looked at me. "I will answer him because he is mated to you, but if you change your mind about him at any time, I will be happy to—"

"Thanks," I said quickly, figuring we were all going to be happier if he didn't finish that sentence. "About the releasing thing?"

He shrugged. "You are a goddess—you must know best how to do that."

"But I'm not a goddess," I protested.

"You bear the *Vikingahärta*, and you called us to rise. Only a goddess could do such a thing," he insisted.

Great. Now what do I do? I'm so not a goddess.

"You don't know how she can release you?" Ben asked as I gave a mental groan.

"No," Eirik answered, looking slightly bored. "We are warriors, Vikings, children of the gods—not the gods themselves. Such things are no concern of ours."

Clearly the answer lies in the pendant, Ben said. *The blond man said earlier that it was responsible for raising the ghosts—perhaps if we knew more about it, we could discover how to use it to release the ghosts.*

Good idea. I'll ask Tibolt.

"What *are* your concerns?" Imogen asked, her voice silky as she stroked the Viking's chest.

"War!" Eirik shouted.

"Pillage!" another one answered.

"Women," the ghost Imogen was touching said in a near purr. They smiled again at each other.

"Oh, for Christ's sake—" Ben muttered to himself.

Would you like me to touch your chest like that? I asked him, watching Imogen as she murmured in the Viking's ear. He laughed and leaned down to whisper in her ear as well.

Ben's eyes, normally a delicious brown with gold and black flecks in them, went the color of honey oak. *Sweetheart, that would lead to us really being mated, which would mean we were Joined. And I don't think you're ready for that yet.*

Gotcha. No chest touchies.

A little sigh of unhappiness swept through him, but he cut it off before I could say anything. "Let's go find this Tibolt."

"OK," I said, turning toward the camp, but Ben didn't follow me like I expected. Instead he and Eirik were toe-to-toe. "What now?"

"He was going with you," Ben growled, doing the macho bit I was starting to think he really loved. I sighed to myself. That was one of the things we had yet to work out, but I figured right then was not the time to do it.

"You guys don't want to stay here?" I asked Eirik, waving my hand to indicate the dig site. "You said this was your home, right?"

"Until you summoned us. Now we follow you," Eirik answered, and sure enough, they all got in line behind him, Imogen's Viking giving her a steamy look as he did so.

"You are not going to annoy Fran in any way," Ben said stubbornly, crossing his arms over his chest.

I walked back to him and put a hand on his arm, giving his biceps a little squeeze (which, I had to admit, made me do a little inner girly squeal, but he didn't need to know that). "Remember rule number one—Fran can take care of herself. Good. So you can stop being all manly and stuff and let *me* worry about me."

Ben shot me an outraged look that pretty much told me what he thought of rule number one.

"Hey, Imogen and I beat up a demon last month all by ourselves!" I stopped squeezing and whapped him on the arm. "We stopped him from killing you, too!"

"I had the situation fully in my control," he answered, his voice low like he was growling. For some reason, that just made me want to kiss him. "If you and Imogen hadn't interefered—"

"Oh, for heaven's sake, little brother," Imogen said as she strolled over to us. "This is 2006, not 1806. Fran and I are quite capable of taking care of not only ourselves, but you, as well."

"I don't need anyone to take care of me," Ben sputtered, his eyes going black as he glared at his sister.

Imogen smiled at him and kissed his cheek. He growled some more. "So typical of Moravian men. I've done my best with him, Fran, but clearly you have a lot of work ahead of you. I believe I shall drive over to the mainland and see what's happening at the local nightclub." She cast a glance over her shoulder at her friendly Viking. "If anyone would care to join me, I'd be happy to have the company."

Ben opened his mouth like he was going to forbid her, but I dug my nails into his wrist, so he just glared at me instead.

Imogen's Viking looked first at Eirik, then at me. I realized with a bit of surprise that he was waiting for permission. "Sure," I said, waving at Imogen. "Knock yourself out. All of you. I . . . er . . . hereby do solemnly give you permission to do whatever you want to do without asking me first. Unless it's, like, some-thing bad—then don't do it. OK?"

The Vikings scattered like pool balls, a couple of them go-ing off with Imogen to the nearest town on the mainland, a cou-ple heading for the main tent, the rest off to wander around the fairgrounds. Only Eirik remained standing with Ben and me.

"Don't you want to go to town with Imogen and the oth-ers?" I asked, kind of surprised that he'd want to stay behind.

"No. My duty is to stay near my goddess in case she has need of me," he said, falling into place on my left side as Ben walked on my right. We were headed toward the lights and noise of the Faire, which still had a few hours to go.

"I will take care of any needs Fran has," Ben said stiffly.

We are so going to have a little talk later, I told him.

Yes. Yes, we are. It's about time we have a few things out.

I sent him a mental frown, and decided he needed to be ig-nored for a minute or two. "So, you guys all died together here?" I asked Eirik. "Was, it . . . um . . . bad? Dying?"

"We fought and died with much honor," he said proudly. "There were twelve of us to the Norwegians' ten score. We sent three times our number to Valhalla before they finished us."

"Wow. That's a lot of killing."

"We are Viking. It's what we do best," he said modestly. "There is a priestess in your group, is there not? I have seen her. She has hair the color of a crow, which stands up in unruly clumps. If I cannot rut with a goddess, a priestess would do."

"That would be Mikaela, but she has a husband," I said, sliding a quick glance toward Ben. "There's a girl working for the Faire who doesn't have a boyfriend, though. Her name is Desdemona. She's a personal time-travel counselor."

"Hmm." Eirik looked thoughtful.

"Fran? Where did you—oh. Hi, Benedikt. Who's that?" We'd reached the edge of the fairgrounds, keeping to the shadows as much as possible because of Ben. Soren popped out of the main tent and stood with his hands on his hips, squinting first at Ben, then at Eirik. "Why is he dressed so funny?"

"He's a ghost, and a Viking, and I'm sure it's not funny to him," I said, making warning eyebrows at Soren. "Eirik, this is Soren. He's the son of one of the owners of the Faire, and is a magician in training. He's also teaching me to ride. Soren, this is Eirik Redblood, leader of the Vikings who were killed over at the dig site. He's . . . uh . . . been called back accidentally."

Soren blinked twice, then nodded. "A Viking ghost. OK. How long will he be here?"

"Er . . . we're not quite sure on that. There are eleven others, as well, although some went off with Imogen to the local disco." I wrinkled my nose as something occurred to me. "What are people in town going to think of a bunch of guys dressed in leather and leggings?" I asked Ben.

He shrugged one shoulder. "It could start a new fashion trend."

"Where is this Desdemona you speak of?" Eirik asked me, scanning the crowds wandering around the fairgrounds. Even though he stood a good head higher than everyone else, and was dressed like ye olde Viking, no one seemed to be paying him any attention. Everyone milled around the various booths and stalls that formed an alley, slowly drifting past us into the main tent, where the second round of magic acts was about to start.

I pointed down to the far end of the right side of the booths. "See the big hourglass above the green-striped awning? That's

Desdemona's booth. The second show is about to start, so most people will go watch that if you wanted to talk to her. Although I should warn you—she's a bit wacky when it comes to the subject of time travel."

Soren snickered. "You just say that because she insists you're the reincarnation of Cleopatra."

Ben laughed, taking my hand and rubbing his thumb over the ring I wore, a ring that had once belonged to his mother, but which he'd given me last month. "Fran?"

"Hey, you don't have to say that in such a disbelieving tone," I said. "I could be Cleopatra!"

"I don't believe in reincarnation," he said, smiling at me.

"I don't know what this time travel is, but I like to sail. I will try it," Eirik said, and without another word he went marching off down the row toward Desdemona's booth.

"He's in for a surprise," I said, smiling.

"*Ja*. Big surprise." Soren looked up as his father and my mother walked over to us.

I flinched. Mom had a really unhappy look on her face, but all she said was, "I will speak to you later about your behavior in the circle."

"Soren, is Bruno ready?" Peter asked, cocking an eyebrow at his son. "No? Then go—the show is about to begin. Ah. Ben, you are back with us?"

"I am," Ben said, shaking Peter's hand. "I will probably be around for a while. I'm staying with Imogen, so if there is something I can do to help out, let me know."

"I will, thank you." Peter yelled something at one of the guys hauling in a crate containing his illusion equipment. "I must go now. I have told them a hundred times how valuable that equipment is, but they do not listen—"

Peter hurried off to set up the second show. Mom gave me a warning look and drifted off. Ben rubbed his chin as he looked after her. "I wonder what was going on with her invocations."

"Probably that huldra. Or the ghosts. Her invocations can go wonky if there are unsettled elements in the area." I shrugged and smiled. "So, you're going to be here for a while this time? No running off without a word to anyone?"

His thumb rubbed over my knuckles. My knees went a bit weak at the touch, but I told them to knock off the girly stuff. "I'm sorry about that. It was unavoidable, but I regret not being able to tell you I had to leave before I was called away."

"Called away by who?" I asked, throwing grammar rules to the wind.

He just rubbed my fingers and didn't answer. I sighed. Just because he couldn't lie to me didn't mean he had to keep silent whenever I asked a question he didn't want to answer. I mean really.

"I'm not going to tell anyone if you've been off doing something, you know"—I made bitey claw fingers—"vampy. You can trust me, Ben. I'm not going to give you away."

"I trust you with my life," he said, pulling my hand up to give my fingers a kiss. My stomach did a happy backflip. "But this situation concerns someone other than me, and I am not at liberty yet to tell you about it."

I sighed again. "OK. Mom says I have to respect your privacy, although she did say a couple of snarky things about guys who run off without a word. But I trust you, too, so I'm not going to say anything more about it. For now."

He smiled and kissed my fingers again, his breath warm on my suddenly sensitive knuckles. Who knew a hand could be so sexy?

"But . . . um . . . that brings up another subject." I bit my lip, a little embarassed. I reminded myself that there was nothing wrong with it, and blurted it out quickly, before I changed my mind. "I know that a guy normally asks this, but I'm into equal rights and stuff, so I was wondering if you'd like to go on a date with me? A real date, not a ride on your bike like we did in Hungary, but a real date date, the kind where I dress up and stuff. Maybe we could get some dinner and see a movie or something, if they have English movies here. Or whatever. If you don't want to, that's fine, too. I just thought maybe—"

He laughed and gave me a quick kiss, almost a non-kiss, just a brush of his lips. It was enough to stop me from blathering on and on, but not enough to make anyone notice us. "I would love to go on a date. Dinner and a movie sounds great. When would you like to go?"

It took me a few seconds to get over the kiss. "How about on Sunday? There's just one show on Sunday nights, and we can go after the last magic act."

"Three days from now?" he asked, smiling.

"Yeah, well, I'm kind of booked until then," I said, trying to sound sophisticated. What I didn't tell him was that my stomach was turning somersaults at the idea of a real, honest-to-Goddess date with him. I'd need those three days just to get myself to the point where I could go out with him without spending the entire time kissing him. Which was what I wanted to do now. Just standing near him made me feel tingly, kind of the same way the pendant felt.

"Very well, Sunday it is." He stepped back behind the demonology booth, pulling me into the shadow with him. "Perhaps we should seal the deal with a kiss?"

"Sounds good to me," I said, leaning up against him, drinking in the wonderful leather/spicey smell that was pure Ben.

"Let's hear the name of that Welsh place again," he said, his eyes going almost golden.

I was just about to say it when Soren ran out into the main aisle, yelling my name. Soren doesn't run well because of his leg, so for him to be moving that fast had to mean something was up. "I'm right here—what's going on?" I asked as Ben and I stepped into the aisle.

"It's Tesla," Soren said, limping toward me, a lead rope in his hand.

"Oh, no, is something wrong with him? Is he sick?" I asked, starting toward the area where the horses were kept.

"I don't know," Soren yelled after me as Ben and I ran toward the pasture. "He's not there. He's gone. I think he's been stolen."

CHAPTER FIVE

Soren was right. I had my doubts when he said he thought Tesla had been stolen—who'd want an old dirty white horse? But the area where Tesla and Bruno had been hobbled was empty. Tesla's hobble was sitting neatly on a rock, right next to the water bucket.

"Someone took this off," Ben said, fingering the open buckles. "It didn't come off on its own."

"Do you see?" Soren asked as he puffed his way up to us. "He was taken, *ja?*"

"Looks that way." I hesitated a minute, then stripped off the layers of latex and lace gloves I wore to keep from reading everything I touched, and held out my hand for the hobble. Ben placed it across my palm, careful to keep from touching my hand. Although he was one of the few people I didn't mind touching, I didn't want to confuse my psychometry abilities by picking up on something he was feeling rather than the person who unbuckled the hobble.

"Well?" Soren asked as I sorted through the images that came to mind as soon as my fingers closed over the leather cuff.

"Who took him? Is Bruno in danger? I should tell my dad if there is a horse kidnapper around."

"I don't think this is a horsenapper," I said, focusing on the hobble.

"Who touched it, Fran?" Ben asked, his voice quiet but full of concern. He knew how much Tesla meant to me.

"Ben, Soren, Peter, Karl . . ." Those last three made sense. They all helped take care of the horses, loading and unloading them in the horse trailer when we move to another town, so it was no surprise that at one time or another they'd picked up the hobble. But it was a fifth person who'd touched it that worried me. ". . . and someone else. Someone I don't know. Someone . . . *different*."

"Different how?" Ben asked. I handed him back the hobble and turned to scan the open field. I didn't think Tesla would be hidden away in the shadows, but I had to look anyway.

"Different as in not human."

"What?" Soren asked, his mouth hanging open. "Not human? You mean like a ghost?"

"I don't know what he is, other than he doesn't have any feeling whatsoever."

"No feelings?" Soren frowned.

"Yeah. None whatsoever. Everyone leaves some sort of re-sidual emotion behind when they touch something—even Ben does when he tries to close off his emotions—I can feel that it's him that touched it. But the guy who touched the hobble wasn't normal. Not human."

"Or heavily shielded," Ben said, looking thoughtful. "There are people who are able to block themselves completely. Mages and the like."

"Mages?" I looked down at the hobble. "Mikaela said Tibolt was a mage."

"You'd know if it was him who took Tesla, though," Soren pointed out, slapping at a mosquito on his arm.

I shook my head. "I haven't touched him with my bare hands." Something occurred to me then. "Oh great. I haven't touched a bunch of people working here—that means I'm going to have to go around doing the touchy-feely thing with every-one. I hate that!"

"That may not be necessary," Ben said, an odd, abstracted look on his face. "There's a Diviner here, isn't there?"

"Diviner? Not that I know of."

"Hmm. Perhaps there's one nearby we can ask for help."

"Whatever," I said, anxious to find Tesla. "All this standing around talking isn't finding him. He could be out there all alone, or being abused or something. Ben? Can we go find him, please?"

"Absolutely. I'll get my bike and pick you up." He tossed the hobble next to the bucket and ran off to get his motorcycle.

"I'd help look, too, but the show is about to start," Soren said, casting a worried look over his shoulder toward the main tent. "In fact—"

"Go," I said, making shooing motions with both hands. "Don't be late with Bruno or your dad will kill you."

He hurried off, leaving me standing alone in the empty field. I tried to open myself up to it. Mom said it was the proper way to get in touch with other beings and weird things like that, but I guess I lack the "opening up" gene or something, because all I felt was the night breeze and a couple of residual itchy spots.

"Ready?" Ben asked. I gave up and ran over to the field where people parked. He was on his bike, fiddling with one of the levers (it had to be a guy thing—I didn't hear anything wrong with the bike at all), his long black hair pulled back into a ponytail.

"I'm ready, although I don't know where to start looking. I guess we're going to have to check out everywhere we can— Ugh. Not that!"

I made a face at the helmet Ben held in his hand.

"It's your mother's rule," he said, giving it to me. I glared at it. I hated wearing a helmet, but my mother had put her foot down after she'd caught me riding around with Ben without one.

"You're not wearing one," I pointed out, knowing it was stupid to pout, but feeling like it anyway.

"That's because I'm immortal." He zipped up his leather jacket and held out his hand for me. "If we crash and I smash my head in, it won't do anything but make me pissed for a while. You're a bit more fragile."

"Well, you keep telling me I'm your Beloved and all. I thought they were immortal like Imogen?"

"Beloveds are immortal like female Moravians, yes, but you're not my Beloved yet. At least, not officially. Unless you want to do the blood exchange?"

I thought for a moment he was seriously pressing me to do the whole "save his soul by binding myself to him forever" thing, but his dark eyes were twinkling from under the shadow thrown by the brim of his hat.

"Another time, vamp boy," I said, giving him a little punch on the arm just to let him know I cared. He laughed and scooted forward a bit as I crawled onto the seat behind him, thankful I'd worn shorts instead of a skirt.

He glanced back at my bare knees, moving back until I was pressed up tight against his back. "I hope you won't be too cold."

"I figured you'd keep me warm." I leaned into his back, wrapping my arms around him as he gunned the bike and pushed off. It took me a few minutes to get my mind off the really delicious scent of leather jacket and Ben (he had to be wearing some sort of spicy aftershave or something), but eventually, I stopped snuffling his neck and ponytail, and started looking around as he drove us through the countryside.

We searched for Tesla until two in the morning. Because of the white night, we could zoom around and look for a horse being horsenapped pretty easily, but unfortunately, whoever took Tesla hid him well. By the time we got back to the fair, I was upset, mad, and frustrated.

"I'm sorry, Fran," Ben said as I climbed off his bike. I felt like crying, but I knew that was stupid—Tesla hadn't been hurt (at least I didn't think he had); he was just stolen. "I'll keep looking for him."

"Look where? We looked everywhere within a two-hour radius. If someone had driven off right away with him and kept driving, we'd never be able to find him anyway."

Ben got off the bike and pulled me into a hug. "We'll find him, Fran. I promise you that we'll find him," he said, his breath ruffling my hair.

I leaned against him, an odd sense of rightness creeping over me that distracted me for a minute from Tesla. I had told Ben the previous month that I was willing for us to try the girlfriend/boyfriend thing, but I had said that just because I liked him so much. I didn't honestly buy into that whole Beloved bit—although it gave me a warm feeling to think about it—but right after we'd left Hungary for France, Ben disappeared to do whatever the mysterious thing was that he couldn't tell me, so we really hadn't had much time to be together.

And now there I was standing in his arms, leaning against him, feeling warm and happy despite the fact that I was worried sick about Tesla. I couldn't help thinking things were pretty wonderful because we were together, and also, I'm ashamed to say, I was more than a little smug because out of the millions of girls wandering around the world, Ben had picked *me*.

Life is kinda weird that way.

"Fran, are you ready for your regression? Oh, hello, Ben. We haven't been properly introduced, have we? Imogen has told me so much about you, though, I feel like I know you. I'm Desdemona. I'm a personal time-travel consultant. Did you know that in a past life Fran was Cleopatra? It's so very exciting. I've promised to regress her again so we can get some more fascinating details of her life in ancient Egypt."

Life just got a whole lot weirder.

Ben unwrapped his arms from around me as soon as Desdemona started to talk, but he didn't move away as I turned around to face her. Part of me was embarassed that anyone had caught us together, but the other part was annoyed because it was clear the way Desdemona was smiling at Ben that she had purposely interrupted us.

"Hi, Des. About the regression—could we do it another time? I'm a bit busy right now."

"Yeeees," she drawled, giving Ben another long look. Her tone made me grit my teeth. And it didn't help that she was wearing a leather waist cincher and short skirt that let everyone see just how different her five-foot-nothing, one hundred-pound self was from mammoth, six-foot-tall me. "I can see you were."

"No, not us. Um. That is, Ben and I weren't . . . well, we were, but that's not what I'm talking about."

"Fran is distraught over the theft of her horse," Ben said, smoothly interrupting me. *Are you by any chance jealous?*

Me? You're kidding, right? I'm so not jealous. Although she definitely has the hots for you, the wench.

Ben laughed in my head.

"Oh, your horse was stolen? I'm so sorry. Of course the regression can wait for another time." Desdemona smiled at Ben. "How would you like a personal time-travel experience, Ben? It seems I have an opening, and since the fair is just now closing, I could get you in quickly."

Oh! She didn't just say that!

Calm down, Fran. She's harmless. "Another time, perhaps. I've promised Fran to continue looking for her horse, and I doubt if I'll be done before daybreak." Ben glanced toward where the sun was barely beneath the horizon. "Or as close to daybreak as it gets around here. Thank you anyway."

"No problem. I'll be happy to do you anytime," she said, giving us both a little wave as she strolled off toward the main tent. Ben watched her walk away from us for a second before looking back at me.

"Why are you making that face?" he asked. "Why are your eyes narrow little slits of ebony that look like they want to shoot lasers at me?"

"You watched her walk away," I said, struggling to keep my voice jealous-free. I lost the fight. "You deliberately watched."

"Yes, I did. I looked at her breasts, too, but despite that, you're still the only girl on the planet for me."

"Nice try, Vlad," I said, slipping out of his arms when he tried to pull me into another kiss. I stalked toward the trailer that Mom and I shared. "*My* boyfriend isn't going to be aware there's anyone else around but me. Since you have other ideas, so long. Hasta la vista. Don't let the door hit you on the butt going out."

Ben stood where I left him, his arms crossed over his chest. I smiled to myself where he couldn't see it.

Fran?

Hmm?

Are you seriously jealous of Desdemona, or are you ragging me a little?

What do you think?

I smiled even more at the pause that followed that. He wasn't one hundred percent sure, something I was perfectly happy about. I entered the trailer, absently moving Davide from the couch that turned into my bed at night.

I think you know full well how much you mean to me. I think you know that I'd do anything to make you happy. I think you know I can't exist without you, that you are heaven and earth to me, my salvation, my joy, my life.

This time I let him feel my smile.

The brush of his mind against mine had a decidedly disgruntled tone to it. *And I think you're enjoying every minute of keeping me on tenterhooks about whether or not you're going to be my Beloved.*

Good night, Ben, I said, laughing into his head. *Thank you for looking for Tesla.*

Sleep well, sweet Fran, he answered, and I gave in and had a lovely sigh of happiness over him.

Even with the Tesla problem, life was looking pretty good at the moment. Ben was back, and as yummy as ever. I had settled into life with the GothFaire, and actually enjoyed doing the palm readings. Mom was happy with her new group of friends, the Faire was doing well, and even Soren was happy these days.

"Things are looking up for a change," I told Davide as I flipped off all the lights but one so Mom could see her way past me when she finished for the night, and settled into my make-shift bed. The big cat sauntered over, jumping up on me so he could sleep on my hip. It was his favorite spot, despite the fact that we didn't really like each other. "Not even poor Tesla gone missing, and half-naked Viking ghosts running around are going to ruin my date with Ben day after tomorrow. That is going to be the most perfect event of my life. I just know it."

Which just goes to show you I'm *not* clairvoyant in any way.

CHAPTER SIX

The first inkling I had that something was wrong the next morning was the war ax embedded in the wooden door of my closet.

"Hrung?" I asked in no known language as I squinted at the wood and steel weapon that still vibrated slightly. The blade of the ax, mostly buried in the door, was curved on the edges. "Wha'?"

"Goddess, have you seen—oh, there it is." The Viking Imogen had been flirting with the night before stood at the open window right next to me. I glared at him, pulling the thin blanket covering my legs up over the jumbo T-shirt I wore to bed. "Would you mind giving me back my Hanwei ax?"

"You threw an ax at me?" I asked, my brain still sleepy and thus not much able to make sense of what he was saying.

"Me?" the Viking asked, pointing at himself in disbelief. "I would never do that! You are a goddess, and I am merely Finnvid, your devoted servant and the slayer of many hundred Huns."

"Then what is that doing in here?" I pointed to the ax. He looked a bit abashed.

"It . . . er . . . slipped. I was aiming at a usurper, and it went through your window rather than cleaving his brain in two, as it was meant to do. "

It was at that point I realized the sounds that had vaguely registered on my brain weren't from someone's portable TV or radio. I distinctly recognized Absinthe's brusque German voice as she yelled orders.

"What the bullfrogs—" A woman's loud scream from nearby had me jumping out of bed and racing to the door. Davide and my mother were gone, which meant they had probably already left to do their morning rituals to the God and Goddess with their Wiccan friends. Since closing time wasn't until two in the morning, most of the GothFaire and Circus of the Darned people didn't get up until after noon, but there were a few hardy folk up earlier. I figured it was about nine in the morning as I flung open the door to the trailer. "Holy crap!"

The sight that met my eyes was not one I ever expected to see—only a handful of GothFairians were up, but they were active . . . very active. Running around screaming with various Vikings chasing after them.

"Is it?" The Viking ghost named Finnvid, who still stood by the open window, looked around, finally spotting a nearby pile of dog poop (probably made by Tallulah's pug, Wennie). "Ah. It looks like dog shite to me, but if it's holy, I will not rub someone's face in it."

The Faire was usually set up in the shape of a large U, with the big tent at the bottom, and two arms of vendor tents and booths. To the far side of one of the arms was what Mom called

Trailer Town—where Faire and Darned people set up their trailers and RVs. In the center of the vaguely circular arrangement
of trailers were a couple of portable picnic tables and chairs, a
small barbecue, and three folding chaise lounges that everyone
used to work on their tans. The chaises weren't being used for
suntanning now—one of them was acting as a trampoline for a
red-haired Viking, while another was tipped up on its end, the
elasticy plastic webbing being used by another Viking to catapult
overly ripe peaches at Tallulah. She had taken refuge behind a
plastic picnic table, but every time she popped her head up to see
if the coast was clear, the Viking launched another peach at her.
The trailer behind her was a slimy mess of gooey, dripping peach
blobs that slumped their way to the ground. Peter would be furious. He had bought the peaches to feed his fruit addiction, and
now they were smeared everywhere.

"What in the name of all that is good and glorious is going
on here?" Mikaela emerged from the trailer next to ours, wearing a pair of jeans and a tank top. She held a bottle of water in
one hand, and a candle and a couple pieces of lavendar in the
other.

"Brutta!" Finnvid shouted, and leaped past me to scoop
her up.

Mikaela screamed and yelled for Ramon, her husband,
while simultaneously beating Finnvid on the head with her
water bottle. Beyond her, Absinthe had somehow made it to the
top of her trailer, where she stood yelling what were no doubt
rude things in German down to the three Vikings trying to
scale the trailer to get to her.

Ramon burst out of his trailer with one leg in his pants, hopping on one foot while he tried to get the other leg in, at the
same time dodging peaches from the Viking at the catapult.

Circus of the Darned ✎ 245

"Fran!" Absinthe shrieked, jumping up and down on the trailer as she pointed at me. "These ghosts are yours! Control them!"

"They're not mine—" I yelled back, pausing for a minute as Peter emerged from between trailers. He walked backwards, a two-by-four in his hands to parry blows from a long, heavy sword. The owner of the sword lunged toward him, sending Peter falling over a lawn chair. While the peach-throwing Viking's attention was focused on Ramon, Tallulah ran to her trailer. But she stopped in the doorway and sent me a look that raised goose bumps on my arms. Although her lips didn't move, I swear I could hear her voice on the wind saying, "This is your doing. Fix it!"

"Hey!" I bellowed, and threw myself off the trailer steps when I saw that the person about to gut Peter was Eirik. "Stop that! I said no killing!"

Eirik paused in the act of beheading Peter. "No, you didn't. You said you didn't have anyone you wanted us to kill for you. There is a difference."

"No killing! No killing of anyone, anywhere! Is that clear?" I fell to my knees and hovered protectively over Peter, who watched with huge eyes as the sword tip waved back and forth over his face. "And while you're at it, call your buddies off my friends!"

Eirik frowned, giving me a blue-eyed glare. "You are a strange goddess. You do not want us to kill anyone in your name, and you will not allow my men a little fun . . . what is next? You will not allow us to have a *spritfest* and wench and gamble?"

"*Spritfest*?"

"Drinking party."

"Ah, OK. I don't care about drinking and . . . er . . . whatever else you do so long as it's not trying to kill anyone," I said, glaring back at him.

Eirik snarled something under his breath, but pulled back his sword. "As you command," he said in a grumpy voice.

I blinked a couple of times, not sure whether he was kidding me or not, but it turned out he meant what he said.

"You're serious about this whole goddess thing, aren't you?" I asked, patting Peter on the shoulder to know he could sit up. He did so as I got to my feet. I helped him brush off the bits of dirt and dried grass.

Eirik shrugged. "You are a goddess. We are bound to you until you call the Valkyries to take us to Valhalla."

"In that case . . ." I stopped brushing Peter's back and jumped onto the nearest picnic table. I put two fingers in my mouth to do the earsplitting whistle my dad was famous for. "Vikings!" I bellowed, and to my surprise, they stopped catapulting, fighting, climbing, and groping.

Mikaela kicked Finnvid in his happy zone. He doubled over and fell to the ground.

"Right, Eirik says you have to listen to me and do what I say. So, I'm saying knock it off! There will be no killing anyone! No hurling of fruit, peaches or otherwise. No climbing on any furniture in an attempt to get to someone."

Finnvid writhed on the ground. Mikaela emptied her water bottle on him, and rushed over to help Ramon up from the mass of peach pulp.

"No picking up women."

A huge Viking with long blond hair walked around the corner with Soren slung over his shoulder.

"In fact, no picking up anyone!"

"Hail, Ljot," Eirik called to his buddy. "The goddess is giving us orders."

"Oh?" Ljot, the giant Viking, turned to face me, a happy smile on his face. Soren's legs kicked feebly. "Who do we kill?"

"Sheesh, what is it with you guys?" I asked, slapping my hands on my thighs in exasperation. "Don't you know how to do anything other than fight and kill people? And put down Soren—he doesn't look like he's breathing."

The Vikings, every single one of them, looked thoughtful. Ljot the friendly giant plopped Soren into a lawn chair. "We wench well," one of them offered.

"Aye, that we do, Gils," Eirik agreed, and all the Vikings nodded (except Finnvid, who was struggling to get to his knees, his hands clasped over his groin). "And we can outdrink anyone, even a Finn."

The Vikings yelled their war cry. I squatted next to Soren and asked him if he was OK.

"Yes, I'm fine. Just a little windy," he said, rubbing his ribs.

"Winded, I think you mean. Windy means something else." I stood up again and looked at the Viking ghosts, my hands on my hips. "All right, so we need to have some ground rules—"

"I can geld stallions with just one hand," one of the Vikings said. The others looked impressed.

"Ew!" I said, giving him a glare. "I don't know who you are—"

"His name is Isleif," Eirik said helpfully, strolling over to stand next to me.

"—but that's just gross. Moving on . . . you're all going to have to behave yourselves, or else I'll . . . I'll . . ."

Eirik raised an eyebrow. "You'll what?"

"I won't call the Valkyries to take you to Valhalla," I said "So everyone had just better straighten up, OK?"

"What is she talking about?" one of the shorter Vikings asked another.

"We're supposed to be good," the second Viking answered with a disgusted look on his face.

"That sucks," the first answered.

I raised an eyebrow at him. "Sucks?"

"Just because we're dead doesn't mean we don't keep current on what's going on in the world, goddess," Eirik answered. "Would you like to see us line dance?"

"No!" I shuddered to myself. "Just . . . behave, OK? I'm working on getting you to Valhalla as soon as I can. I just need to figure out how to summon the Valkyries first. Hopefully, that'll be before tomorrow night."

The Vikings looked disapointed, a couple of them pouting, but they did as I asked.

"Why tomorrow night?" Eirik asked as his men started cleaning up the mess they'd made. Peter gave Eirik a wide berth as he went to check on Soren.

"That's when I have—" Everyone, and I do mean everyone— from Absinthe climbing down off her trailer to Ramon, who was helping Mikaela pick off sticky blobs of peach—stopped what they were doing and looked at me. It was like a TV commercial or something. "Er . . . I have a thing I'm doing."

"A thing?" Eirik frowned, scratching his chin with the handle of his sword. "What sort of thing?"

"Kind of a date," I said as quietly as I could. I may have to live and work with these people—the ghosts aside—but they didn't need to know every little thing about me.

"A date?" Eirik asked in a voice that could probably be heard in Denmark. "You have a date? You mean with the Dark One?"

"You're going on a date with Benedikt?" Soren asked, limping over, an odd expression on his face. Peter went to check on his sister and the others. "A real date? Not just hanging around with him?"

I sighed. "Yes, I'm going on a date, a real date."

"The kind where you—" he waved his hands around vaguely—"do things?"

"How do I know? I've never been on a date before!" I said, just wishing everyone would leave me alone. Honestly, it was just a date!

"You've never been on a date before?" Eirik asked, pulling up a chair. "You need advice." He said something in what I assumed was ancient Viking to the others. They stopped what they were doing and made a circle around me. "The goddess is going on a date. Her *first* date."

"Ahh," the Vikings all said, looking at me like I was a boar about to be roasted.

"A first date. That is very important," the one named Isleif said. He was just as tall as the rest, but really big around, as well. Unlike most of them, he also had a beard, the sides of which were done up in a braid. He plopped down on another chair and put his hands on his knees. "I will give you the same advice I gave my daughter Anna."

"This I *have* to hear," Soren said, his arms across his chest as he gave me a belligerent look. I wanted to tell him to knock it off, too, but I didn't. I've never had a crush before—Ben aside, and he wasn't exactly a crush—but I imagined it wasn't a good feeling if the person you were crushing didn't feel the same way about you.

"I appreciate the offer for advice, but I don't really think I need—"

"'Anna,' I told her—you understand this was close to nine

hundred years ago, but you girls never change—'Anna,' I said, 'you are twelve now, ready to be wed. Your skin is the color of the richest curd, your teeth are strong enough to tear a leather thong, and your breasts are like two little apples, ripe for the plucking.' Then I told her—"

"Twelve?" Soren interrupted, looking shocked.

"OK, no plucking stories," I said, waving my hands for Isleif to stop. "Dating advice from a Viking ghost I can just barely survive, but no apple plucking! I don't want to hear anything about your daughter's boobs."

Isleif looked insulted. "They were very nice. High and firm and—" I started to walk away. Isleif yelled for me to stop. "I have not finished! As I said, I told Anna the time was right for her to be wed. I had always intended that she marry Ljot's son, but he went and got himself killed by a mad boar. Ljot had another son, but he was a bit light in the head."

"Daft." Ljot nodded. "No brains whatsoever. He got that from his mother."

"Anna insisted she be allowed to look around for a husband," Isleif continued. "But she didn't know how to proceed with the one she'd chosen. So I told her—and this is the wisdom I'm passing along to you—the best way to catch yourself a husband is to rip his clothing off, and have your way with him." Isleif sat back, a pleased look on his face like he'd just explained the greatest mystery of the universe.

"Um," I said, not wanting to insult him. The other Vikings were nodding their agreement.

"That's how my second wife caught me," Finnvid said. "She followed me to the lake one summer morn, wrestled me to the ground, stripped me naked, and sat—"

"Thanks for the advice," I said really loudly, giving Finnvid a look that he evidently didn't get, because he just grinned at me. "I'll . . . uh . . . take it into consideration."

"You're not really going to rip Benedikt's clothes off, are you?" Soren asked a few seconds later as I was walking back toward my trailer.

"Of course not! I'm brand-new to this whole girlfriend thing. There's no way I'd attempt as advanced a technique as clothes-ripping-off."

Soren shot me a questioning look from the corner of his eye. "You're joking, *ja?*"

"Yes, I'm joking." I stopped at the steps to the trailer. "Honest, Soren, it's not a big deal. Ben and I are going out on a date, just a date. Probably dinner and a movie. No biggie at all."

Soren didn't say anything, but his eyes were troubled. I didn't know what I could say to him that was the truth and yet would help him get over the crush, so I didn't say anything. I socked him on the shoulder and told him he could help me find Tesla.

"I thought you and Benedikt already looked for him?" he asked, socking me back.

"We did. But I was thinking last night—here we are in a fair full of people with all sorts of freaky powers, and I'm not using any of it."

"You touched the hobble," he pointed out.

"Yeah, but that didn't tell me much. I'm going to see if Tallulah can tell me anything."

"She's a medium, not a diviner. What you need is someone who can tell you where to find Tesla."

"Tallulah has Sir Edward. She says he can see everything from the Akashic Plain."

"The what?" Soren's nose scrunched up in confusion.

"Akashic Plain. It's kind of like limbo. Imogen told me about it last week. I'm going to see Tallulah later. You want to come?"

"Sure, if I have my chores done."

"No prob. My mom should be back any minute, and then I'm going to have to spend some time dealing with leaving her circle last night. I'm lucky she didn't slap the itching spell on me this morning."

Soren trotted off and I used the next half hour to wash and get dressed, taking a few minutes to scarf down some green tea, toast, and two apples. I felt a twinge at the last one, since I automatically set one aside for Tesla. "Poor old boy. I hope you're all right," I said just as the door opened and my mother came into the trailer.

"Oh good, you're up," she said, a glint in her eye warning she was going to read me the lecture of a lifetime for leaving her circle before she'd broken it. She plopped down her bag of Wiccan stuff on the table, along with a familiar nylon object. "I found this halter in the clearing. I assume it was Tesla's."

I burst into tears. I know what you're thinking, but it wasn't an attempt to distract Mom from the lecture—just the sight of seeing the halter I'd bought him before we left Hungary broke my heart, driving home the point that some stranger had my horse. "I don't know where he is," I said in between sobs as Mom tried to comfort me, murmuring things about it being all right. "I don't know who has him, or if he's hungry, or in pain, or being made to walk too much—you know he's not supposed to get anything but a little gentle exercise! He's too old for a lot of running around. He could be dead and I wouldn't . . . wouldn't . . ." I couldn't go on. It was too horrible to think about.

"Aw, honey, I know it's hard, but you really can't believe the worst. If this Lars Laufeyiarson person wanted Tesla enough to offer you so much money for him, he's not going to be abused or mistreated."

"But we can't find Lars Laufeyiarson," I said, sniffling into a couple of tissues. Yes, it was stupid to cry, but sometimes you just have to give in and have a good sobfest. "We checked all the phone books in the area. There are a couple up the coast, but Ben called them and they weren't the same guy."

Mom frowned. "I thought he gave you his card? What happened to that?"

"It disappeared."

She gave me a look.

"No, I'm serious—it disappeared. I put it in my bag when I got back to the trailer that night, and when I went to look last night, it was gone. Poof. Vanished into nothing."

"Or someone took it," she said slowly, shaking her head as soon as she spoke. "No, no one would come into our trailer and touch our things. You must have lost it or misplaced it somewhere, honey."

I bit my lip to keep from telling her I distinctly remembered putting it in my purse where it would be safe. Although Mom was Wiccan and had seen all sorts of strange things, she never believed any of them could happen to me.

"Now, about you leaving the circle last night—"

I sat back and let her give me the old "why it's wrong to leave a circle" lecture, glancing out of the open window when I thought I heard someone calling my name. There was no one out there but one of the Viking ghosts sweeping up peach debris. I nodded at the appropriate times, shaking my head when that was called for, looking out the window again when I could have sworn someone was calling me.

"—and to think you'd been raised to honor and respect our practices. I was appalled by your abrupt—Franny, I am speaking to you. I would appreciate having your attention." Mom stopped her pacing up and down to glare at me, her hands on her hips.

"Sorry. I thought someone was calling me," I said, hurriedly turning back toward her and putting on my "being lectured yet again" face.

Fran, the wind whispered.

"Honestly, Fran, I have no idea what you thought you were doing—"

I tuned her out to listen as hard as I could for the elusive sound.

Fran.

Ben?

Fran. You . . . help . . .

"Absolutely," I said, leaping to my feet and heading for the door. "I'm so sorry about the circle, Mom. Never happen again. Promise. Gotta run now."

"Francesca Marie Ghetti—"

"Sorry, sorry, sorry," I yelled as I flung myself out of the trailer, running toward the center aisle of the Faire, stopping to get my bearings. *Ben, where are you?*

Woods, the answer came in kind of a gasp. My heart leaped at the sound of it—Ben was in trouble, serious trouble if he was asking for help. Part of his Mister Macho act was that he never, ever asked for help from anyone. *West.*

I raced down the aisle, ignoring the shouted question from Soren as he tended to Bruno, past Tallulah as she took her pug for a walk, down the slope that led to the parking area, and into the sparse fringe of woods that ran like a spine down the center of the small island. *Ben? Whereabouts are you? I don't see you.*

Here, a faint voice whispered in my head. *Left.*

I spun around and ran into the woods, beating back stray branches as they slapped at my face. I figured he wouldn't be at the edge, where the sunshine could get him, so I went for the darkest part of the thin stretch of woods. I wouldn't have seen him slumped up against a giant fir tree if he hadn't moved, but fortunately I caught the movement in my peripheral vision. "What's wrong? Why are you hiding in the trees? Where have you—oh, Goddess! What's happened to you?"

My skin tightened and tingled with goose bumps as Ben slumped to the ground. He wore the tattered remains of his leather jacket, his shirt completely gone, but that wasn't what made my stomach freeze into a solid block of horror—his face, arms, and torso were bright red with blood, as if he'd been dipped in a blood bath. Beneath it, I could see a horrifying criss-cross pattern of slash marks on his chest and arms. I lunged for him but couldn't catch him as he hit the ground, his head lolling backward. I touched his throat, feeling for a pulse, but there was nothing. His chest didn't rise with breath. His heart didn't beat. And his being, his self that I was always subtly aware of when he was around, was utterly and completely gone.

I sat on the ground, clutching his lifeless body to me, my mind shrieking in horror. How on earth was I going to go on without Ben?

CHAPTER SEVEN

"I'm never going to forgive you for this," I said, throwing a pillow down onto the floor.

An eye the color of dark oak opened and rolled over to look at me for a second or two before closing again.

"You've died twice in my arms. Twice! There's not going to be a third time, do you understand?"

The man-shaped lump on the bed grunted.

"Dark Ones can't die unless they're beheaded," Imogen said, bustling into the bedroom of her trailer with yet another jar of cow's blood (I know, major ick, but this was an emergency). She stopped for a moment and looked thoughtful. "Or burned—they can be burned, too. And if they lose all the blood in their body, that's as good as dead since they are more or less comatose. But they can't die just from a few cuts."

I glared at her for a moment, before looking over to where Ben lay, swathed in bandages, propped up on a pyramid of pillows. He looked awful, his skin gaunt and gray as if he was every single one of his three hundred and twelve years. He'd lost so much blood, Imogen couldn't replace what he needed, so she had sent Karl into town to buy some blood from the local butcher.

Imogen sat on the edge of the bed, tucking a blanket around his hips. She was about to offer him the mug when she looked over to me. "Do you want to do this, Fran?"

"I'm sorry. I can't," I said, throwing another pillow around. I picked up Ben's bloodstained jeans and shook them at him. "I'm too busy being furious at him to pour blood down his throat."

Ben opened his eye again and looked at his sister. "She's picking on me."

"As you well deserve. I can't imagine what you were thinking collapsing like that on poor Fran. You scared her to death! You should have seen her face when she came dashing back here to get help for you. She was devastated, her face the very picture of horror and agony. I wanted to weep just seeing the despair in her eyes."

Ben looked at me. "You were that worried about me?"

"Yes, I was." I picked up his bloody, shredded jacket, narrowing my eyes at him. "That was a horrible, horrible thing you did to me! And I'm telling you right here and now that I'm never going to go through that again! No more, got that? No more scaring Fran to death! Twice is enough, thank you!"

"The first time wasn't my fault," he protested in a weak voice that just about broke my heart. "I'm not to blame if a demon tried to kill me."

"I suppose it really wasn't his fault last month," Imogen said, thrusting the mug of blood at Ben. He shot her a narrow-eyed look, but obediently sipped at the blood. I was glad Imogen knew what to do for him—when I had staggered back into our camp earlier, my brain was frozen solid, locked on the thought that he was dead. I had no idea what to do to help him—assuming help was possible. But thankfully, Imogen took charge of the situation immediately, helping Kurt to bring Ben back while Karl went for some take-out blood.

"Maybe not directly, but he was pigheaded enough to get himself ambushed."

"Pigheaded!" Ben sputtered around the mug.

"That's what I said. Are you done?" I asked when he pushed Imogen's hand holding the mug away.

"Yes."

He didn't look much better, but at least he'd had a couple of pints of blood, and his wounds had stopped bleeding. "Good. Now you can tell us what happened to you."

The silent, stony look I received was a familiar one.

"Oh, no," I said, hands on hips again (I seemed to be doing that a lot lately). "You're not going to give me the silent treatment. I order you to tell me what happened to you."

Ben glared. Imogen made a little face. "Fran, dear, a word of advice—never give Benedikt an order. He doesn't like them."

"I'm not one of your ghosts, Fran," he said, having finished his glare. "You cannot compel me to tell you where I've been."

"I can't, huh?" I sat on the bed, stripped off a glove, and took his hand in mine. His fingers, as always, fascinated me. They were long and slender, the hands of a musician. These hands had been around for more than three hundred years, buttoning fancy Victorian waistcoats, loading muskets, holding on to the side of a sleek, polished carriage—and so many other things, I couldn't even begin to imagine. And yet with all that history behind them, they were just hands, warm, supportive hands that gave me a little zing of pleasure each time they touched me. "What if I ask you to please tell me what happened? What if I remind you that I was absolutely devastated when I saw you so weak and injured." *What if I let you see how much it broke my heart to think you were gone?*

He closed his eyes for a minute, his fingers tightening around mine. "I was helping my brother."

My eyebrows shot up in surprise. "You have a brother?"

Imogen shook her head.

"Dafydd is my blood brother, not an actual relation. He saved my life once. I am bound to return that debt." Ben's eyes were still shut, but his thumb stroked over mine. A little warm glow of happiness filled me at his touch, joining with the massive well of relief and gratitude that he hadn't died.

"Oh. What exactly were you helping him with?"

He shook his head. "That I cannot tell you. I swore an oath of secrecy to him."

"Poop. Well, how were you hurt? Those slash marks were deep and jagged, like something with really big claws got you."

His eyes were dark when they opened, the lovely little sparkly gold bits dull and flat. "I can't tell you that, either."

"What can you tell me?" It took an effort, but I managed to keep from strangling him. Long exposure to Wiccans had taught me the importance of honoring an oath, although that didn't make it any easier on me when I was dying to know what happened to him.

He said nothing.

I counted to ten. "OK, how about this—does whatever you're doing tonight have to do with you disappearing in Hungary last month?"

"Yes."

I don't know why, but that actually made me feel a bit better. Not that I was jealous or anything, but I wouldn't be human if I didn't admit that a couple of times, the horrible thought had occurred to me that Ben might have taken off with someone much thinner, smaller, and all-around less weird. But if he was off helping his blood brother . . . well that, too, I could understand. Wiccans are very big on bonds of blood.

I sighed. "OK. I won't ask you any more about that. But this obviously means our date tomorrow is off."

"Date?" Imogen asked, puttering around the tiny bedroom. She fluffed up one of Ben's pillows, tucked the sheet around him tighter, and readjusted a curtain so the tendril of sunshine that sneaked in was eliminated. Her eyes went from me to Ben and back. "You two are going on a date? A real one?"

"We were. Dinner and everything." I gave Ben's hand a final squeeze as I stood up. He needed to rest and let his body heal all those horrible wounds, and me sitting there wouldn't do him any good. "But now we'll have to wait until he's better."

"I'll be fine by tomorrow night," he said, giving me a feeble smile.

"Uh-huh."

"I will. I should be back to normal tonight, as a matter of fact."

I made a face that let him know I thought that was a bit optimistic, told him to get some sleep, and left Imogen's bedroom.

"Oh, Francesca . . ." She followed me out of the bedroom, carefully closing the door behind her. Her forehead was wrinkled with a puzzled frown. "About this date . . ."

"What about it?" I asked.

"It's just . . . you've never been on a date before, have you? I seem to recall you telling me that."

"Yeah, but it's not like I have to pass a test or anything to do it."

She met my smile with one of her own. "No, but I thought you mightn't mind a little advice."

"Sure," I said, taking a seat at the semicircular table. "I'd be happy to get some advice from the queen of dating. It has to be better than what the Vikings told me."

"Tea?" She bustled around the tiny kitchen area.

"Just a fast one. I have to visit Tallulah, and then give Tibolt his necklace back."

She paused for a moment at the mention of Tibolt, sighed heavily, then shook her head and reached for the electric tea-kettle she had plugged in earlier. "I wouldn't quite call myself a queen of dating—just someone who has learned a few good tips over the centuries. First, you naturally want to ensure that your date worships you as is your due."

"Uh . . ." I thought about Ben arguing with me.

"That is not a problem with Benedikt, as you are his Beloved."

That had me laughing a little as I sipped the cup of Earl Grey she set down in front of me. "I may be his Beloved, but I don't think *worship* is the word I'd use about his feelings. More like pushy and bossy, although admittedly really, really hot."

"That aside, you must remember what you are owed. Allow him to open doors for you, and pull out your chair. Beyond that, just smile. If something doesn't please you, don't ruin the evening by whining—just keep smiling and ignore the problem. And above all, don't resist if Benedikt wishes to give you a memento of the evening."

I opened my mouth to tell her there was no way I'd do half the stuff she said, but stopped because I knew she was trying to be helpful. "Memento?" I asked, instead. "What sort of memento? Like a picture or something?"

"Oh, goodness no. Something sparkly," she answered, absently turning the sapphire tennis bracelet on her wrist. "Benedikt has excellent taste in jewelry. You may trust him to pick out something that will be in style for many, many years."

I choked on my tea at the thought of letting Ben buy me jewelry. He'd already given me his mother's ring, and my mother just about had a hissy at that. I couldn't imagine what she would do if he gave me anything sparkly. Not to mention I wasn't a sparkly kind of girl.

"Well, thanks for that advice. It's very helpful," I said without even giggling, getting up to set my cup in the tiny sink. "I have to run now. I'm hoping to catch Talullah before she goes to town. Let me know if you need help with Ben."

"You'll remember what I said?" she asked, coming to the door as I hurried down the couple of steps.

"Absolutely. Sparkly. Smile. No whining."

She beamed back at me. "It'll be a lovely date, Fran. I just know it will."

I was a bit less optimistic, but I still waved cheerily to her as I trotted toward Talullah's trailer. Soren was still busy, so I was on my own with Talullah.

Even though she was older than my mother, Talullah had a little blue Vespa that she used to zoom around wherever we were staying, strapping Wennie the pug into a basket on the front of the scooter so he wouldn't fall out and get run over.

I found her just leaving her trailer, her shopping bag tucked under one arm, Wennie in his lightweight travel jacket in the other.

"Good morning," she said, her black eyes carefully looking me over. "I see you have your ghosts under control at last."

"Yeah, well, I didn't know they were going to cause any

trouble." I'd given up trying to get everyone to realize the ghosts didn't belong to me. Evidently everyone, including the Vikings themselves, thought they did. "I'm sorry you were attacked with peaches."

She looked at me silently for a moment, then turned back and opened the door to her trailer. "You wish for me to conduct a reading."

"Yeah, if you don't mind. I know you're about to leave, but I promise it won't take long."

"I am happy to help you," she said primly, and sat on a bench couch that was almost identical to ours. "You have been troubled of late. I have not been pleased to see that. You are young, too young to be burdened with the cares you have."

"Like Viking ghosts?" I asked, taking a seat when she waved toward the opposite end of the couch. Tallulah was a Gypsy queen—at least, that's what my mother said—and looking at her I could believe it. It was hard to tell exactly how old she was, although her jet-black hair had a streak of white slightly off center. It wasn't her appearance that always made me feel slightly uncomfortable, like I'd been called into the principal's office to find out what I was in trouble for . . . it was the natural dignity and grace that she wore almost as an aura that made me believe the rumors that she had been a powerful queen in a Romany tribe, but had abdicated to lead a quieter life.

"Pfft," she said, pulling out a small flat black bowl. Its surface was mirrored, so shiny I could see the details of every line in her face as she set it down before her. "The ghosts are not what is troubling you. Your auras are muddy, but I can see that at least one thing is giving you much concern."

"One?" I would've thought there'd be two—Ben and Tesla— but then I realized I wasn't really worried about Ben anymore.

I knew he would recover just fine. "Yeah, I guess just the one thing. But—auras? Plural? I thought I just had one?"

"That is a common misconception. You can manifest up to five auras under the right circumstances, but most people only show three. Have you never been to the aura photography booth?"

I shook my head. "I never really wanted to know."

One of her eyebrows rose in question. "I see. Well, I will save you the trouble by telling you now that your inner aura is white, indicating purity and chasteness, your middle aura is blue, indicating dissatisfaction with something in your life, and your outer aura is a sharp red, all of which tells me that you have a pure heart, are on the beginning of a path to enlightenment, but your energies now are focused on the problem which troubles you."

"Tesla," I said, sighing.

"Ah, your horse that was stolen?" She nodded and tilted the shallow black mirror bowl so she could look into it. "Let us consult Sir Edward and see what he has to say about Tesla."

When Mom first dragged me to the GothFaire a month ago—committing us to traveling around with them for half a year—I made the big mistake of asking Tallulah why she didn't use a crystal ball like a normal medium. Her response still made me squirm uncomfortably—she had pinned me back with a glare and said in a voice that had the faintest touch of an accent, "I am *not* normal. Normal is for lesser people."

Although I didn't diss normal the way she did, I couldn't dispute the fact that she seemed perfectly happy the way she was. I watched her now as she hummed softly to herself, swaying slightly, her eyes fixed on the bowl. It never failed to amaze me how normal everyone looked on the outside, but inside they had some really jaw-dropping abilities.

"Sir Edward is with us," she said suddenly in a singsong voice.

"Oh, good. Hi, Sir Edward."

A little breeze whispered by me. I got goose bumps from it even knowing that Sir Edward was a good spirit.

"He is pleased to see you, although he, too, notes that you are troubled, and is displeased by that."

"Sorry about that. I'll try to be less . . . er . . . troubled."

The Sir Edward breeze gently touched my face. "He wishes to help you with your troubles. What do you wish to ask him?"

"I want to know where Tesla is. I want to know who took him, and why, and whether Tesla is OK."

The breeze caressing me stilled for a moment, then went whipping past me with enough velocity to ruffle my hair.

"Oh," Tallulah said, her eyes distant and unseeing as she maintained her trance by staring into the bowl.

"Uh . . . oh?"

"Yes. Sir Edward is distraught. He is not making sense. One moment while I commune with him."

I sat quietly while she stared into the bowl. The only sound in the trailer came from Wennie as he snored, stretched out on his belly next to her.

"Ahhhh," Tallulah said on a long sigh, blinking as she came out of the trance. She set the bowl down and gave me a long look.

Despite my best intentions, tears pricked behind my eyes. Something was wrong with Tesla. I just knew it. "He's hurt?"

She shook her head.

I swallowed back a big lump in my throat and croaked out the next word. "Dead?"

"No. Fran, do not weep. I do not know how Tesla is—Sir Edward could not see him."

"He couldn't?" I sniffed and used the back of my hand to wipe off a couple of sneaky tears. "Why couldn't he see him? I thought Sir Edward was a scout or something."

"Guide, he is a spirit guide, which means he exists in the Akashic Plain and can see all, but this even he could not divine."

"Why?" I felt slightly better, although my worry level increased a few hundred notches.

"He said the vision of Tesla was blocked, hidden by a being much more powerful than he had seen before."

My skin crawled. I swear it positively crawled up my arms. "What sort of a being?"

"Sir Edward did not know. It was not a being he has encountered before." The look she gave me was long and full of unspoken warning. "But he did say the being seems to have great power, and it would be the sheerest folly for you to pursue it. I'm afraid for all intents and purposes that your horse is lost to you, Fran. To attempt to regain it from this being would likely result in your death."

CHAPTER EIGHT

here's nothing that ticks me off more than being told I
can't do something. I'm not talking about obviously stupid
things like walking out in front of a moving semi truck, but
things like "Don't stay up late on a school night," "Don't go
swimming right after eating," and most of all, "Don't try to get
your elderly horse back from the weirdo being who stole him
from you."

I'm not an idiot, however. "If Sir Edward was scared by Mr.
Laufeyiarson—assuming he was the one who stole Tesla, and
it's not likely he is a coincidence—then that meant Mr. Laufeyiarson isn't what he appeared. Then again, who *is* around
here?"

Soren nodded. We were perched on a fallen tree, watching
Bruno graze by the light of the afternoon sun. I had a few painful minutes when I had a little pity party about Tesla not being
there, but one thing I've learned—crying about something sel-
dom makes it change. Therefore, it was up to me to find Tesla,
and get him back.

"That's true." Soren chewed one of the curried chicken

sandwiches I'd made for us both, picking out the bits of celery, which he didn't like. "But if a ghost is scared of him . . . well, that says something, right?"

"Kind of. It says I'm going to need some help getting Tesla back." I popped a couple green grapes in my mouth and wondered whether Ben really was going to be well enough to go on the date tomorrow night. I'd already done the angsting over my wardrobe—I had exactly one skirt—and managed to beg a little spending money from Mom for a trip into town. "But that's one of the benefits of having a vampire for a boyfriend. Ben will help me tackle Mr. Laufeyiarson. They had something going on earlier, when he tried to buy Tesla. Ben never did tell me what Laufeyiarson said to him."

"Maybe Benedikt is in on the theft," Soren said, his eyes narrowing. "Maybe that was a setup."

"Why do you insist on calling Ben by his full name?" I asked, tipping my head to the side to look at Soren. "Imogen does, but she's his sister, and you know how it is with family. But no one else calls him Benedikt. Well, OK, my mom does sometimes, but she has that whole mom thing going on. Why do you do it?"

Soren shrugged and looked away. "When are you going into town?"

"As soon as Imogen is ready." I smiled to myself about the quick change of subject. "You want to come?"

"I should give Bruno another bath, but he had one three days ago," Soren said, looking indecisive for a moment. "Meh. I will go with you two. If Papa is mad, he's mad. It's not as if he can fire me."

"*Vive la résistance,*" I said, having watched an old black-and-white movie called *Casablanca* the other night with Imogen.

"*Ja.* What did Tibolt say about the necklace?"

I stuffed the last bit of sandwich in my mouth and dusted off my hands before pulling out the pendant from where it lay beneath my T-shirt. "He didn't. I couldn't find him this morning. Ramon said he was off communing with the gods, which Mikaela snarked meant he was working on his tan. I didn't want to disturb him, so I'll just catch him tonight."

"Snarked?" Soren's face wrinkled as he tried to figure out the word.

"It means said snarkily. You know, kind of smart-ass. Not quite mean, but not nice, either. Snarked."

"Ah. You are good for my vocabulary." He tossed a couple of grapes in the air and tried to catch them in his mouth. They bounced off his face and rolled into the grass. "If all he is doing is lying in the sun, you could ask him to take the necklace back."

"No, I don't think so," I said, smiling.

"Ah? Why not?"

"Because evidently he's working on an all-over tan." Soren blinked at me in confusion for a moment. "You know, nude sunbathing?"

"Oh!" His eyes got big as he nodded. "No, you do not want to disturb him. I'm surprised that Imogen isn't with him."

My smile turned to a grin. "Evidently Desdemona beat her to it. Imogen had a couple of really interesting things to say about that, but in the end she decided to go shopping rather than duke it out with Desdemona."

"Ah."

"Anyway, Mikaela said Tibolt would be back around supper time, so I can catch him—oh, there's Imogen. Let's get this over with."

"I thought most girls liked to shop?" he asked as we followed Imogen to the parking area.

I tipped my chin up so I could look down my nose at him, doing my best to sound like Tallulah. "*I* am not most girls."

He snorted as we approached Imogen's white car. "You can say that again."

I punched him in the arm.

"Goddess! Where are you going?"

I stopped and glanced over my shoulder at where Eirik was yelling at me. He and Finnvid and Isleif were squatting around a small fire, roasting something that looked like it had once been a cute little bunny. I decided I really, really didn't want to know, so I kept my eyes on Eirik. "Shopping with Imogen."

"Shopping?" He frowned for a moment, then said something to the other two. Finnvid jumped up immediately, Isleif waiting before he pulled the dead thing off the makeshift spit before following the other two. "We will come with you."

"Um," I said, not wanting to offend them, but not particularly wanting an audience of Vikings while I tried on dresses. "Imogen's car is kind of small."

"Not that small," Finnvid said with a knowing smile. I figured that was just something else I didn't want to know.

Imogen raised her eyebrows as we approached. "You gentlemen are all coming with us?"

"Yes. We wish to shop." Eirik took the front seat. I guess he figured that as head Viking, he got to ride shotgun. "There are many things we need."

"Er . . . I don't think there's enough room for everyone," I said, looking at Soren, Finnvid, Isleif, and the backseat.

"You may sit on me," Isleif said. "You are big, but I am bigger."

I bit my tongue, fighting back the urge to snap back something mean about his "you are big" comment.

"Soren will sit on Finnvid," Eirik said, playing with the air conditioner. "He is small, and Finnvid won't mind."

"I am not sitting on anyone!" Soren said, backing away as Finnvid tried to grab him.

"You can sit up front, between Eirik and me," Imogen told him, pushing him toward the front seat.

"There, you see? Everyone fits. Let us go," Eirik said. "Are we going to McDonald's again, as well? Last night Isleif ate ten Big Macs. I will show him that I can eat eleven."

I sighed, wondering, if anyone else ever got stuck with Viking ghosts that were addicted to McDonald's. I climbed onto Isleif's lap, apologizing to Finnvid when I inadvertantly kicked him in the knee. I didn't mind sitting on Isleif because he had a daughter my age—or he did at one point, several hundred years ago—but it was a tight fit getting the two big Vikings and me into the back of Imogen's car.

"What exactly—oh, sorry again, Finnvid. My foot was cramping—what exactly do you guys want to buy?" I asked as we crossed the causeway over to the mainland. The town of Benlös Vessla was just a few minutes away, a nice enough place with a couple of streets of shops, suburbs, even a couple strip malls.

"Finnvid wishes to visit Kärleksgrottan," Eirik answered, leaning back as the air-conditioning blew on him.

"Kärleksgrottan?" I asked.

"Yes. It means love grotto. Finnvid has heard of something called a motion lotion, and wishes to try it."

I peeked at Imogen. She was blushing faintly, but kept her eyes on the road and said nothing. I added Finnvid's quest to my Too Much Information list.

"I wish to get a new bow," Isleif rumbled behind me. "I have seen pictures of modern bows in a catalog. I want one with a laser sight. No moose would ever escape me then!"

"Er . . . I don't think hunting is allowed now," I said, crossing my fingers because I had no idea whether or not that was true. I just didn't want to see Isleif hauling in the corpse of a moose some morning.

"It isn't? What is this country coming to?" Isleif grumbled under his breath for a few seconds. "Then I will get a new hunting knife. A sharp one, with a compass in the handle."

Soren turned around just enough to raise his eyebrows at me. I shook my head slightly, telling him it was useless to get into a lecture against hunting with guys who spent their entire lives doing it.

"And I wish to get a Game Boy," Eirik said, his eyes still closed, a look of bliss on his face as he wallowed in the cold air blowing from the front vent. "I have seen many tourists with them. I wish to blow up tiny little people as they do."

Soren snickered.

"It sounds like you guys will be busy for a while buying all your stuff."

"Buying?'" Finnvid asked. "We do not buy. We are Vikings! We pillage!"

"Pillaging is also outlawed now," Imogen said, winking at Finnvid in the rearview mirror. "You must buy things or the police will lock you away in a very small room. It is not pleasant."

"You don't have any money?" I asked Eirik, who was sitting up now, looking around the town as Imogen drove us down the main street.

He frowned. "No. We will barter."

"Barter what?" I asked, chewing on my lower lip. I didn't

want the ghosts glommed onto me forever, but neither did I want to see them end up in jail for shoplifting.

"We have gold and silver," Finnvid said nonchalantly, rolling down his window in order to stick his head out of it.

"Oh. Well, that should do. OK, so you guys do your bartering thing while Imogen and Soren help me pick out a dress, and then we'll all head back to the Faire in time for the opening."

"A dress?" Eirik asked, his head swivelling around to look at me.

"For your date with the Dark One?" Finnvid asked.

"Yeah, but —"

"We will help you pick out a dress. This date, it is important to you." Eirik pointed out an empty space in the parking lot. "Vikings have good taste. You will trust our opinion."

"I will?" I asked, unfolding my legs to get out of the car. My left foot had gone numb, causing me to do a little pins-and-needles dance. "Uh . . . Imogen has had a lot more experience picking out clothes, and she said she'd help me first, so it's only fair —"

"Bah," Eirik said, grabbing my arm and hustling me down the sidewalk. I have to give the people in Benlös Vessla credit — they didn't bat a single eyelash at the sight of three Vikings walking around town. Imogen was giggling with Finnvid behind us as I was marched between Eirik and Isleif to a ladies' clothing shop. Soren rolled his eyes and followed. "Imogen is a woman and thus does not have as much good taste as we do. In this, we are superior. We are Vikings!"

"That's what you said about killing people and stuff," I said, resisting as best I could even though I knew it wouldn't do me any good. I was right. Isleif and Eirik just pushed me into the shop.

"We are superior in all things," Eirik said, looking around the store. Soren wandered in, found himself directly in front of a table mounded high with panties, gawked at them with a horrified look on his face, and ran to the other side of the store.

"Finnvid, fetch the slave—"

"Sales assistant," I corrected, spying a middle-aged lady in the back of the shop that I took to be the owner or a salesperson.

"—to attend the goddess. We will pick out something for you. You sit until we're ready."

"I don't *think* so," I said to their backs as they went over to a rack of dresses. A few seconds later, I had to apologize profusely when Finnvid plopped down the saleslady he'd picked up and carried from the back of the store. "I'm so sorry. My . . . *friends* . . . are a little enthusiastic. Do you speak English?"

"Yes," the woman said in a heavy accent, her eyes huge as she looked from Finnvid to Eirik and Isleif. Luckily, there wasn't anyone else in the shop. "Yes, I do. Er . . . you wish to buy something?"

"These are charming lace panties," Imogen said, coming up with a handful of underwear. "Do you have matching bras? I do like my undergarments to match."

"Yes, behind you," the woman said, nodding toward the chair into which Soren had slumped. He looked even more horrified as he followed the woman's gaze and turned his head to find a wall of bras next to him.

"I'll be outside," he said quickly, dashing for the door.

"Sales slave! Do you have nothing with ermine or squirrel?" Eirik called, holding a horrible slinky purple disco dress.

"Er . . ." the saleswoman said, her mouth hanging open slightly.

"I've found it works best if you just ignore them," I told her quiet voice. "They really do mean well, but they can be a bit much if you let yourself think about them."

"Er . . ."

"The goddess has a date with a Dark One. She must be dressed according to her station," Finnvid said, holding up a pair of moss green linen capris to his waist as he checked his reflection in the mirror.

"Eh . . ." The saleslady looked like she wanted to bolt.

"Fran, you must come look at these lace bras. They are extremely well made. I'm sure if you were to wear one of them you'd feel much more confident. Oooh! Strapless!"

"I found something," Isleif said, pulling a pink maribou baby doll nightie from a rack. He fondled the maribou feathers. "This is very goddess-like. It's short, and it will show her breasts well."

"Let me see that," Eirik said, tossing aside a taffeta promlike dress. He groped the maribou, too, for a few seconds before holding the nightie up against himself, smoothing it down this chest. "Yes, this is good. I like it. Do you have bearskin boots? Ones that lace up the thigh?"

"Erm . . ."

"The goddess Fran will need an ax, too," Isleif told her. "A nice little ladies' beheading ax with matching baldric. And a skinning knife to tuck into her boot, for emergencies."

Imogen shoved a periwinkle blue bra into my hands. "Wireless underwire. Truly one of the seven modern miracles of man. Is that a negligee Eirik has? Where did he get it? Oooh, they have it in peach!"

The saleslady made an *eep*ing sound, and started backing toward the door. Imogen hurried past Isleif to pounce on the rack of nighties.

"Good point, Isleif," Eirik said, nodding. "She must be protected. Sales slave! I have gold Arabic coins. I will give you two of them for this goddess dress, and one more for the beheading ax and skinning knife."

That turned out to be the straw that broke the sales slave's back. The lady ran for her life as I slumped down into the chair Soren had so quickly vacated, wondering if I was going to go through the rest of my life accompanied by twelve Viking ghosts, clad in a feathery pink nightie.

It was beginning to look like I was.

CHAPTER NINE

"There you are," Ben said, giving me a long look as he stood next to where Imogen had parked her car. "I thought you were going to be back early. Your mother has been looking for you. You only have a few minutes before the Faire opens."

GothFaire is a popular show even though it goes to most places just once a year. People come to it from all around the countryside, which is why we tend to stay parked for a week in smaller towns, sometimes two weeks in big ones. So I wasn't surprised to see that the parking area was already filling even before the Faire was officially open, although it was a bit embarassing having an audience as we all piled out of Imogen's car.

"It looks like a clown car," Mikaela said as she strolled past swinging two chain saws.

I had to admit, she was probably right. As Isleif, Finnvid, and I tried to squeeze our way out of the back, laden with packages that didn't fit in the trunk of Imogen's car, I just knew the people waiting in line for the ticket booth to open were getting a good show.

"Goddess, you are on my hand—"

"Sorry. Isleif, my shirt is caught on the edge of that bow. Can you—ow! That was my head!"

"Who has the french fries?" Eirik asked, peering out from beneath a mound of packages. The Vikings were not content with their success at the dress shop (although they pouted over the skirt and top I finally picked out, claiming they were lacking in both the feather and breast-presentation departments), and had spent another three hours going to just about every store in Benlös Vessla. We might have been able to stop them after just a couple shops since the shopkeepers didn't take ancient gold coins, but then they spotted a coin dealer who bought precious metals, and all bets were off. "Soren, you are spilling my McShake. If it stains my new silk suit, I will gullet you and hang your intestines to dry in the sun."

"I hear eating," Isleif said behind me. He shifted and the huge hunting bow (with laser sight) smacked me in the head again. "Finnvid is eating our Big Macs!"

"I told you boys, no eating in the car," Imogen said. As the driver, she alone was not laden with packages, but she had been wedged in pretty tightly next to Soren and Eirik. She yanked open the car door behind me, sending me spilling out with my bag containing my date outfit (including a new pair of shoes, nylons, and a froufrou undie set Imogen insisted I have), two bags of men's clothing, a box containing five different flavors of fudge, a Game Boy box and several cartridges, and a cup of Diet Coke. I fell onto the grass with Isleif not far behind me.

"Aha! I knew it! Finnvid is eating our Big Macs!" Isleif shouted as he got to his feet. Finnvid looked guilty with a french fry hanging out of his mouth, but he didn't wait around to explain why he was scarfing down the Vikings' dinner. He threw down all the packages but the seven McDonald's bags, and bolted.

"*Tors vänstra tånagel!*" Eirik erupted from the car, bags and boxes and packages scattering all over the place as he ran after Finnvid. He almost reached him when Finnvid suddenly turned invisible. Eirik shouted again, then did the invisible thing himself. Isleif grunted as he got to his feet, fading away to nothing.

The line of people waiting to get in applauded, evidently believing the Vikings dematerializing was part of the show.

"*Tors* what?" I asked, brushing off myself as I stood.

"*Vänstra tånagel.* It means 'Thor's left toenail.'" Ben handed me one of the bags that had fallen with me.

"Oh. Thanks. You speak Swedish?"

"Yes. You're late," he said again.

"We were delayed by the Vikings," Imogen answered for me, coming around the car with her arms laden (she did as much shopping as the Vikings did—it's a wonder even half of it fit in the car). She kissed Ben on the cheek and hurried off toward her trailer, calling for Soren to bring her things quickly. He limped past me carrying the remains of Imogen's shopping, giving Ben a dark look as he went by.

"So was it Swedish Mr. Laufeyiarson was speaking to you the other night?"

Ben looked surprised for a moment. "Yes, it was. Why?"

"I'm curious why he was talking to you when he knew I was Tesla's owner. What did he say to you?"

It took a few seconds for him to answer. I knew for some reason he didn't want to tell me, but I was less worried about offending him than finding Tesla. "He asked if you were my Beloved. I told him you were. That is all."

"Hmm. You look better," I told him, heading for my trailer.

I had just enough time to drop off my things and get my palm reader's clothes on (basically, a Gypsy outfit that I'd bought in Hungary).

Ben walked beside me, holding himself stiffly, as if he still hurt. "I told you I would be fine."

"Was that before or after you died?"

"Fran." Ben stopped me, sighing. "I'm sorry I frightened you, but you of all people should know it takes more than a little blood loss to kill me. You overreacted to the situation. Despite appearances, I was not near death."

I shook his arm off and reached for the trailer door. "Oh really? Is that why you didn't answer me when I did the mind thing with you?"

He blinked but said nothing. I gave him a knowing look and ran up the steps to the trailer to change my clothes.

During the summer, GothFaire ran from six at night until two in the morning, which seems like a weird time to run a fair, but given the bizarre nature of the attractions—most popular were the piercing booth (couldn't get me near that with a ten-foot pole), aura photographs, and my mother's potions and spells—the fairgoers liked that we were open so late. I only worked four hours, from the Faire opening until ten. After that I was free, although the rest of the Faire was going full blast.

How is it going? a voice asked me a couple of hours later.

I looked up from the hand I was reading, smiling at Ben standing next to the line of three people waiting to have their palms read. *Are you checking up on me?*

Yes. Do you mind?

I thought about it for a moment as I explained to the man in front of me what his lifeline showed. *That depends. Are you checking* up on me to see if I need anything—like a break, or a drink, or something like that—or are you checking up on me just to see what I'm doing?

The former.

Then I don't mind.

Do you need a break, or a drink, or something like that?

Naw. I only have an hour to go, and things will slow down in a half hour once the magic shows start. What have you been doing?

Are you asking because you are concerned about my well-being, or are you inquiring as to how I've kept myself busy?

I smiled. *I wanted to know if you're all right.*

Ah. I am, thank you. I feel much better. And since I can feel your curiosity, I'll add that I've been sleeping since you and Imogen returned. I woke up a short while ago, and now I'm here to see how I can help you. Do you wish for me to continue hunting for Tesla?

Hmm. I finished the reading for the man before me, smiling when his girlfriend, who was next in line, told me she liked my lace gloves. *I think that's pretty much a lost cause, don't you? We both looked last night; then you looked some before you went all mysterious and almost got yourself killed.*

I think Laufeyiarson has hidden himself and Tesla very well, but if it would make you happy, I will continue to search for them.

No. I don't think searching is going to find them. I spent the next few minutes simultaneously reading a woman's palm, and telling Ben what happened with Tallulah.

Sir Edward didn't say what sort of being the thief was? Ben asked when I was finished.

No. He just said powerful. Tallulah made it sound like bad news. You didn't . . . er . . . you know, kind of know what he was? Because you're a vamp and all?

Ben gave me a look. *Being a Dark One is not synonymous with omnipotence, Fran.*

I love it when you talk with big words. OK, so how do we hunt him down?

I will try to talk to Sir Edward and meet you in an hour, when you are finished.

OK. But I'm going to find Tibolt between shows and get his help getting rid of the ghosts. I don't think I can go through another day like today.

Ben laughed into my head and did something he'd never done before—kissed me. Mentally. Or rather, he remembered what it felt like for him to kiss me. I gasped as the sensation filled my head of just what he felt when we kissed.

"Are you all right?" the girl in front of me asked as I grabbed a palm-reading flyer and started to fan myself.

"Just a little hot." I made a face at Ben, then turned my attention back to the girl's hand. "Let's see, we were on the Mound of Venus, weren't we?"

An hour later I folded the midnight blue velvet cloth that I used to read people's hands ("Make your space your own," Mom always said), counted out the money, putting it into the GothFaire bag before tucking it away in a lockable metal box I'd picked up in Berlin.

Soren was giving Bruno a last-minute check to make sure the horse's harness was clean. I waved at him as I hurried to drop off the cash box at the trailer. "Have you seen Tibolt?" I asked, stopping for a moment.

He pointed past me. "They just finished their act."

"Thanks!" I popped into the trailer, stashed my money box in its usual place, hurriedly gave Davide some cat food and told him that no, he couldn't go outside when the Faire was open, and hurried out to find Tibolt.

Circus of the Darned people didn't have trailers like the

Faire folk. Tibolt had a sleek black RV with a satellite dish clamped onto the top. Ramon and Mikaela had a silver RV, and the three people who worked behind the scenes for them—I never was quite sure of their names since they didn't speak much English—all shared a third RV, much more battered than the other two. I knocked on Tibolt's door, a little surprised when Mikaela answered it.

"Hullo, Fran. Have you come to see Tib?"

"Yes, if he's not busy."

"Sure. Tib? Fran is here for you."

I climbed into the RV, making a mental note that this was what Mom and I needed if we were going to stay with Goth-Faire. The interior was done in black and red, with gold trim on the black wood paneling. Overhead, a long light hung from the ceiling, while a full couch, two recliners, and a TV made up the living room part. Tibolt was stretched out on the couch, sipping a drink while Ramon sat at the table going over a map of Europe.

"Hi, everyone," I said, feeling a bit out of place in all this opulence. "Tibolt, I came to give you back your pendant, and also to ask if you wouldn't mind using it to get rid of the Vikings. I like them and all, but they pissed off Absinthe this morning, and raised a bit of hell in town, so I think it's best if they were sent to Valhalla."

Tibolt waved his drink at me. "The pendant is yours now. I meant to tell you that earlier, but forgot."

"Mine? I don't think so," I said, pulling the chain over my head. "It's gotten me in enough trouble."

"Regardless, the *Vikingahärta* is dead to me now. It has forsaken me for you."

"Dead?" I looked at the pendant in my hand. It vibrated

slightly, as if it was charged with power. "It doesn't feel dead. It's kind of . . . humming."

"Yes. Let me see it." He held out his hand for it. I plopped it onto his palm. He closed his eyes for a second, then opened them and shook his head, offering me the pendant again. "No, it's as I thought—the *Vikingahärta* has no power for me. It can serve me no purpose now, so you may have it."

"I don't want it!" I said, protesting when he sat up to shove it back into my hands. "It looks valuable and really old. My mom would freak if she found out you gave it to me."

He made a funny little half smile. "Then your mother must understand that in this, we have no choice. The *Vikingahärta* cannot be used by just anyone—the bearer must be sympathetic, open to its abilities. It has chosen you to act through, which is why I said earlier that only you can get send the ghosts to Valhalla. I can do nothing."

"But—I don't have the slightest idea what to do to get them there," I said, my heart sinking. I'd never be rid of the ghosts without help!

"Tib, there has to be something you can do," Mikaela said as he stood and stretched. I narrowed my eyes for a moment, wondering again why the Tibolt magic seemed to have faded. Ever since he'd given me that pendant . . . hmm. Unobtrusively, I set it down on the back of a chair.

"No, and I'm tired of you nagging me about it. Isn't it enough that I'm being unfairly punished by the master?" Tibolt snapped, turning to scowl at me. My knees almost melted at the sight of him—he was gorgeous, so very gorgeous even when he was mad. I wanted to run over and throw myself on him . . . eek! Quickly I grabbed the pendant, sighing in relief when Tibolt's attraction faded into normalness.

Clearly he'd cast some sort of glamour on himself to seem irresistible. I wondered if a bit of that had wonked up my mom's invocation, or if it was the valknut that had thrown her off?

"You're being punished for your own folly," Mikaela said, frowning just as much as her cousin was. "You have no one to blame but yourself for what happened, so blaming Loki or anyone else for your troubles is just denial."

"I know that, you stupid witch!"

Mikaela gasped. Ramon stood up and said, "You will not talk to her that way."

"Don't tell me what to do!" Tibolt yelled as he went toe-to-toe with Ramon. "I'll call her whatever I like!"

"Er," I said, uncomfortable. I had a feeling I was indirectly the source of the argument—or rather, the pendant was—and I would be better off elsewhere. I tried to edge around the two men but they blocked the aisle to the door. "I think I should probably leave now. If you'd let me past . . ."

"You're lucky I am a priestess and not the witch you claim, because if I were, your ass would be so cursed!" Mikaela said, poking Tibolt in the chest and ignoring me just as the other two did.

"You have no powers over me," Tibolt answered, narrowing his eyes at her. "I am a mage of the fifth level."

"And I am the high priestess of Ashtar," she snapped back, giving him another poke in the chest. "Your magic has no effect on me."

"Um, guys? Can I get by, please?" I asked.

"Magic is wasted on the ignorant," Tibolt said as he slammed down his drink and started toward the door. His insult made Mikaela gasp in surprise again.

"Tibolt—" Ramon started to say, but stopped when Tibolt snarled something in Swedish and slammed his way out of the RV.

"I'm sorry," I said quietly, slipping the pendant over my head and scooting past a black-faced Mikaela. "See you guys later."

Mikaela muttered a few things in Swedish, stopping suddenly to call me back. "No, Fran, wait! I will help you with the ghosts."

"You will?" I climbed back into the RV, hesitant because I didn't want to cause any more problems.

"Yes, I will. Tibolt is not the only one in the family with powers, and since he is to blame for the situation, and he refuses to help you, I will." She looked at Ramon, who nodded. "And so will Ramon. We will help you send the ghosts to Valhalla."

"That's awfully nice of you," I said, touching the valknut. "But how are we going to do that?"

"It's very simple," she said, pushing past me to leave the RV. Ramon and I followed. "You know about the Valkyries, yes?"

"Yes," I said, though I was far from an expert on Norse mythology. "Kind of. Ben told me the other night that they're warrior maidens who swoop down on horses and pick out dead warriors to take to heaven, which is called Valhalla."

"Close enough. Queen of the Valkyries is Freya, goddess of love."

"Oh?" I wondered what the goddess of love had to do with dead Vikings.

"Yes. So there's our answer." She ran up the steps to her RV, quickly returning with a tapestry bag. She hurried around the front of the trailer, toward the stretch of woods in which I found Ben. "Come on, we don't have long before our act is on again."

I looked at Ramon. He took my arm and hustled me after Mikaela.

"There's our answer? What answer?" I asked, stumbling over an unseen root. "You don't mean—"

"Yes," Mikaela said, spreading out a cloth and laying out a bowl, candle, and small bouquet of flowers. "We're going to summon Freya and ask her help."

CHAPTER TEN

Crash!
"I was at a party!"
Bang!
"A very nice party!"
Kerwhang!
"In Venice! The city of love! And there were four lovely mortal men practically *drooling* on me with desire!"
Crack. Tinkle, tinkle, tinkle.

I peeked through the fingers I'd slapped over my eyes when Freya, goddess of love, warrior queen, and evidently Venetian partygoer started her hissy fit. The tinkling sound came from the crystal goblet Mikaela had set out as part of the summoning equipment. Freya crushed the goblet between her hands and sprinkled the glass shards on the grass at Mikaela's feet. I had to give Mikaela credit—it took guts to stand up to a really pissed-off goddess (even if she did look like she belonged on the E! channel modeling the latest fashions), but Mikaela didn't budge an inch when Freya got mad at her for being summoned.

"Goddess Freya, I am sorry for disturbing you—"

"And you, you mortal priestess of Ashtar, you think nothing of summoning me from *the* party of the year? Did I mention Elton John was there?"

Mikaela flinched slightly when Freya shredded her invocation cloth. "I'm very sorry, goddess, but this is an emergency."

Freya threw down the cloth, spinning around to glare at Ramon, who stood a few feet away from Mikaela. "You! You are a priest?"

"Yes." Ramon looked like his usual implacable (and silent) self. He didn't even blink when Freya marched over to him.

I was having a hard time wrapping my brain around the idea that first of all, all those Norse gods like Odin and Thor and Freya really existed, and second, that they would look like fashion models. Then again, maybe it was just Freya—beautiful, raven-haired, elegant Freya—who looked like a model. Maybe the rest looked all wispy, and had big beards and wore horned helmets and things.

"Hrmph. Not worth my time." Freya dismissed Ramon and turned to consider me. I thought about clamping my fingers together again so I wouldn't have to see through them, but decided that was too cowardly. Instead I dropped my hands and tried to smile at the irate goddess.

"Hi. I'm Fran," I said politely as she stalked over to me. "I'm not a priestess or anything."

Her eyes narrowed as she examined me from head to foot. "You are something. You are mortal, but you have been touched by an immortal being."

"Well . . . my boyfriend is a vampire," I told her, praying she didn't call down lightning to smite us, or any of the other god-like things that I'd read about a few years back in a mythology class.

"You are a Beloved? You do not look like a Beloved."

"We're not to that point yet," I said with a kind of cheesey smile. "We haven't even gone on a real date yet, although we're going to do that tomorrow."

She looked interested. "Ah, a first date! I am the goddess of love and romance—you seek my advice, naturally."

"Well—"

"Let me see, a first date . . . " She tapped a finger to her chin while she thought. "Ah, yes! You must seek many lovers."

"Uh . . ." I snapped my mouth shut as soon as I realized it was hanging open. "I must?"

"Yes. As many as you can find. For how else will you know that this Dark One is truly meant to be your soul mate? I made the mistake of marrying young, and without sampling as many men as I could. Luckily, Od left and I was able to see what I was missing, but I would not have you make that same mistake. 'Try before you buy' is one of your mortal sayings, is it not? You must try as many men as you can before you settle for just one."

She looked pleased with herself as I stood in stunned silence, not knowing what I was supposed to say to that. Evidently nothing was expected because she started toward Mikaela, but stopped, looking back at me. "Why do I feel power from you? Nordic power?"

I chewed my lip for a moment before figuring out what was probably bothering her. I pulled the chain around my neck up, displaying the valknut. "Maybe it's from this?"

She hissed and took a couple of steps back. *"Vikingahärta!"*

"Yeah. Is it bad or something? I raised a group of Viking ghosts with it, which is kind of annoying, but it didn't do anything evil or anything like that."

"It is not bad in itself." She tossed her head and her hair, long, wavy, and black, swung backward to lie in perfection along her silver cocktail dress. The dress itself was studded with crystals (or diamonds—I couldn't tell, although I wouldn't have been surprised to find out they were real diamonds), as were her ankle-strap silver stilettos. "It's the source rather than the pendant itself I would prefer to avoid."

"Fran inadvertently used the *Vikingahärta* to raise a dozen warriors," Mikaela said carefully. "We desire them to be sent to Valhalla, but are unable to do so. We hoped you would help us."

"Bah," Freya said, using Mikaela's mirrored scrying bowl to check her reflection.

"Er . . . if you don't mind, what is the source of the necklace?" I had to ask the question, although I was a bit worried she'd start breaking things again.

Evidently she'd worked through the worst of her anger, though. She stopped primping in the bowl and tossed it at Mikaela. "That is Loki's valknut. The power comes from him. And because you used it rather than a pendant made in my image, I cannot help you with your warriors."

"But you're the queen of the Valkyries, right?" I asked.

She brushed a speck of something off her dress. "Yes. I am returning to my party now, and if even one of those delicious mortal men who were swooning over me has left, I shall make plain my anger."

"But—but I really do need help with the Vikings," I said, stepping forward to block her as she started to walk past Mikaela. Her eyes widened like she couldn't believe I was obstructing her (she wasn't the only one—my stomach was doing flip-flops at the thought of pissing her off any more). "I understand you can't do anything about the raising of them since it was with this Loki guy's necklace, but you are the queen of the Valkyries, so it seems to me you could help me get them into Valhalla."

"I don't do that sort of thing now," she said, waving a hand at me. A big puff of air suddenly swept up and pushed me aside. "The mortal world offers so much more than the immortal one—television, movies, Hollywood, fashion houses—I spend little time in Valhalla anymore. No one there has been on *CSI: Miami*!"

"But—"

"Remember, seek as many lovers as you can find! You will be much happier for that. And you—do not summon me again, priestess," she warned Mikaela, and without another word, she was gone in a sunburst of light.

"Oh great. Now what am I going to do?" I asked, plopping down onto a tree stump. "I don't even know this Loki person. Now I have to hit him up for help, too?"

"Loki?" Eirik and a couple of the Vikings emerged from the woods. Eirik was wearing a sleeveless black mesh muscle shirt, and pair of tight leather pants. Gils had on a red T-shirt with the word SEX made up by lizards shaped like letters, and Ljot evidently wanted to go swimming, because he wore a pair of speedos, flip-flops, swimming goggles . . . and nothing else. "You are summoning Loki? It is Freya you want. She is the queen of the Valkyries."

I gestured toward Mikaela and Ramon, who were on their knees collecting the debris from Freya's hissy fit. "She was just here. She told us she doesn't go to Valhalla anymore because there are no *CSI* guys there, and that we'd have to ask Loki for help."

"*CSI*?" Ljot asked, adjusting his swim goggles.

"TV show."

"Why did the goddess Freya tell you to summon Loki? " Eirik asked, slapping at a mosquito. I don't know why, but the thought of a ghost with a mosquito bite had me giggling to myself.

"Because this is evidently his. Or was his. Or has his power or something," I answered, standing up to show him the valk-nut. "So I'll have to try to get him to help, whoever he is."

"You do not know Loki, god of mischief?" Gils asked, disbelief plastered all over his face.

"Nope. I'm not really hip to all the gods. Who is he? And why didn't Freya like him?"

"That would be because of Asgard. Sit, and I will tell you the story of Loki and Freya," Eirik said, making himself comfortable on a fallen log next to me. Ljot and Gils sat on the grass, putting on comfortable "about to hear a story" faces. Mikaela rolled her eyes as she dumped all the debris into a cloth bag, but she and Ramon sat cuddled on her casting blanket to listen.

"Who's Asgard?" I asked, taking my seat again on the tree stump.

"Asgard is a place, not a person. It is where the gods live. Loki was at first a god of much mischief, always pulling jokes on the others, using his powers of transformation to get himself out of trouble. One day, when the gods were constructing Asgard, they found they needed more money to build the wall around it. Loki had the idea of hiring a giant to do the work, and thought up a plan to have the giant work without paying him. He offered the giant the goddess Freya if the wall was completed on time. At first the gods were skeptical, but Loki assured him that he would make sure that the giant did not complete the task on time, so that the gods would not have to pay him for his work."

"What a creep," I said before realizing I was talking about a god. "Er . . . nice creep, of course."

"No, he was not nice," Ljot said grimly, shaking his head.

"The giant had a stallion to help him build the wall. Three days before it was to be finished, the giant was almost done, and the goddess Freya was beside herself with anger at Loki. With the gods behind her, Loki had no choice but to transform himself into a mare, and entice the giant's stallion away. The giant missed the deadline, and was furious. He tried to take Freya anyway, but Thor stopped him. Freya never forgave Loki for using her in such a way."

"Ouch. It was nasty of him to set that up, knowing the giant was going to do all the work and not get paid. I don't blame Freya for being ticked at him." I was about to add that he'd get sued up the ying-yang if he tried something like that now, but remembered in time that we were talking about stuff that happened probably thousands of years ago. Now you see why my brain had such a hard time coping with the fact that all these Norse gods were real people. So much for mythology. "Well, I don't look forward to having to ask him for help, but if there's no other way to get you guys to Valhalla, I'll just have to gird my loins and tighten my belt and grit my teeth, and all that stuff."

I stood up and stretched. Even though it wasn't yet midnight, I was tired.

"We will help you," Eirik said, standing and carefully brushing off the seat of his pants. "Since you will need Loki's goodwill, tonight we will offer a sacrifice in his name to make sure that he views your request for help with favor."

"That would be a nice change," I said, stifling another yawn.

"But what sort of sacrifice are you talking about? More mead like Tibolt used?"

"Traditionally we sacrifice a slave," Ljot said, peering through the goggles as if he expected a slave to pop out of the woods and volunteer.

"But you have decreed we not kill anyone," Eirik said quickly when I turned around to yell at him. "So we will, instead, offer a smaller sacrifice."

"Like what?" I asked, suspicious. "You guys aren't going to kill another rabbit like you did earlier?"

"The rabbit was on the stringy side," Gils said, picking his teeth.

"No, no rabbit. The sacrifice has to be something worthwhile," Eirik said, shooing me toward the trailers. Mikaela and Ramon had already gone off to get ready for their next show.

"What, exactly?" I asked. "You can stop trying to shove me, too. I'm not going anywhere until you tell me what you guys are going to sacrifice."

Eirik sighed and looked up at the stars for a couple of seconds, like he was *so* put upon. "I hope the next goddess who binds us to her is much more reasonable. You need not worry, goddess Fran. We will sacrifice no mortals—only many Big Macs will be offered in the name of Loki."

"And McNuggets," Gils added. "With dipping sauces."

"Yes, McNuggets as well," Eirik said with an "are you happy now?" look on his face.

I smiled. "OK. That sounds fine. Knock yourselves out. I'm a bit tired so I think I'm going to find Ben to say good night, then go to bed early."

"Good night, goddess," they called to me as I headed for the Faire.

"Get the rest of the men together," I heard Eirik say to his men as I left. "Tonight, we pillage McDonald's!"

"I really do not want to know," I said to myself, hurrying so I wouldn't hear them making plans for taking the McNuggets hostage. "It's just better if I don't know."

"What is?"

A man's voice emerged from the dark time-travel booth. Most of the booths, including Desdemona's, had closed during the magic shows.

At least I thought it had closed. "Ben?"

"Oh, Fran!" A light clicked on to show Ben and Desdemona standing much closer than I would have liked. Screw jealousy, Ben was mine! How dared she stand around in a dark booth with him. And how dared he allow her to do it! "I was just showing Benedikt my moonstone. If the moon is in the right quadrant, it casts a light in the darkness. Would you like to see it, too?"

What's wrong? Ben asked, his eyes watching me carefully.

Oh, like you don't know.

"No, thank you," I said politely. "I'm tired. I'm going to bed. Enjoy your moonstone watching, or whatever it is you're doing."

I spun around on my heels, my hands fisted, my jaw tight. And worst of all, my eyes were watering. I was so mad, I didn't know whether I wanted to hit Ben or cry.

Are you going to be jealous every time I'm next to another female?

This is not jealousy. I ran up the steps to my trailer. Thankfully, Mom was still out doing things. *This is righteous indignation, Mister You're-the-Only-Woman-for-Me-I'd-Die-Without-You. You know what I say to that? Bullfrogs!*

Fran, Ben said, sighing into my head. *You are the only one for me. I would die without you. And I wasn't doing anything with Desde-mona despite her manuevering.*

Davide squatted on top of the counter and flattened his ears as I paced up and down the narrow aisle.

Oh, I am so not going to believe . . . wait. You knew she was deliber-ately luring you into her dark booth?

Ben laughed. *Of course. I'm not an idiot, sweetheart. I know when a woman desires me. But that doesn't mean I feel the same way toward her.*

I thought about that for a minute. Davide's ears straight-ened up as I stopped to think. *You knew and yet you went anyway?*

I didn't know until I was there.

Oh. There's such a thing as being too passive, though. Did you just stand there while she put her lips all over you? You could have left, you know. You could have said, "No thanks, not interested, and by the way, keep your hands off me or Fran will have a hissy." You could have told her to leave you alone.

You really are silly when you're in the throes of jealousy. I can't de-cide if it is flattering or annoying.

Annoying? Annoying! Oh! I'll give you annoying, buster!

Davide hunkered down as I stormed past him and yanked open the door to the trailer. I intended to run back out to find Ben so I could punch him in the belly, as he deserved. In-stead I stopped as he came up the steps.

"If I were to raise hell every time you spent a few minutes alone with Soren, what would you do?" he asked, walking to-ward me. I took a couple of backward steps past Davide, who was watching us with interest. "If I screamed and yelled and forbade you to spend time with any man, anywhere—your ghosts, Peter, Karl, and Kurt, anyone—would you mind?"

"Soren is a child. He doesn't have the hots for me."

"Like hell he doesn't. His crush on you is evident to every-one." Ben kept walking toward me, his face unexpressive, but his eyes were glowing a rich browny-gold.

"Kurt and Karl are having a fling with Absinthe," I said, backing up another couple of steps.

"Doesn't matter. They could still be attracted to you, and you likewise."

"Peter is old enough to be my dad."

I bumped up against the door that led to the tiny bedroom at the end of the trailer.

Ben put his hands on each side of my head and leaned in, his breath brushing my face in a soft caress. Despite being angry at him, my stomach was twisting and turning happily because he had that look in his eye that he got whenever he kissed me. "How could any mortal man resist such a beautiful, alluring girl as you?"

"I don't care about the mortal ones," I said, my breath coming short and fast as he leaned in even closer. I put my hand on his chest and let his feelings flow into me.

Tell me I'm interested in anyone but you, he commanded, and as an answer, I brushed my lips against his, sliding my arms under his until we were pressed so tightly together, I couldn't tell where I ended and he began.

I might have overreacted a little, I admitted as his tongue flicked over the corner of my mouth. I'd never been one for French kissing before Ben because, I mean—tongues! But it was different with him. It was exciting and wonderful and he tasted like the spicy mulled wine Mom had let me have a sip of last Christmas. My whole body went up in a rush of tingles as I kissed him back, intent on showing him that I appreciated his honesty.

And?

All right, I take your point. I wouldn't like you to be jealous of me being around other guys. So I will try very hard not to care if Desdemona corners you again.

His lips curved against mine in a smile.

But you could tell her hands off, you know! It wouldn't hurt.

He pulled away enough to laugh. "Ah, Fran, you never fail to delight me."

"That's me, good ole entertaining Fran . . . oh. Hi, Mom."

Over Ben's shoulder, my mother's face loomed angry and scowling. He pulled away and half turned to see her.

She tossed down her bag of Wiccan stuff and stood glaring at Ben. "I thought we had an agreement?"

Ben inclined his head slightly. "My apologies. Fran was upset with me, and I was simply trying to straighten things out."

"Agreement?" I asked, licking my lower lip. I could still taste Ben on it, which made my legs feel like they were made of Jell-O. "What agreement?"

"If it happens again, you will leave me no choice," Mom said in a cold voice. She moved aside so the open door could be seen, her arms crossed over her chest.

Ben turned back to me for a moment, caressing my cheek. *Good night, sweet Fran. Sleep well.*

"Hey, wait a sec — Ben! You don't have to leave."

He nodded at my mother, said good night to her, and without another look at me, left the trailer, closing the door behind him.

"What agreement?" I all but yelled, so frustrated I wanted to scream.

"I have told you before that he is not allowed in our trailer," she answered, snatching her bag and brushing past me to get to her room. "I won't have you putting yourself in a dangerous position."

"Dangerous position?" I said, following her to the door to her room. "With Ben? How dangerous can he be? I'm his frickin' Beloved!"

"He's a man," she snapped, whirling around and marching back over to me. "I've seen the way he looks at you, and I will not allow him to use you that way."

My mother has gone insane, I told Ben.

She's concerned for you.

Did she tell you that you couldn't come to our trailer?

We have an agreement, yes. I am allowed to continue seeing you so long as I abide by the boundaries she has set for you.

"You set boundaries for me?" I yelled, so angry I felt like I was going to burst. "I am not a child! You can't treat me like one!"

"You are a minor and my daughter, and I will continue to look out for your interests so long as I need to," she said, slamming her things into a drawer. "Yes, I set boundaries. Someone had to. It was clear to me that you are naive enough, and smitten enough, to allow Ben any liberty."

My mouth hung open for a few seconds. "This is about sex, isn't it? You think I'm going to have sex with Ben? I just barely learned how to kiss him!"

"From what I saw a few minutes ago, you're very well along in your lessons. I will not have you throwing away your life on a . . . a . . ."

"Dark One?" I said, my arms wrapped tight around myself. I was so angry, so hurt that my mother didn't trust me one little bit, my body was shaking, my eyes puddled with tears of frustration.

"Vampire." Mom spat the word out. "He may try to wrap it up in clean linen, but he's a vampire, Fran. Born of the dark powers, he is a parasite on the living, an abomination in the eyes of the Goddess."

I grabbed the doorknob. "You can take your Goddess and stick her up your —"

"Fran!" Mom shrieked, her face black with anger.

"Ben is not evil. He is not a parasite or an abomination. He's a guy who just happens to be made a little different from most people. And he's my friend. No, he's my *boy*friend. And you can make all the agreements you want with him, but I am not going to honor them. You may not have any trust in me, but I believe in Ben. He'd never hurt me. Never!"

"You foolish, stupid girl," Mom said.

I slammed the door closed, tears running down my face. I thought for a few seconds about running to Imogen's trailer and demanding to stay with them, but I knew my mother would drag me back, and I'd die if anyone saw that. Instead I grabbed my iPod, blanket, and pillow, and curled up on the couch, ignoring my mother when she came out a few minutes later.

CHAPTER ELEVEN

"Good morning, Fran." Imogen stopped on her way past where I was slumped at one of the tables. She looked around the area, then glanced at me, her eyes widenening. "You look horrible."

"That's always so flattering to hear," I said, trying to shake my grumpy mood to give her a smile. It wasn't Imogen's fault my mother was so biased she couldn't understand about Ben and me. "If you're looking for Tibolt, he went off for his run about half an hour ago. Mikaela and Ramon went into town to have something with one of the chain saws fixed. Peter is off buying supplies for the horses . . . horse."

"I've always felt flattery wasn't needed between friends," she said, setting down her latte and taking a seat opposite me. Imogen wore a pair of white linen shorts, white tank top, and gauzy white and silver blouse over it. "You must have been up early to see everyone about their business."

I eyed the tan leg she swung next to me. "Why is it that female Moravians can get a tan, but the men can't tolerate the sunlight?"

"It has something to do with the nature of the original curse, I believe," Imogen said, shrugging slightly as she sipped her latte. "Now, are you going to tell my why you look so horrid this morning, or shall I have to guess?"

"Mom and I had a fight over Ben."

"Ah," she said, nodding.

I flicked a piece of orange peel from my breakfast into the nearby trash. "You're not surprised?"

"That your mother is threatened by Benedikt? No. She would not be a loving parent if she wasn't concerned for you."

"Oh, not you too," I said, rubbing my forehead. "I'm sixteen. I'm not a child! I don't need someone watching out for me. I'm perfectly able to take care of myself. I'm a Beloved, for heaven's sake!"

"No, Fran, you're not," she said, setting down her cup and taking my hand in hers. I'd only recently started allowing Imogen to touch my hands. She had a lot of emotions that I didn't think were any of my business, but I knew she loved Ben, and liked me a lot, so I didn't flinch when she took my hand, giving it a little squeeze. "You were born to be his Beloved, yes. But you have not yet completed the seven steps to Joining with him, and until you do that, you cannot comprehend what it is to bind yourself to one man for an eternity. You cannot imagine what you will be sacrificing in order to be his Beloved. Your mother understands some of that, and she's just trying to protect you as best she can."

I made a face. "I doubt it. She's just being a control freak and trying to keep me under her thumb. She still thinks I'm a little kid, and I'm not!"

"Of course you're not. You have great powers, but more important" — Imogen drew a ward over my chest — "you have a large caring heart. You put other people before yourself, and no child would do that. But you do have to give your mother a little credit for wanting to keep you from being hurt. She has seen more of the world than you have."

"I know." I sighed, my anger melting slightly. "Although she hasn't raised a herd of Vikings, or killed a demon. And she's not dating a vampire."

Imogen smiled. "I have an uncle she might like—but that's neither here nor there. Now, other than your fight with Miranda, what are you looking so very blue about?"

"Oh . . . everything." I flicked the last bit of orange skin into the trash. "The date tonight. The Vikings I can't seem to send home. Tesla missing, and me helpless to find him. Ben keeping secrets from me."

"Very well. I was going to have a swim with Tibolt today, but you need my help far more than he needs to pay attention to me." Imogen set her cup down.

I giggled at the way she phrased her plans for Tibolt.

"Let us take this step by step. Your date tonight with Benedikt—your mother has not forbidden you to go out with him?"

"No. And she'd better not," I said, thinning my lips.

"Good. Your outfit you have taken care of. That just leaves the setting, and that's up to Benedikt. I have given you valuable advice on how to act, so I don't see that you have any worries where the date itself is concerned."

"Well . . . I'm a bit worried about the Vikings."

"Why?" Imogen asked. "I haven't seen them attack anyone lately."

Timing is everything. At that moment Isleif strolled by,

wearing a pair of scarlet-and-orange-striped biking pants and purple tank top. In one hand he had his hunting bow, the other a book of dog breeds. "Good morning, goddess, Imogen. I'm going hunting for poodles. Would you like to join me? I hope to get enough to make a pair of poodle-fur leggings."

I looked at Imogen.

She sighed.

"If we run across a herd of them, I should have enough pelts to make you a pair as well," Isleif generously offered.

"Are there any poodles on the island?" I asked Imogen under my breath.

"Not that I've seen. No one lives here but the archaeology people, and they only have golden retrievers."

"Knock yourself out," I said to Isleif. He stared in surprise. "Um. I mean, go right ahead. Have fun. Happy . . . er . . . poodling."

"Very well," Imogen said as he walked away. "I concede that the Vikings are an issue, although I'd like to point out that Finnvid has not been any trouble, and has a most delicious way with . . . but that's beside the point."

"Not to mention way too much information." I smiled.

"Next on your list is Tesla, and I believe you and Benedikt have done all you can there. I wish there was something I knew of to help, but short of hiring a detective to investigate — something that would be bound to cost a great deal of money — I'm at a loss."

I rubbed my forehead again. The headache I thought I'd gotten rid of this morning was back. "Yeah, me too."

"And as for Benedikt keeping secrets — you must realize, Fran, that he has commitments to people other than yourself."

"I know that. He told me about his blood brother. Or rather, he told me that he couldn't tell me about him. Something about an oath. Which I understand, I really do. But it's still kind of annoying to have him disappear for a month and pop back up and not say where he's been. Or go off for the night and come back almost dead!"

"I admit that last annoyed me, as well," she agreed. "But you must learn to trust Benedikt. He would never do anything that would harm you."

"I know that. I just hate that he's off doing probably really neat things without me."

She smiled. "I sense that your feelings for him are becoming deeper than perhaps you realize."

"Not going there," I said, sighing again. Sometimes life seemed so overwhelming.

"All right, we won't. Out of your four issues, I believe only one is a legitimate concern, and I can help you with that."

"With the Vikings?" I stopped rubbing my forehead to squint into the morning sun that shone over her shoulders.

"Yes. You wish to send them to Valhalla, correct?"

"Yeah." I told her what had happened the night before. "I was going to summon this Loki god guy, but Mikaela went off to get a chain saw fixed, so I'm stuck waiting until they get back."

"Nonsense," Imogen said, drinking the last of her latte and throwing the paper cup into the trash. She stood, dusting herself off. "You have me."

"I do?" I got up slowly, not sure what she was getting at.

"Yes, you do. I shall summon the god Loki, and you will lay your case before him."

"But . . . you're not a witch. Or a priestess, for that matter."

"No, I'm Moravian. That is infinitely better," she said without the slightest trace of arrogance. I followed her to her trailer, and waited while she dug out a book of invocations and grabbed a few odd items from one of the drawers under her couch. I glanced a couple of times at the door to her bedroom, knowing Ben must be in there since he usually slept through the early part of the day, when the sun was at its strongest.

"Shall we?"

I nodded and trotted obediently at her heels as we made our way through the just-waking-up fair to a small sandy area that jutted out of a rocky stretch of beach.

"This is a nice quiet place where we shouldn't be disturbed," she said, nodding at me to set my armload down. I helped her spread out a blanket, pour a little water into a metal chalice, and lay out some flowers, a big black feather, and a large curved animal claw.

"Have you done this much?" I asked, chewing my lip a little as she consulted her book.

"Not with Norse gods, no. But it can't be that hard if Mikaela did it. Now, let's see . . . for the earth we have purified water and—just grab a handful of dirt, would you? Set it in that little cup. Perfect. Nature is represented by the flowers, and the animal kingdom by the feather and bear claw. Hmm." She looked up, her lips pursed. "It says to summon a god we must first be in a religion that honors the god, or possess a personal talisman of the god himself. Did Freya say that amulet belonged to Loki?"

I shook my head. "She just said it had his power in it."

She looked thoughtful for a second or two before closing the book. "That sounds good enough to me. You'll have to do the invocation since the amulet is yours."

"Um . . . I don't know what invocation to use for him."

She flipped through the book for a few minutes before closing it again. "I believe we just make something up. So long as it's about Loki, asking for his help, and using the amulet to reach him, it should be all right."

"OK. I'm not very good at this, but anything is worth a shot to get the Vikings on their way."

"I'll help. How do invocations usually start?"

I thought for a minute, then knelt behind the arrangement of elements that we'd laid out. "By leaf and flower, by water and earth, by feather and claw, I do invoke thee, Loki."

"Oh, that's very nice," Imogen said, looking impressed.

"Thanks. I do sometimes listen to my mother."

She smiled at my grin, then looked serious. "How about this next—'shape changer, sky traveler, god of fire riding in the sky, descend upon your daughters, we beseech thee.'"

"Wow. You're good," I said, then repeated the words to make sure I remembered them. The valknut started glowing hot under my shirt. I pulled it out, showing it to Imogen.

"Oooh, it's glowing! That must mean it's working."

"I hope. Let's see . . . 'aid me in my time of need, oh Loki whose power moves the universe.'"

"Appealing to his vanity—excellent choice," Imogen said, nodding.

"Um . . . what next? I'm drawing a blank."

"Oh, let me. I know a little something about Norse mythology. I must know something about Loki that we can use . . . hmm. Let's try this: 'Loki Laufeyiarson, full of fire, strong in spirit, searing all with your splendor, grant me your presence!' Then repeat the first part again."

"Eh . . . did you say Laufeyiarson?" I asked, wondering if that was a common name.

"Yes. Loki is the son of Farbauti and Laufrey, if I remember my mythology correct. Why?"

"It's just that I know someone with that name . . . naw. It's got to be a coincidence. OK, here I go. Let's hope this works."

I spent a few moments clearing my mind of extraneous thoughts, took a couple of deep breaths as I got a firm grip on the valknut, mentally spelled out the word Loki in my head to use as a focusing image, and then spoke the full invocation.

". . . by leaf and flower, water and earth, feather and claw, I invoke thee now!" I finished, staring at my hand where the valknut suddenly burst forth with blinding light.

"Imogen?" I asked, trying to shade my eyes against the bright light. It was like staring into one of those huge arc lights they use for movie premieres—or so I imagined, never having been idiot enough to do that. "Are you OK?"

"Yes. Did it work? I can't see anything."

"I think it's fading," I said, squinting. The light in the center of the starburst changed, turning black as a man's shape formed and turned into a person.

"Who summons me?" the furious voice of a man asked. I still had sunspots in my eyes, but as I blinked them away, I got a good look at the god we'd summoned.

"'You!" I yelled, gritting my teeth. "I want my horse back!"

The red-haired man who'd offered me a thousand bucks for Tesla looked startled for a moment, his eyes quickly narrowing. "I don't know what you're talking about."

"Yes, you do," I snarled, marching up to him, shaking my

fist at him. "I want Tesla back! Don't you dare deny you took him, because you're the only one who has been interested in him. Now, where is he? What did you do to him? Is he all right? Is he getting enough to eat? I swear by all that's holy, if you've hurt him, I'm going to kick you in the happy sacks so hard, you won't be able to walk for a week!"

"Fran!" Imogen shrieked, running to stand next to me, pulling down the fist I was waving under Mr. Laufeyiarson's nose. "One does not threaten to kick a god, let alone to emasculate him. I take it you know Loki?"

"I have never met this deranged, violent young woman before," Loki Laufeyiarson lied. He didn't seem to be overly concerned about my threats, either, but I didn't let that stop me.

"Oh, I know him. He offered me a thousand bucks for Tesla, and when I wouldn't sell him, he stole poor Tesla! You may be a god, but you just can't go around stealing other people's horses!"

Loki pulled himself up until he was several inches taller than me. I wondered for a moment how he did that, then remembered—Norse god. Probably growing a couple of inches was no big deal to him. "I am one of the Elders, mortal. I can do whatever I desire."

"Yeah? Well, maybe I should just call Freya back. I bet she'd have something to say about that. And maybe that Odin guy, too. Isn't he supposed to be the head god?"

A little something flashed in his brown eyes, something like worry. I smiled to myself, happy I'd found a pressure point.

"All right," he said, kind of grinding his teeth as he spoke. "Since you summoned me for this purpose, I will put your mind at rest and admit I took the horse you call Tesla. But I had a very good reason for doing so."

"Yeah? What would that be?" I asked, worried he was going to say he used to own Tesla. One of the problems of getting a horse without its history is that you never quite know just who owned him over the years.

"He is an offspring of mine."

CHAPTER TWELVE

❧

I goggled. I just opened my mouth and let my eyes bug out in a good old-fashioned goggle. "He *what?*" Loki was clearly insane.

"He is the descendant of Sleipnir, the eight-legged horse I bore and gave to Odin. Only a few horses exist today that can trace their heritage back to me—the white stallion Tesla is one of them."

"OK, OK, time out here," I said, freaking out a bit. "You're a god, a male god, and you gave birth to an eight-legged horse? Wait! This wouldn't have been when you were trying to make some giant mess up his work schedule with Asgard?"

Loki looked down his nose at me. "The events at Asgard have been skewed out of proportion, but yes, it is while I was in the form of a mare that I became pregnant with Sleipnir. Now you see why the white stallion is valuable to me."

"To be frank, no. I mean, the whole thing about you changing yourself into an animal and giving birth aside, Tesla has to be . . . what—a couple of hundred generations away from Sleipnir?"

Loki waved away that point. "The fact remains he is an off-spring, and I have precious few of them left these days."

"Yeah, but . . . you're Loki. God of mischief, the trickster. You do all sorts of mean things to other gods. It's a little hard to believe that all of a sudden you've turned into a family guy."

He shrugged. "People change with time. So have I."

"You're a god," I pointed out yet again in case he'd forgotten that point, or thought I was so stupid I had.

"And who is to say gods cannot have a change of heart?" he asked, one eyebrow going up in question.

He had a point there.

"Tesla is just an old horse. He needs to be taken care of. He doesn't need some —" I bit off the phrase "deranged old man who thinks he's a god" and replaced it with, "—one who is busy with other things. Besides, I promised I'd take care of him, and I don't go back on my promises."

"I believe the phrase 'too bad, so sad' comes to mind," he answered, examining his fingernail like he needed a manicure. "Tesla is mine now."

"Oh, you . . . gah!" I yelled.

"You're being terribly inconsiderate of Fran," Imogen said. She had on what I thought of as her haughty face, the one she used with guys who got rude with her. "All she's doing is trying to get her horse back, and help some ghosts to move on to Valhalla. She has a very important first date with my brother to-night, and because you're being obstinate and obstructive, she's not going to enjoy it as she should because she'll be worrying about Tesla, and what the ghosts are doing while she's on the date."

"A date?" Loki asked, looking from Imogen to me. "You have a date with a Moravian?"

"Yes, Ben's a Dark One, but that isn't really important—"

"A Beloved on her first date," Loki interrupted, stroking his chin as he gave me a speculative look. I groaned to myself. I knew that look. I knew what was coming next. "How well I remember the courtships of all three of my wives. I will give you some valuable advice."

"I have already advised Fran as to the best way to enjoy her date," Imogen pointed out. "Input by a man is hardly necessary."

"First, you test this Dark One to see if he's really faithful to you," Loki said, totally ignoring Imogen. "I recommend playing a trick or two on him to see if his heart is true, or if he's a lying dog."

"My brother does not lie!" Imogen said, outraged.

"Next, take something away from him that he values greatly. When the time is right, pretend you found it, and he will be grateful to you forever."

"Oh!" Imogen gasped. "That is completely out of line! Fran, don't you listen to a word this man is saying!"

Loki continued to ignore her. I just hoped the advice would end soon, so I could get back to the topics of Tesla and the Vikings. "Finally, you must bring him many gifts. Something to give you value in his eyes, and make him cherish you as the source of great fortune."

I couldn't help but roll my eyes at his advice. I may be naive where dating is concerned, but even I knew what he was recommending was downright stupid.

"You need some serious psychological counseling," Imogen told him with a sniff.

"I am finished," Loki told me. "Now that I have given you the gift of my advice, you may thank me and then I will leave."

"Thank you for the advice." No matter how awful it was. "But I'm not quite through talking to you about Tesla and the Vikings."

"I've told you my answer," he said, starting to walk away. "There is nothing left to discuss."

Just in time I remembered that I wasn't as powerless as he thought. I whipped the amulet out and held it up so the sunlight glinted off it. "Recognize this?"

His eyes widened as he took a step toward me, his hand outstretched. "The *Vikingahärta!* What are you doing with it? It is mine!"

"Nuh uh." I held the valknut close to my chest and gave him a victorious smile. "'Too bad, so sad,' remember? The *Vikingahärta* is mine now."

"Fran," Imogen hissed between her teeth as she came to stand next to me. "It is not wise to tease a god!"

Loki said something in a language I didn't understand, but the mean tone of his voice was enough to tell me he wasn't offering up a prayer for my good health.

"Don't worry. I'm in control," I whispered to Imogen before turning back to Loki with a pleasant smile. "However, I'm willing to let you have it if you give me back Tesla, and send the Viking ghosts I raised with it to Valhalla."

"No," Loki said, and took another step toward me.

"No? Like . . . no?" The *Vikingahärta* glowed warm in my hand, but whether it was heating up because I was suddenly starting to sweat, or if it was warming of its own power, I didn't know.

"No. No, I will not release my descendant into your custody, and, no, I will not help you with any warriors. You will give the *Vikingahärta* to me now, or you will suffer the consequences."

"That would not be fair to Fran," Imogen said, her chin held high. "You would take everything from her and give her nothing in return. I cannot allow you to do that."

"You cannot *allow* me?" Loki said, his voice suddenly getting very deep and very big. So big it echoed off the rocks behind us, scaring the seagulls above into silence. "You would threaten me, immortal?"

Imogen gave him a look I'd seen bring other men to their knees. "I would protect my friend's best interests from a greedy god, yes."

"Bah!" Loki waved a hand at Imogen. Without a sound, she fell over backward onto the sand, narrowly missing hitting her head on a large chunk of driftwood.

"Imogen!" I screamed, falling to my knees next to her to see how badly she was hurt. I felt for a pulse, and was relieved to feel it beating away strong and steady. Her eyes were closed, her face peaceful, but it was as if she'd fallen asleep standing there. "What did you do to her?" I asked, looking up at Loki, ready to call for backup help if he'd harmed her.

"Merely stopped her squawking for a few minutes. She is immortal. She is not harmed, merely sent to sleep."

"If she doesn't wake up in a minute, you're going to be one very sorry god," I promised, slowly getting to my feet.

He sighed, his eyes hard and glinting with anger. "More threats. Very well, I have one for you, mortal. If you do not return to me the *Vikingahärta*, I will take that which you most value."

Cold gripped my heart, a number of images chasing each other through my mind—Ben, my mother and father, Tesla, Soren and Imogen . . . I valued all of them highly. "Take? Take them where?"

The look he gave me made the cold in my heart turn to ice.

"Give me the valknut now, mortal Fran." The voice coming out of his mouth seemed to be amplified, as if he was speaking through a bullhorn. It was so loud, it hurt my ears.

I took a couple of steps backward, shaking my head slowly, the pendant clutched tight in my hand. "Not unless you give me back Tesla, and take the Viking ghosts to Valhalla."

His eyes narrowed. "You would sacrifice that whom you hold most dear for one small, insignificant piece of jewelry?"

"No, I would not." I glanced quickly at Imogen, but her chest rose and fell normally, so I figured Loki was telling the truth and she was just asleep. "I would, however, fight with every last breath in my body for them. If you want this valknut, you're either going to have to take it from me, or give me what I want."

Loki snarled something under his breath and lunged for me, but the valknut, despite being his and seeped in his power, evidently didn't like him much, for it suddenly blasted out a reddish gold light that had Loki leaping backward.

"Very well," he growled, his body starting to shimmer. "We shall do things the hard way."

He shimmered off into nothingness before I could say anything. One second he was there; the next he was gone, just a few sparkly bits in the air left to indicate that a god had been standing there.

Imogen moaned.

"You OK?" I asked her, kneeling next to her. "How do you feel?"

She rubbed her head. "Like someone struck me. What happened? Ew. I'm lying on seaweed."

I brushed her off and helped her pick seaweed from her long silver blond hair, explaining what Loki had done and said.

"Oh! He is not going to get away with treating us this way," she said, her eyes fired with anger. "Just wait until Benedikt hears about this!"

"Um. Yeah." A chill rippled down my arms at the memory of Loki swearing he would take whoever mattered the most to me. "Maybe we shouldn't tell him about this."

"Not tell him?" Imogen paused in the middle of gathering up her Loki invocation things. "Fran, you cannot keep secret from Benedikt something of this importance."

"Why not? He doesn't seem to have any problem in keeping secrets from me." I handed her the chalice.

She dumped the water from it and frowned at me. "That's different, and you know it."

I didn't see the difference, actually, but an argument about that wasn't going to do either of us any good at that moment. I stayed silent as we walked slowly back to the trailers, Imogen lecturing me the entire time about having confidence in Ben.

"Fran!" Imogen said as she stopped next to the steps to her trailer. I handed her the things I'd picked up. "You haven't listened to a thing I've been saying, have you?"

"Actually, I have."

She opened the door to her trailer, glanced inside to make sure Ben wasn't up and about, tossing the things onto the seat nearest the door. "You can't just do nothing about this! Ignoring it won't make it go away."

"Oh, I know that. And I'm not going to do nothing."

"What are you doing, then?" She asked.

Finnvid and Gils were lying out on the chaises in the center area, a boom box between them, getting a tan while listening to music and swigging back what looked like a case of Swedish beer.

"I'm going to ask Sir Edward for help. Now that I know who I'm up against, I just need to figure out a way to make Loki do what I want."

"Loki?" Finnvid asked, looking up from a magazine with topless women all over its pages. "Did you summon him? Did he like the sacrifice of many small hamburgers we made in his name? Will he help us get to Valhalla?"

"Yes, I have no idea, and no. He's being really annoying, and I'm going to have to get tough with him," I said as I marched past the two ghosts.

"Gils, wake up," Finnvid said, smacking his friend on the head with the magazine. "The goddess Fran is going to war against Loki. We must help her!"

"No, it's not a war—"

"*Idag dör vi!*" Finnvid shouted at the top of his lungs. "*Nästa hållpats: Valhall!*"

"Shhhh!" I hissed, clapping a hand over his mouth. "Some people sleep in late! And what did you say?"

"Today we die. Next stop: Valhalla," Finnvid said from beneath my hand. I pulled it back to let him speak since he wasn't bellowing anymore. "Ah, see? The others come."

"Oh, great, just what I . . . no, no, put down the bow, Isleif."

"Finnvid called us," Isleif said, puffing a little since he had run up from the shore. Behind him were Ref and Ljot, with Eirik emerging at a full gallop from the woods, tucking his shirt into his leather pants. "We go to battle?"

"No! No battle!"

"Yes!" Finnvid said, waving his arm at the other Viking ghosts as they materialized and emerged from various parts of the island, all attracted by his war cry. "The goddess Fran goes to war against Loki! It will be a battle like none other!"

"You can say that again," I muttered under my breath.

CHAPTER THIRTEEN

"First, we must draw Loki into an area where he is unprotected," Eirik said, shaking a ballpoint pen that wouldn't write. He made an annoyed sound and threw it down along with the tablet of paper he'd taken from my trailer. "Gils, do you have your laptop?"

"Yes, right here," Gils said, hauling out a small white laptop. He sat down with it at one of the picnic tables. The rest of the Vikings clustered around him to watch over his shoulder.

"You guys bought a laptop yesterday?" I asked, having a bit of a problem trying to cope with the thought of one-thousand-year-old ghosts with computers.

"Two. Mine is getting a memory upgrade and a Firewire card, and should be ready later today," Eirik answered as Gils booted up a graphics program. He directed him to draw a rough map of the area. "We need a nice spot to ambush him. How about behind the main tent, where the Wiccans hold their circle? It is enclosed on three sides."

"Look, I really appreciate everyone thinking they have to help me, but you know, it's probably going to be easier for me to do it myself," I told them, but no one paid the least bit of attention to me.

"The goddess Fran can draw him into the area tonight, when the sun is at its lowest, so Loki's power will be at its ebb," Isleif explained. "Then when he is in position, we will strike."

"I will cut off his head," Gils said.

"And I will cut out his spleen." Ljot brandished a hunting knife with great pleasure.

Isleif's eyes lit up. "I will shoot him full of arrows that will pierce every major organ."

"That's a really sweet thought, guys," I said, trying again to make them see reason. "But this is a god we're talking about, remember? I know the twelve of you are big and bad Vikings, but Tallulah's boyfriend Sir Edward said that Loki was like nothing he'd seen before, and he had a whole lot of power. So I don't think you guys are going to be able to defeat him even if you do ambush him."

"The goddess Fran has a point," Finnvid said thoughtfully, looking at Eirik.

"Hmm. Perhaps she does. Loki still has much power. It couldn't hurt to have some help. Very well—Thorir, you and Ref summon the Vangarians."

"The who?" I asked.

"Vikings, of a sort. They sailed primarily into Russia," Eirik explained. "We used to war with them, but they will join us in a battle against Loki. Tonight, when the sun is at its lowest, the goddess Fran will drawn Loki into our trap, and we will spring it on him, killing him once and for all."

The others made happy noises of agreement. I wanted to whap them all on the head with a lady's small beheading ax.

"Sheesh! What part of 'he's a god' do you not understand? You can't kill him! And even if you could, I don't want him dead—I just want him to give me back Tesla, and to send you all on your way."

Instantly twelve Viking faces turned pouty.

"Oh, for heaven's sake . . . look, even if I agreed to this plan—and I'm not!—I couldn't help. I've got a date with Ben tonight, remember?"

"The big date," Gils said, pursing his lips. "The goddess should not miss that."

Isleif nodded. "It is important."

Eirik paced back and forth for a few seconds. "Very well. We will use some other bait than the goddess to ensnare the god Loki. Then when we have him—"

"I will cut out his liver, cook it before him, and make him eat it while it's still smoking," said an enthusiastic Ljot.

"No liver cutting!" I yelled.

"Then we will hold him prisoner until the goddess is done with her date and can force him to her will," Eirik said, shaking his head at Ljot. I could have sworn I heard him muttering something to Ljot about how later they would cut out Loki's liver, but it could have been my paranoid imagination.

"Whatever. Just so there's no killing, no liver cooking, and no messing with anyone in GothFaire. If hear one more complaint from Absinthe about you guys . . ."

I shot them all meaningful looks. They all, every single one of them, tried very hard to look innocent.

"We haven't raped, pillaged, plundered, or murdered anyone in days," Finnvid grumbled. "Well . . . we did pillage the McDonald's last night for the sacrifice."

324 ∽ Katie MacAlister

"And see how much good that did," I answered, making a mental note to find out if they had left any money for the hamburger sacrifices.

"You will go now, goddess, and get ready for your date," Eirik said, shooing me away when I tried to see what Gils was busily typing in on his laptop. Just when did he learn to use one? Not to mention learn to type? "We will take care of everything here."

"That's just what I'm afraid of."

"We will summon the Vangarians to help us catch the god Loki. We will not kill anyone. We will wait for you to come back from your date before torturing him. You see? All is in hand. Go have your date."

I glanced at the sun's position in the sky. "I have about five hours before I have to get ready for my date. Why don't I help you guys, instead?"

"You are a goddess!" Eirik said in a voice filled with fake shock. He grabbed my elbow and hustled me off in the opposite direction from Gils and his laptop. "We would never ask you to work. That would be wrong."

"Uh-huh." I let myself be manuevered, but only because I didn't think there was much the Vikings could do to screw things up so long as they promised no one would be killed and flame-roasted.

"We'll see you later, when the trap is ready for the god Loki." Eirik released my arm and gave me a gentle shove.

I stopped and let him have a bit of a glare. "Fine. But stay out of trouble! I'm going to talk to Sir Edward while you guys are making your big plans. Just remember! No killing! No maiming! No general destruction."

"Be on your way, goddess," Eirik said with one last shove. "We have work to do."

I had work too, but I put that thought aside as I trotted over to Tallulah's trailer. I figured it was much more important to talk to Sir Edward about what he knew about Norse gods than cleaning the trailer.

My mother had other ideas.

What are you doing?

Cleaning the bathroom in our trailer. Mom caught me as I was leaving Tallulah's. How are you feeling?

As good as ever. What were you talking to Tallulah about?

I was talking mostly to Sir Edward about Norse gods. I gave the shower wall one last wipe with the sponge, and called it good, tossing the cleaning things into a bucket we kept in the cupboard under the sink.

Ah. Imogen told me what happened between you and Loki this morning. You should have called for me. I don't like the idea of you two standing up to a god.

I snorted as I glanced outside. The Vikings had long since disappeared. They were gone when Mom found me and dragged me in for some forced cleaning. I figured they were out calling up all their ghost friends to help them with Loki. *Right. First of all, it was early morning and you were asleep.*

Fran, you can wake me up if you need me.

I know that. But we didn't need you. We were in control of everything.

It was Ben's turn to snort. *That's why Imogen was struck with a sleeping spell?*

She wasn't hurt. I would have called you if she had been hurt.

Nonetheless —

Sir Edward said the only way to get a god to comply with your desires is to use his power against him, I said, interrupting what was sure to be yet another macho guy lecture.

You're changing the subject. Irritation seeped into my head with the words.

I giggled and started on the tiny kitchen area of the trailer. With just a couple of counters, a miniscule stove, and tiny sink, it wouldn't take me long to clean it up. *Yep. Do you think the valknut is going to be power enough to use against him?*

Ben was silent for a moment. *I will see that it is.*

I frowned as I wrung out the washrag. *Is something wrong? You sound distracted. What are you doing?*

Taking a shower.

Oh! For some bizarre reason, a little tiny blush warmed my cheeks. *Right this second?*

Yes. Why? Don't you believe me?

Sure. I just . . . it's kind of odd talking to someone while they're naked and soapy.

His slow smile stole across my mind. *Would you like me to prove it?*

Prove it? What do you mean?

Sensation flooded my head, the feeling of Ben stroking his hands down his wet, soapy chest, his long fingers leaving a trail as they slid down his breastbone to his belly. The image was so strong, so clear in my mind, my own fingertips tingled as if it was my hands touching him.

Oh man. You're . . . oooh.

I was thinking about kissing you a few seconds ago. Now I'm imagining it's you touching me. His fingers spread out over his belly. The combination of what he was thinking and feeling made my own stomach turn over in excitement. *But what I'd really like is for you to touch me here.*

His hands slid lower, the soap turning his skin into wet, slippery silk. I gasped, my eyes almost bugging out when he started washing his guy parts. OK, I'm no idiot. I knew he had those parts. I knew what they were and all, having had to sit through a couple of years of sex ed and things like that, and didn't think they were that big a deal. And although I was secretly interested in knowing what Ben—all of Ben—looked like, I wasn't ready for *him* to know that I wanted to know.

Is this too much for you? he asked as he soaped himself up. *If you want me to, I'll stop.*

Well . . . you have to get the soap off, so I don't think you can stop right now, I said, my mouth hanging open as I stood there trying not to let him see how interested I was.

I meant I'd stop sharing myself with you. His voice was warm in my head, reassuring, and yet stirring something deep inside me.

My mother entered the trailer, Davide at her heels. "Done already? That didn't take you long."

Just because I don't want to have sex with you doesn't mean I'm not . . . um . . .

Curious?

Yeah.

"Fran? Are you all right? You have an odd expression on your face."

The sensations of warm water that cascaded down his body were as vivid in my mind as his. *There are some things I cannot share with you, Fran. But everything else I have is yours, including my body. Whenever you're ready for it.*

"Honey? What's wrong?"

I blinked a couple of times to get rid of the vision of a wet, naked Ben. My mother stood directly in front of me, staring. "Are you all right? You're panting. If you don't close your mouth, you're going to catch flies."

"Yeah. I was just . . . uh . . . thinking of something."

"Hmm." She gave me a suspicious look, but moved past me. "Why don't you put those things away. I want to have a talk with you."

I put the last of the cleaning things away, and sat down on the couch while she unloaded her invocation items. She chatted about how the day's circle had gone, just the same old stuff I'd heard a hundred times. I mentally turned down her voice a couple of notches.

How about in two hours? I asked Ben, trying for a light, playful tone, but I suspected he knew I was reeling in my tongue and drying not to drool.

For our date, you mean?

Yeah. Not anything else. I'm not ready for that yet.

I know, sweetheart. And you know that I will not rush you. I've waited more than three hundred years for you. I can wait a few more until you are comfortable with the thought of physical intimacy.

I'd never talked like this with anyone before, and I had an odd feeling I should be embarassed to be talking about sex, not to mention more or less watching Ben take a shower, but I wasn't. Ben was different from every other person, and not just because he was a vampire. He was . . . right.

Thank you.

Huh?

I think you're the right person for me, too.

Stop eavesdropping! I yelled, mortified.

He laughed. *I wasn't. You're projecting to me. If you don't want me to hear your thoughts, you'll have to shield them.*

Oh great, now I'm a radio station. Well, WFRAN is going off the air now. I'll see you in a bit.

"Fran? What is wrong with you today?"

I dragged my mind back from Ben and realized that once again my mom was standing in front of me, having evidently been waiting for me to answer a question I didn't hear. "Sorry. Just thinking about things."

Her lips thinned. "It's Ben, isn't it? You were thinking about him."

I decided what could work for Ben could work for me. I said nothing, just looked at my mother.

Her lips thinned even more. I swore to myself that no matter how much she ragged on Ben or me, I wasn't going to get into another knock-down, drag-out with her. Things between us had been strained and tense since the last fight, and although I knew she was wrong about Ben, I didn't see that there was going to be any way of convincing her of that. She'd just have to see for herself what a trustworthy guy he was.

"Very well," she said, sitting down on the opposite side of the little table. "Now is as good a time as any to discuss this date you have with him tonight."

I continued to say nothing. I sure thought a whole lot of things, though. I thought so many, and thought them with so much mental hand waving and general freaking, I had to double-check first to make sure that I wasn't broadcasting to Ben.

Mom took a deep breath and let it out slowly. "I'm not going to say I'm sorry about the argument we had the other night, primarily because I don't believe I have to apologize for caring about my daughter and worrying about her health and safety, but also because I can see by the sullen look on your face that it wouldn't do any good."

I fought down the urge to touch my face. Sullen? Me? I wasn't feeling sullen. Tired, yes; wary, oh yes. But sullen? Nope. Not this girl.

"However, I believe one good thing came out of that ugly scene—I know now the depths of your feelings for Benedikt."

It was on the tip of my tongue to tell her that I didn't think she did, because not even I knew how I felt for Ben, not in the way she meant, at least. My feelings for him were still confused and more or less up in the air. Oh, I liked him. I liked how he shared himself in the shower. I *really* liked kissing him. But anything beyond that was still unknown territory.

"As for your accusation that I don't trust you—" Mom paused a minute and frowned at me.

So much for not talking about the fight.

"—I want you to know that I do trust you. If I didn't, I wouldn't allow you to go on this date."

My back straightened up at that "allow" business, but I decided to let it go. A fight now would only piss us both off even more. "Good," I said at last, figuring she'd get snarky if I kept up the Ben-trademarked silence.

She took another deep breath and used the knuckles on one hand to rub her temples. "As a woman and a mother, however, I know what sort of trouble you can get into placing yourself in a position of weakness with a man. Any man—I'm not speaking specifically of Benedikt here. Going off with a man on a date is one of the times when you are vulnerable to assault: sexual, physical, and mental."

"I've already told you," I said, deliberately keeping my voice calm. "Ben and I aren't going to have sex. He's not going to physically or mentally assault me because I'm his Beloved. That means he pretty much can't, even if he wanted to, which he doesn't."

Mom flinched at the word "Beloved" but didn't say anything about it. "There are such things as date rape, honey. There are drugs that men can give girls to knock them out so they can rape them." I started to open my mouth to protest Ben's innocence in anything so ridiculous, but she raised a hand. "No, hear me out. I know you don't think that any of this will ever happen to you, and Goddess only knows I pray that it doesn't. But I want you to be prepared for any sort of attack on you, no matter whom it's from."

I bit my lip to keep from telling her I could take care of myself. She reached behind and grabbed a small bag, pulling a couple items from it.

"This," she said, holding up a small black canister, "is pepper spray. It won't cause any permanent damage, but it should slow down anyone who attacks you."

I took the pepper spray without comment. I had actually kind of wanted some before, but never had the need for it.

"This is a Green Tara amulet." Mom held up a chain with a small stone amulet hanging from it. She slipped it over my head. I held the stone amulet up so I could see it—it was a woman who sat lotus style, kind of like a female version of Buddha. "It is warded and spelled for protection. It should keep you safe from any being from the dark powers. Keep it on you at all times. And last . . ." She pulled out of a long leather case a big herkin' knife. "If the pepper spray and Green Tara aren't enough to stop someone, this should. I don't condone violence against others, as you know, but self-protection does not fall under those precepts."

"OK," I said, pushing the knife away when she shoved it at me. "The pepper spray I'll take because it's cool. The green Buddha lady I'll take too, because it will make you happy. But I am not going to walk around with the equivalent of a sword on me!"

"Fran, it's for your own—"

"I know," I said, standing up. "And I appreciate it. The first two are fine. I won't let Ben slip me any pills, not that he would. I won't go into a dark alley with anyone. And I won't get in any strangers' cars, OK? Are you done? It's almost six, and I have to get changed for the palm reading, so I can end early and get ready for my date."

She wasn't done, of course, but I didn't wait for her to finish before I got dressed for my time at the palm-reading table. She continued to warn me right up to the moment I left the trailer.

"Mom, it's just a date, one little date, not the end of the world," I said as I opened the door and started down the stairs. She stood in the doorway giving me the same worried look she'd been giving me for the last half hour. "Stop worrying. Everything is under control, OK? Nothing bad is going to happen."

"Women and children to the hills!" Finnvid yelled as he raced by, clad in his original Viking outfit of leather and wool, his huge shining sword in one hand as he ran for the beach. "*Anfall! Anfall!* Every man to arms—we're under attack by the Vangarians. To Valhalla!"

"Except, of course, if the Vikings Eirik called for help attack us instead," I said with a lame smile.

Mom just stared.

CHAPTER FOURTEEN

"How bad is it?"

Eirik looked over his shoulder at me. He was half-hidden behind a rock, shouting orders to his men as they took up defensive positions. "Goddess Fran, you should not be here. Go back to your camp."

"Weren't these guys supposed to be helping you with Loki?" I peered over the rock at the five boats that were bobbing up and down on the waves, about twenty yards offshore. "Are those whatchamacallit . . . dragon ships?"

Eirik rolled his eyes for a moment before snatching up a walkie-talkie and barking an order into it. "You have seen too many movies. Those are longboats, traditional Viking ships. Yes, we called the Vangarians to help us, but evidently they were jealous when they heard how you took us shopping, and now they wish to pillage our many fine possessions."

An arrow whizzed past us with an odd humming noise.

"Arrow," Ljot said helpfully as he trotted past us, an air horn in one hand, a paintball gun in the other.

I closed my eyes for a minute. "Please tell me you're not going to let them get past you to the Faire."

"No, of course not," Eirik said, shooting me an irritated glance. "There are only twenty-five of them. We will take them easily."

The walkie-talkie came to staticky life again. Eirik listened intently for a minute, then answered in Swedish.

"Good, because if there is one more incident, I don't think Absinthe is going to be very happy. Crap, I'm late. I'll check on you later to see how things are going."

"Enjoy your date. We will be here with Loki when you return," Eirik said, sticking a knife between his teeth as he grabbed his sword and leaped over the rock to race down to where the longboats were landing.

I shook my head and hustled back to the Faire, wondering for the umpteenth time why things never seemed to go easily for me.

An hour later I was in the middle of explaining to a woman that I was not responsible for her hand saying she was going to have three kids when a man jumped up on my reading table and cut off my head.

Or rather, he tried to.

"Hey!" I yelled as the sword swung straight for me. I threw up my hands to protect myself, only realizing as he started a second swing that I could partially see through him. I narrowed my eyes at the Viking. "I don't recognize you. You're not one of Eirik's men, are you? I bet you're one of those Vangarians he called. Will you stop swinging that sword through me? It's annoying!"

There were three people in line behind the woman seated at my table. All four people stared in amazement as the Viking ghost turned toward them. He was dressed similarly to Eirik and his men in that he had a bare chest, wore a bit of fur strapped around his back, and had cloth pants tied on with leather leggings, but unlike my Vikings, he was partially translucent. I took it to mean he wasn't grounded the way the local ghosts were.

The people in line gasped as the Viking ghost flung himself off the table to race into the crowds wandering up around the Faire. A couple of people shrieked as he tried to behead one person, disembowel another, and hack to bits a Goth guy and girl with matching face piercings, but most people applauded. Just like with Eirik and his men the previous day, the visitors thought the Vikings were part of the GothFaire performers.

"I'm sorry. I'm going to have to close early," I told the people waiting for me to read their palms. "We're having a bit of a problem with our . . . er . . . Vikings. Sorry. I should be here again tomorrow night."

Two more strange Vikings raced down the aisle, screaming what I assumed were Viking war cries, trying to kill as many people with their phantom swords as they could.

"Fabulous special effects," I heard one guy say in an English accent. "Straight out of Hollywood. Are they holograms, do you think?"

"Have to be," his friend answered, watching curiously as one of the Viking ghosts stabbed a sword into his body a couple of times. "Bloody good ones, too. I wonder where the projectors are?"

"Top of the light poles," I lied, pointing to the nearest tall stand of lights that lit the aisle.

"Ah." Both men nodded. I spied a familiar, much more solid-looking Viking, and ran to intercept him. "Isleif, what's going on? I thought you guys were going to hold your buddies at the beach?"

"They're not grounded," he answered, slinging his bow over his shoulder. "We are. We can't stop them any more than they can hurt us."

"Oh, for heaven's sake . . . what are we going to do?"

"Ref and Gils and I are trying to round them up. Once we have them together, Eirik can tell them about our plan to battle Loki. They'll like that. We'll summon Loki then, and hold him for after your date."

My date was beginning to look like it would never happen. "How are guys who can't interact physically with us going to help you with Loki?"

"He's a god," Isleif said, yelling something and pointing in the direction of the last two Viking ghosts as Gils ran by. "Gods have a presence in both the spirit and mortal worlds. An ungrounded ghost can touch him."

In the distance, a horn sounded.

"Oh, great, now what's that?" I asked, glaring at a ghost as he paused long enough to try to cut off my legs.

Isleif tipped his head to the side as he listened to the fading horn blast. "More Vangarians."

"More? No! We have enough!"

"I'd best go help Eirik," Isleif said, spinning around. "Things could get ugly if everyone decides not to cooperate."

"All right, all of you, stop it," I yelled, clapping my hands together in hopes the ghosts would pay attention to me. It was hopeless. "You there, in the leopard skin—knock it off! Stop stabbing people."

Desdemona burst out of her booth directly in front of me,

her eyes wild. The leopard print ghost looked at her as she went racing off toward the trailers.

"Well, OK, you can stab her. But leave the tourists alone!" The Viking grinned and dashed off after Desdemona.

Ben! I yelled, desperate for some support.

He didn't answer for a couple of seconds. *What's wrong, Fran? Is your mother giving you another lecture?*

She did that earlier. It's the Viking ghosts! They're running amok! I'll talk to Eirik, he said.

No, not those ghosts . . . these ones are friends of theirs. Or enemies, I'm not sure. They're not grounded so they can't do anything physically, but they're running around the Faire trying to kill everyone and attracting attention, and any minute now Absinthe is going to notice—

"Francesca!" a familiar female voice tinged with a German accent bellowed. I twitched.

Too late. Where are you? What are you doing?

I was having dinner, he said wryly. I had a moment of squirminess as I realized what that meant, but his choice of food wasn't of concern at the moment. *I'm on my way to help you.*

Thanks. We're going to need it.

"Vhat is going on with your ghosts?" Absinthe demanded as she stormed toward me. "Did I not tell you to make them stop these behaviors? They are bothering the customers!"

"I'm sorry. These aren't really my ghosts. They're . . . uh . . . friends. We're trying to get them contained, but—"

At that moment, a pack of women on motorcycles roared onto the fairgrounds. They didn't stop at the parking area; they went right through it and into the center aisle.

"Fran!" A woman riding double on the first motorcycle leaned out and waved. Imogen wore a helmet, but I recognized her even through the smoky faceplate. She plucked the helmet off and smiled broadly. "Look who I found for you!"

The first motorcycle came to a stop directly in front of Absinthe and me. The woman riding it nodded at me. "I understand from Imogen that you need some help with lost warriors?"

"Er . . ." I looked from the blond woman—about six foot three inches tall, taller than me even—to Imogen.

"This is Gunn," Imogen said, introducing her friend. "She's a Valkyrie."

"Oh! Excellent! I was wondering how to get hold of you guys."

Gunn nodded. "We were at a resort in San Tropez having a little retreat, but Imogen convinced us this was an emergency. Where are the warriors?"

"Valkyries?" Absinthe asked, looking as all the other ladies on motorcycles pulled up. "You bring to my Faire the Valkyries?"

Five Vikings chased a group of tourists past us.

"Valkyries," Gunn said, turning to her sisters in arms. She pointed to the tourist-chasing ghosts. "Warriors!"

I won't say I'll never see a stranger sight than ancient female Nordic gods in leather jackets and spike-heeled boots riding motorcycles, chasing down equally ancient Nordic ghosts, but it was something I won't forget in a very long time. The Valkyries didn't have any trouble grabbing the Viking ghosts as they zoomed in and out of the crowds, picking off the ghosts. They just reached out, grabbed, and did an odd little shake that dissolved the ghosts into nothing. Most of the tourists were clumped together in groups watching, applauding and cheering every time one of the ghosts was snagged.

"What are they doing?" I asked.

"Sending them to Valhalla," Gunn answered.

Imogen, who had taken Absinthe aside and was explaining to her what was going on, turned to beam at me. "Am I not the cleverest person ever to find Gunn and the Valkyries to take care of the problem? Now you will not need Loki's help."

Except, of course, I wanted Loki in my power so I could force him to give me Tesla.

"Brilliant," I said, summoning a smile I didn't particularly feel. I wouldn't hurt Imogen's feelings for the world.

"Now," Gunn said, turning to me. "While they are taking care of the Vangarians, why don't you take me to the group Imogen told me about. We'd like to get back to our resort as quickly as possible. There's to be a wet T-shirt contest tonight that I just know my girls can win."

Gunn looked down at her chest fondly for a moment.

I blinked at her boobs. "Um . . . yeah. My Vikings are on the beach, trying to control the others so they can trap Loki, but once they're done with that—"

"Trap Loki?" Gunn yelled.

"What can I do to help?" a deep, smooth, velvety soft voice asked behind me.

"Ben!" I whirled around, smiling with relief to see him. "Nothing right now. Imogen brought the Valkyries to help with the ghosts."

He raised a dark eyebrow and looked at his sister. "I didn't know she knew how to call them."

She smiled back at him, winking. "You don't know what you can do until you try. Actually, Fran gave me the idea by summoning Freya. I called a few friends in Italy and managed to track her down, and she gave me Gunn's mobile number. I called and told her you needed help, and voilà! Instant backup!"

I opened my mouth to ask how on earth she knew that a

Valkyrie would have a cell phone, but decided not to. If my Vikings could be addicted to McDonald's and use a laptop to plan battle strategy, what was so strange with Valkyries being summoned by a phone call rather than an invocation?

"My Vikings are over there, beyond the main tent, down at the beach," I said, directing Gunn to the area where I'd last seen Eirik.

"Groovy. Let's go get them," she said, propping her bike up against the light pole. She peeled off a pair of leather gloves and marched off, Imogen in tow. Absinthe blinked a couple times, shot me a look, and hurried off in the other direction.

Ben looked at me. "Aren't you going as well?"

"Yeah, I am. It's just . . . " I bit my lower lip. Ben gently pulled it from between my teeth with a brush of his thumb.

"It's just what?"

"I almost hate to see them go. They're nice. And they've tried to help."

Ben laughed and put his hand on my back, giving me a little push forward. "You have such a soft heart. It's one of the things I admire most about you."

I sighed as we made our way through the crowds toward the beach. I knew I was being foolish—Eirik and his men *wanted* to go to Valhalla. It was only right that they should get there. "I'm glad you admire it, but it's annoying most of the time. Things matter so much . . . oh, no, now what?"

Ben and I started running when we heard three Viking horns go off simultaneously. It only took us a few minutes to reach the area on the beach where I'd last seen Eirik. Just as we were leaping over a couple of downed trees that were on the fringe of the beach, the remaining Valkyries roared up behind us, passing us and coming to a stop on the beach.

"Oh . . . bullfrogs!" I swore at the sight of the number of ungrounded ghosts milling around. The small stretch of beach was elbow-to-elbow with Viking longships, and there had to be at least a hundred ungrounded ghosts roaming around. In the center, a ring of Eirik's men stood, all of them looking at a red-headed man who was swearing up a blue streak at Gunn.

"I will not be summoned this way! You have no right to call me here now, and for that, you will pay!"

"Oh, blow it out your butt," Gunn said.

Loki's mouth hung open for a moment.

Gunn turned to Imogen and said in a lower voice, "I've always wanted to tell him that, the self-aggrandized little twit."

Loki roared in anger.

"Get over yourself already, will you?" Gunn asked. "No one is impressed. Eirik asked me to summon you, so get a grip and do whatever it is he wants so I can get my girls back to the T-shirt contest."

"Wow. Tough chick," I said in an undertone to Ben.

"They have to be. They're warriors, too, remember."

"Yeah. I just wish she wasn't pissing off Loki. I'm going to have a hard enough time to get him to hand over Tesla as is."

I'm here with you, he said, making me feel almost invincible. *Would you like me to deal with Loki for you?*

No, it's my problem. Tibolt gave me the valknut, so I have to do this, but thank you for asking and not just going ahead and doing it.

He smiled. *You are welcome. Imogen lectured me earlier about not allowing you to grow. I am trying to give you the space you need to learn about your powers and abilities.*

Thanks. I really appreciate that. And I appreciate more you being here when I need you. I stepped forward, pushing between Isleif and Gils to enter the ring of Vikings. Gunn looked at me curiously.

Loki snarled when he saw me. "You again?"

"Yes, me again." I raised my chin and tried to look as tough as Gunn. "I want my horse back, Loki. I want him back now. In exchange, I will return to you this valknut."

Loki laughed, his voice booming back from the rocks in a horrible double echo. "You foolish mortal. What do you think you can do to force me to give you my descendant?"

I gestured toward the ring of Vikings. "My friends are here to help me take you down if you won't cooperate."

He sneered at them. "A handful of long-dead warriors. They are no match for me."

The Valkyries stepped forward, joining the Viking ring.

"Valkyries . . . bah. A bunch of women playing at being men," he snorted. Imogen grabbed Gunn as she spat out a curse and started toward Loki.

"There are also other Viking warriors here," I said, nodding at the groups of ghosts that Eirik had convinced to help him. They stood in clusters in a semicircle around us, watching everything silently.

Loki sent them a mocking glance. "I fear no man, dead or alive. Is this all you have, mortal? You're wasting my time."

Uh-oh. He doesn't seem to be worried at all, I told Ben. *I thought seeing all those Vikings would have him changing his mind.*

You made him listen to you before, he answered. *What did you do?*

I showed him the valknut. But he just seemed mad I had it more than he feared it or anything like that.

If he wants it, that means it has some power. Use it, Fran.

Use it how? I don't know how to do any of that sort of magic. I'm just a psychometrist!

It was given to you for a reason. It has power that you can use. You just have to figure out how to access it.

I pulled the valknut from beneath my top, holding it in my hand for a moment. Ben was right—it did have power. It tingled against my palm as if it was waiting to be used. "I have the *Vikingahärta*."

Loki's smile got a whole lot nastier. "But you do not know how to use it. You have twice engaged my anger, mortal. Now you will feel my wrath." He raised his hand like he was going to smite me, or do something equally godlike, but Ben stepped in front of me.

"You will have to go through me, first."

Loki laughed again. "As if a Dark One could stop me? Prepare for annhiliation."

I thought you were going to let me do things my own way? I asked, poking him on the shoulder.

There are limits to my patience. This is one of them.

I can't make him do what I want if you won't let me try, I pointed out.

And I cannot allow him to harm you. If you are dead, you won't help Tesla.

He had a point. *OK, how about this—we do it together.*

Ben didn't like that. I could feel the need within him to protect me, but he isn't my boyfriend for nothing. He pushed back that need and said simply, *Very well. We will do this together. You will attempt to barter—if he refuses or attacks, then I will take over.*

Deal.

I moved around to his side, letting my arm brush his just because I liked the feeling. "Loki Laufeyiarson," I said in a loud voice, pulling the valknut over my head and laying the chain and pendant across my palm. The tingle changed in quality, becoming more intense until it buzzed on my hand like a joybuzzer. It also grew hot, very hot, almost too hot to hold. "Return to me the horse known as Tesla, or else I will unleash your own power against you."

Loki's hand dropped from smiting position, his eyes narrowing.

Good girl. Now you have his attention.

Yeah, but what should I do to prove to him I can use this darn thing? I have no idea how to use power. I'm not a Wiccan like my mom.

Mold it, Ben advised. *Hold it and shape it, making it take the form you want, then when you're ready, fire it at Loki.*

"You don't know how to use it," Loki said, suddenly relaxing.

I looked at the pendant glowing on my hand, my arm starting to burn from the energy and heat it gave off. I gathered together all the feelings it gave me, added to it my own anger and frustration and worry about Tesla, and formed it into a giant glowing ball.

"I want my horse," I yelled, slamming the ball of energy into Loki. To my surprise, he reeled backward, his image shimmering for a few seconds. It must have taken him by surprise, too, because the look he shot me was one of sheer fury.

Excellent, Fran. That was very well done. Ben's arm slid around my waist, under the edge of my shirt, his hand warm and comforting against my skin.

"Give me Tesla," I shouted again, getting ready to slam Loki with another jolt of power.

He leaped to the side, snarling. "You believe you have won, little mortal, but you have not. You may have your horse back, but it will be at the cost I warned you of earlier. Enjoy your defeat."

The air beside Loki shimmered and seemed to twist around on itself, forming into the shape of a familiar white horse.

"Tesla!" I tried to run forward to grab him, but Ben held me back.

"Wait until Loki is gone," he said softly. "He is the trickster. It might not really be Tesla."

"I have fulfilled your demand. Give me the *Vikingahärta*."

I didn't want to, but I had agreed to hand it over to him in exchange for Tesla. I took a few steps forward and held it out to him. "Thank you. I promise that I will take very good care of Tesla."

Loki tried to snatch the valknut from my hand, but the second his fingers touched it, it burst into flames.

"*Häxa!*" he screamed, leaping back as I dropped it onto the sand. "You have enchanted it!"

Do I want to know what he called me?

Witch.

"No, I haven't, honest. It just did that on its own." The flames died down, leaving the valknut glowing slightly against the silvery sand.

"You have done something to it to keep me from taking it."

"I haven't! I swear!" I held up my hands to show they were empty.

"We will meet again," Loki warned, his voice low and ugly. His body started elongating, as if he was being stretched. "And I will not be nearly so merciful when we do."

He blipped out as the last of his words were spoken, just as if he was a picture on the TV someone had turned off. The air was heavy with his words, however, leaving a grim feeling. I ignored it, hurrying forward to Tesla, not absolutely sure he wasn't just an illusion.

He wasn't. Tesla nickered softly and rubbed his head on me, searching for apples. I blinked back a couple of happy tears, hugging his neck and rubbing my face in his mane for a moment to reassure myself that he was real.

"Thank you," I said finally, turning to face the Vikings, Valkyries, and ghosts that had gathered to help me. "Thank you all so much. I can't tell you how much it means to me to have Tesla back."

My Vikings grinned. "We were happy to help, goddess, although sad we could not disembowel Loki," Eirik said. "Perhaps you are having trouble with another god?"

I shook my head. "No. Everything's fine now. Thank you. I'm going to miss you guys. I hope you enjoy Valhalla. Gunn?"

She stepped forward, waving her warrior sisters on as well. "Absolutely. Valkyries! We have warriors to escort!"

The Vikings smiled. In less time than it took to say *smorgasbord*, the beach was empty of everything but one white horse, Imogen, Ben, and me.

"I hope they got to take their stuff with them to Valhalla," I said, stroking Tesla's neck. His eyes were half closed as he leaned into the petting. He looked fine, not like he'd been overworked or underfed. His coat was shiny and clean, and someone had worked a few braids into his tail and mane. "I can't believe it, but I'm going to miss them."

"They have gone on to their reward," Imogen said, consoling me. She patted me on the shoulder and even gave Tesla's ears a quick rub. "They will be happy. I shall miss Finnvid greatly, but I am pleased for them. And for you, too, Fran. That took much bravery, facing Loki as you did. I am very proud of you."

"Thanks," I said, giving her a quick hug. "I couldn't have done it if you hadn't brought the Valkyries."

"Pfft," she said, waving a hand. "You didn't need them. You would have simply made Loki send the Vikings on first. Ah well, it has been an interesting evening." She sent Ben a little smile. "And I'm sure it will become even more interesting. I'll see you both later."

"You're awfully quiet," I told Ben, looking at him over Tesla's neck. He stood in the same spot, not moving, not saying anything, just watching me with dark, black eyes. "Is it because I didn't thank you yet for helping me? I was going to do that later, on our date."

"No," he said, and for a second, I felt a wave of concern and worry come from him.

"What's wrong?"

"What exactly were Loki's words to you the first time you summoned him? When you refused to give him the valknut?"

I glanced over to where the valknut lay innocently on the sand. It was cool to the touch. With nothing else to do with it but leave it—something I didn't want to do—I slipped it back over my head next to the Green Tara, and thought back a couple days. "He said that if I didn't return it, he would take that which I most valued. But that is you, and you're standing here, fine as can be. In fact, everything is fine. The Vikings have been sent on to Valhalla, Tesla is back, and there's still time for us to go on our date. I'd say things are looking up for a change."

Ben gave me an odd look. "Fran—" he started to say, but was interrupted by a shout from Soren at the edge of the beach.

"Fran! Benedikt! You must come! Something terrible has happened."

A chill rippled down my back and arms as I grabbed Tesla and urged the horse into a trot.

"What's wrong? Are there more Vikings? We can call the Valkyries back—"

"No, it is not them," Soren said, turning as we reached him. "It's the troll."

I stopped dead in my tracks. "The *what?*"

Soren grabbed my sleeve in order to drag me to the other side of the island. "A troll. It kind of looks like a wrinkled-up TV actress. He says he's looking for the goddess who sent the Vikings on to Valhalla because he wants to be released as well. You'd better come quickly before he gets annoyed. He's already talking about making you take him shopping first."

I took a deep breath and shot a glance at Ben.

He looked at me without expression for a minute, then burst into laughter, wrapping his arm around me and pulling me up close. "Ah, Fran. I can see life with you is going to be anything but dull."

ACKNOWLEDGMENTS

I took a lot of poetic license with my interpretation of Viking ghosts, and Nordic gods, but I hope that devotees of Nordic history will forgive any trespasses. If you have a comment you'd like to make about that, or anything else in the book or series, feel free to e-mail me. Links to my e-mail and mailing address can be found on my Web site at www.katiemacalister .com.

And finally, I'd like to thank my friend Tobias Barlind for answering my endless questions about Sweden and Vikings, and providing translations. No matter what time of day I asked him for help, no matter how strange the request (and how many people have the opportunity to translate the phrase "legless weasel"—the name of the nearby town in *Circus of the Darned?*), Tobias always came through for me. *Tack så mycket*, Tobias.

GLOSSARY

Akashic Plain aka Akasha. What is referred to by mortals as limbo, banishment to the Akasha is the ultimate punishment.

Asatru A Nordic- and Germanic-based neopagan religion that honors the Norse gods.

Asgard Home of the Aesir (the Norse gods and goddesses), and also the location where Valhalla is situated.

Ashtar (priestess of) Practicing members of the Asatru religion, priestesses are responsible for communing with the gods and goddesses.

Blot An old Norse tradition of offering a sacrifice to the gods, blots in modern times are more a celebration of the gods with sacrifices mostly consisting of ale and mead rather than animals. Pronounced "bloat."

Circus of the Darned A traveling performance act consisting of Mikaela and Ramon Jupiter and Mikaela's cousin Tibolt.

Demon Minion of a demon lord, demons can take whatever shape they desire, usually human. They cannot be killed, although their mortal forms can be destroyed, returning the demon to its demon lord.

Sir Edward Deceased Englishman who serves as Tallulah's spirit contact, as well as being her boyfriend.

Freya Norse goddess of love.

Miranda Ghetti Mother of Francesca, and a renowned Wiccan who sells various items of magic at the GothFaire.

GothFaire The fair that travels around Europe offering performers and vendors with a Gothic twist.

Gunn Head Valkyrie.

Holle Goddess who presides over the part of Asgard containing the souls of the dead.

Joining The seven steps that a Dark One and his Beloved complete in order to redeem his soul. The steps are: 1. Dark One marks the heroine as his own; 2. Dark One protects heroine from afar; 3. Dark One conducts the first exchange of bodily fluids (usually a steamy kiss); 4. Dark One entrusts the heroine with his life by giving her the means to destroy him; 5. Second exchange of fluids (usually sexual in nature); 6. Dark One seeks heroine's assistance to overcome his darker self; 7. Exchange of lifeblood: the heroine redeems his dark soul by offering herself as a sacrifice.

Mikaela Jupiter One of the three members of Circus of the Darned, she is married to fellow performer Ramon.

Ramon Jupiter One of the three members of Circus of the Darned, he is married to Mikaela Jupiter.

Kurt and Karl Brothers who perform a magic act at the Goth-Faire. Both are reputed to be involved romantically with Absinthe Sauber.

Lars Laufeyiarson One of the names of the Norse god Loki.

Loki Norse god of mischief, frequently referred to as "the Trickster."

Mage A person who can perform arcane-based magic.

Moravian Females and redeemed males are referred to simply as Moravians. Female Moravians such as Imogen Sorik do not need to drink blood to survive, although they do so if they desire.

Moravian Dark One Males who are either born cursed or created as one via a demon lord or other Dark One. They can be saved only by Joining with their Beloveds, and are referred to by the mortal world as vampires.

Psychometrist Person who can make associations from the emotions and significant events related to an object simply by touching it.

Eirik Redblood Leader of a band of ghostly Vikings raised by Fran.

Rune Stones Small stones with runic symbols that are used for divination purposes.

Absinthe Sauber Co-owner of the GothFaire with her twin, Peter, she is the business manager of the Faire, as well as a mind reader.

Peter Sauber Co-owner of the GothFaire with his twin, Absinthe, he is also the headlining magician who periodically performs real magic.

Soren Sauber Son of Peter Sauber, and Fran's friend. Soren is training to be a magician and spends his time at the Faire helping his father.

Imogen Sorik Older sister of Benedikt Czerny, Imogen reads rune stones and palms at the GothFaire. She is a Moravian and more three hundred years old.

Tallulah A medium of Gypsy ancestry, she communicates with the dead, including her boyfriend, Sir Edward.

Tesla An elderly Lipizzan stallion who Fran rescues in Hungary.

Tibolt A mage of the fifth class.

Wards Magic in symbol form. Most, but not all, wards are protection-oriented, and all are customized by the individual drawing them. The most important element of a ward is the drawer's belief in his/her abilities.

Valhalla Heaven to Viking warriors, Valhalla is located in Asgard, and consists of a hall where fallen warriors may drink and fight all day.

Valknut A symbol containing three interlocked triangles, it represents the slain, the afterlife, and eternity.

Valkyries Females charged with bringing fallen warriors to Valhalla.

Vikingahärta A valknut created by Loki that bears his power. Its name means "Heart of the Viking."

Wiccan Modern-day witch who worships the God and Goddess and performs nature-based magic.

Wiccan circle A gathering of Wiccans to perform magic and rituals.

Growing up in a family where a weekly visit to the library was a given, **Katie MacAlister** spent much of her childhood with her nose in a book. She lives in the Pacific Northwest with her husband and dogs, and can often be found lurking around online game sites, indulging in world building of another sort. To contact Katie, visit www.katiemacalister.com. Fans of the Otherworld are invited to stop by www.drag onsepts.com.